Cathy Williams can remember reading Mills & Boon books as a teenager, and now that she's writing them she remains an avid fan. For her, there is nothing like creating romantic stories and engaging plots, and each and ever̶ ̶b̶o̶ok is a new adventure. C̶a̶b̶y̶ lives in London. H̶ ̶ ̶ ̶ ̶ ̶d̶aughters—C̶ ̶ ̶ ̶ ̶ ̶, Olivia and Emma—h̶ ̶ ̶e̶ al̶w̶ ̶ ̶ ̶ ̶ ̶, an̶d̶ continue to be, the greatest i̶ ̶ ̶ ̶ ̶ ̶ ̶ ̶s̶ in her life.

Growing up near the beach, **Annie West** spent lots of time observing tall, burnished lifeguards— early research! Now s̶h̶e̶ ̶s̶pends her days fantasising about gorgeous me̶ ̶ ̶ ̶ their love-lives. Annie has been a reader all he̶r̶ life. She also loves travel, long walks, good company and great food. You can̶ ̶ ̶ ̶ ̶ her at annie@annie-west.com or via PO Box ̶ ̶ ̶ ̶ Warners Bay, NSW 22̶ ̶2, ̶ ̶stralia.

THE ITALIAN'S INNOCENT CINDERELLA

CATHY WILLIAMS

THE HOUSEKEEPER AND THE BROODING BILLIONAIRE

ANNIE WEST

MILLS & BOON

First published in Great Britain 2023
by Mills & Boon, an imprint of HarperCollins*Publishers* Ltd,
1 London Bridge Street, London, SE1 9GF

www.harpercollins.co.uk

HarperCollins*Publishers*, Macken House, 39/40 Mayor Street Upper, Dublin 1, D01 C9W8, Ireland

The Italian's Innocent Cinderella © 2023 Cathy Williams

The Housekeeper and the Brooding Billionaire © 2023 Annie West

ISBN: 978-0-263-30672-9

04/23

MIX
Paper | Supporting
responsible forestry
FSC™ C007454

This book is produced from independently certified FSC™ paper to ensure responsible forest management.
For more information visit: www.harpercollins.co.uk/green.

Printed and Bound in the UK using 100% Renewable Electricity at CPI Group (UK) Ltd, Croydon, CR0 4YY

THE ITALIAN'S INNOCENT CINDERELLA

CATHY WILLIAMS

MILLS & BOON

CHAPTER ONE

'NOT WHAT I was expecting...'

Mateo's dark, lazy voice from behind feathered along Maude's spine and she turned around slowly to look at him.

Ever since this arrangement had been made the evening before, Maude had had time to ponder and had come to the conclusion that it was just a terrible idea.

What had possessed her?

Mateo Moreno was her boss. Her billionaire boss. She had spent the past two years climbing the career ladder, doing her utmost, as one of five structural engineers at his prestigious London firm, to impress him with her initiative and drive.

She was thirty-two years old with an exemplary record when it came to productivity and already in charge of a small team. She had always made sure to keep her professional life separate from her private one so why on earth had she been crazy enough to succumb to this reckless adventure? If it could even be called 'adventure', as opposed to 'hare-brained scheme that defied all logic and would end in tears'.

She knew why. Of course she did.

He had caught her in a weak moment. There they'd

been the evening before, long after everyone else had left the towering glass building that housed his lavish offices, discussing the latest project and inspecting the scale replica village on the concrete table in his office, when her phone had pinged and she'd read the text that had sent her into a tailspin.

Angus, the plus-one she had roped into her brother's pre-wedding party the following evening, had bailed on her at the last minute. Maude was mystified as to why her brother had to have a pre-wedding party when the actual wedding was only a matter of weeks away, but it had been unavoidable and, that being the case, she had asked Angus to help her out. Matter sorted...until she'd got that text.

His boyfriend had fallen off a ladder. He had decided on a whim to paint the ceiling in their bedroom and had fallen, splintering two bones in his ankle. Why on earth Ron had wanted to paint the ceiling in the first place was a mystery, because he loathed anything to do with DIY. Naturally, there was no way Angus could possibly go to the party while Ron was laid up in hospital, being patched up.

And, in response to a couple of sympathetic questions from Mateo, Maude had done what she had vowed never to do—she had opened up to her boss. He had noted the dismayed expression on her face and had perched on the edge of his desk, tilted his head to one side, pinned those devastating dark eyes on her and had asked what the problem was. And she had opened up.

It was a first. Conversations between them had always revolved around work. Mateo owned multiple companies around the globe. He might be based in London, but he travelled extensively, so their contact was limited to when he was around.

Once a month, he would have a group meeting, and every so often he would summon her to find out the ins and outs of particular projects she had been put in charge of. He seemed to know every detail of every project in her remit, regardless of whether he was physically in the office checking on her work or not. She knew that he was pleased with her progress, because her pay had increased five times in two years, and she now had her own fabulous office with sprawling views across to the Tower of London and the hectic streets below.

Maude had always respected the boundary lines. She had *enjoyed* those boundary lines. Her sights were fixed on her career, and fraternising with the boss had been a big no-no.

But Angus's text...

The prospect of facing eighty-five people...the general chaos...the expensive caterers vying with the expensive florists to see whose creations would be the most admired...not to mention her mother, her gran and various aunts clucking at her unmarried status and asking when she was going to meet some *nice young man*...

A migraine threatened just thinking about it.

Angus as the plus-one by her side would have made the whole extravagant do a little more bearable.

No Angus and the weekend of fun-filled festivities had suddenly loomed like an impending storm.

Thank goodness she had held back from a full scale, hand-wringing confession about her own insecurities, about the way she would be confronted with her life choices and put on the spot by her mother—who always managed to make her feel horrendously self-conscious and a bit of a loser, successful career or no successful career... But she had still confided enough for her to be here now, in a tangle of her own making.

Of course, as Mateo had thoughtfully told her, for him a plus-one situation would come with certain advantages, so the tangle was not *entirely* down to her, but still...

They were here. A party was in full swing. And it was a bad idea.

She plastered a bright, breezy smile on her face and stepped towards him.

Her heart sped up. The broad patio, spacious enough to house several sitting areas, was beautifully lit with fairy lights and lanterns and, in the semi darkness, Mateo was all shadows and angles. Most of the time, Maude could side-line his extraordinary looks. But here, close enough to breathe him in, and without a comforting desk and computer in the background reminding her of those all-important boundaries, her eyes widened and her mouth went dry. He was just so drop-dead gorgeous.

It was a hot, still summer evening and he was wearing a pair of hand-made cream linen trousers, a white shirt cuffed to the elbows and tan brogues. The whole ensemble shrieked the sort of vast wealth that most people could only dream about, including her own comfortably off, middle-class parents. The man was built to turn heads.

He was six-foot-three of dark, brooding, uncompromising Italian beauty, with pitch-dark hair that curled a little too long at the collar and dark eyes that always managed to be expressive without revealing anything at all.

She was suddenly conscious that she was no longer in her usual work uniform. She was wearing a *dress*, something floaty and blue which her mother had bought for her and had then guilt-tripped her into wearing, much to Maude's grudging amusement.

She would have to make sure that this interaction was kept as crisp and formal as possible, given the circumstances. They might not be in an office but it would be a mistake to think he had stopped being her boss. Why compound one mistake by foolishly adding to the tally?

'What were you expecting?' She turned and felt him move to stand next to her as they both surveyed the lavish spectacle in front of them.

'Not this.'

'You mean nothing so lavish?'

'I guess that's one way of putting it.'

'Because I got a first in Engineering at Cambridge, you somehow expected me to come from a more humble background? Maybe a couple of professors for parents and Bunsen burners everywhere...?' Knowing that she sounded defensive, she added with a wry, humorous sigh, 'Believe me, I very firmly cracked the mould when I decided to do engineering at university and then, horror of horrors, put a career at the top of my to-do list.'

Mateo slid a curious glance across to the woman standing next to him. In heels, she was almost as tall as him.

Well, who would have thought...?

This was not the Maude Thornton he knew.

The Maude Thornton he knew was the archetypal, besuited, impeccably but dully clad professional who did everything to an exceptionally high standard, but with her head down and in a way that attracted no attention to herself whatsoever.

He couldn't remember ever having had a conversation with her that hadn't focused on work.

She was exceptionally clever, highly creative, sharp as

a tack and easily the most promising of the very bright intake working at his London branch.

She was a career woman with a glittering future ahead and that that was where his observations of her had begun and ended.

Until yesterday.

Until he'd glimpsed a side to her previously hidden from casual viewing. He'd seen her unflappable, professional demeanour suddenly morph into dismay and vulnerability. When she'd told him about her brother's party, and the fact that her plus-one had let her down, he'd glimpsed even more of that dismay and vulnerability.

And then he'd noticed a bit more.

Not just the height—that was something unavoidable. She was probably five-eleven, much taller than the small blondes he went for. No, he'd noticed the glossiness of her chestnut-brown hair scraped back into something contained. He'd noticed the blue of her eyes and the contrasting darkness of her eye lashes. He'd noticed the fullness of her mouth and he'd taken in the suggestion of ripe curves underneath the boxy skirt and loose blouse tucked into the waistband.

In the space of forty minutes, she had gone from the consummate professional—who had never, not once, roused his curiosity—to a living, breathing human being and he had responded in kind.

Why?

Mateo was at a loss to work that one out. Was it because her sudden burst of honesty had taken him off-guard and, in that fleeting moment, he had acted out of character?

Or had he, on the hoof, seen an unexpected opportunity for an arrangement that would serve both their purposes at a particular point in time? An arrangement that would cost nothing and have no consequences?

She wanted a plus-one to make an event she seemed to be dreading a little easier. He hadn't quite understood why she was dreading whatever party was lined up, but not his to question why.

And for him?

He'd thought of the thorny problem with his ex. Cassie had turned out to be the ex from hell. He'd broken up with her over two months ago, and since then she had developed a messianic zeal to cling on to him. She'd texted... she'd phoned...she'd started showing up at his home at random times with a list of so-called forgotten items she needed to collect from his penthouse apartment.

She had the tenacity of a barnacle and, whilst Maude had been contemplating the gloomy prospect of a pre-wedding party she didn't particularly want to attend, he had likewise been contemplating an equally gloomy scenario. Cassie had informed him that she would be popping over to get some shoes and a bracelet she needed and could he please be around to let her in.

Yes, he would. Because he felt guilty—that was the long and short of it. Guilty that he had taken his eye off the ball, guilty that he had been sucked in by a helpless fragility and a touching back story of having been bounced around between angry, divorced parents from the age of three. Not his back story, but there'd been enough misery there to match his own, and he'd fallen for it.

He'd fast discovered that her fragility had concealed a core of pure steel, but by then he'd somehow become her saviour, and she had refused to listen when he'd patiently explained that his qualifications to save anyone were sadly non-existent. He was no knight in shining armour.

Not only was it an almighty nuisance for him—and not only was it teeth-clenchingly frustrating to consider the prospect of having to set her straight in language she would be forced to understand—but he had one or two dark misgivings about whether he would be able to deter her in her desperate efforts to reignite what had turned to ashes.

He did, however, suspect that the one thing that might work would be if he were to become involved with someone else.

And over his dead body was he about to go down that road. After Cassie, a spate of celibacy felt like an extremely good idea.

But then...he'd gazed thoughtfully into blue, blue eyes and it had occurred to him that they could both do one another a favour. Truth would blend seamlessly into a tiny white lie and no one would ever be the wiser.

He would be Maude's plus-one and he would tell Cassie that he was involved with a woman. He knew that the mere fact that he was going to a wedding party with Maude, a party where family members would be present, would have the desired effect because that sort of thing was something he had adamantly refused to do in all the time he had spent with Cassie.

He had bought three cases of the best champagne on offer to take with him. He didn't think for a minute that his ex would think he was deceiving her and, if she did, then Mateo was confident that he could erase any such doubts from her head because, after all, truth was largely on his side.

'Can I ask you something?' Maude murmured, taking

time out to have a private conversation with him before entering the fray.

'How did your...er...ex-girlfriend take the news?'

'About my new-found love interest?'

'Well...'

'No point skirting round with niceties.' Mateo's eyebrows shot up but his voice was thoughtful. 'Varying degrees of incredulity, fury and teary-eyed sorrow.'

'Poor girl.'

'Come again?'

'She was obviously in love with you.'

'Do I detect a hint of disapproval in your voice?'

'Not at all.'

'Is that diplomacy talking by any chance? Because, now that we're this week's hottest item, then it's fair to say we can dispense with the usual employer-employee, duty-bound responses...'

'It's none of my business.' Maude shrugged. 'As we agreed, this arrangement...well...it suited us both. I suppose I feel sorry for her. Getting in too deep and then having to go through the trauma of being side-lined because you're no longer wanted.'

Maude thought of her own moment of disillusionment once upon a time.

She'd spent all her adolescent years with her head firmly screwed on. She'd come to terms with the fact that she was taller and bigger than all her friends...that she just wasn't the sort of girl to bring out the much-vaunted protective instinct in boys.

For a long time, she'd actually been taller than every single boy she knew and even after, when their growth spurts had kicked in, only some of them had caught up.

No, she'd dealt with her own gnawing insecurities

under a glossy façade of indifference. She had listened to the ins and outs of her friends' teenage relationships and had never let slip any of the hurt that she was excluded from those youthful, heady first steps into love. Then she had hit university and within three months had fallen hopelessly in love with a guy on her course.

He'd been tall dark and handsome. He'd been someone who hadn't seemed daunted by her towering height and the fact that she wasn't model-thin. Maude had thrown herself headlong into a relationship that had lasted a handful of months, as unprotected as a tortoise shorn of its shell. With no teenage flirtations, no youthful broken heart, there'd been nothing to prepare her for the sudden storm of emotions or the crushing feeling of loss afterwards.

Small and blonde had won the day. The Perfect Guy had apologised profusely and dumped her for someone she could have popped in her pocket.

Since then?

She had been single minded. But she could still remember the hurt when that first tentative relationship had fallen apart around her ears, with all her deeply embedded insecurities about her looks crawling out of their hiding places, mocking her for being an idiot to have thought the cute guy could actually fall for her. Something inside her had broken and she'd known then that putting it back together would never happen. Her happy-ever-after would never involve all that starry-eyed nonsense about giving your emotions over to someone else's safekeeping, lock stock and smoking barrel.

Thank God the guy in question hadn't had to lie to her just to get rid of her! Maude cringed when she thought of what Mateo's ex had gone through, and some part of her wondered why the woman couldn't have read the writing on the wall from day one.

Mateo Moreno was a player.

Even if someone was buried under a mountain of books, and only surfaced now and again to take a breath of fresh air, they couldn't have missed the pictures in the tabloid press of the most eligible bachelor on the planet with some ridiculously beautiful blonde draped on his arm, gazing adoringly up at him.

Who in their right mind would ever get involved with a guy like that?

'You haven't met my ex. She's no shrinking violet,' Mateo murmured with wry amusement, and Maude looked at him, prepared to defend the female race from womanising men without a care for diplomacy. But he continued thoughtfully, 'I may have a reputation that precedes me, but believe me when I tell you that I never give any woman I date any promises I know aren't going to be fulfilled—and Cassie was no exception to that rule. Permanence? No. Not going to happen. Not in a month of Sundays. I lay my cards on the table from the start.'

'I'll bet that's a popular move with the ladies.'

'Where have you been hiding that sense of humour, Miss Thornton? I'm very happy you've decided to bring it out for some fresh air. Just for the record, I spoil the women I date—whatever they want, they get. Cassie, however...'

'Your ex?'

'Cassie wanted a whole lot more than that. She wanted the real deal, and my fault, but I should have backed off the minute I got a whiff of just how dependent she was going to be.'

'And why didn't you?'

He'd told her that she was funny...

Maude tried and failed to stifle the rush of pleasure that remark had given her. She turned to look at him and was entranced by his profile, by his dark, dangerous brand of beauty and by his casual indifference to it.

She blinked but discovered that it was harder than she'd thought to tear her eyes away.

He was compelling.

'I felt sorry for her,' Mateo surprised himself by confiding. 'She's a fragile person from a broken home and I foolishly ignored the warning bells when they started going off.'

'That's nothing to be ashamed of,' Maude countered gruffly. 'There's nothing wrong with empathy.'

'There's not a lot right with it when the outcome involves being stalked, and worse when the stalker risks her own mental health by not letting go.'

'What do you mean?'

'My amateur interpretation is that Cassie needs therapy. It's the only way she's going to solve ongoing issues, and that's exactly what I suggested, along with an offer to pay for the best money can buy.'

Maude was impressed. Something shifted under her feet. She was barely aware of it. No more was he 'just the boss' and even less just the cardboard cut-out, one-dimensional womaniser.

'Being told that I'm involved with someone else will be step one towards her letting go.'

'Except you're not.'

'That's a technicality she'll never know about. That's why this arrangement is such a good idea. I get to set my ex on the right track and you get your plus-one whose role is to...what, exactly, Maude? Pretend to be your boyfriend? That I understand. What I *don't* get is the *why*. Why do you need someone in this role?'

His voice was a low drawl, and Maude could feel his warm breath against her, because he had half-turned to face her.

She faced him and her mouth went dry.

The sounds of laughter and merriment faded, as did the spectacle of the marquee, the assembled party, the boys and girls weaving through with their huge, circular trays laden with delicacies...

Confused and alarmed, Maude sucked in a shaky breath and snatched at the self-control that had momentarily deserted her.

'I...it's always easier dealing with these sorts of things with someone at your side,' she stumbled.

'Still not really getting it. I can understand a large event where you don't know anyone. Could be a bit daunting, I imagine. But presumably you know most of the people here? And it *is* on home ground, after all.'

'I...'

Their eyes tangled and the breathless feeling was with her again.

'Yes?'

He leant into her and the hairs on the back of her neck stood on end as she did her utmost to wrest herself out of the shaky, sinking feeling trying to stage a takeover. He was so cool, so collected, asking questions that were only mildly curious...while she suddenly felt as though she were trying to balance one-legged on quicksand.

Was this what had propelled her into her initial foolhardy foray into confiding in him yesterday at the office—a sudden weakness when his attention was directed exclusively on her? When he asked her something personal while pinning her to the spot with those dark, brooding, mesmeric eyes?

'Angus was going to be my plus-one for the weekend,' she confessed a little breathlessly and then added, surprising herself, 'It's not that I'm anxious about being here, or nervous about having to socialise with all these people—I'm not. It's just that... I wanted to convince my mum that I'm not throwing my life away because I don't have anyone in my life at the moment.'

'Come again?'

Maude smiled sheepishly. 'Ever since I was a kid, my mother has been determined that I follow in her footsteps. She loves socialising and networking and having parties. She can honestly throw herself into the business of planning a dinner party with the attention to detail of someone running a military campaign.'

Mateo's lips twitched and Maude relaxed and grinned back at him.

'She wanted a "girly girl" and, well, what can I say? She got me.'

'I can tell you that *that's* the one thing you should *never* say,' Mateo murmured.

'My brother is six years younger than me,' Maude continued, staring off into the distance. 'And he's going to be married in six months. I'm thirty-two and my parents are still waiting for Mr Right to come along. My dad is okay with the road I've chosen to take, but my mum is convinced that I just won't find true happiness until I settle down. I think she's scared that I might end up on the shelf, gathering dust, because all the decent young men have been taken. So tonight...'

'Tonight you decided that a plus-one in this situation,

with friends and family everywhere, would be just the trick.'

'Something like that. We should head down. I'll introduce you to everyone.'

'Before we go...'

He reached to stay her, his hand resting gently on her arm, and his touch sent a frisson of heat coursing through her body.

'Yes?' Out of the corner of her eye, she could spot her mother making a beeline for them.

'What exactly is the agenda here?'

'You... I've implied that we're an item.'

'And have you told your mother that you work in one of my companies?'

'I haven't told her anything. My theory was to keep it vague and play it by ear. She doesn't even know that my plus-one was called Angus. I just told her that, yes, I'd be bringing someone, but it was a new relationship so she wasn't allowed to pry. I thought that would do away with...you know...'

'Nosy questions about whether the time might be right for her to start thinking about hat-buying?'

'Something like that.' Maude smiled. He was a quick study.

'And they know that I'll only be sticking around for a handful of hours?'

'You're a very busy man. There's no chance you would be able to stay for the entire duration of the weekend. We can both make that clear from the start.'

'Must mean a lot to you,' Mateo murmured, 'Heading your mother off at the pass, if you're willing to go through all of this just to buy a little time.'

'You don't get it.'

'What? What don't I get?'

Maude turned to him and looked at him with clear-eyed honesty. 'I adore my mother, and I know she loves me dearly, but I've been a disappointment.' She blushed when he looked shocked, but it was the truth, a sadness she had never been able to completely bury. It was also something she had never said aloud to anyone. In a rush she continued, voice low, 'Nick, my brother, was always the one who slotted in easily—outgoing and sporty, and always with a string of girls phoning him up. Me? Not so much.'

Their eyes met and she said hurriedly, embarrassed at this rush of unwarranted truth-sharing. 'It's no big deal. This bash will probably wind up early, around ten, as some of us—my brother and his friends and Amy, his fiancée, and hers—are splitting and heading off in different directions. Nick and his lot are going to head to one of the bars to play snooker in a room they've reserved, and we're going to a club to fritter the rest of the night away.'

'And I will be...'

'Long gone—because you're a very busy man, like I said. Early mornings to get through emails and make... er...important calls.'

'On a Sunday? I risk sounding more of a crashing bore than a workaholic, with no choice but to abandon the love of his life in her hour of need...'

Maude glanced at his dark, amused face and thought that the last thing Mateo could ever be accused of being was a crashing bore.

'Anyway.' She quickly glanced away to where her mother was bearing down on them at speed. 'My mum's spotted us.' She plastered a smile on her face, and the smile broadened into genuine amusement when she took in Felicity Thornton's double-take as she closed in.

'Ah… I'm beginning to get the picture…' Mateo murmured.

Before he could expand on that, Felicity was with them, a force of nature, laughing and confident, giving her daughter a warm hug and openly inspecting Mateo, not caring one jot for politeness.

'Maude never told me that she was going out with a hunk!' She burst out laughing and patted Maude's arm with warm approval.

'Mum!'

'Don't you *Mum* me, darling. Honestly…' She leaned towards Mateo and whispered, more than loud enough for Maude to hear, 'This daughter of mine is *such* a dark horse! But, no fear, you're here now…' Without standing on ceremony, she swept round to link her arm through Mateo's. 'And I intend to introduce you to *everyone.*'

She affectionately scolded her daughter. 'The time is over for you to be Little Miss Secretive! You're not keeping this dashing young man under wraps a minute longer!'

And Mateo allowed himself to be swept along, down the bank of shallow steps and away from the house, straight into the thick of things.

All the pieces of the jigsaw puzzle were beginning to fall into place. One glance at Maude's mother had answered a lot of questions. Maude had quite simply grown up somehow thinking that she was a disappointment because she wasn't like her mum—she towered over the tiny blonde.

The plus-one conundrum…why? Who would be desperate enough to entice someone into pretending to be their partner for a situation that should have been well within their comfort zone? That had puzzled him, to start with.

As Maude had explained uncomfortably, a thirty-two-year-old woman who needed to convince her parents that she wasn't about to end up gathering dust on a shelf, bereft of all options, as thirty-two turned into forty-two and then fifty-two...

Which still begged the question...why did a grown woman have to explain her choices to her parents? Why the need for approval? That was something Mateo genuinely didn't understand.

He had no parents. His mother had jumped ship when he'd been a baby, leaving him with his father. He had no memories of her whatsoever. He had no anecdotes about her at all. The only received information he had was that she had bailed for someone richer. She'd never looked back.

His father had done the best he could and, in return, he had gained his only son's fierce loyalty. There had not been much money to go round, but that had been fine, because impoverishment had been an excellent teacher. Mateo had learnt that the only thing that counted in life was hard cash, and his father had made sure to move mountains so that his son could get an education to give him a head start.

The worst time of his life had been when his father had died. Eighteen at the time, Mateo had hurt in places he hadn't thought possible. In the very moment of hurting, he had made his one and only mistake and had given his heart to a woman who had seemed so right at the time and had ended up proving so wrong.

Like his mother, she had not been bowled over by the

proposition of having no money long-term, even though he'd told her that he was going to make it big. When someone with a bigger bank balance had blown in six months after they'd become lovers, temptation had proved irresistible. She had walked away and, if Mateo hadn't been hardened enough by lessons learnt in his childhood, that experience had hammered the final nail in the coffin of any lingering illusions he might have had about love.

Mateo thought he had consigned those memories to a safe place from which they could never escape, but for no reason, as he listened to Felicity chattering merrily next to him as he was absorbed into a crowd of family and friends on a balmy summer evening, they crawled out of their prison to show him all the things he had never had.

And that was when he really understood why Maude had wanted her plus-one. Not only was Felicity the polar opposite of Maude—diminutive, blonde, impeccably groomed and every inch the bubbly socialite—but it was clear that she absolutely adored her daughter, whatever concerns she might have about the path she had chosen.

He glimpsed the swirling complexities of an insecure Maude, raised in a middle-class background for a future she didn't want, defensive about the route she had chosen but compelled through love to try and please her mother. And, on this big occasion, the easiest way had been to conjure up a boyfriend that would make her parents happy.

She didn't want to disappoint. Next to her mother, she felt ungainly, too tall, not polished enough…a disappointment. And Mateo felt an odd sense of pain on her behalf, which was ridiculous, but did make him realise that this arrangement wasn't quite as business-like a situation as perhaps either of them had imagined.

When he glanced at Maude by his side, reaching with nervous hands for a flute of champagne from a passing waitress, on impulse he reached out to link his fingers through hers, giving them a brief, reassuring squeeze while Felicity chattered away on the other side, dragging them along with breezy confidence to meet yet more of her friends.

'Don't worry,' he whispered to Maude with a smile in his voice. 'You wanted your plus-one? Trust me, you won't be disappointed...'

CHAPTER TWO

HE WAS HOLDING her hand.

Her ear tingled from where he had leant into her, whispering and reassuring. How had he known that she was nervous? He must have sensed something because, truthfully, she *was* nervous. Did the man have X-ray vision, enabling him to see what was going on in her head?

This was the first time she had ever brought anyone to her family home for an event like this, where so many family members and old friends were present. Sure, she'd had some passing dates in the past, and her parents had met one of them—a guy called Steve with whom she had had a half-hearted six-month fling until the whole thing had devolved into them being good friends.

But this? This was different and she *was* nervous. She was very much aware of the glances in their direction. Her mother was in her element. No guest was left unbothered. If there had been a Tannoy system in operation, Maude was convinced her mother would have used it to bulk-introduce him to everyone there in preparation for face-to-face meetings.

'Sorry,' she whispered, en route to yet another cluster of people—this time family from Yorkshire who had packed their bags and as they'd laughingly put it, headed off for 'those foreign shores called Down South' for the weekend.

'What are you apologising for?'

'I didn't expect all of this, and I don't suppose you did either.'

'All of what?'

'The attention.' She was on her fourth glass of champagne. Fortunately, food was also doing the rounds, soaking up the alcohol.

'What were you expecting when you arranged to bring the original plus-one?'

'Less of all of this,' Maude confided truthfully. She grinned and waved at some childhood friends, who made lots of gestures about wanting to meet her, whilst vigorously pointing at Mateo and mouthing questions.

'Why?'

The conversation was put on hold while the Yorkshire faction was introduced by a beaming Felicity. As the evening wore on, Maude was a little alarmed that Mateo seemed to be morphing from plus-one boyfriend to, 'Darling, is there another engagement on the cards?' boyfriend. She would patch that up later with her parents, make it clear to them that this was no more than a fling.

'Well?'

He had adroitly led them away from the pack towards a quiet corner of the garden and they now returned to the conversation they had earlier abandoned.

Food had been laid out on a succession of long, dressed tables in the marquee and a lot of people were inside as night fell and the summer heat faded. There was a small band playing in the marquee, easy-listening stuff guaranteed not to have the older contingent covering their ears and running for the hills.

Outside little groups had gathered, some sitting on the sofas on the broad patio. The fairy lights strung along the trees and foliage twinkled like little stars, mirroring the stars studding a velvet-black sky. Her mother had done a brilliant job of bringing their garden to life, turning it into a wondrous, magical backdrop for Nick's party. The food was amazing and the attention to detail was fantastic. If any of these guests weren't attending the actual ceremony, then they weren't going to be deprived of a similarly pleasing experience.

And Mateo...here with her... Maude was guiltily aware that she had enjoyed his presence way too much. For the first time in her life, she had dazzled, with him at her side. Her mother's eyes had shone with unabashed pride at her unexpected conquest. Yes, she had known with some unease that it was all a charade, and it was a charade that had a shelf life, but the temptation to relish it had been too much.

She looked at Mateo from under lowered lashes. So tall, so dark...so undeniably sexy...

She shivered, sipped from the flute and realised that it was empty.

'Why did you think it was going to be different?' he quizzed, and she shook herself back to reality and away from rampant female appreciation of his masculinity.

'Angus wouldn't have created quite the same...um... stir...'

'Poor Angus. Something of a bore?'

'He happens to be a very nice guy!'

'Damning words indeed. Can I ask you something?'

'What?' Maude narrowed suspicious eyes on him. He might have been by her side all evening, and holding her hand for most of that time much to her consternation, but they had had very little time on their own and personal interaction had been limited. This was the first time no one was around and the sudden intimacy of their surroundings made her shiver.

She nervously smoothed her dress and fiddled with the champagne flute, heartily wishing it contained some fortifying alcohol.

He was within touching distance. She looked at the brown column of his neck and hissed in a breath.

'I'm puzzled as to why you don't have a genuine partner to bring here.'

'Sorry?'

'You're a beautiful woman, Maude. So why isn't there a suitable guy on your arm? Why do you have to audition for someone to fill the role so that you can keep your parents happy?'

'I...'

Mateo watched the play of emotion criss-cross her face and marvelled that he could ever have thought that she had only that one, business-like image she presented to the outside world. That was the image she had chosen to present, the highly professional career woman, but he felt as though he was seeing the real Maude for the first time, with all her hang-ups and doubts.

Or maybe that woman had always been there, lurking just beneath the surface.

He could remember a meeting some time ago, attended by various legal and technical bods there to cross and dot what needed to be crossed and dotted before the closure of an unusually big sign off. One of the guys had done his best to chat Maude up and Mateo had been amused at her body language. She'd posted so many *Do Not Tres-*

pass signs around her that he'd been amazed at the guy's persistence.

Had the guy just not been her type?

At the time, Mateo had assumed so, but now he wondered...had she just not noticed?

Seeing her out of context here, he could see all those nuances that she had taken such care to keep hidden. For someone so confident on the work front, she was endearingly tentative elsewhere. Certainly she lacked the booming self-assurance that usually accompanied a comfortably off background.

'Broken heart?' he queried softly.

'What do you mean?'

'The lack of a man in your life.'

'That's none of your business!'

'Or maybe...' His voice lowered as he leant even closer towards her, and there was thread of lazy teasing in it that sent ripples of forbidden excitement racing up and down her spine. 'Maybe there *is* someone lurking in the background...'

'Someone lurking in the background?' Maude squeaked, genuinely confused at this tangent. 'What on earth are you talking about?'

'Undesirable...? Ex-con...? Married father of four...?' He did a casual sweep of his surroundings with his eyes and then lasered them right back to her flustered face. 'Coming from a middle-class background as you do, that's the sort of thing you might find handy to keep under wraps...although, as they say, the truth will out sooner or later.'

She blushed like a virgin. In the semi-darkness, he noted her nervous swallowing, her wide, alarmed eyes, her breasts heaving as though she'd run a marathon.

The dress was by no means revealing, and yet he was finding it very effective when it came to stirring his imagination.

What was happening here?

Accustomed to exercising complete control over his responses to anyone and anything at all times, Mateo was disconcerted by his own wayward reaction.

Yet...wasn't there a novelty here that was oddly invigorating? When was the last time he'd been confronted by the unexpected? The tough bit of his life was over. The hunger and the searing ambition that had propelled him from nothing to everything had faded. He had the world at his fingertips now. Hardship had been the whip driving him forward and he had got everything he'd ever wanted—money, power...and everything that came with it.

Mateo had grown up witnessing his father in a never-ending cycle of trying to make ends meet. He had lacked a mother figure to put a perspective on things, to comfort him, because his father had never found anyone else. He was tough, had had to be, but on the way things had been sacrificed. He now had the world at his feet but this...this feeling of seeing things through different eyes...hadn't happened for a long, long time.

He was here for a couple of hours more. Why not relax and go with the flow until he left? He would never allow himself to get into any situation he couldn't control, so there was no need for any kind of alarm bells to start going off.

'Don't be ridiculous!'

'My sincere apologies if I've offended you.'

'Really?'

'Have I offended you?'

'You...you've jumped to all sort of ridiculous assumptions! Of course there's no one undesirable lurking in the background!'

'Perhaps you have no interest in men?'

'Yes, I happen to be *very* interested in men!' Maude spluttered. 'I don't have a boyfriend because...because...'

'Tell me. Why? I'm curious.'

'Because I'm not the sort that guys go for!'

Maude covered her mouth with her hand and looked at him with horror, because her own outburst had taken her by surprise.

Confession good for the soul? Since when? What had possessed her to say what she'd just said? It was something deep and fragile inside her that she'd always kept to herself, a little kernel of truth that lay at the very heart of her.

'What I mean...' She rushed into speech. Right then, if the ground had opened up beneath her feet, she would happily have helped matters along by jumping in. 'Is that I've always been quite a bookish sort and I've discovered, growing up...'

She licked her lips and dragged her eyes away from his dark, interested gaze to stare at something and nothing in the far corner of the garden, where the mellow lighting receded into darkness. Her heart was thumping hard and her mouth had gone dry. Her desperate attempts to explain what she'd just stupidly come out with tapered off into silence. Her eyes skittered across to his face to find him staring at her seriously.

The noise of everyone at the party having fun had receded. Of course, no one would question them being here, closeted away on their own because they were supposed to be a loved-up couple desperate for time out after hours of doing the rounds. Hopes of being saved by a nosy guest were therefore dashed before they'd even begun to take shape.

'Because you're too bookish?' Mateo queried quietly. 'Since when is intelligence a turn-off? Because you're tall? Many would find that striking. Maybe you've spent a lifetime living in your mother's shadow, but I don't get the impression that she would ever have made you feel so self-conscious that you ended up keeping men at arm's length.'

'I don't want to talk about this.'

'Why not?'

'Because none of this… This isn't *me*. I… I work for you…'

'Let's say that this is an unusual situation,' Mateo murmured, 'So the normal rules of engagement are put on hold.'

He was intrigued. He wanted to hear her story. It was unusual for him, because he was usually immune to back stories, or indeed any kind of touchy-feely stuff that could take him to places he had no interest in exploring. But he was finding that he just couldn't fight the curiosity tearing through him. In many ways, she was proving to be the most *natural* woman he had ever met.

Had he become jaded over the years?

He was thirty-six years old, but had years of being master of his universe, having whatever he wanted whenever he wanted, made him world weary?

With no one to answer to…no parents propelling him in any direction…had he become somehow adrift in an ivory tower of his own making, living a gilded life that was controlled and predictable to the point where nothing new was ever allowed to break through?

It was an uncomfortable thought which Mateo immediately shoved aside.

Self-control was the way you conquered the vagaries
of life. That was something he'd accepted from a very
young age and it had always served him in good stead.
Naturally, he wasn't going to abandon it now because of
an unexpected hiccup.

'I'm interested,' he urged in a roughened undertone.

'Do you ever give up?'

'That's not my profile, no.'

'Well…' One slip, Maude thought, and it felt as though
a dam had burst inside her. 'My mum's a tough act to
follow.' She smiled. 'You've met her. She's…she's always been the sort who sets a room alive the minute she
walks in.'

'Maybe that's just the way you saw it when you were
a kid and things have become stuck in that place.'

Maude shrugged. Was that what had happened? She
had *always* known that her mother longed for a little girl
she could dress up and Maude had not been that little girl.
She'd been a tomboy as a kid and then, as a teenager, a
bookworm who'd grown too tall and too buxom to fit
into skimpy cropped tops and tight jeans.

Had she got stuck in a groove somewhere along the
way, imagining that that was who she was when, in
fact, that kid was long gone? Had she somehow rebelled
against an image her mother had not actually been interested in perpetuating? Had her own lack of self-confidence made her overlook the very simple truth, which
was that love was accepting and her mother loved her?

'Maybe.' She sighed. 'But I suppose I did feel…as
though I didn't really fit in. Living in a goldfish bowl

has its down sides and my life has always felt a bit like being in a goldfish bowl.'

She offered a tiny smile to detract from the sudden dive into seriousness. 'Anyway...' She threw a look over her shoulder. 'We should head back to the marquee. Part two of the evening is going to begin any minute now.'

She spun round on her heels but, before she could move away, Mateo had circled her arm with his hand, tugging her back to him.

'I meant what I said, Maude. You're a beautiful woman. Because you don't fit what you think is the mould doesn't mean you're not beautiful in your own right.'

'Thank you for that,' Maude said with sincerity. 'I know you mean well, but Mateo, what sort of women do *you* go for...?' She grinned when he flushed darkly and raked his fingers through his hair, and then she burst out laughing. 'I think I've proved my point,' she said drily.

Mateo watched as she began to walk away. He sprinted after her and caught up with her in a matter of strides.

'Wait,' he murmured. 'Is the love of my life now walking out on me? What's the world going to think?'

He slung his arm around her shoulder.

'Mateo...' Maude stopped abruptly and placed her hands palms-down against his chest. For a few seconds her mind went a complete blank at the sensation of hardness under her fingers, then she blinked and said crisply, 'No one's going to think anything. This is all make believe, remember?'

'Ah...but only the two of us know the truth.'

They were closer to the marquee and the scene of the action now. People were coming and going, the older ones on their way home, heading to the door to get their carriages, the younger ones already preparing for more of the same until the early hours of the morning. Someone called out to her but she was in the moment and didn't turn round.

'Which is that there's *no need* to pretend anything when we're on our own.' Her skin tingled from where he had touched her. It had felt so stupidly natural just for a moment...so dangerously *good*.

The voice behind them got closer and then a smiling blonde was standing next to them, gathering a silk shawl over her shoulders on her way out while talking at the same time—rueful that she hadn't got to meet them properly, maybe another time, as Amy talked so much about Nick's fantastically clever sister...

She turned to Mateo.

'You don't remember me, do you?'

'Should I?'

He was frowning. For a few seconds, Maude wondered whether he was about to be accosted by an ex, but then the blonde introduced herself as, 'Georgie, one of Amy's friends from when she spent those six months in LA.' Her head tilted to one side, she said, 'We met ages ago at that art exhibition thing...you were going out with Cassie Fowler?'

Mateo smiled politely. It was obvious he had no inkling who the blonde was but good manners forced him to murmur something affirmative, at which the blonde burst out laughing.

'It's okay.' She winked at Maude. 'He'll keep you on your toes!' Then she turned back to Mateo to say with a hint of surprise, 'I had no idea you and Cassie weren't... going out.'

'We ended our relationship months ago.' Mateo's voice cooled and he glanced at his watch, an invisible signal that the conversation was terminated as far as he was concerned.

In fairness, the blonde laughed again and smiled with a touch of puzzlement, murmuring, 'Blow me, she never said...' And then she nodded goodbye and headed towards the bank of shallow steps leading up to the house.

'Well, ' Mateo mused thoughtfully, 'That was unexpected.'

'I don't know quite a few of the younger crowd here,' Maude admitted. 'I've never met that girl in my life before. She'll be with Amy's party. Amy's a fashion journalist so they probably met through fashion. She seemed nice.'

Mateo shrugged and gazed down at the woman by his side.

'Penny for them.'

'Sorry?'

'You're lost in thought.'

'She's at the top of the steps with a few of Nick's pals and they're looking in this direction.' Maude sighed. 'She's probably wondering what the heck you supposedly see in me after Cassie... Wasn't Cassie a model? Look at me. I couldn't be a model if I spent the next decade on a two-hundred-calorie-a-day diet!'

'There you go again. Why don't we show them all and prove a point?'

He didn't give Maude time to object. He barely gave her time to think at all. He leant towards her, hand rising to cup the nape of her neck, gathering some of her long, thick hair between his fingers and tugging her close to him.

She wanted this. He could feel it in her tremble and the soft sigh that escaped her lips. And he wanted it too, more than he could have imagined possible. He'd wanted to touch her all evening. Only now, when he was actually touching her, did he realise that.

And it felt as if he wanted more...more than just a kiss. He wanted to silence her self-consciousness, make her know in her gut that she was as stunning as the rest of them. He wanted to make her feel really good about herself, as confident in her looks as she was in her professional abilities. Where was that urge coming from? For now, this was enough...

His mouth covered hers in a kiss that started gentle but then grew hungry, demanding, wanting more of the sweetness of her tongue against his.

The shooting hardness of his erection made him stifle a groan, but common sense wasn't making an appearance.

Not yet. He was lost and it was up to her to shakily pull back, eyes wide as she stared at him.

Maude could hardly think straight.

He'd kissed her!

Her mouth tingled. She wanted to trace her lips with her finger, but she kept her hands by her sides and somehow managed to weave a path through her confusion back to the reality of the situation.

Mateo had kissed her to prove a point. He'd felt sorry for her—wasn't that the truth of the matter? Confident in her work and clever at her job she might be, but she'd done what she always did when it came to that uncertain side of her—she'd laughed at herself, joked about the way she looked. And he'd automatically done the one thing that had occurred to him to do in front of an audience... he'd kissed her. Because he was a nice guy, underneath it all, and because he felt sorry for her. And, yes, because they were pretending to be an item and he'd been swept away by a bit of method acting because she'd pointed out their audience.

Maybe she'd given him some kind of invisible signal that she wanted him to kiss her.

Maude was mortified to think that.

'That wasn't necessary,' she said briskly. She wondered whether he could detect the slight wobble in her voice and hoped not. Her eyes were glued to his face, but in the darkness she couldn't begin to see what he was thinking.

Was he embarrassed that he had acted on impulse and done something he knew hadn't been necessary? Now he was staring at her—was he making comparisons between her and the supermodels he was fond of dating?

No. Maude knew in her heart that was an uncharitable accusation, but she didn't want to assume that he might have been attracted to her, even if it was for just a moment in time, caught up in the romance of a situation they had engineered. There lay a dangerous road—some gut instinct told her so.

'Not necessary,' he parroted huskily.

'No. Not at all. I mean, I know you kissed me to…to show them that we were really an item…but there was no need at all! I doubt they were even looking in this direction.'

'Is that what you think?'

'What do you mean?'

'You think I kissed you because I wanted to confirm the story we'd told everyone?'

'Y-yes…why else?' Maude stammered. 'Unless you felt sorry for me. I know I have a few hang-ups.'

'Shh.'

Maude trembled when he held one finger over her

mouth as he continued to pin his dark, pensive gaze on her face.

'No,' she whispered, tugging aside his finger, but then keeping it linked with hers. 'This isn't me. I'm one hundred percent the professional.'

'Maybe I kissed you because I wanted to.'

'Of course you didn't. You're teasing me.'

'I never lie about things like this. I kissed you because you turn me on.'

The breath left Maude in a whoosh and the dangerous ground she feared trembled underneath her feet, like a sudden earthquake.

How was this possible? How could she turn him on? Men ran to type, and his type was blonde and sensational. Was it because she was a novelty and, as they said, a change was as good as a rest? Had she awakened something in him, some kind of sexual curiosity, because he was seeing a different side to her, just as she was seeing a different side to him?

If that was the case, then the best and only thing she could do was to set him straight, because she wasn't born yesterday. The guy could have any woman he wanted with the crook of his finger. Very few would be able to resist. It wasn't simply because he was good-looking, or rich, or smart. Independently, those were traits that a lot of men possessed, and indeed some possessed a combination of all three, but not like Mateo Moreno.

Mateo Moreno was in a league of his own, and being swept up in the moment like an infatuated schoolgirl because he'd happened to pay her the compliment of the decade would be a big mistake.

'Do I turn you on?' he asked roughly, interrupting her thoughts with that single, devastating question.

'That...doesn't matter.'

'What do you mean?'

'It means that that's not what we're about.'

'Because I own the company you work in? Because I'm your boss?'

'Amongst other things,' Maude muttered, horribly uncomfortable but driven to stay and finish the conversation she had started.

'Believe me,' Mateo ground out with utter sincerity, 'I don't get it either. I have never believed in mixing business with pleasure. In fact, the opposite. I've always made sure to keep my private life out of the office.'

He raked his fingers through his hair and took a step back. The very fact that she felt the void and missed the heat of his proximity was enough to get the alarm bells sounding ever louder.

'But we're here,' she shot back urgently. 'It's out of the ordinary...*this*...and I guess it's taken us both unawares! It's been pretty stressful, having to keep up the charade. I didn't think... Well, you know, I didn't think that there would be this much attention directed at us, but maybe I should have known. We're both out of our comfort zones and we did something we would never have done in a million years!'

For a few seconds, Mateo didn't say anything.

She was flushed, her eyes bright. Frankly, she was desperate to shove this small indiscretion some place where it could never see the light of day again, and she was right. Everything she said made sense. They were both out of their comfort zones. With typical self-assurance, he had assumed that this brief adventure would be a situation over which he would have ultimate control, and why not? He had ultimate control over every aspect of his life, didn't he?

But he hadn't banked on the woman gazing earnestly up at him having so much sex appeal, nor had he catered for his legendary cool being sideswiped by feminine charms he hadn't come close to glimpsing in all the time they'd worked together.

Life, for once, had taken him utterly by surprise and he'd acted out of character.

This was the time to back away at speed—Mateo knew that. Maude Thornton wasn't like the women he was accustomed to dating. She was serious, about her work and about life in general. She wasn't someone to yelp with joy at the prospect of a fling with him and he wasn't the sort to declare intentions he knew would never materialise to get a woman into bed with him, however much he knew that she would enjoy every second of the experience as much as he would.

In every respect, they stood on opposite sides of a divide, and it was a very important divide. Forget about the fact that he was her boss—they were two consenting adults at the end of the day. No, this divide was a more fundamental one. This was a divide anchored in a difference of mind set, a difference of goals, hopes and expectations.

She expected love.

It was who she was.

She might have her personal insecurities, but she was a woman who wanted it all, or at least all the things he didn't want.

And she deserved to get everything she wanted without him messing with those dreams simply by taking her down a path she might end up regretting having taken.

'You're right,' he agreed. He glanced around him, suddenly restless and out of sorts.

'I know I am!'

'It's late. I should start thinking about heading back to London.'

'You should.'

He hesitated, shifted, glanced at her, looked away and then pinned his dark eyes on her face.

'You're…okay?'

'Why wouldn't I be?'

'You're right. What happened just then…should never have happened.'

'I hope the traffic back is okay.' She smiled a glassy smile and fiddled with her hair, which had unravelled over the course of the evening.

Mateo made an effort not to let his eyes drift down to her mouth…or dwell for too long on those chestnut tendrils of hair that had escaped the little chain of thin plaits forming a crown from which her long, wavy hair cascaded past her shoulders. He certainly didn't glance further down to the full breasts, more than a handful, or the slender waist curving out to rounded hips.

She was as cool as a cucumber while he…

Horny teenager sprang to mind. It was infuriating.

'Why don't you take next week off, Maude?'

'Whatever for?'

'Relax after the party. Surely you're due some time off?'

'Maybe next Monday,' Maude agreed thoughtfully. 'I can help Mum tidy up here and spend a bit of time with Amy. But I'll be in from Tuesday. I have a meeting with Doug Smith about the project we're working on at Canary Wharf.'

Back to business, Mateo thought, and it got on his nerves, because he was still in the grip of a physical response he had no time for. He tilted his head to one side and forced a grim smile.

'Have fun tonight.' He began to walk and she fell into step next to him.

'I'll do my best,' she said politely. 'Although, I quite fancy ditching it and going to bed instead.'

Mateo nearly groaned aloud at the image that suddenly flashed through his head.

'No need to see me to my car, Maude.'

'Okay.' She stopped abruptly. 'Safe drive back, Mateo. And thanks for this evening!'

Maude was held captive by the glitter in his eyes, the angled shadows of his handsome face.

That kiss still burnt her lips but it was something to be forgotten. They'd agreed.

She backed away then gave a small, stilted wave before spinning round on her heels and hurrying back to the house into which everyone had disappeared, no witnesses anywhere to their abrupt, detached parting.

The night air was still and humid, and for the life of her Maude couldn't work out why it suddenly felt as though the fairy dust had been blown away.

Maybe, just maybe, her mother had a point and she should start to think about finding Mr Right after all...

CHAPTER THREE

MAUDE SURFACED THE following morning to urgent knocking on the bedroom door.

It took time for her brain to engage and even longer for her body to follow suit.

What a night. There'd been too much of everything—nerves…tension…anxiety about playing a role to which she'd signed up on the spur of the moment, only to regret it when she'd stood in front of the mirror, looking at her reflection in a floaty blue dress that was so unlike the outfits her boss was accustomed to seeing her in. *What had she done?*

But of course, the second she had confirmed to her parents that Mateo would be coming, there had been no turning back. Had it been Angus, as originally planned, then it would have been fine. Angus she could have handled. Mateo, on the other hand, had kept her nerves in a state of high-wire tension so that, when she'd hit the club with Amy and her friends, the release of no longer having him at her side had catapulted her into just a little too much of everything—too much drink, too much loud music, too much dancing.

And too much of a raging headache at three in the morning when she'd just about managed to stagger to the bathroom and swallow a couple of tablets before crawling back into bed.

On the plus side, heading straight out to the club after Mateo went meant her parents had not had the opportunity to quiz her. Yet. Time wasn't on her side when it came to that thorny problem but Maude would cross that bridge when she came to it.

More immediately, the knocking on the bedroom door wasn't going away, and she eventually dragged herself out of bed, caught a glimpse of the time on her mobile and with a groan realised that it was after ten.

She flung on her dressing gown en route to the door, unlocked it and peered out, expecting to see her mother, bright-eyed, bushy-tailed and with a list of questions about Mateo filling a side of A4—none of which she felt equipped to answer when she was still nursing the remnants of her hangover.

She wasn't expecting Mateo.

In a rush, the dull hangover disappeared and she was suddenly as sharp as a tack, open-mouthed and stunned into shocked, disbelieving silence.

She was frazzled and bleary-eyed, her hair a tangled mess, while he looked as though he'd just stepped off the cover of a magazine. He was unfairly and sinfully sexy in black jeans, a faded grey polo and handmade loafers.

Maude yanked the bathrobe tightly around her and arched her eyebrows.

'What are you doing here?' Her mouth was dry and her crisp greeting emerged as a croak.

'You look lousy.'

'Thanks very much, which doesn't answer my question.'

'Can I come in?'

'No!' In case he had other thoughts on the matter, she inched the door shut a little more.

'You might want to rethink that, Maude.'

'Why? And you *still* haven't answered my question. You should be in London! When did you get here anyway?'

'Over an hour ago, to answer your last question first. Let me in.'

'Over an hour ago?'

Her heart was beating like a sledgehammer. She had no idea what was going on and the expression on his face was hardly reassuring.

'And before you ask,' Mateo continued in a low voice, 'I've been downstairs, chatting to your parents, having three cups of coffee and declining several offers of a full English breakfast. You really have to let me in, Maude. There's been...what shall I say...*an unexpected development.*'

Maude fell back. Her wide blue eyes were glued to his face as he brushed past her and strolled into the bedroom before swinging round, urging her to close the door behind them with a nod and a gesture.

She leaned against the closed door, folded her arms and stared at him.

'I'd sit if I were you,' Mateo drawled.

'You're panicking me. What's going on?'

'Before I launch into that, is there anything you want me to get for you?'

'Anything, like what?'

'Mug of strong, black coffee? Paracetamol? A glass of whisky, in case you want to try some hair of the dog? How much did you have to drink last night?'

'Not a huge amount—and I'm fine.' She'd subsided onto the chair by the bed and now stared at him in discouraging, stony silence. He was still standing in the middle of the room, elegant, sophisticated and utterly in control, whatever slice of bad news he happened to be bearing.

More than ever, Maude was conscious of her state of undress. Aside from knickers, she was naked under the thin bathrobe, and she was aware of the weight of her breasts and the push of her nipples against the abrasive towelling fabric of the robe.

They tingled, making her want to fidget.

'Just say what you have to say.' Her voice was gruff.

For the first time, Mateo looked uncomfortable. He sighed and moved to the bed to perch on the side so that they were on eye level, his thigh almost touching her knee.

'Where to begin? To cut a long story short, Maude, I woke up this morning to find a text from Cassie telling me that I might want to buy one of the Sunday rags because there was something about me in it.'

'You came all the way back here to tell me that?' She was genuinely confused. 'I don't understand. What would that have to do with me? Look, whatever went on between you and your ex is your business, Mateo. Yes, we embarked on this *arrangement* because it felt like it suited both of us, but I don't want to hear about what your girlfriend has to say about it.' Maude frowned. 'Why is that in a tabloid newspaper, anyway? I'm not getting any of this.'

'You also happen to feature in the article.'

'What do you mean?'

'I mean my ex has decided to have a little fun at my expense.' His voice was grim and his mouth had thinned, but his dark eyes remained fixed on her face, steady and grave.

'Explain,' Maude whispered, already predicting what he was about to say and dreading confirmation of her suspicions.

'The blonde who approached us yesterday clearly decided to find out first-hand what was going on, and she got in touch with Cassie to tell her about you.'

'She said that she didn't know the two of you had broken up…'

'I'd told Cassie that I was seeing someone but I never mentioned any names. Heck, Maude, it was just a piece of spectacular bad luck that someone at that wedding party knew my ex. Who the hell would have thought?'

'Amy knows anybody who's anybody in the world of fashion,' Maude said dully. 'That would have been the connection. What…what was in the paper, Mateo?'

'I debated bringing it, but in the end I thought better of it.'

'Why?'

'Because we're engaged.'

Maude's mouth fell open and she stared at him in utter shock.

'Sorry?'

'It would seem that I have found the love of my life with you and we're engaged.'

'No. No, no, no, no, *no*…'

'Believe me, I'm as horrified as you are by this development.'

'Have you spoken to her?'

'She's diplomatically not picking up,' he said drily. 'Although what would be the point of a conversation? She wanted to punish me for ending things and she chose the most effective way of doing it. I drove here at lightning speed on a damage-limitation mission.'

'My parents!' Maude squeaked.

'Thankfully, they don't subscribe to any Sunday tabloids, but they're going to hear the glad tidings sooner rather than later, I should imagine. I wanted to wait until we had this conversation before saying anything to either of them.'

'What…excuse did you give them for showing up at the crack of dawn?'

'Impulse decision to ditch the work commitments for the day.'

'I need to think and I need to get dressed.'

Maude realised that she was clutching the bath robe so tightly that her knuckles were white.

'We need to decide what we plan on doing before we go down,' Mateo said calmly, and Maude looked at him with disbelief.

'How can you be so…so…*cool* about this?' she cried.

'Would you rather I descend into screaming hysteria?'

'This is a catastrophe!'

'It's an inconvenience,' Mateo ground out in response. 'And one that will obviously be sorted, if not this instant, then certainly in the coming days.'

'And how do we set about doing that?' Maude demanded. She leapt to her feet but then remained rooted to the spot, glaring at him as the situation developed in her head in all its horrendous glory. 'You don't know my mum. This is what she's been waiting for…for *ever*! If we go down there and announce that we…that we're *engaged*…then it'll be all around her friendship group by this evening and there'll be an ad in the local newspaper by lunchtime tomorrow!'

'That's surely a bit of an exaggeration?'

'I'm thirty-two years old and she's been desperate for me to get married since I was in my early twenties.'

'You've really had to buck against the trend to develop your career, haven't you?' Mateo murmured, side-tracked by the image of a youthful Maude, digging her heels in and refusing to go down the prescribed route.

Strong, smart, feisty and a whole lot more.

He'd struggled to get where he was, had sacrificed a lot and had had to toughen up even more. They might have come from wildly different backgrounds, but in her own way she had faced her own struggles, and he admired her for that. That admiration was in his eyes as they briefly rested on her flushed face.

'Yes, I have!' Maude's head was all over the place. This was exactly what happened when she jumped in the deep end without doing her due diligence! It had all seemed so simple when they had thought up the idea. She'd been in a tizzy because Angus had let her down, and in Mateo had stepped with what had seemed a perfectly sensible solution. One that worked for both of them and would involve no more than a couple of hours with them both playing a part.

In some insane part of her she had actually thought that it might benefit her chances at branching out into more client-facing work if he got a chance to see her away from the confines of an office environment!

It had all seemed so straightforward.

It hadn't occurred to either of them that nothing in life was as easy as it seemed.

'Like I said, this will get sorted, but...' Mateo frowned, thinking. 'It doesn't have to be the end of the world.'

'I'm going to change. You should go downstairs and... and...'

'Break the news that it was all a misunderstanding? That, in fact, we've never had a relationship? It was all a case of smoke and mirrors?'

'Well...'

'Isn't that going to lead to a flurry of questions? The main one being why you allowed everyone to think that we were an item in the first place?'

Maude hesitated. She tugged the robe tighter and glared. Shorn of the constraints of their normal working relationship, they were now two people, man and woman, without the divide of their established roles separating them.

It was just something else she had failed to predict.

His dark eyes roved over her, ponderous, lazy and doing all sorts of things to her body, making it respond in ways she didn't like and didn't trust.

She turned her back to him, rustled briefly in her chest of drawers, grabbing the first things that came to hand, and informed him with a toss of her head that she was going to shower and change and he was to wait for her downstairs.

She pulled on jeans and a tee-shirt. She would have to think about an outfit for lunch when she managed to get her head around what was going on.

She emerged from the bathroom to find Mateo still in the bedroom and as relaxed as he could possibly be on the bed, half-lying down as though he hadn't a care in the world.

Before she could utter a word, he held up one hand and drawled, 'I have a suggestion.'

'You were going downstairs.'

'Incorrect,' he said gently. 'I was staying right here until we hashed this thing out.' He shrugged but there was amusement on his face as he held her gaze. 'I'm just far too much of a gentleman to contradict you when you ordered me to leave.'

'You're…you're *impossible*!' Maude snapped, moving towards the bed to stand at the bottom of it, arms folded. 'Okay. I have no idea what your suggestion is going to be, but I might as well hear it.'

Mateo crossed his legs loosely at the ankles. Maude, arms still folded, tried not to watch compulsively because the man was just so compelling, so charismatic, so ridiculously addictive to look at.

The jeans emphasised the length of his muscular legs, pulling taut across the thighs and riding low on his lean hips, and the polo had ridden up a bit. With not too much squinting, she could see a sliver of bronzed belly, and the sight made her feel all hot and bothered.

'By the way,' she snapped, 'Shoes aren't allowed on the bed. It's a house rule.'

'My apologies.'

She expected him to move and sit on the chair, which would have been a lot more calming on her fraying nerves. But instead he kicked off the loafers and they dropped to the ground, leaving the sight of bare feet, which was a thousand times more disconcerting.

'Think about it, Maude,' he said seriously. 'Your

mother is fully engaged with your brother's up and coming wedding. She's put a huge amount of effort into making sure that everything is perfect.'

'She *has* been in her element,' Maude admitted.

'With the big day so close, would you want to ruin things for her now? And for your brother and his fiancée?'

'I beg your pardon? What on earth are you talking about? Why do you think I would want to *ruin* things?'

'If we go down and break the news that this was all a charade, then your parents are going to be shocked. Your mother...' Mateo paused. He thought of his own mother, missing in action. 'Your mother loves you, and for that you should count your blessings.'

'Why do you say that?'

'Because I never had one around to give a damn.'

The silence settled between them.

What the hell had possessed him to say that?

Mateo scowled. He waited for her to jump on his casual admission, to try and prise confidences from him that he had no intention of sharing, but she remained perfectly silent with her head tilted to one side and her cornflower-blue eyes, so calm and intelligent, holding his but without asking any questions.

He vacated the bed in one easy movement and strode towards the window to perch against the sill, arms folded, as were hers. He was filled with a sudden restlessness.

'My mother walked out on me and my father when I was a baby,' he said gruffly, still scowling, still completely bewildered by this departure from his normal behaviour.

'I'm sorry,' Maude said quietly.

'A better prospect rode into town and she decided to hitch her wagon to his and take off. She never looked back.' He raked his fingers through his hair and prowled the room, absently taking in the bits and pieces of Maude's past that were there in the framed photos and the children's books from a long time ago.

When he finally came to a stop, it was to stand in front of her, staring down and feeling a tug of *something* at the empathy in her eyes. He'd never in his entire life needed empathy from anyone, so why wasn't he turned off by what he saw now?

In fact, he'd never needed to talk about his past with anyone in his life before, so why now?

For a split second he felt vulnerable, and it was anathema to him.

'None of this matters.' He waved aside his momentary lapse with a dismissive gesture. 'You know what I'm getting at.'

'I do.' Maude sighed. She'd brushed her hair in the bathroom but hadn't tied it back and it fell over her shoulders, halfway down her back. Distracted, she scooped it up, swung it over one shoulder and then toyed with the ends, chewing her lips, not looking at him but instead staring out of the window with a frown. It was another lovely day with the summer sun glinting on the huge gardens outside and streaming into the bedroom.

Mateo's startling admission had taken the wind from her sails. How she longed to ask more questions. She was in the grip of driving curiosity but there was no way she intended to breach boundaries. Enough had been breached already!

'I know it would stress Mum out...would stress both my parents out...if they were to think that we'd concocted the whole thing. You're right. There would be questions and all sorts of soul-searching.'

She made a decision. 'Perhaps it might be an idea to play along with the gossip. The wedding is in a matter of weeks. When you think about it, nothing really has to change. You disappear and, when I do come back here, I can always say that you're abroad.'

'The vanishing workaholic,' Mateo murmured.

'That's right. In the meantime, I'll get the opportunity to quietly start laying the foundations...'

'For our eventual parting of ways?'

'Relationships come and go.'

'Is that your experience?'

Maude frowned at the sudden change of subject. How did he do that? How did he manage to take her down one road and then, when she was dutifully following him, swing down a side alley and lead her completely astray?

Maude hated that sort of thing. She liked to know where she stood. Growing up had been an insecure business, a balancing act between displaying the confidence she knew was expected of her while tackling the uncertainty of never quite fitting in. And then that painful episode at university, when she had foolishly given herself to a guy who had ended up rejecting her...

Over the years, she had got her act together. She was in charge of her life. Was that why she did what she did—a job driven by the precision of numbers and equations? When it came to structural engineering, there was no room for uncertainty or doubts. Either the maths worked and the structure was solid or it wasn't. She liked that.

It was so different from the business of emotions and all the angst that came along with them. When she'd been studying design and the dynamics of concrete and timber, those days of being painfully shy—of growing up so much taller and bigger than everyone else, of avoiding parties because of the gnawing fear that she would be the wallflower glued to the side—had gone and were long ago and faraway.

'What do you mean?' Her voice cooled.

'Remember I asked you why you were still single at your age?'

'I'm not yet over the hill!'

'Remember I said that the reason I was puzzled was because you're a beautiful, intelligent woman? Did you get your fingers burnt in the past?'

'My private life is none of your business!'

'It is now that we're engaged.'

'We're *not* engaged!'

She glared at him and in return he slowly grinned back at her, his expression suddenly relaxed, amused and *boyishly* appealing.

'You're teasing me.'

'Partially,' Mateo admitted. 'Maybe I like the way you blush. Like you're doing right now. Really, though, we need to know a bit about one another if we're supposed to be a serious item. Your parents might think it odd if they ask a question only to find that we have completely different answers. They might also find it odd if I don't seem to know the slightest thing about your personal life.'

Maude hesitated. She'd embarked on this charade without thinking through the possible consequences and now, as she stared at him, she had a feeling of sinking further into quicksand.

Yet what he said made sense. He would have to know the bare bones about her and vice versa. In truth, she already knew the bare bones about *him*. He was a player who went for blondes and had made a fortune from ground zero.

And he was also a guy who had lost his mother... Who had grown up with all the insecurities of knowing that he had been abandoned, whether he ever admitted to those insecurities or not...

Looking at her with brooding intensity, Mateo was riveted by the expressions flitting across her face. He knew that he was shamelessly fishing but he wanted to know more about her and, if *he* was unrevealing, then she wasn't too far behind.

What she gave away, she gave away without really verbalising any of it in passing remarks…a look on her face…the way she turned her head to the side, shied away from whatever she didn't want to answer.

She wasn't interested in trying to garner his attention and so, rather than the usual coy remarks and flirtatious, targeted innuendo, she preferred to say as little as possible. And therein lay what, Mateo was discovering, was an irresistible appeal.

'You must have had dozens of boyfriends in the past,' he murmured encouragingly, and watched as the blush deepened.

'I've been busy with trying to forge my career!'

'Too busy for…?'

'Okay, I've been out a few times, but nothing serious!'

'Ever?'

Maude shrugged, mouth set in a stubborn line, and Mateo backed down, knowing full well that he would pick up the thread of the conversation at a later date.

'We should go down.' Maude interrupted the stretching silence. 'Face the music. We can decide what happens next...well...maybe before you leave.'

'There's a big lunch, I hear?'

'It's the last thing I fancy.'

'Your parents can't wait. I suspect announcements might be made.'

Maude groaned aloud as yet more tangled, complicated strands wove in front of her, strands that would need unpicking just as soon as Nick and Amy were married off and her mother's attention was no longer focused on the big event.

'This feels like it's all getting out of control.' Maude looked at him with shooting despair.

She had gone to the door and was standing with her hand on the knob, watching as he slowly moved to join her.

'You're the inveterate bachelor,' she tacked on acidly. 'Your ex really knew how to interfere with the smooth running of your life.'

'Is there anything more dangerous than a woman scorned?' He was standing close to her, gazing down, and Maude was held captive by his eyes.

A frisson of *something* whispered through her and she stumbled a couple of inches back, heart picking up speed.

'I've never understood why a woman would want to get revenge if she's been dumped,' Maude mumbled. 'The

CATHY WILLIAMS   61

best revenge you can ever get is by moving on with your life and showing the guy who dumped you that you really don't give a damn.'

'Is that right?' Mateo murmured.

Maude yanked open the door and stepped out into the corridor, which felt huge, light and airy after the enclosed intimacy of her bedroom.

She sucked in a deep breath and spun round on her heels, feeling his soft tread at her side and wondering what he was thinking.

She found out soon enough when he whispered into her ear, 'We have parts to play. I'll let you take the lead when it comes to being as vague or as graphic about the details of our searing, sudden love. Trust me, I'll be as curious as your parents to hear about how we fell deeply in love in the space of…how long? Not hours, I would suggest.'

Maude stopped abruptly, on the verge of reminding him that there was nothing funny about the situation. But before she could say anything he continued, his voice firm, inflexible and suddenly very serious.

'But, trust me when I tell you that I don't like this situation any more than you do. I also realise that I carry the full brunt of the blame for what's happened.'

'What are you talking about? We both entered into this…arrangement of our own free will.'

'I should have…' Mateo raked his fingers through his hair and skewered his eyes onto her, only the tic in his jaw giving away the fact that he was furious at what had happened out of the blue. 'Foreseen certain possible outcomes.'

'How on earth were you to predict that one of my brother's fiancée's friends would know your ex because she works in the fashion industry?' Maude sighed. 'I don't blame you. We overstepped, you know, boundary lines… and maybe that was the mistake we made.'

'And yet…' Mateo breathed '…what's the point of boundary lines if you can't occasionally step over them? I didn't get where I am today by obeying every single rule in the book.'

Maude shivered.

He was being honest. Mateo Moreno was the maverick whose genius had got him to the very top and mavericks had their own rule books.

'I'll try and be as vague as possible.' Her voice was a little shaky and this time it was because of the effect he was having on her, his proximity, his uncompromising masculinity and the way it made her feel—soft, fluttery and feminine in ways she had never felt before.

'If the tabloids have an angle on this, then the paparazzi won't be too far behind. I know how they operate. I also know how fast these stories die down.'

'Okay…'

'It would work for us to disappear for a few days. I have a place close to where I'm planning an ambitious project—a select housing development using the local natural resources and making every building as green as possible. It would be quite easy to take some time out there in the safe knowledge that prying eyes and wide-angled camera lenses won't be able to pay any unwelcome visits.'

'A place? An office? Is it the Scottish branch you're opening up, to explore expanding communities up there? Sounds perfect. We could work on whatever project this is in the meantime.' It sounded like manna from heaven to Maude—no conflicting emotions, back to an office environment where normality could be resumed. She could stay somewhere local, where no one knew who she was, and if Mateo said there would be no paparazzi, then there would be none.

She thought wistfully of an outpost in deepest Scotland where she could pick up being the woman she was and not the one who had suddenly decided to make a disruptive appearance in her well-ordered life.

'That's a really good idea.' Maude relaxed. Her parents could also be put on hold for a bit, as well as friends. By the time she returned to London the fuss would have died down and, as he said, they'd be yesterday's news. Gossip had a way of doing that.

They headed down to the kitchen, following the sound of voices.

Everyone was there—her parents, Nick and Amy and several family members who had stayed over.

The large kitchen, with its long, rectangular wooden table, bore the remnants of the full English Mateo had earlier refused. Amy was by the sink, rubber gloves on, stacking the dishwasher.

As they entered, however, all heads swung in their direction. Catching her mother's eye, Maude wasn't surprised to see pleasure on her face mixed with bursting excitement and the gleaming look of someone with a million eager questions. Even her dad, normally the more sanguine of the two when it came to digging deep into her private life, looked thrilled to bits.

It was clear that the tabloid press had landed squarely in the lap of Amy and, sure enough, her mother's opening words were, 'Engaged! I *knew* it, my darling! What did I say to you, Richard? Didn't I say? A mother can tell! Oh, Mateo, you darling man! I'll bet you were horrified that whoever spilled the beans took the wind out of your sails! Were you going to surprise us with an announcement after the wedding was done and dusted?'

'You dark horse, Maude Thornton! You didn't breathe a *word* when we were out last night and we wanted to find out all about the dashing chap in your life! Now you'll have to confess all. Details, please, and spare me nothing!'

'Sorry, Mateo mate, you're going to have to get used to my wife-to-be telling it like it is. Congratulations, man!'

Champagne was brought out of the fridge and Maude let herself be swept along on a tide of goodwill and questions, questions, questions. But she could see light at the end of the tunnel and that fortified her. They would disappear on their work trip to Scotland...and everything would be calmer when she returned. So his hand casually draped over her shoulders as she fielded the Spanish Inquisition, not a problem.

And when eventually the questions slowed, she tried not to beam as he said, ruefully, that he wouldn't be making it to lunch.

He gave her shoulder a reassuring squeeze and Maude already had her response on the tip of her tongue when he continued smoothly, 'And you may have to release this wonderful woman from her lunchtime duties as well. The next few days might, regrettably, require some Houdini escapology, so we're going to disappear and miss the fun.

'By which I mean...' his audience was hooked '...reporters standing outside houses making a nuisance of themselves. The quicker we leave, the better.'

Maude's ear tickled when he continued, his dark, velvety voice as disconcerting as a physical caress, 'I hope your passport's in order?'

'Huh?'

Maude whipped round to gaze at him with genuine surprise.

'Your passport.' Mateo smiled and touched her nose with the tip of his finger in a gesture which she knew was designed to show just the right level of loving affection. The guy could have won an Oscar. 'We're heading to my place in Italy!' He raised his flute in a toast and everyone else followed suit.

'Italy?' Maude parroted.

'I think you'll like it there, my darling. And key priority? Pack swimsuits. I'll make sure my private jet is ready and waiting for us by nine in the morning!'

CHAPTER FOUR

MAUDE DISCOVERED WHAT it would feel like to be swept along on a rip tide.

One minute, she'd been bobbing along as comfortably as she could, given the circumstances, and the next minute…? Life was moving at warp speed and she was playing catch-up.

They had remained in the kitchen for another hour before everyone had started drifting off to get ready for the fancy lunch, which she would now not be attending. As soon as the last person had vacated the kitchen, she'd shut the door and spun round to face Mateo, hands on her hips,

'*Passport? Swimsuits? Private jet?*' She'd seethed as he'd calmly strolled to the fridge to help himself to some orange juice. 'You *told* me that we were going to *Scotland*!'

'Did I?'

'Don't you *dare* look at me as though I've suddenly taken leave of my senses!'

'If you recall, I didn't say a word about Scotland. I admit, it would certainly fill the necessary criteria about being out of the way, but that office is far from finished and the development is still in the embryo stages. I think the locals might be a little alarmed if we were to show up with mock-ups of what their new housing might look like.'

'Very funny.'

She'd frowned and had had to concede that he hadn't confirmed where they would be going for their brief disappearing act. She had jumped to conclusions and he had cheerfully allowed her to.

With a thousand other questions to ask, Maude had found herself shuffled out of the kitchen without pinning him down on anything at all because, he'd pointed out, he would have to return to London to get various things sorted before they left.

'Time,' he'd said, 'Is of the essence.' This, as he'd been scribbling something on one of the paper napkins—the name of the airfield where she was to meet him.

'Don't worry,' he'd then reassured her. 'We *will* be working, and where we're going will be one-hundred-per-cent journalist-proof. There will be other people around, so don't be alarmed at the prospect of being secluded anywhere with me.'

'You still haven't told me where exactly we'll be going…' His words had gone some way to banking down her flights of fancy.

The truth was, she *had* catapulted herself into a state of panic at the thought of leaving the country with Mateo. Swimsuits, private jets and passports…they'd formed a picture of a holiday abroad and she had reacted with instinctive horror.

Why?

Because he got to her in ways that sent alarm bells ringing. Whatever simmering attraction that had been there all along…whatever inappropriate *awareness* of his sinfully potent good looks…had been manageable in the contained environment of an office, with the bustle of other people around, the hum of computers and the buzz of phones. But take that safety net away...

She had reacted with immediate horror.

She'd thought back to that kiss and had then projected to a few days spent lazing around somewhere with a pool, and her nerves had gone into instant freefall.

She was thirty-two years old! She wasn't a teenager swooning over the hottest boy in the class! She knew better than to let her emotions rule her head again. She was mortified because she knew that he had no such qualms about being anywhere with her, whether there were chaperones around or not.

Yes, he had told her that she was beautiful, but Maude knew to take that compliment with a pinch of salt. In the wake of her having confessed her insecurities to him, he had responded with kindness, as many would in a similar situation.

Left with no option, Maude had decided that she would simply have to accept the break with routine but treat it as work related.

And now she was here. At the designated airfield not a million miles away from where her parents lived, as it happened.

And their destination?

Italy.

She'd packed the minimum. He had sent a car for her and she had stepped into the sleek, black Range Rover, with its privacy glass and breathed a sigh of relief—because, as it had sped away, she had spotted two cars parked half on the grassy kerb outside the gates of the house.

Maude had had a comfortable life, but nothing had

prepared her for the feeling of stepping out of that chauffeur-driven car to wait for a private jet to whisk her away.

The place was crowded. Small light-aircraft were lined up, booked for flying lessons. People were spilling out of the café, drinking coffee and gazing at the planes from behind a protective wire fence.

There were several private jets, and she was staring at them when she heard Mateo say, right next to her, 'I see you're travelling light. That's a first, in my experience, when it comes to a woman...'

Maude spun round, heart beating fast, and shielded her eyes from the glare of the sun.

He oozed sex appeal in a pair of faded jeans and a white, collared tee-shirt. At his feet was a well-used luxury leather holdall and he was wearing dark sunglasses, although he removed them to gaze down at her.

'I...just threw in a couple of things. We're not going to be there long. Your jet...'

'Will be here.' He glanced at his designer watch and then she followed his gaze to where a black speck was approaching the airfield, filling the air with the distinctive roar of its powerful engines. 'Right about now...'

Maude's mouth fell open.

The black beast dominated the airfield, a shark among minnows, and there wasn't a face in the crowd that didn't turn to stare.

'Come along.' Mateo jostled her briskly. 'I can't waste too much of this day. I have meetings lined up and I want you along for a couple of them.'

'Of course!' This was more like it—thank goodness. She would have to stop fretting about things that weren't going to happen.

Behind them, the driver had taken their bags. The crowd parted as they walked through to the jet. This was what immense wealth felt like, Maude acknowledged. Everything paled in comparison. It was the material manifestation of his ruthless drive towards the top.

He'd gone from an impoverished background to having everything at his fingertips. The ultimate maverick who had defied the odds to become the biggest lion in the jungle.

What had been sacrificed along the way?

Curiosity had no place here, but Maude was suddenly consumed with it. What had life been like for him? He had let slip that confidence about his mother...had shown her a glimpse of a boy who had grown up with the notion that he had been abandoned. Some things were very hard to paper over with common sense and grown-up logic—that was one of them. To think that you'd been left behind by your own mother, that she had chosen another life rather than the one with you in it, would have cut deep.

Was that why he was so detached from women? Why he could have countless relationships without ever allowing any of them to become a permanent feature in his life?

It was funny to think that, for all their backgrounds were so different, she too had absorbed things as a child that she had not been able to shake. She had had love and all the privileges of a middle-class background. Yet she had never been able to forget the way the other kids had looked at her when she had started shooting up—the giggles behind their hands, the invitations that hadn't dropped on the doormat.

She'd developed lots of coping mechanisms but had

those experiences, like his, followed her into adulthood, defining what she did and how she reacted to stuff?

Had she spent a lifetime shying away from giving herself to anyone because of her own insecurities, which had been compounded by a youthful misjudgement with a guy, the sort of thing that happens to everyone at least once in their lifetime?

Of course she had. Maude knew that, just as she knew that time had gone by and the past should never dictate the present or, worse, the future. But what was to be done about it?

Her love life had frankly been non-existent for years. The occasional date, boyfriends here and there, had always taken second place to her career.

Had she been too scared to jump in at the deep end? Should she have done that ages ago? Maybe if she had taken a few risks, allowed herself to be hurt a couple of times, she would now be in a different place, emotionally less fragile. She wanted kids. She wanted a partner at her side. How long would she carry on searching for the one guy who wouldn't hurt her?

She surfaced from uncomfortable thoughts to find herself in the cabin of Mateo's private jet and she gasped and stood stock-still.

'Wow.'

'First time in a private jet?'

'No, I hop on these all the time when I have to travel short haul.'

Mateo burst out laughing. 'Why did I never see that sense of humour before? Help yourself to anything you want to eat or drink. I'm going to spend the time working.'

'You haven't told me much about where I'll be staying.'

'Haven't had the opportunity.' Mateo moved to one of the leather sofas, a pale-green affair that looked elegant enough for a five-star hotel, and Maude sat in a cream one opposite. 'And now...? Well, we'll be there very shortly. It's as safe as Fort Knox when it comes to ensuring privacy. I haven't had a chance to ask...but were discussions ongoing about this situation after I left?'

Maude sighed. 'It was all a bit of a rush, to be honest. Everyone was heading off to lunch, and of course, by the time they all returned, I was already back in London.'

'Good. Give it a few days and the fuss will have died down considerably.'

'Not with my parents. But when they next see me it will probably be the night before the wedding, and I can always make up some excuse for you not being around. It'll be hectic anyway. No one will have time to analyse why the guy I'm supposed to be engaged to has better things to do than to accompany me to my brother's wedding. And afterwards I can begin laying the foundations for it being a relationship that was never going to work.'

'You're very level-headed, aren't you?' Mateo murmured and she reddened.

'Yes, I am.' *Not his type*—that much she could tell from the amused expression on his face. 'Can I ask what the project is that we will be working on when we get to...er... Italy? How big is it?'

'All in due course, Maude. Why don't you try and relax for a couple of hours, instead of diving into work-related matters before we've even landed?'

It felt like a reprimand, a gentle, amused reprimand, and she nodded and looked away. She had come prepared for a reset. No more blushing Maude but back to the Maude he knew—composed and ready to pick up the baton with whatever work issue he threw at her. She'd even dressed the part, in a neat grey skirt, a white blouse and her flat pumps, no concession made for the heat, and certainly no hint that she might interpret this as anything but a necessary detour which would involve work.

She pursed her lips and made a show of looking around her whilst she felt like a fool. The space was compact but beautifully and lavishly furnished, with leather seating and small walnut tables dotted in convenient places for computers and drinks. A partition in the middle sectioned off a desk and chair and behind it Maude could glimpse a pale sofa that would double as a bed.

The pilot stopped by to chat for five minutes, and they were offered whatever they wanted by a young man smartly attired in blue and white, but largely they were left to their own devices.

Mateo submerged himself in work, oblivious to his surroundings as the jet took off...and Maude contemplated how the next few days were going to be spent.

It took Maude under a day and a half to realise that this was not going to be the working retreat she had originally hoped for.

They emerged after their luxurious flight to a rolling panorama of hills creeping up to sharply peaked mountains. She had expected the bustle of an airstrip somewhere, only to discover that the runway was actually on Mateo's own estate, which seemed to go on and on and on as far was the eye could see.

It was breathtaking.

He casually pointed out his acreage of vineyards

stretching off into the distance and told her that the wine produced, fine though it was, was purely for local consumption—and of course his, whenever he found the time to return here.

She was led into an enormous villa, sepia-coloured and fronted by a sprawling, circular courtyard, which was dominated by a fountain.

Inside there was pale wood, pale marble and pale furnishings and, at the back, a splendid infinity pool. It was cleverly sunken into a carefully tended area that was contrived to look like a garden left to grow wild, from the dancing, coloured flowers to the artful planting of shady trees.

Of course, there were people around, staff to take care of everything, from the cooking to the cleaning. And in a building tucked to the side were offices where the people who ran the vineyards took care of business.

There were chaperones aplenty and yet, from the start, it didn't *feel* like work—not in these surroundings. Not with the sun pouring down like liquid honey on a lush, green, hilly vista.

Now Maude gazed from the window of her bedroom to the pool which she planned to avoid at all costs.

It was a little after six and she would be heading down shortly for drinks.

'Work talk again, I'm afraid,' Mateo had apologised. 'The project, as you saw from yesterday's drawings, will intersect the town close to the local church. We need to work on a way around that, making sure that every single thing is done harmoniously and is in keeping. Alberto Hussi is in charge and he'll be joining us for dinner.'

Maude's heart had lifted. *More work? In the most stun-*

*ning place on the planet? Where lush, peaceful surround-
ings beckoned one to explore and relax? A place where
computers should be hidden away and mobile phones
stuck in drawers, out of sight? Perfect.*

There'd been no blushing when their eyes had tangled,
his dark and unreadable. A crisp nod had said it all.

'And Maude,' he had added in a lazy drawl, 'I know
that, now we're here, there's no game playing but there's
really no need for you to dress formally.'

Standing out on the wide, marble-floored veranda that
gave onto views of the open countryside, with nightfall
throwing everything into dark relief and with the last of
the guys from the vinery gone for the evening, Maude
had shivered.

Behind them, two of the practically invisible members of staff were clearing away the vast array of wine
glasses which had been used to taste various reds—two
from Mateo's own estate, the rest from other vineries in
the area. An elaborate meal had been served earlier in a
formal dining room.

'I wasn't dressed formally. I didn't think so,' she had
responded, and his eyebrows had shot up.

'Don't forget,' he'd murmured, the hairs on the back
on her neck standing on end, 'That I know what you look
like when you decide to do away with the starchy outfits. I know this isn't officially a *holiday*, and I realise
that work is on the agenda, but you're in my home and I
would like you to try and unwind as much as you can.'

The gauntlet had been thrown down.

Stiff and formal would signify that the problem was
definitely on her side, that she couldn't relax around

him…and, if that were the case, would he read anything into it?

Yes, he would. He would wonder why she was suddenly so skittish around him when she had been the ultimate professional in the past. And how long would it be before he concluded that he got under her skin because she was attracted to him? He was quite accustomed to those reactions from women, after all.

On the spot, Maude decided that she would ditch the three prissy skirts and the two loose, comfortable, buttoned-up blouses and resort to the culottes, khaki shorts and tee-shirts she had added to the pile on the spur of the moment.

Stepping out of her comfort zone, she resolved, would be good for her…

Mateo was waiting on the veranda for Maude to join him. He had forgotten how much he enjoyed the privacy of this sprawling villa, and the vineyard, which had been his life's ambition from when he'd been a kid. He came at the most a couple of times a year and never for longer than a weekend. He'd never brought a woman here. As he gazed over the dark shapes of the hills, and the marching silhouettes of the grape vines, he couldn't help but think how ironic it was that the first woman to come here was someone he was supposedly engaged to, to dodge the sort of tawdry publicity that would have prolonged a situation not of their making.

The breeze was cool. He could detect the rustle of trees, leaves and grapes swinging on vines. The smell was fragrant. How could he have forgotten what peace felt like? Naturally, there was work to be done here.

He hadn't been lying when he'd told Maude that it would be something of a busman's holiday. He and three high-profile businessmen with small but profitable vineyards were planning to expand into the community and breathe much-needed extra life into the area that had been good to them over the years. It had been something in the making for the past year and a half. This was a perfect opportunity to start the groundwork, but right now...?

He had the strangest urge to *play truant*.

He'd never had that urge. Even as a school boy, playing truant hadn't been on his radar. Playing truant was for losers whose life ambitions were no higher than the gutter.

For Mateo? He had always been far too driven and far too focused to go down that road. Even to contemplate it.

So why now?

Because his mind was preoccupied with other things... With a woman who had taken him by surprise and was now holding him captive to an attraction he couldn't seem to sideline...

It wasn't going to do.

He straightened as he heard the soft pad of her footsteps behind him, pausing by the bespoke glass doors that opened out concertina-style to the back veranda, a seamless divide between exterior and interior.

He turned around and hissed under his breath.

How the heck was a man supposed to concentrate on anything when he was confronted by a woman with those assets?

She was in pale-green loose culottes and a simple, white V-necked tee-shirt. But under those culottes he could define the length of her legs and, under that tee-shirt, the heavy swing of her generous breasts.

He lowered his eyes and moved towards her, aware of his body reacting against all the diktats of his brain.

'I hate to break the news,' he opened, reaching for a bottle of white from the silver wine-cooler on one of the many tables on the veranda. 'But Alberto isn't going to make it tonight. Problems with his mother. She's been taken to hospital with pains in her chest.'

'Oh, my. I'm sorry to hear that.'

'Wine?'

'A small glass, if we're going to be working…'

'Might be a bit of a stretch without his input, but of course. I see you've come equipped with your laptop.'

'Well, yes.'

'Sit, Maude.' There was only so long they could discuss work-related issues before the conversation dried up. He didn't want her to feel uncomfortable here. Whilst they had entered into this arrangement, having mutually agreed at the time that it was a good idea, it was his fault that they were now having to duck for cover from the slings and arrows his ex had decided to let loose. She didn't deserve to feel awkward or, worse, trapped into having to work because she didn't think she had a choice. She was in his villa, in his territory…the last thing he wanted her to think was that she was at his mercy.

'There's work to get through here.' He waited until she was sitting opposite him, then he leaned forward, his elbows resting on his thighs, his dark eyes serious. 'But, like I said, I want you to take time out and relax. The weather's good…whatever you want is on tap…' He slanted a slow smile at her. 'No one's going to be following us out here. I can show you the vineyard, take you to some of the local beauty spots...'

'You don't have to, Mateo.'

'I know.'

'I...it's...very beautiful here.' She reached for the glass of wine being offered and turned as a platter of canapés was placed on the table between them.

She made herself forget about the unnerving effect he had on her and gazed at the view.

'How long have you had this place? All this land...the vineyards...it's a world away from the rat race.'

'Yes. It is.'

'You sound surprised.' Maude sipped the wine and smiled.

'I'd forgotten how serene it is,' Mateo admitted.

He'd angled his chair so that they were both contemplating the same view, watching the same stars studded against the velvet darkness of the night skies.

A wave of utter peace crept into him, slow and steady, filling every part of him. For the first time, Mateo went with the flow and allowed himself to kick back.

'How often do you get to come here?' Maude murmured.

They both reached for a canapé from the table between them at the same time and their fingers touched.

He didn't pull away. Nor did he look at her. His hand lingered. Or was that her imagination?

The brush of his finger was as hot as the mark of a branding iron.

That dark, treacherous excitement she had felt before sizzled in her blood. She *wanted* to leave her hand right there, wanted the thrill of it touching his.

She had to force herself to bring the canapé to her mouth and then keep her hand on her lap as she continued to stare straight ahead, heart thudding in her chest.

'Not often enough.'

'Why not?'

'Work. Too much of it.'

'I suppose that's a blessing and a curse.' Maude smiled, darted her eyes across to his aquiline profile and shivered. 'If you don't work, how can you become...er...as wealthy as you have?'

'And is that where you're aiming to go?'

'What do you mean?'

'To the top...in pursuit of wealth?'

'Not at all.' She sipped the wine and let the alcohol loosen her. It was excellent wine. 'Money doesn't mean anything to me.'

'That's because you've always had access to it.' Mateo glanced at his glass to see that it was finished so he helped himself to another and topped up Maude's as well.

He found himself thinking about his childhood, the road he never went down, and knew that the last thing he wanted to do was go there in yet more confessional mode.

'Maybe. Probably. It would have been a lot easier to have become a spoiled brat.'

Mateo grinned, admiring her honesty. He looked at her and, when their eyes met, he held her gaze.

'I've met a lot of those in my life,' he said huskily.

'Trust me. So have I. Why here? Can I ask?'

'What do you mean?'

'Why do you have a house here? In this particular place in Italy? Is this where you grew up?'

And, just like that, Mateo knew that he was going to

CATHY WILLIAMS 81

do the unthinkable and lower his defences. Something about being here, perhaps, with the silence around them and the memories this place stirred...*and being in this place with this particular woman.*

She was so measured, so intelligent...so unlike the women he went out with.

He brushed aside the whisper of what a threat might feel like, because it was only what he didn't know that might prove dangerous. Everything else—people, women, business—you were in control of, once you knew what you were dealing with. And, despite surprises along the way, Mateo knew Maude. There might be many sides to her he hadn't seen before but that was true of everyone. The fact was, she remained his cool-headed, dependable employee—serious and dedicated, risk-averse and sensible.

She couldn't have been more different from Cassie. She wanted nothing from him and was sharp and insightful enough to know that, as two human beings went, they were worlds apart, whatever heat had burned between them when they had kissed.

'Not a million miles away,' Mateo confessed. 'My father worked at a vineyard. Not one of these local ones, but a bigger, more commercial concern. He was housed there. He never owned his own place because he was never paid enough.'

'Did that bother you?' Maude asked curiously.

'It made me realise,' Mateo said drily, 'That, when I got older, the only vineyard I would ever stay on would be one I owned.'

'And you did it.'

Mateo looked around him, the master of all he surveyed. He'd put in the blood, sweat and tears and he'd done it. This vineyard was his crowning glory even though he had many other properties and holdings all over the world.

So how was it that he so seldom made it over here?

This place was in his blood.

'Food beckons.' He stood up and then turned to look at Maude as she hurriedly scrambled to her feet.

He reached out, an automatic gesture to help her up, and she linked her fingers tightly with his as he pulled her up towards him so that she stumbled forward into him and against him, hard chest against the soft swell of her breasts...

Mateo's breath caught sharply in his throat. His body fought against his brain and he heard his own raspy breath as the heat poured through him, staying his hand on hers and keeping her against him.

He was only inches away from kissing her.

'My apologies.' Mateo barely recognised his own voice because it was so unsteady.

'What are you apologising for?'

'You really want to know?'

Maude knew. He could see her body trembling with knowing. *Temptation.* She'd seen it in the dark flare in his eyes and felt it in the heat from his body that matched hers. But he was sensible enough to know that, alone out here, they should fight the temptation. There was no one looking this time, demanding a kiss to prove a non-existent relationship.

There was just the two of them, and no...

They couldn't let themselves be swept away by this. Could they? Could she? She'd been swept away once by a guy she'd thought was right for her. It would be crazy to let herself be swept away by a guy who was so, so wrong for her in every way...wouldn't it?

She stepped back but her eyes were still held captive by his.

'Dinner,' she croaked. 'We should go in.'

Their eyes held for a few seconds and then he nodded, raked his fingers through his hair and did her a favour by not saying anything at all. Because she had no idea what she would have done if he'd actually come right out and dealt with the elephant in the room.

CHAPTER FIVE

MAUDE WAS ASTOUNDED at how easy it was to forget about London, her parents, her brother's imminent wedding and a phoney engagement story doing the rounds courtesy of Mateo's spiteful ex.

The truth was he could not have brought her to a more perfect spot when it came to escaping those thorny problems. His beautiful villa, with its stretching vistas of rolling hills and trellises heavy with grapes disappearing into the horizon, was so wonderfully peaceful that it was hardly surprising that her brain was finding it very easy to shut down.

It was also making Maude realise just how little time she had ever taken to really unwind. She had spent so many years keen to prove that she could pursue the career she wanted and be happy that most of her time was devoted to work.

Her degree had been enormously difficult, and afterwards she had launched herself into the job market without pausing for breath. While friends had taken a year out to travel or pick up casual work in new cities, she had been filling out online application forms for jobs and, once she had landed her first job, she had had no time to surface.

Total peace would have been achieved now had she

not been so acutely aware of Mateo and the disturbing effect he had on her. For the past two days they had circled one another, making no mention of those fraught few moments when the world seemed to have stood still and she had had to fight off the yearning to drown in the temptation of touching him.

She'd pulled back. He'd pulled back. Common sense had been reinstated...

And since then work had continued, interrupted by a trip to three of the local towns, where she had wandered around on her own, dazzled by a scenery of jumbled sepia houses clambering up hills, nestled amidst lush greenery. Mateo, on one occasion, had joined her, taking her to a quaint antiques market and an ancient church, its walls decorated with Mediaeval and Renaissance art.

He had been informative, knowledgeable, charming and very, very polite, and Maude had hated it.

How on earth could she *miss* the treacherous excitement of the forbidden? She just *did*. He had awakened something in her and she was helpless to fight it.

Clearly, he had no such problem. Maybe he had sensed the attraction and was now in a hurry to ensure it came to nothing.

For the past two evenings, there had been company, one or other of his associates from the nearby estates, and as soon as they had gone he had excused himself and disappeared into the bowels of the villa to work.

Where was he now at a little after five in the afternoon? Giving her time to relax, he had said first thing that morning, over a breakfast of fresh breads served on the veranda by Luisa, the young girl who was the resident chef.

'I won't be back until reasonably late,' he had apologised, glancing at his watch and rising to his feet, his body language letting her know that he was a guy who didn't have time to hang around chatting. 'But you can instruct the chef to prepare whatever you want for yourself this evening.'

He'd dispensed politeness and she'd responded in kind, murmuring something and nothing about a salad, while her eyes had skittered away from the temptation to drink him in. He was so dark, virile and stupidly sexy in a pair of cream chinos and a white linen shirt cuffed to the elbows and hanging over the waistband of the trousers. He should have looked sloppy but instead he looked way too hot for her peace of mind.

She should have been grateful for the brief reprieve from being in his company but instead, as she'd heard the purr of his sports car leaving, she'd felt a surge of silly disappointment which she'd had to squash by bracingly telling herself that the less she saw of him, the better.

In the morning, she would ask him about leaving. As in...*when*?

It was something they hadn't discussed. He'd become submerged in work and she had fallen in step, working alongside him with the ease of familiarity, and enjoying the vision he was creating with the other vineyard owners for some of the tiny villages they did a lot to support.

On one occasion, she had met some of the people who had jobs in the various wineries. A spread had been laid out under an awning in the centre of one of the villages, in a square surrounded by old stone buildings with a tiny, well used church in the corner. Maude had become consumed by the sort of community spirit that was very hard to find in London. The sun had poured down from a milky blue sky and, intrigued, she had seen a different

Mateo, a more relaxed Mateo, one who listened to everything the locals were saying and who communicated with them with curiosity and interest, keen to hear what had been going on. She had smiled when he had apologised for having stayed away for far too long, his Italian fast and his gestures so typically, exotically foreign.

Meanwhile, her mother had texted daily, filling her in on progress with the wedding and keeping a dignified and tactful silence on the subject of the engagement. Although, the day after they had arrived in Tuscany, she had confessed that she had got hold of the tabloid where the gossip had first hit the press and just couldn't help being thrilled that her baby had finally found the man of her dreams.

And who could blame her? Because Mateo was a dream.

Maude fretted over what the next step in their ill-judged charade would be but, oh, how easy it was to put those niggling anxieties on hold over here.

How easy to live in this parallel universe, where life had taken on a technicolour clarity, and every minute was spent in a state of illicit heightened excitement.

And the surroundings... They were like nothing she had ever experienced, a world apart from middle class suburbia, which looked mundane in comparison.

Maude paused where she was for a few seconds and breathed it all in. For the first time, she was going to use the swimming pool. Mateo wasn't going to be around, and she had told Luisa that she could head off early, as there would be no need to prepare an evening meal. After a lot of gesticulating, she had also managed to communicate to the smiling Italian *nonna* who was the daily help that she too could leave ahead of schedule.

It was slightly cooler now but still very warm and the sky was a watercolour blend of deep blues, light blues and tinges of streaky orange.

In the distance, the hills were vague shapes cutting across the horizon, framing the rustle of green that fanned out in waves across the acres of Mateo's estate.

The pool looked amazing and Maude walked towards it, not bothering to test the water or let her body adjust to the cold. She tossed her towel on one of the wooden loungers, along with the bag she had brought containing her sun block, her shades and a book she was having trouble finishing and dived in.

She was a strong swimmer. She had always loved the way she could hear herself really think when she was under water. She had no idea how many lengths she was doing. She picked up speed, slicing through the crisp, cold water, her body remembering all the flips and turns from way back when.

She was clearing her eyes, surfacing at the deep end, ready to do a few more laps before calling it a day, when she realised that she was no longer alone at the pool.

She swiped wet hair from her face and saw his feet first.

No shoes, just brown ankles… As she raised her eyes, she saw lean, muscular calves…up and up to his thighs… and then a pair of black swimming trunks.

She was getting a little breathless from treading water in the deep end but there was no way she was going to heave herself out in front of him.

'Are you coming out?'

Maude gazed up and her mouth dried at the sight of his bare torso. He had a white towel slung over his shoulders and he was staring down at her through dark, reflective sunglasses.

On every level, Maude felt disadvantaged.

'Give me your hand. I'll help you out.'

'I was about to swim a few more lengths, as it happens. What are you doing here? I didn't think you were going to be back until...er...much later.'

'Disappointed?'

'This is your house!' Her voice rose an octave higher. 'You can come and go as you please!'

'Many thanks for that.' He grinned, slid the towel off and tossed it onto the nearest sun lounger. 'The pool was beckoning. It's not often it gets used and I decided it would be more fun to test the water than sit through another meeting that can wait until tomorrow. Mind if I join you?'

'Your house! Your pool!' Her voice was squeaky and high, and she was bright-red and uber-conscious of her body on show, distorted in size because of the water.

In an embarrassed rush, she struck out, swimming fast to the opposite end of the pool and then resting on the steps with the sun on her shoulders, watching as he slid into the water to swim lazily towards her, with perfectly modulated strokes.

As he closed the distance between them, more and more her stomach tightened into panicked knots.

The muscles rippled in his broad shoulders. It was a fascinating sight.

Her breathing slowed as he joined her on the steps, lying back on his elbows for a few seconds, eyes closed to the sun.

They flew open when he turned to face her and Maude hurriedly looked away.

'How long have you been out here?'

'Forty minutes or so.'

'It's nice to see you relaxing, Maude. You've been working a lot while you've been here.'

'Wasn't that part of the deal?'

'Was it?'

'Of course it was,' she confirmed stoutly, still staring straight ahead, glassy-eyed and uber-conscious of him so close to her and of the water lapping around them.

She tried not to look at herself.

She could feel all her hang-ups about her appearance waiting in the wings, and that was the last thing she needed.

'I thought the deal was basically to clear off for a few days until the fuss died down and, coincidentally, there was work that could be done over here.'

'Which reminds me, I've been meaning to ask—how much longer do you think we should stay here? Amy's been keeping her ear to the ground, and there's lots of gossip in certain circles, but I can handle that if you can. I mean, I would rather not have people coming at me with cameras, but I expect that'll have disappeared by the time we get back to London.'

'There's a celebrity marathon for charity happening next week,' Mateo told her. 'Once that hits the streets of London, all cameras will have moved in that direction.'

'I'd forgotten about that. I'm surprised you take an interest.'

'I was invited to the big opening event.' He shrugged. 'Not my thing. At any rate, I propose we stay out here for another week. A celebrity marathon is one hundred percent guaranteed to throw up a lot more fodder for the rumour mill. That aside, the work out here can be finished in another week, with sufficient instructions in place and signatures on dotted lines for work to begin.' He turned to her and grinned. 'It's not that much of a hardship being here, is it, for a few more days?'

'No, of course not.' Maude could feel his eyes on her. He was close enough for her to feel his warm breath on her cheek as well. Both were horribly disconcerting. 'I just thought that you...well...might want to get back to work.'

'Like I said... I'm working here.'

'Yes, I get that.'

'If you want the truth, I'm finding it oddly relaxing being here. It's been a while.'

Maude shifted and looked at him, and he turned and looked right back at her.

He had ditched the sunglasses and she could see sincerity in his eyes mingled with that most human of traits: hesitation.

Why did she feel so comfortable with this man?

Why did she lecture herself about being professional around him only to jettison her fine intentions the minute he got close?

He made her weak and she hated it.

Yet she found herself saying, 'I've wondered about that.'

'Have you, now?'

'It's not my business...'

'Despite the fact that we're engaged?'

Maude went bright-red but held her ground, ignoring his gentle teasing. 'Why would you have this wonderful place out here...all these acres of vineyard...and then delegate it to other people to run so that you can spend time holed up in cold, busy, grey London?'

'There's money to be made holed up in cold, busy, grey London.' Mateo relaxed back. 'I like your choice of wording, Maude. Very evocative. I've never thought of living in London on a par with being in a prison cell.'

'You know what I mean.' But she was smiling, enjoying this return to cordiality, and realising just how much she had disliked the abrupt remoteness between them earlier.

'I do, as it happens. But I meant it. These vineyards... Yes, they're profitable, but they're a hobby. A sentimental hobby. My only one. However, it's not real life being out here, and I can't afford the time to laze around for weeks on end watching the grapes swell and grow.'

'It sounds pretty perfect to me.' Maude heard herself sigh.

She shook herself and sat forward. The sun was beginning to fade.

'I'm sorry, but I had no idea you were going to be back, so I sent the ladies home. I just fancied something light for dinner and I didn't want anyone fussing around.'

'Excellent plan!'

'A couple more laps and then we go in?'

He didn't reply, instead propelling himself forward to slice through the water, making light work of one length and then effortlessly turning around to swim back.

Maude was spellbound by the power and the speed.

She'd always fancied herself an excellent swimmer but, when she pushed off to join him for some remaining laps, she found that it was a struggle to keep up when he seemed to be doing no more than barely breaking sweat.

She'd forgotten all about her inhibitions and self-consciousness when, fifteen minutes later, she stepped out of the pool at the shallow end to fetch her towel from the deck chair.

Mateo, reaching for his own towel to sling around his waist, stopped dead in his tracks and stared.

She was all woman.

He'd always gone for slender little blondes. He now had no idea why when an earthy, rounded, well-built brunette was doing all sorts of crazy things to his body.

He felt the heat of an erection and he immediately made sure the towel was very securely fastened around his waist. Too much more of an eyeful and God only knew what might push up against it, embarrassing them both.

He flushed when she turned to him to ask, innocently, 'Where did you learn to swim like that? You're amazing.'

For a few seconds Mateo was deprived of speech. She was drying her hair, body tilted, her heavy breasts practically spilling out of the very sober, very old-fashioned one-piece swimsuit. She stood at nearly six feet and her legs were long and well-shaped, her hips rounded and feminine, dipping to a narrow waist, and he could see her way-more-than-a-handful breasts. It was sheer torture, not giving in to the urge to stare like a teenage boy with no self-restraint.

He looked away hurriedly and began strolling towards the house. He breathed more easily when she fell into step alongside him—just about.

'Self-taught,' Mateo said in a roughened undertone. He cleared his throat. This was about as *un*-cool as he had ever felt in his life.

'Wow. I'm impressed! I had tons of lessons growing up and I always thought I was pretty decent. I used to out-swim the boys in my class most of the time, but I'm green round the ears compared to you!'

They were back in the villa, front door closed and the pale marble flooring generating wonderful cool. He turned to her, still fighting his own rebellious body, knowing that it was imperative to keep some distance at the moment or else make a fool of himself by gawking. Damn it, he wished she would just *cover up*. How much more could a red-blooded male deal with?

'You barely looked as though you...'

'I'm going to head upstairs, Maude. Also, I have work to catch up on—emails. Probably a good idea for you to carry on without me this evening as planned.'

'Oh, yes, of course...'

'Right.' Mateo took a couple of steps back. 'I'll head up now. I will see you in the morning.'

He swung round on his heels and Maude watched him vanish into the bowels of his mansion with a sinking heart. What on earth had possessed her to start feeling as though they were best friends, relaxed, chatting and swimming in his pool without a care in the world...*as though they really were the couple they were pretending to be?*

Mortified, she raced up to her bedroom, towel clutched tightly around her, locked the bedroom door and leant against it, calming down.

Her bedroom was more of a suite, with a seating area and a giant *en suite*. Pale wood made the floors underfoot cool, as did the overhead ceiling fan which she immediately turned on, finding the whirr of the blades soothing.

She forced herself to have a long bath and to relax but, by the time she made it to the kitchen an hour and a half later, she had determined that hanging around for another week or so, until reporters might or might not have lost interest in their stupid phoney engagement, wasn't going to do.

Indeed, there was no reason for her to stay on at all. Yes, she was sure he had work to do out here, and it was convenient being around to get through it, but what did that have to do with her? She wasn't needed for consultation on any of the engineering issues because they had their own guy out here who had covered all of that.

She could return to England, go and stay with her parents and there she could start laying the groundwork for the house of cards that would come tumbling down approximately one day after Nick and Amy were safely married off and her parents' attention was no longer focused on the wedding.

And if there were reporters lurking behind bushes? They would soon lose interest when they clocked that there would be no pictures of the loved-up couple, but just of her. And if they wanted to ask intrusive questions then she was fully capable of smiling, nodding and saying absolutely nothing at all.

She would also take a couple of weeks off, which she was entitled to. At the end of it, and by the time she finally clapped eyes on Mateo again, she would hopefully have rid herself of her inconvenient attraction.

After all the formal evening meals prepared by a qualified chef, it was fun rooting through the fridge and larder for bits and pieces with which make herself something to eat.

She had washed her hair but not bothered to dry it and she knew that it would get very curly as it dried. On her own, and with no need to dress to impress, she was in cut-off jeans, a tee-shirt and some flip-flops. She had brought down her mobile and was playing some music, half-humming along even though the audio was poor, so only became aware of Mateo's looming presence when she swung round with a plate of salad in one hand and a glass of wine in the other.

She had no idea how she retained a grip on both as she stopped dead in her tracks to stare at him, utterly confounded by his unexpected appearance.

He had vanished earlier, leaving her with the impression that she was the last person he wanted to spend time with. He had shut down her friendly chit chat in mid-flow and stalked off without a backward glance, leaving her to assume that he was bored with her company and keen for her to realise that he wasn't her pal, let alone anything else. Possibly just in case she started getting ideas.

Yet here he was, and Maude could feel a sense of fury building because him just standing there, darkly, dangerously and thrillingly sexy was scuppering all her carefully worked out plans.

'I thought you were working,' she said tightly. She galvanised her body into motion, walked towards the kitchen table and sat down with her plate and glass of wine. She didn't look at him. This was his house, and she could hardly stop the man from moving freely inside it, but her heart was thumping and she could feel her resentment ratcheting up.

'I couldn't.'

Maude shrugged, eyes fixed on her plate as she dug into the salad which tasted of cardboard.

She switched the music off and then wished she hadn't because the sudden silence was now deafening. She glanced up when he dragged a chair over to where she was sitting, positioning it so that she had absolutely no choice but to be aware of his proximity.

'I'm sorry I haven't prepared any salad for you,' she said politely. 'You made it clear that you weren't going to be around.'

'I don't like salad. I prefer to leave that stuff to the rabbits to dispose of. I needed to talk to you.'

'Good. Because, actually, *I* need to talk to *you*.' Maude pushed the plate to one side, sat back and folded her arms. 'I've come to the conclusion that this trip might have been a good idea at the start, but it's been a number of days, and I feel it's time for me to return to London. If you don't mind, I will take a few days off work, perhaps as much as a couple of weeks. I'm actually due the time off. I have holiday accrued since...'

'You think I vanished because I didn't want to spend time in your company?'

'Don't be nuts. Why would I think that?' But she went beetroot-red. 'I know this is a working holiday for you! And I hope you haven't come in here because you...because you feel guilty at leaving me to my own devices.'

'You were hurt. I could see it on your face.'

'I was *not*.' Maude wondered whether this conversation could get any worse.

'I had to leave because I wasn't sure whether I was going to end up making a nuisance of myself.'

'I have no idea what you're talking about.'

'When I came back here earlier and saw you in the pool, Maude...' He raked his fingers through his hair and sat back, briefly closing his eyes. 'I don't think you have the slightest idea how you look.'

'How I *look*?' Maude was prepared to be indignant

but something about those dark eyes fastened on her was bringing her out in a cold sweat.

She found that she was fidgeting with the wine glass and sorted that problem by gulping down the lot and pushing the glass to one side.

'Sexy,' Mateo muttered huskily. 'That swimsuit…your body…'

'*Me?*'

'You. Don't look so shocked. You must have known that I am attracted to you, Maude? You must have felt it when we kissed at the party and then later…?'

'You *can't* be attracted to me! Not really.'

'What does that mean? I'm sitting here and it's all I can do not to reach out and touch you.'

'You're *you*, Mateo,' Maude said helplessly as she grappled to keep a hold on common sense.

'What is that supposed to mean?'

'You could have anyone you want. I *know* the sort of women you want. I know the sort of women men go for and it's not strapping brunettes with careers!'

'Maude, you've lost me. What the hell are you talking about?'

'I lost my heart to someone once!' she burst out impulsively. 'It was when I first went to university. His name was Colin and he was just about everything I knew wouldn't look at me twice…he was tall, dark and handsome and smart…but he *did* look at me and we went out for a few months before…'

She felt her eyes sting and was cross with herself because that was all a lifetime ago, and afterwards, she'd known that she hadn't been in love with the guy at all. She'd just had a coming-of-age moment, destined to be lost in the mists of time.

'Before…?' Mateo prompted gravely. He leant towards her, reached for her hand and she didn't pull away.

'Before he found true love with a petite blonde.'

'What happened years ago has nothing to do with what's happening right here, right now. Nothing to do with what my body feels whenever you're around. I'm not comfortable telling you this, because I don't like not being able to control my own responses, but it seems like in this instance my body has other ideas. I couldn't stay away today like I'd planned, and I couldn't work for the rest of the evening knowing you were around, also like I'd planned.'

Maude looked away, face burning, and her body aflame at what he was saying.

'Look at me, Maude.' He gently tilted her chin so that she was staring at him, wide-eyed and in a state of shock. 'I'm attracted to you, it's as simple as that. I don't know what to do with this attraction but I felt I had to get it out in the open.'

He paused and tilted his head to one side, his eyes searching hers. 'You had a crap experience with a guy you met when you were younger and you've let that play into a narrative about the way you look. For reasons that baffle me, you somehow never gained self-confidence when it came to appearances, so you relied on your brains instead to see you through. I'm guessing you don't want to be hurt by anyone again. Am I right?'

'No one mentioned anything about that,' Maude muttered.

'That's as may be but…' He hesitated. 'This thing I feel…this isn't about love, Maude.' He smiled crookedly. 'Despite the fact that we're supposed to be a pair of love birds on course to a lifetime of happy-ever-afters. This is about attraction. It's about my eyes following you and my hands longing to touch. It's about having to take cold showers because when I think of you my body goes into overdrive. The world may think one thing but we know different. We've found ourselves in a peculiar situation but this isn't about love, is it?'

'No. No, it's not. Of course it's not!'

'People get hurt because they hand their emotions over to someone else's caretaking. That's not what this is about. For me? This is about a pull I can't shake. I want to sleep with you, and I'm telling you this because if you're not of the same mind set then tell me. Tell me and you have my word that this conversation ends here.'

'I...'

'Are you attracted to me, Maude?'

Maude squirmed. She was a grown woman and yet she felt like a teenager dealing with feelings and emotions for the first time. But, truthfully, this *was* a first, wasn't it? All her life she had linked sex with love. After Colin, she had made up her mind that she would never compromise when it came to guys. She had her checklist and she had ticked off their suitability as long-term partners—even the handful of guys she had dated casually had been ticked off. They'd been found wanting before bed had ever reared its head.

But Mateo...

He was so unsuitable, sitting there, luring her into something that promised nothing...just a couple of ships passing in the night...

Her body tingled at the thought of him touching it and she breathed in deeply, shakily.

Was this what she had been missing in her life? Had

she wasted too much time searching for Mr Right, when Mr Utterly Wrong might be just the tonic she needed?

Had she spent way too long living in her comfort zone, too timid to venture out?

Heart beating like a sledgehammer, Maude lowered her eyes and then said, 'Yes. Yes, I am, Mateo Moreno. I'm attracted to you...'

CHAPTER SIX

'So what do you think we should do about this?' Mateo murmured huskily.

Sweet anticipation filled him but there was no way he was going to rush anything. Instinct told him that she wasn't tough like the women he was accustomed to dating. She said she was attracted to him and, leaning into him as she was, her eyes bright with tentative sincerity, there was not a bit of him that doubted her.

But he wanted her to feel secure enough with him to follow through with what she'd said. Whether he spontaneously combusted out of sheer frustration didn't matter.

'There's no one here at the moment, aside from us...'

Mateo relaxed. His smile was slow and wicked. 'Deep down,' he murmured, 'Maybe you decided to be prepared to seduce me when I got back... Get rid of the staff, and you would be free to pounce on an innocent guy...'

Maude burst out laughing. Moving closer seemed the most natural thing in the world to do because here they were and, against all odds, he made her feel utterly relaxed and comfortable with his light teasing.

She'd just made a monumental, earth shattering decision to *live in the moment* and, if she'd thought that she might be riven with self-doubt, then she was proved wrong as he stood, pulling her towards him as he did so, and then cupped her buttocks with his hands and shifted her so that she felt the stiffness of his erection.

Maude's legs turned to jelly. Her hands were flat on his chest and she worked them slowly and cautiously over his shoulders, and sighed at the packed muscle under her fingers.

His mouth when it touched hers was soft and gentle and she relaxed into a slow, lingering kiss, the kiss of someone with all the time in the world and in no hurry.

The yearning for more built as they continued to kiss. His tongue meshed with hers in a lazy exploration of her mouth and her hands crept from his shoulders to his neck, caressing and feeling the warmth of his skin with something akin to wonder.

His hair was springy when she sifted her fingers through it, just as he brought his hands up to curve her waist and then to rest lightly on her breasts.

'Upstairs…please…' She struggled to gasp the words out and Mateo drew back and smiled.

'Your wish is my command but…are you sure about this, Maude?'

'I'm sure.'

She met his eyes steadily. Whatever the carousel that could be called his love life, and however much she had always disapproved of men who veered from one woman to another like a spoiled toddler given free run in a candy shop, she couldn't help but be impressed by his genuine concern for her.

She knew that, if she were to slap him down now, he would do just as he had said. He would walk away and he would never, ever mention it again.

She held his hand and tugged him behind her towards the kitchen door.

'I've always loved a woman who takes the lead,' he said. 'It fulfils my craving to be dominated.'

Maude laughed again over her shoulder. 'You should be careful what you wish for,' said this reckless, daring young woman she barely recognised as herself.

'Why? Are you promising me some kinky stuff between the sheets?'

Maude paused, suddenly worried, and she moved to gaze at him with serious eyes,

'I should warn you, Mateo…'

'Shh.' Mateo placed a finger over her lips and smiled. 'Don't say a word. We're going to have fun and that's it. If you want to tie me to the bed posts and have your wicked way, then I'm more than willing to give it a go, but there'll be no pressure on you to do anything at all you don't feel comfortable doing.'

'How do you do that?' Maude whispered.

'What?'

'Make me feel so at ease.'

'There's no need to be nervous. What's happening between us is perfectly natural.'

He led the way this time and she fell into step with him, her hand around his waist, his slung across her shoulders, two people at home with one another, their bodies in sync.

'Haven't you ever been here before?' he asked. 'By which I mean, in a place where you just can't fight the pull of sexual attraction?'

'I…' Maude thought of Colin and struggled to recall his face. She certainly had never felt this way with him. What she'd felt back then had been gentler and a heck of a lot more polite. This...*this*...was like being thrown into the eye of a hurricane, catapulted this way and the other, in the grip of something so powerful all you could do was go along for the ride. 'Not really,' she admitted.

'Not even with the university chap you were in love with?'

'That was ages ago.' Maude marvelled that he had zeroed in on just what had been going through her head. But somehow admitting that this was a first for her, when she knew that it would hardly be a first for *him*, stopped her from telling him the blunt truth. Instead, she laughed and said wryly, 'I'm guessing that being overwhelmed by lust isn't exactly a first for you?'

Why did that hurt?

They were outside his bedroom door.

Mateo paused, hand on the door knob, stilled by her laughing, teasing remark.

Was this just more of the same for him? Mateo had never been a shrinking violet when it came to the opposite sex. He enjoyed women and women enjoyed him. But had he ever been knocked for six like this by any woman? He didn't think so and he frowned because that made no sense.

In passing, he noted that she hadn't expanded on the ex from way back when. Had he been her one big love, leaving a scar that no man had ever been able to smooth over? When Mateo thought about that he felt a stab of something, but he'd never been a jealous guy, so surely that couldn't be it?

This was too much introspection. There was a reason he didn't go down that road. Nothing good ever came from dwelling on things you couldn't change or looking for answers where none were to be found. He'd spent a childhood trying to find out why his mother had walked out on him, and of course there'd been no answers to be found. Since then, he'd accepted the futility of a task like that. He'd learned his lessons and that was the important thing.

'No more talk.' He purred, pushing open the door and stepping aside for Maude to precede him into the bedroom.

A cool breeze blew through a bank of floor-to-ceiling doors that opened out onto a private black-and-white-tiled patio that housed casual seating. The bedroom was twice the size of hers, and hers was enormous.

She looked around her and he smiled at the direction of her gaze.

'For when I've worked through the night here and couldn't be bothered to use the main offices downstairs.'

She was looking at an impressive desk that sat in its own sectioned space surrounded by a bookcase to the back and a bank of hand-made teak cabinets to one side.

'Do you ever stop working?'

Mateo shot her a slashing, sexy smile that turned her legs to jelly and he strolled towards her.

'You're about to find out.' He played with the lobe of her ear, eliciting a sigh of capitulation, before tracing the outline of her mouth with his finger, then his tongue, before picking up kissing where they had left off.

Maude wound her arms around his neck. She was a tall, well-built woman and yet, mysteriously, he made her feel ultra-feminine and protected. His arms were bands of steel. When her hands slid to feel him, softly exploring over his shirt, she felt hard muscle and sinew.

The heat and damp between her legs made her squirm.

Maude, who had spent so long single-mindedly pursuing her career, was an innocent when it came to the opposite sex. She'd genuinely had no idea that she could be so overtaken by desire that she could barely keep a thought in her head.

He tilted back her head and trailed hot kisses along her neck, one hand coiled into her hair, the other sliding along her side, dipping into her waist and skimming over her thigh.

They staggered to the king-sized bed and Maude fell back on the softest of silken covers, immediately propping herself up to watch as Mateo reached for a remote, pressed a button and activated the smooth glide of shutters across the open windows, blocking out the light and plunging the room into cosy semi-darkness.

He didn't head for the bed—not yet. Instead, he stood, his back to the windows, hand on the zipper of his trousers resting there and teasing her so that she wanted to yell at him to *hurry up.*

He took his time undressing, and Maude didn't want to blink because she didn't want to miss a thing.

The shirt came off and he flung it to the ground, then the trousers, and when he stepped out of them only the boxers were left, through which she could detect the bulge of his erection.

He adjusted himself, cupping his erection and then leaving his hand on it before ridding himself of the last barrier to total nakedness.

Maude drew in a sharp breath.

Mateo Moreno, the guy she had surreptitiously looked at for so many months safe in the knowledge that he would never glance twice in her direction, was now standing in front of her completely naked.

And what a magnificent sight he made.

'Like what you see?' He half-smiled as he walked towards the bed to stand right next to her. 'Feel free to touch me wherever you like...'

Maude moaned softly, fell back against the pillows and shut her eyes as she heard him laugh under his breath.

'Everything about you turns me on,' he said, sinking onto the mattress alongside her. He positioned her so that they were facing one another. She still had all her clothes on. How did that make sense?

But instinct told her that he wasn't going to rush. She was here because she wanted to be here—she had told him that, had practically led him up to the bedroom and was now going crazy with wanting him—but still...

He would give her all the time in the world because he wanted this to be just right, wanted her to feel safe, and she really did feel safe.

Moreover, she didn't feel self-conscious. How had he made that possible?

'Like what?' she asked, and he grinned and kissed the tip of her nose.

'You're smart, you're funny and you're sexy as hell. What's not to like?'

'I'm new,' she challenged with a smile. 'I'm a novelty.'

'And maybe that's what I am as well,' he suggested.

'Maybe you are.'

'Which brings me to the fact that, once again, we're talking too much.'

'Is that something you're not into doing when you're in bed with a woman?'

'As a general rule, I tend to leave the chit chat at the bedroom door.' He slipped his hand under her top and rested it on her stomach, feeling her quiver. 'One more thing to add to the list of things about you that turn me on—I like the way you respond to me.'

'That's very egotistic,' Maude said lazily, her breath catching in her throat when he cupped her breast and began massaging it.

'I'll take that as a compliment. Now, enough! I want to go slow but, hell, I want to see you delectable and naked on my sheets a whole lot more.'

He stripped her of her clothing.

Bit by slow bit, she was shorn of her top, her trousers, until he was gazing down at her and she was in just her undies and her bra.

He was straddling her and he was turned on, his erection bold and throbbing. She sensed that he was hanging on by a thread and she felt a heady power that this beautiful, sexy guy could be so hot for her.

He groaned, cupped her breasts and said something thick in Italian that she didn't understand, but didn't need to, because his expression was saying everything she wanted to hear.

She was every single thing he'd never known he needed. That was going through Mateo's head as he toyed with her nipples, large, circular discs that were testing his resolve to the max. He desperately wanted this to last, wanted to take his time, but he knew he wasn't going to.

He sank into her breasts, teased the bulbous nipples with his tongue, nipped them gently with his teeth and felt soaring satisfaction at the mewls of pleasure that came from her as she tossed underneath him, her eyes shut, her mouth parted, her breathing fast and shallow.

He reached behind and groped to feel her underwear then pushed his hand underneath until he found the slick, wet groove between her legs.

He worked his magic in two different places, sending her into another world.

'Please stop or I won't be able to…to…'

'To come against my finger?' Mateo asked huskily and she nodded, face burning as she sped towards the point of no return. Their eyes tangled and he kissed her, a thorough, heated kiss while he continued doing what he was doing, bringing her to the peak of satisfaction until she spasmed in an orgasm that took her away.

Mateo let her cool down. He was so turned on, it was a physical ache. He forced himself to go slow, built himself up bit by bit in stages, stilling her hand when she wanted to touch him because he knew that, if she did, he would go the way she just had, and he wanted to be deep inside her for his release.

Maude's body was so in tune with his. *She* felt so in tune with *him*. She didn't understand how that was possible. She didn't get how he could make her feel so comfortable, so uninhibited, when everything inside her said it should be just the opposite.

She stroked him, she let him take his time, murmuring into his ear; and, when he reached for protection from the bedside drawer, she was blossoming once again inside, yearning for him, her body tingling all over.

He took her to heights she'd never imagined possible. Her fingers dug into his back as she writhed under him and, when he came, arching up and straining with the force of his orgasm, she followed shortly after.

Spent, she flipped onto her back and stared up at the ceiling.

'Regrets?'

She turned when he asked this to find him looking at her with brooding intensity.

'No.'

'Sure?'

'I'm not a kid, Mateo. I'm good at following through when I've made my mind up about something.'

'I know.' He smiled. 'Just for the record, no regrets from me either.'

'I guess I should head back to my room—or we could go downstairs and have something to eat. It's still quite early.'

'I'm relieved you didn't suggest doing some work.'

'Am I that boring?' Her voice was light but there was hurt underlying it. He wasn't to know that *work* was the wall she had built around herself to protect her from the slings and arrows of doubt and uncertainty. It always had been.

'Anything but.' He smiled and tucked her hair behind her ear, then left his hand there to cup her cheek. 'You can try as hard as you like to duck behind that professional mask you enjoy wearing, but I've seen behind that mask now and the woman there is the least boring woman I've ever known.'

Maude reddened.

'I don't duck behind anything...' she protested, but feebly, and his eyebrows shot up.

'Don't you? I think, whenever you're confronted with anything you find a little too much out of your comfort zone, you revert to work because that's your safe place. I'm not sure you even realise it, Maude. Perhaps it's a habit that's become so ingrained that it's part of you, but maybe it's stopped you from the business of going with the flow and seeing what happens next.'

'There's such a thing as doing too much of that *going with the flow* stuff,' Maude muttered uncomfortably, because he had hit the nail on the head, and he burst out laughing.

'My darling, you're so very right.'

Which for some reason made her feel very good inside. He added casually, 'Now that we're engaged…and these are my personal thoughts, to be shot down in flames if you so wish… I think we should carry on with what we have here.'

But for how long…?

This was what Maude thought as she lounged back in her chair, Mateo next to her, both sipping iced coffee and people-watching, backs to the bustling chi-chi café as they looked at the people coming and going.

Both were behind dark sunglasses.

Undoubtedly, he looked considerably more sophisticated than her, his skin burnished bronzed from the time spent under Tuscan skies. She noticed how people, both men and women, slid sideways glances at him when they walked past, as though wondering whether he was famous, whether they should recognise him behind those dark sunglasses.

'This is the longest I've ever been out of an office for a while,' he had confessed only the night before, lying in bed after a session of passionate sex.

They had only been in Tuscany for ten days, and it beggared belief how little time he seemed to spend relaxing.

But he was relaxing now. So was she—bliss. She was enjoying the heat of the sun and the pleasure of being in Siena, sitting in a mediaeval square surrounded by buildings that looked as though they had been there since time immemorial, all of them weathered and the colour of faded, water-coloured sepia, each so exquisitely fashioned that it was a feast for the eye.

They had spent the day shopping. It was the first time she had ever shopped with a guy and she had loved the way he'd made her feel when she'd paraded outfits for him.

He'd made her feel special.

He made her feel special now, their fingers loosely entwined on the wrought-iron table between them, an intimate gesture that warmed her.

But for how long? For how much longer could this continue...?

Reality awaited them. As predicted, they had been a flash in the pan when it had come to the tabloids, soon overtaken by celebrities doing stupid things or getting into trouble.

And what about his ex? From even further away in LA, where she was apparently back on the catwalk and doing the social scene, she had sent a text telling him that she'd met someone and sarcastically wishing him the best with his new woman.

Maude had done her bit and, if Cassie was poised in the wings, waiting for the fallout of her mischief-making to rain down, then this charade had served its purpose because Cassie had apparently given up the ghost when it came to trying to climb back into a relationship with Mateo. She would have the last laugh when the engagement she had engineered came to its predictable end. She'd think he would be massively inconvenienced and she would be rather pleased with herself.

And her family... Maude had sent a couple of sneaky selfies to them, but her mother was busy with the finishing touches to the wedding and just content that her daughter was doing a bit more than working eight to eight in an office, ignoring her pleas to find herself a good man.

She'd found the good man and all was right in the world. Except, it wasn't, was it?

'Penny for them.'

Maude felt Mateo's eyes resting on her and she sighed. 'I'm thinking how wonderful all of this is,' she said truthfully.

'Don't tell me you've never been to Italy before?' he said gently. 'Isn't this the playground for the English middle classes?'

'You're very cynical, Mateo Moreno.'

'Old habits die hard. But am I right?'

'I've been before,' she confessed. 'But not for a long time and never like this.'

'Like this?'

With someone I'm falling for...

'Not...being shuffled here and there by parents who want to cram in as much as they can with two pre-adolescent kids.'

Her heart was beating fast and she felt a slick of perspiration form a film over her.

Was that what was happening—was this a slow path towards falling in love with this guy? Yes. How and when, she didn't know. She just knew that this was where she'd ended up—on track to losing her heart to a heart breaker, to becoming another notch on the bedpost. Because, however much of a gentleman Mateo could be, he was still the inveterate bachelor who had no intention of settling down.

She'd disobeyed every rule she had ever taken care to lay down for herself and had drifted into love—and what a hopeless love it was.

He was smiling, his voice a lazy drawl as he sympathised with a twelve-year-old Maude wanting to wriggle out of traipsing around churches and looking at boring old statues.

She wasn't even listening. Appalled, her mind was throwing up a series of scenarios, each worse than the one before. How desperate he had been to get rid of his clingy ex—would he be equally desperate to get rid of *her* should he find out what she felt for him? She pictured him fleeing into the dead of night and then disappearing without a trace.

'My mum wants me to head back home,' Maude said abruptly. She turned to look at him and faked a smile, relieved that she could hide behind her sunglasses. 'Something to do with flowers and bridesmaids.' She smiled ruefully. 'And I guess it's time we left this paradise behind. It's safe to say that the hounds have found other trails to sniff. We're old news.'

'Flowers and bridesmaids?'

'Happens when there's a wedding and your mum is a perfectionist,' Maude hedged vaguely.

'When did you have in mind?'

'Perhaps in the morning?' She smiled again but inside her heart was breaking in two. 'Or is that too soon for... er...things to be put in place?'

'That could work.'

Mateo tried not to scowl. How easy to destroy a good

moment! Of course she was right, he grudgingly admitted—he was a workaholic, wasn't he? And there was work waiting for him in London—lots of it.

So, why exactly was he here, basking in the sun, watching the world go by?

Because of the woman indolently lounging next to him. She'd bewitched him. Little by little, she'd cast a net around him, seducing him into a holiday frame of mind which had made him lazy and...*content*.

Unease slithered through him because this sort of situation was not one he had ever courted, or ever wanted to. As much as she pulled him to her, weaving spells he couldn't resist, so instinct pushed him back, obeying laws of survival embedded inside him.

It was almost as though she had taken sandpaper to him and softened his edges, but Mateo knew that he needed those edges. Without them, life risked losing structure and that wasn't going to happen.

So, did they return to London?

Definitely.

If he wasn't as relieved as he should have been with her suggestion, if there was a scrap of him that hankered for a bit more of this truant-playing, then it was simply because she had beat him to saying what had to be said. He was usually the one who took the lead in this sort of situation.

'And once we're back,' she suggested thoughtfully, 'I'm thinking I could take a fortnight off and head back up home to help.'

'Isn't your mother in control of everything, except whatever's going on with flowers and bridesmaids?'

'She would never actually *ask* for help,' Maude said,

sticking to the truth as much as she could. 'Which doesn't mean she wouldn't *welcome* it.'

She gave his hand a quick squeeze and looked away, detaching her fingers to twine them together while she waited for him to respond, to take the conversation to its natural conclusion, which would surely be a discussion about *them*.

She flirted with the forbidden hope that, faced with this cautious ultimatum, he might declare undying love for her, tell her that he couldn't bear the thought of them returning. That hope lasted a matter of seconds, while into the silence she read something else, something that made her blood run cold.

What if he asked her just to prolong this? They made great love together. She knew that he enjoyed her as much as she enjoyed him, and she also knew that he was not a guy who was into self-denial. From his point of view, she was on the same page as he was. A charade started in good faith had turned into something else, and now here they were, so why not just 'go with the flow' as he was fond of encouraging her? It would fizzle out in due course, but they would have non-committal fun in the meantime.

Maude could think of nothing worse. The only way she could think to deal with this, to deal with her silly heart which she'd handed over to him on a platter, was to cut herself free. Rip off the plaster, suck up the pain and wait for it to pass.

At the end of a fortnight away from him, she would be in a better place, more able to distance herself. She could request a transfer. She could quit her job and find something else. There were options.

One of those options wasn't waiting for him to suggest something she knew she would be sorely tempted to take.

Before he could say anything, she plunged in.

'Let's enjoy what we have here, Mateo. It's been... time out for us. Weird but invigorating...and no regrets.'

'Explain.'

Around them people came and went, and it felt odd to have this jarring conversation surrounded by such beauty.

'When we return to London...tomorrow...then I think we should end this. It's not as though either of us is in it for anything more than a bit of fun, is it?'

Mateo turned to face her and she likewise looked at him. Now he lifted the sunglasses to his forehead and lifted off hers, so that their eyes tangled, so that he could see what was going through her head. But there was nothing there to see, no thoughts revealed.

He dangled her sunglasses on one finger and with a frown gazed directly into her blue eyes.

'Is this the sound of you dumping me?' he asked softly, with teasing amusement even though he was, frankly, incredulous.

'It's the sound of me doing what needs to be done,' Maude returned. 'Wouldn't you agree?'

No, Mateo thought. It was the sound of her hurting him, because there was a pain inside him, an ache at the thought of never touching her again, never being able to reach for her in the night.

There had been times in the early hours of the morning, still half-asleep in the stillness of the dark, when he had wondered whether he had dreamt some of the sex they'd had.

Sex with no protection.

Once. Twice. The mere fact that he was only think-ing about this now was worrying enough in itself. Never mind the even more worrying notion that he had some-how become stupidly addicted to her nearness, to the sound of her laughter, to the way she enjoyed arguing with him, to her fierce intelligence mixed with that pe-culiar vulnerability that she was always at such pains to hide. There was a chill inside him, something danger-ous and unpredictable stirring, something to be fought against.

Shutters dropped.

'Absolutely,' he drawled, pushing the sunglasses back in place and dropping hers on the table.

He signalled for the bill without taking his eyes off her. 'Tell me what happens next. I like a woman who takes charge. And you're right—absolutely the correct thing to do. Business and pleasure? Never makes for a good mix.'

'Agreed.' Her smile looked frozen. 'I'm glad you're not…not…upset.'

'Upset?' Mateo laughed shortly. 'I think you must be confusing me with someone else. So what's the way for-ward? We head back…you take your time out with flow-ers and bridesmaids and then the wedding…?'

'Which, I think you'll agree, it's probably wise for you to skip. Now that we've decided on a way forward, there's no point feeding the illusion that this is some kind of love match. Which it isn't.' Maude paused just for a few seconds. She could feel the heat burning her cheeks.

'Don't you think your parents might be a bit alarmed that your fiancé isn't around on such an important oc-casion?'

'They'd be more alarmed if you didn't show up at *our* important occasion.' The joke fell flat. 'I've sent them a couple of photos of here and of you, and before we head back today I can get someone to take some shots of us. I'll just tell them that you were called away on business and after that—'

'Bridges to be crossed,' Mateo interjected levelly. He gave her a mock salute but there was no humour in his smile. 'Well, my darling, here's to a short-lived but highly enjoyable engagement. Tomorrow is another day...'

CHAPTER SEVEN

MAUDE STOOD IN front of the wine bar where she had arranged to meet Mateo.

She could have chosen the office. She could have chosen his house in Chelsea. But she had ditched both options—the office because she wasn't sure she could bear the curious looks of the people she had worked with, and his house because that reeked of the desperation of an ex who refused to leave him alone. Besides, she hadn't relished the thought of seeing him in his natural habitat, surrounded by stuff that might weaken her defences.

So here she was. Standing in front of a trendy pub in Kensington, one half of which was gastro, with fashionable rustic tables and cool, colourful mismatched chairs, and the other half pub, with a semi-circular bar and lots of stools by a high counter and squat, square tables and chairs.

It had been nearly three weeks since she had last seen him. They had spent that last night together. They had made love and she had smiled through it all, knowing that she was saying goodbye to a place to which she would never return but one that would leave lasting damage to her heart.

It had been intense. Maude had wanted to take everything she could from that last time she got to feel his nakedness, got to enjoy the way he touched her, the way he responded to her touching him. She wanted to fill herself up to the brim *with him* and commit every single detail to memory.

They had parted on excellent terms. She had kept that smile on her face and he had been perfectly happy with the end of their affair. She suspected that he'd been thoroughly relieved that she had done the dirty work and called the whole thing off, without putting him in the awkward position of having to give her the brush-off.

She'd then headed to Berkshire. She could have popped up there now and again to help out, but she chose to stay instead, because she knew that keeping herself busy would clear her head.

'But honestly, darling, what about your work?' her mother had questioned, for once concerned about the career she had previously despaired of.

'Holiday,' Maude had responded. 'Also, Mateo is… er…away, I'm afraid, for most of the coming month with huge deal in the Far East… Globetrotting…always on the move… Not ideal, to be honest!'

And so his non-appearance at the wedding had been glossed over. And in fairness it had been such a busy time that in-depth questioning had been avoided.

But foundations had been put in place. Amy had casually asked her about an engagement ring. 'Not,' she had hastily added, 'That anyone really cares about that kind of thing any more…'

Maude had looked saddened and had made noises about whether she was doing the right thing with Mateo.

'I want a guy who's going to be around for me,' she had said vaguely but sincerely, which had been nothing but the truth. 'Not a guy who's married to his work. What starts out in good faith can end up crashing and burning in the face of reality.'

Amy had been far too busy to probe but Maude had planted seeds, and what else could she have done? But, in her head and in her aching heart, Mateo refused to be consigned to the past.

The wedding day had been hard as she had watched the joyful couple, the love they shared, cruel reminders of what she so desperately wanted in the end with Mateo— the happy-ever-after future Amy and her brother were united in finding, and what she knew she would never have, because she had foolishly fallen for a guy who was incapable of giving it.

As soon as the wedding was out of the way, she had headed back to London, emailed Human Resources and quit her job.

Tellingly, Mateo had had nothing to say about that.

Had he spared her a second's thought?

He had texted her on the day of the wedding to tell her that he hoped it had all gone well and had sent the couple a ridiculously expensive set of high-end luggage as a present, apologising for his absence.

In return, she had texted him back, informing him that she was going to hand in her notice, that it was for the best and that she knew he would be pleased to hear that she was making great headway in finding an out for their so-called relationship. She had ended the text with a friendly winking emoji, keeping it light-hearted.

Things would all work out in the end, she had told herself. Broken hearts mended. Time was a great healer.

She had been badly prepared for the unexpected.

She had not really paid attention to the fact that her

period had failed to show up when it should have, even though she was as regular as clockwork.

She had not even really braced herself for that little stick giving her a positive result when she had reluctantly decided to buy the pregnancy testing kit.

It had all come as a shock.

Instead of spending the first week on her return to London looking for a new job, she had spent it in a daze doing three more tests, staring at each positive result with the same shock every single time.

Until she had finally done what she knew she needed to do. She had texted Mateo and requested a meeting.

Right here—in a public place, busy but not too busy, quiet but not too quiet.

She propelled herself forward. The sunny skies they had left behind weeks ago were no longer in evidence. Instead, it was a grey day with a light drizzle dampening everything, still warm, but not warm enough for any of the sundresses she had shoved in a trunk and stuffed into a cupboard because they reminded her of Tuscany.

She was wearing a pair of trousers, trainers, a short-sleeved tee-shirt and an anorak. Not exactly chic, but that was the last thing on Maude's mind as she took a deep breath and headed inside to meet Mateo.

Mateo had no idea how keyed up he was about this out of the blue meeting until he saw her.

Three weeks. With a push, and much to his fury, he could practically count the time in minutes and seconds. He hated it because it smacked of emotional weakness which was something he had no time for.

She'd dumped him. That was the long and short of it. The guy who was never dumped had been dumped.

She'd walked out on him and hadn't looked back, and Mateo had not been able to get her out of his mind ever since she'd done that.

Why?

Was it because he was so damned arrogant that his pride had been wounded? He liked to think himself bigger than that, but then the only alternative was one he had no intention of accepting—she was still in his head because he missed her. He'd grown accustomed to her being around. He no longer enjoyed the solitude of an empty bed. She'd opened his eyes to the joy of spending the night with someone sleeping next to him, and then she'd vanished and taken that joy away with her...

Mateo had buried himself in work and taken himself out of the country, returning to bury himself in work once again, but for the first time in his life it had failed to do the trick.

And then she'd texted him to meet up.

She'd had time to think, had time to work out just how good what they'd shared had been—that was the obvious and only conclusion he could read into her desire to meet him. Because he knew that everything had progressed and finalised when it came to her handing in her notice. He hadn't stood in the way, hadn't demanded she work out her notice, but indeed had given her a glowing reference. He expected some people might think he'd been biased, because they'd been an item, but Mateo could not care less because he'd never allowed other people's opinions to influence his behaviour.

So, she obviously wanted to pick up where they'd left off, at which point Mateo was torn.

He wanted her back.

They'd had a good thing going and it was only natural to want to prolong it. Why not? And, on the plus side, wasn't it always better to let things reach their natural conclusion? If he didn't, wasn't there the danger of experiencing the frustration of an incomplete situation? A painful, driving need to see things through?

But Mateo knew that this was not a normal situation. In truth, his preoccupation with Maude had made him uneasy and wary. It would be important to lay down ground rules just in case they had become blurred in the interim. He wasn't into longevity with any woman and nothing had changed.

All these things had gone through his head when he had read her brief text. A 'when and where' text, brisk and to the point, which he had appreciated. No need to state urgency when it was a given.

For the first time in weeks, he had felt...*content*.

Now, as he watched her glance around, frowning as she tried to locate him, anticipation rippled through him.

God, he'd missed her body—her generous curves, the feel of her breasts weighing heavily in his big hands...

All of her... He'd missed the whole package deal.

She was dressed in the sort of frightful outfit that had become a thing of the past when they'd been in Italy but, for some weird reason, he found he didn't mind. The fewer stares she got, the better, as far as he was concerned. He almost laughed at that sudden bout of old-fashioned possessiveness.

Since when had he morphed into a chauvinist? Not him at all!

He signalled to her and saw a shadow of hesitation cross her face before she headed to where he was sitting at one of the low tables in the bar area.

He'd ordered a bottle of wine in advance of their

meeting, an excellent red. Not one from his vineyard, of course, but from the region. He'd be interested in hearing what she thought of it. For someone who wasn't particularly interested in drinking wine, she had a pretty good palate, as he had discovered in Tuscany.

'Maude...' Mateo rose to greet her. He reminded himself that, however satisfying it was to know that they were once again on the same page, he would still have to lay down his boundary lines. He might feel oddly out of control when it came to her, but laying down those lines would be a reminder to himself. He was still a guy in charge.

'Hi.'

Now that she was here, standing in front of Mateo, overwhelmed by him once again, she was wondering whether she'd done the right thing in coming.

'Don't look so apprehensive. Shall we retreat to the dining area? Are you hungry?'

'It's fine here. I... I won't be here long.'

Mateo frowned. 'There's no rush.' He delivered one of those killer smiles that always made her weak at the knees and which made her go weak at the knees now. 'I've cleared my calendar for you.' He waited until she was sitting, until wine had been poured for both of them and the hovering waiter had left, with an order for some tapas, before he continued, the killer smile abruptly dropping to be replaced by an expression of deadly seriousness.

'Look, I know that you're finding this awkward.'

'You do?'

'Yes. It's written all over your face. Don't forget, I know you as well as I know the back of my hand. At least it seems that way to me. You're finding this awkward, and I don't blame you, but I'm glad you're here. Glad that you've come back to me.'

'Come back to you...'

'I've been thinking about you as well. I'd go so far as to say that I've been missing...our passionate nights together. And days.' The smile returned and his eyes darkened. 'I've discovered that an empty bed is way too big when the woman I should be sharing it with is no longer in it. Which is why I don't want you to feel awkward. We're in the same place, Maude, we want the same thing. And I think we can both be honest and admit that giving one another up was good in theory but crap in practice.'

'Hmm.'

'But...' Mateo let that single word hover in the air between them, inviting her to look at him with questioning blue eyes.

'But?' Maude politely parroted.

'*But*...this is the first time I've ever done anything like this.'

'Anything like what?'

'For me,' Mateo elaborated, 'When a relationship ends, it ends. There's no going back.' He smiled wryly. 'I would say even more so in the case of a relationship that ends because a woman has been the one to do the walking. Not that I would know that for sure, because it's never happened before.'

'I'm sure,' Maude said, even more politely.

'But because this is a first for me...well, how do I put this?... I don't want you to read anything into it.'

'Read anything?'

'What we had was pure and simple. We had great sex. I'm very happy to pick up where we left off.'

'Ah. I understand. You want to make sure I know that this is just a meaningless affair that has a timeline.'

Mateo frowned and shifted.

He had finished his glass and poured himself another, but realised that she had failed to take a single sip of hers, sticking to water instead. The tapas had been delivered to them. He had barely noticed the arrival of the waiter. He'd been utterly wrapped up in the glow of anticipation and the urgency of making sure he told it like it was, no room for misunderstandings.

Now, he realised that she had contributed remarkably little to the conversation and she certainly hadn't shown any of the enthusiasm he had expected.

Why? It wasn't as though he had tried to dissuade her, was it? The contrary! He had been open and honest about wanting her back in his life as much as she clearly wanted him back in hers.

'That's not how I would have phrased it,' he said stiffly.

Maude shrugged.

'I'm not here to get back together with you, Mateo,' she clarified.

'What? Come again?'

Their eyes tangled and Maude could see his puzzlement. Why else would she possibly have arranged this meeting if not to coerce herself back into his life?

Yet she could see why he thought as he did. There had been no need for her to sit through the past forty minutes of him telling her that he wanted her back, and she was ashamed that she felt something warm and satisfying inside at the thought that he still wanted her, still desired her. Nothing to do with love, of course, because that was not what they had ever been about. He had stated that boldly and clearly.

Yet how wonderful it felt to be wanted by him... To have those husky words wash over her, reminding her of how they had made one another feel, how he had made *her* feel—alive for the first time in her life, a woman encouraged to enjoy her sexual appetites with a man who couldn't get enough of them.

Surely she was only human in greedily wanting to take those titbits and hold onto them for a bit?

'Mateo, I'm pregnant,' she said flatly and watched as the colour drained from his face.

'Sorry, I don't think I quite caught that.'

'I'm having a baby. That's why I arranged to see you.'

'But...*no*. That isn't possible. It can't be. *No.* Impossible!'

He flung himself back and raked his fingers through his hair, and for a few seconds he looked away from her and stared blindly over to the bar. Maude read that as the reaction of a guy desperately trying to find a way out of a nightmare he hadn't invited.

She felt for him. She knew that this was the last thing in the world he would have expected to hear and, even as those words had left her lips, she knew that they would shatter the world as he had knew it.

But not for a single second had she considered *not* saying anything to him. That would have been utterly unfair. How he dealt with the news would be up to him, but she had to let him know, in a hurry, that she hadn't dropped this bombshell to mess up his life.

'How could that have happened? How? I was careful...'

'There were a couple of times,' Maude murmured, 'When being careful wasn't top of the agenda. In the early hours of the morning. I didn't make a note of dates and times but I'm sure you can remember...'

'It felt like a dream, that one time...twice...' Mateo
muttered. 'This can't be happening.'

'I came here because it was the right thing to do, not
because I want anything from you.'

'I'm not following you.' Mateo frowned. Everything
felt disjointed. He looked at her. What he saw was a
woman with his baby inside her, and it was tearing him
apart, because a child had never been in his game plan.
But *his* child! He could barely follow what she was saying.

'I won't need rescuing,' Maude said gently. 'I know
this has probably blown your world apart, but don't think
that you owe me anything. Neither of us is to blame. In
the heat of the moment, things happen, and sometimes
those things have consequences that are unexpected.'

'I can't believe this is happening. When did you find
out?'

'A week ago.'

'You've known about this for *a week*? And it took you
that long to make your way here?'

The incredulous condemnation in his voice made her
hackles rise and she narrowed her eyes.

'I was adjusting to the situation myself,' she said
coolly. 'Your world's been tilted on its axis but so has
mine. You're not the only one who's been knocked for
six, Mateo.'

'No,' he apologised roughly. 'I get that.'

'The point I'm making is that I don't need anything
from you. I can manage financially and I can make a loving and rock-solid background for this baby.'

'I really can't believe I'm hearing this.'

'How many times do I have to tell you that mistakes
happen?' she said, patience wearing thin, because there

were only so many times she could listen to him try and pretend she hadn't said what she had.

'Not that,' Mateo returned with driven urgency. 'What I can't believe is that you actually think that I'm the kind of guy who would walk away from taking responsibility for a child I fathered, with or without planning.' *A baby...a child.* A different world opened up at his feet, and in that world nothing obeyed the laws that had always guided his life choices.

'Well...' Maude went bright red. 'Of course I expect you might want to...take an active part in his or her life...'

'That's very noble-minded of you.' He rallied even though his head was still spinning.

'There's no need to be sarcastic.'

'I think there's every need,' Mateo countered coldly. 'You drop this on me and then, without pausing for breath, you tell me that you don't expect me to do anything with what I've been told. What was your plan ahead, Maude? That I would just conveniently vanish from the scene, letting you do your own thing once your conscience had been cleared?' Shock was still there but fading, giving way to acceptance of a new reality.

'Of course not! I...'

'Have you told your parents?'

'No. Like I said, I've been adjusting to it myself.'

'Good.'

'What do you mean?' Maude was ensnared by the expression on his face, captivated by all the old attraction she had hoped to navigate her way around after three weeks. It was hopeless. Would she ever be able to get beyond the devastating effect he had on her? Was this what love was all about—exquisite pleasure and then this terrible pain? She felt tears trying to push their way through, and blinked rapidly, because she didn't want to break down.

'Good that you haven't told your parents. We can tell them together.'

'I beg your pardon?'

'We're still engaged, I believe. It shouldn't come as too huge a shock when they find out that we're going to have a baby, or maybe a better way of putting it is that it shouldn't be as much a bolt from the blue.'

'But we're *not* engaged.'

'Let's not lose focus, here, Maude. We're having a baby and I will be at your side when we break the news to them.' He paused. 'And my guess is they will be over-joyed when we tell them that there will be another wedding on the way, and sooner rather than later.'

'What?'

'You came here to tell me that I was allowed to disappear, leaving you to bring our baby up on your own. I'm here to tell you that no such thing is going to happen. The opposite—we're going to be married, Maude.'

He raised his glass and met her gaze with steely determination. 'A champagne moment but, in the absence of champagne, I'll toast with this excellent wine and you can with sparkling water. A toast to *our* impending big day...'

Maude gaped.

If there were links to what was going on, then she didn't see them.

Hadn't she just been given a speech about his enthusiasm to resume a sex-only relationship with her, no strings attached, because he was a commitment-phobe who wanted nothing more than a bit of fun? How could she now compute that he was sitting here telling her that he wanted to marry her? Since when had 'I'm not into longevity with you' tallied with 'I want us to be married'?

'I'm not following you,' she said slowly. 'You thought I came here to reignite what we had, and you were happy to do that provided I knew that it wasn't going to go anywhere...'

'That was before you told me about the baby.'

'I've already said that I would never get in the way of you seeing him or her. I can manage financially on my own, but likewise, if you want to donate money to the baby's upbringing—'

'Donate? *Donate?*' Mateo exploded with icy fury. 'We're not talking about a local charity here, Maude.'

'Yes, I know that.'

'You're right,' he ground out with wrenching honesty. 'I never thought about a wife or a family but, now that this has been sprung on me, then there's only one solution as far as I am concerned.'

'Which is fine, but it's a situation that involves the two of us, and as far as *I'm* concerned marriage isn't the solution at all, whether or not this has been *sprung* on you.'

'Why not?'

It wasn't just a question, more a challenge contained within a statement, and deep underneath was a barely discernible hint of genuine bewilderment. And it was that bewilderment that softened something inside her and sapped her temptation to argue with him.

'Because we don't love each other,' Maude said huskily. It hurt to say that aloud because it just wasn't true. Her heart was full of love for him.

'But this isn't about us, Maude.'

'It would never work. I look at my parents and they're bonded because they love one another. If they hadn't been, then it would have been a marriage of convenience which would have fizzled out whether kids were involved or not. With the best will in the world, it takes more than a baby to unite two people.'

She looked at him with stubborn determination. 'I'm giving you an out here, Mateo,' she said quietly. 'You can keep the lifestyle you enjoy, go out with whoever you want to go out with, and yet always have however much or little contact with our child as you find comfortable. I really don't understand why you don't find that appealing.'

'You had the luxury of two parents,' he said in a rough undertone. 'You're lucky. Stop to think that there are people like me who never had that luxury. People like me who grew up envious of people like you. I want my child to have what I lacked. I want my child to have the luxury of two parents. When it comes to love, well, it's hit or miss, isn't it? Divorce happens because people get wrapped up in believing in a magic that rarely happens, instead of accepting something that might not be stardust but might just be a lot sturdier. We *like* one another. We *respect* one another. Bring that to the table, and what we would have is a rock-solid union.'

'There would be so much more than that I would expect from a marriage, Mateo.'

Yet what he had said touched her. She had always taken it for granted that marriage was about love, and that without it there could be no such thing. Had she been unrealistic? They were going to have a baby together. For him, above all else, two parents were always going to better than one because he had grown up with just one parent, had lived in the shadow of abandonment. From that had sprung this fierce determination of his to make sure their baby had what he had missed out on.

Two people with two separate dreams.

'What? Tell me.'

'Even if I felt that it was okay to sacrifice my life to a loveless marriage for the sake of a child...'

'Good God, Maude, *sacrifice*...?'

Maude had the grace to flush and when she met his eyes it was to find herself drowning in his incredulous dark gaze.

'Okay, maybe that's a bit—'

'Overblown? Damn right it is.'

'But you know what I mean.'

'Tell me what else you would expect, aside from affection, respect and of course amazing sex. Because let's not beat about the bush here, Maude—we're good in bed together. So tell me what other pieces of the jigsaw have to slot into place before you climb down from a place where only perfection will do.'

His husky reminder of the very thing she had spent the past few weeks trying to shove under the carpet made her go beetroot-red and set up a chain of physical reactions that she couldn't control. Her breasts felt heavy, her nipples pinching against her sensible cotton bra, and there was a shameless pooling of liquid between her legs, an ache there that only served to remind her of just how expert he had been at assuaging it.

And wasn't this why she couldn't end up marrying this guy? The very fact that she loved him made her vulnerable in ways he wouldn't understand.

If she took the love out of marriage, then it would become a business arrangement, and he was right—a business arrangement had a good chance of surviving.

But would *she* be able to survive *it*?

Would she be able to hide her love day after day, week

after week and year upon year and content herself with a guy who *liked her* in return?

At what point would those shoots of unhappiness mushroom into full-blown misery and despair? And would that just mean divorce at a later stage when their baby, then a child, would suffer more from the fallout?

The thoughts whirred inside her brain like angry insects and she held her head in her hands for a couple of seconds. When their eyes met, she saw sudden concern in his.

'This is stressing you out.' He raked his fingers through his hair and shook his head. 'That can't be good for you.'

Maude smiled wryly. 'I'll survive, Mateo. It's important we have this discussion. You asked me what other things I would want in any marriage beyond what you've...er...said...'

Mateo tilted his head to one side, his dark eyes still concerned, but thoughtful, his body as still as a statue. His nod was curt.

'Fidelity. Yes, we have great sex at the moment, but that's called lust, and lust doesn't last. What happens when that fades away, Mateo? You're a guy with a strong libido. Will you start casting your net a little further afield? Because that would be something I would find intolerable.'

'You have my word. I am more than prepared to fold away that net and never bring it out of storage. I would be one hundred percent faithful to you.' He paused and then said in a driven undertone, 'And that's presuming I tire of you. You might find that you're the one who tires of me...or we both might discover that the magic we shared in Italy is longer lasting than expected.'

Maude felt the persuasive impact of his words swirling round her, enticing her to agree with his proposition. Wasn't he right? Wasn't their child the only one that mattered?

But then she thought of her own parents and the love they shared, the intimate jokes between them, the way they still held hands.

Those were the simple things that came with love, things that could never be replicated in a relationship which would only ever be an arrangement, whatever words he used to describe it. *That* was what a child deserved, not a business arrangement between two polite parents, where resentment would most probably find its home in due course, whatever Mateo might believe to the contrary.

'So,' he urged. 'Will you marry me, Maude?'

She looked at him steadily, and then said as gently as she could, 'I can't, Mateo. I can't marry you.'

CHAPTER EIGHT

FIVE DAYS LATER Mateo swept by in his sports car to collect Maude from her house.

During that time, all talk about marriage had been dropped. He'd proposed once, tried to persuade her once, had been knocked back once and had retreated.

Was Maude happy?

Of course she was! Why wouldn't she be? Wasn't this exactly what she wanted? There was no way she wanted to be pressured into a situation that would never make sense in the long run!

Yet, she couldn't stifle a sting of disappointment at his hasty retreat. Obviously, whatever he'd said, once his obligatory offer had been rejected, his conscience had been cleared and he'd probably breathed a sigh of relief. He'd done the honourable thing and it wasn't his fault that she had turned him down.

He phoned her daily. How had her day been? Was there anything she needed?

Maude knew that there was a continuing conversation to be had, but she was putting it off, because she had been knocked for six by seeing him again and had wanted to take a little time out to handle events that seemed to be rushing past her at speed.

They had agreed that they would see her parents together.

'I won't marry you,' she had said five days earlier. 'But, yes, it would be good for you to come with me when I break the news to my parents. We can explain that we've decided that we're better as friends but will remain committed to our child...'

Mateo had looked away, expression unreadable, and nodded. They would visit just as soon as her parents were back from the three-week holiday they had taken post-Nick's and Amy's wedding.

'Your father is very naughty,' her mum had told her with a breathless, girly giggle two days after the wedding. 'He just went ahead and booked it...said I needed to relax after all the stress of arranging the wedding. It's a Caribbean holiday, and he says it's about time he got to see his wife in a bikini on a beach with someone else doing all the running around. You know your father, a hopeless romantic.'

In the meantime, Maude figured, there would be ample opportunity for Mateo and her to handle all the practical arrangements, which had yet to be discussed.

Ample time for her really to gather herself and face the future without qualm or trepidation and to count her blessings—which were many, not least having supportive family around her and, yes, Mateo, who had made it patently clear that he was going to take an active part in his child's life.

She had cruised along, coming to terms with a life turned upside down and accepting that Mateo would now be a permanent feature in it, if from a distance, and one that she would just have to get used to. His casual daily chats had put her at ease and given her hope that her wild heart might be tamed by the time they came face to face again. Which, she'd quietly hoped, perhaps might not be until just before her parents were due to return. After all, it made sense that, if *she* had to retreat to consider an altered future, then surely so did he?

Fat chance.

The evening before, he had phoned and announced that he would be passing by to collect her the following day.

'Around four,' he had said. 'And don't ask. It's a surprise.'

'I've had quite enough surprises to last a lifetime, Mateo,' she had told him. His burst of laughter down the end of the line had reminded her of all those times in Italy when that laughter had thrilled her to the bone, making her breath catch in her throat.

So now, watching the busy streets below from the window of her rented flat, she noted the black Ferrari and her heart skipped a beat.

She watched, savouring those illicit, forbidden few seconds as he swung his lean body out of the low, sleek car and headed for the downstairs front door.

He was dressed in black. Black jeans and a black, long-sleeved tee-shirt that managed to delineate every muscle.

Maude heard the buzz of her intercom and his disembodied voice announcing his arrival, and she took one quick glance at her reflection before taking her time to collect her backpack and run her fingers through her hair.

She wore jeans and a colourful stripy jumper and trainers. There was no sign of any bump and only a couple of days before she'd wondered what he would think as the pregnancy advanced and she turned into a barrage balloon.

It was one flight down to the front door. She paused

and took a deep breath before opening it, and then had to remind herself how to talk in a normal voice as her eyes met Mateo's, pinning her to the spot and depriving her of speech for a couple of seconds.

How could one human being be just so beautiful? A light, cool wind had tousled his hair and he hadn't shaved. The shadow of dark stubble made him look even more heart-stoppingly dangerous.

'Ready?' he drawled, which brought her right back down to planet Earth.

'Where are we going?'

'Haven't I already told you that it's a surprise?'

He walked round, opened the passenger door to his car, waited as she lowered herself inside and then relaxed back in the leather seat.

'I figured,' he said huskily, swinging into the driver's seat and starting the engine, which roared into life, 'That if Mohammed wasn't going to come to the mountain, then the mountain would have to come to Mohammed.'

'What do you mean?'

Maude shifted to look at him to find him gazing at her, one hand resting loosely on the steering wheel and an amused half-smile on his face.

'I mean,' he said softly, 'We haven't had a proper conversation about what happens next, and I was beginning to get the feeling that if I didn't do something about that then I'd be hanging around for ever, phoning you every day and waiting for you to open up the dialogue.'

Maude reddened.

'That's not true,' she protested. 'I just thought that you might need to have some breathing space to digest what's happened.'

'And that's very thoughtful of you but now, for me, sufficient digestion has taken place.'

She felt frustration, bewilderment and restless dissatisfaction butting up against the brick wall of her stubborn refusal to see where he was coming from.

She was no pushover, and Mateo had known to back off, to retreat back into an easy familiarity, because war was not the answer and was not going to get either of them anywhere. He could never give her that one big thing she insisted on.

He eased the car away from the kerb and along the narrow street. It soon became clear that, wherever he was taking her, it was out and away from London because she recognised the artery that led out to the M25 and M4.

Curious, Maude settled back as the fast car picked up speed, clearing the London traffic and heading out. It was a familiar route but, instead of taking the junction to get to her parents' house, he instead began navigating a series of side roads, passing through a couple of small villages which she didn't recognise.

When she glanced across at him, her heart fluttered.

'You're eaten up with curiosity, aren't you?' He half-smiled, glancing at her, but not for long, because the roads were now small and windy.

'I hope I'm dressed for whatever restaurant we're going to.'

'What makes you think I'm taking you out for a meal?'

'Where else?' Maude sighed. 'And you're right. We need to have a conversation about, well, the details… and I'm guessing you wanted somewhere quiet where you can hear yourself think.'

'London *is* an extremely noisy place, now that you mention it,' Mateo murmured. 'Noisy…cluttered…polluted. Actually, I'm not taking you to a restaurant—although, of course, we *will* need to eat at some point. I suggest we wait and see where we land.'

'Where are we going, in that case?'

'Ten minutes and all will be revealed.'

There was something thrilling about this mysterious trip. The car passed through a bank of lush, green trees with fields in the background and through yet another quaint town, big enough for a pretty square with a pond in the middle, white houses jostling in a ring around it with a church dominating the parade.

'I've never been here before,' Maude observed, drinking in the detail and loving what she saw.

'No? I thought you might have explored this part of the world. You know, family days out?'

'It's lovely.'

'Glad you like it.' He swerved away from the town centre, but only for a few minutes, before taking another left and there, in front of them, was a cottage.

It was pink with beams and an upper storey that curved in an arch and glinted with leaded, stained-glass windows. On all sides there were fruit trees and it was protected by a low brick wall, behind which a tangle of hedge seemed to be staging a takeover.

'What on earth is this, Mateo?'

Eyes glued to the picturesque property, Maude let herself out of the car and stood for a few seconds, taking in the sight.

'A recent acquisition, although not finalised, but it's fair to say I see no obstacles.'

'A recent acquisition?'

'Come tell me what you think.'

He had a key and he opened the door to a spacious

hall, with a flag-stone entrance, myriad rooms spreading in various directions and a short staircase that led up to the top.

The smell was musty, the smell of a house that hadn't been inhabited for a while. There were signs of disrepair. Maude could spot each and every one from a mile off because she had a keen eye for those details.

But the musty smell, the flaky paint and the saggy floorboards were all minor technicalities that faded away, because everything else was just so charming.

The dimensions were perfect and she forgot all about Mateo as she embarked on a journey of discovery, looking into all the rooms.

They were cosy rooms with high ceilings, bay windows where a person could sit and gaze out at the tangle of greenery behind, with the creak of ancient floorboards in need of restoration...

There were six bedrooms, three of which were on the ground floor and looped in a horseshoe shape, circling a small, private courtyard with its own gurgling fountain and rose bushes running amok. The other three bedrooms were up the flight of stairs and overlooked the fields at the back. Each room had its own veranda.

Maude's imagination went wild. There was so much to do.

'This is nuts,' she said, tour finished, as he pushed open the door from the kitchen that led out to the patchwork-quilt garden at the back.

'What is?'

'This!' She waved her arms around helplessly and sneaked a look outside at the overgrown orchard and the open space.

'Sorry?'

'You can't just go and buy a house you know I'd like to win me over.'

'Ah…so what you're saying is that you like the place…'

'You know I do! It's…it's wonderful. Lots of work to do. Definite signs of damp here and there that need taking care of, and that staircase has seen better days.'

'Want to have a look around outside?'

'Mateo, it's not going to work!' She folded her arms and made herself look at him with firm resolution. 'If this is about trying to get me to marry you by seducing me with the perfect cottage, then it just can't work.'

'Because of the love angle…' His heart constricted. He was so used to winning yet so powerless to win this one important thing. He banked down the sour taste of impotence.

'Don't.'

'Well.' He leant into her and there was a smile in his voice. 'As it happens, this cottage isn't for you, my darling.'

'It's not?'

'It's for me.'

He took his time showing her round the parts of the cottage she had yet to explore, and the grounds, which were considerably more extensive than they'd appeared.

He had thrown her. He could feel her all at sea and on edge after what he had said.

Did she think that he would sit around passively, waiting for her to take the lead and tell him how she saw things panning out?

She had dropped a bombshell, and he marvelled that she had then seen fit to withdraw from the fray in the expectation that he would play along with that.

She was having his baby! It was a thought that filled his head every second of every minute of every day, and each thought fired him up with a protective longing he had never known existed in him.

Mateo didn't doubt her for a single second that he was the father. Why would he? For starters, he could uncomfortably remember those occasions when taking precautions had not seemed as urgent as it should have; when sheer, blind lust had overridden everything else, including caution.

She also wasn't the sort to fabricate anything because, as she had told him in no uncertain terms, she wanted nothing from him.

Except the one thing he could give no one.

But why couldn't she see everything else that he brought to the table? Not just financial security, but a willingness to put his life on hold for ever for the sake of their child?

How could he have failed to explain to her, to make her see just how important it was that personal preferences be put on the back burner when a baby became part of the equation?

Was he disingenuous in thinking like that? Yet, he couldn't help himself. There was nothing he could ever say in criticism of his father, who had stoically brought him up, sacrificing much along the way, and always doing his best to make up for the lack of a mother figure.

He had had a good upbringing in that respect, yet Mateo was now beginning to realise just how much mother's abandonment of her husband, her marriage and *of him* had affected him down the years.

He had shut the door on love. Had the very fact that he had been born driven his mother away? On every level, that made no sense, but still, buried deep in his subconscious, was that fear which had driven him into barricading himself behind a steel fortress, protecting himself from the vagaries of emotions and everything that went along with succumbing to them.

But, more than that, he had realised just as soon as she'd told him she was pregnant that there was some yearning he had grown up with which he had never recognised to somehow fill the void in his life. He would never have dreamt of courting the rollercoaster ride of fatherhood but, now it had been thrust onto him, he was overwhelmed by a feeling of wanting his child to have what he hadn't had—the stability of a home with two parents.

Yet, Mateo was honest enough to realise that there was justification to Maude's refusal to get on board with that notion. The scars he carried weren't hers and what she proposed was what anyone who wanted more from marriage than a simple, practical, workable union between two people for the sake of the child they shared would do.

They would both be there for their child, which was more than he had had. There would be no shortage of love.

Unfortunately, for Mateo, that wasn't enough because he could easily think beyond that to a scenario he didn't intend to accept. He thought about her finding Mr Right, if such a guy existed, leaving him to be the father who showed up every other weekend while some other man effectively got to bring his child up as his own.

That wasn't going to happen.

But neither could Mateo force her to accept his marriage proposal. These weren't Victorian times, and he certainly wasn't dealing with a wishy-washy damsel who was in search of rescue.

That said, this cottage was step one in persuading her that, whilst it might not be her first choice, what they had was good enough to stay the course. Better, indeed, than merely *good enough*.

He would be patient and let her come to her own conclusions and, in the end, if she dug her heels in, then he knew that he would have no option but to retreat, however much that retreat would feel like a journey walked on broken glass.

But he had no intention of retreating until he had given it all he'd got.

'So, you're saying that this cottage is for *you*...'

'That's exactly what I'm saying.'

'You're a city guy, Mateo. Do you honestly expect me to believe you would be comfortable living out here, in the middle of nowhere?'

'The M4 is a hop and a skip away,' he pointed out, the very voice of reason. 'And, as you well know, a lot can be achieved virtually. These aren't the bad old days when we were all nailed to desks.'

'Were you ever *nailed to a desk*?'

'Fortunately, that fate passed me by.'

'You never told me that you were planning on buying a place out here.'

She'd swung round to look at him, hands on her hips, the overhanging apple tree throwing her into a mosaic of shadows.

Around them the air was rich with the smell of fruit and the dampness of earth, leaves, trees and nature. It was a garden that had run wild.

'I didn't realise I had to, considering we'll be going

our separate ways,' Mateo said with a show of puzzlement, and watched her flush in response. 'While you were doing your thinking over the past couple of days, I was likewise doing something thinking of my own.'

'Oh yes?'

'Is there anything else you want to see while we're here?'

'No. Thank you.'

'In that case—' Mateo glanced at his watch '—we can go and have an early dinner somewhere local before we return to London.' He held up his hand even though she hadn't said anything in return. 'And no point telling me that you want to get back now. Whether the time suits you or not, we have to hammer a few things out, Maude, and I suggest we start doing that today—now that you've been shown around the first step I've taken in dealing with this situation.'

Mateo waited for her to object and, whilst he waited, his eyes drifted over her face and then he lowered them to her still flat stomach and felt the tug of something bigger and more powerful than he could ever have imagined possible.

He clenched his jaw, hooked a finger over his jeans and raked one hand through his hair.

'I suppose you're right.' She sighed and, without realising, cast one last wistful glance at the cottage, which was so damned perfect in every way imaginable.

'Right. There's a nice little place by the village green...'

'You've checked out the town?'

'When I do something, I make sure I do it properly.' He began leading the way back through the cottage and out to the front while she fell into step with him. 'No point liking a property only to discover once you've moved in that the neighbours are too loud and half the town's boarded up.'

It was a short drive to the centre. Along the way, he made sure to point out various plus points, just in case they'd passed her by. There were many ways to get what he wanted, and persuasion could be a powerful tool.

It would be an easy stroll to the centre of the town, even though they'd chosen to drive, Mateo told her. There were scenic parks within shouting distance and a vibrant community spirit, judging from the central square, the array of independent shops and businesses that made such a change from the monotony of chain stores and coffee shops.

He could have gone on, but he felt as if he was beginning to sound like an estate agent with an eye to a sale, so he fell silent as they strolled to the restaurant he'd sourced, letting her make up her own mind about the place.

It was hard not to enjoy the surroundings. They were the very essence of the picture-perfect English market town. They strolled past a butcher, a fishmonger and two greengrocers, all shut at the moment, but all promising top-quality fare, judging from the pristine awnings and cheerful signage. The coffee shops were likewise closed, but a buzzing atmosphere remained because there were restaurants aplenty and at least three pubs that all seemed to be doing booming business.

The restaurant was nestled down one of the side streets and was already filling up by the time they were shown to scats towards the back and orders were taken for some light food.

The garden was coming alive, making the most of

the last of the summer days, with a string of fairy lights hooked up between trees and lanterns on tables.

Mateo was quietly satisfied with the choices he had made.

'So...' Maude said, a little awkwardly. 'You said you were going to surprise me and you did.'

'In a pleasant way, I hope?'

'How did you manage to find that place in the space of a few days?'

'I got a team of people to do it for me,' he confessed. 'I told them the sort of thing I wanted, that money was no object, that I wasn't afraid of renovations from the ground up, that speed was of the essence and hey presto.'

'Hey presto indeed...'

'The way I see it,' he mused slowly, sitting back while the waitress poured some water and a glass of wine for him, 'Is, whilst you haven't yet made clear whether you intend to continue living in London, I certainly think that some open space is a must. London is fine for the urban professional but in a few months' time I will no longer be just that urban professional. I'll be a father and with that comes certain conditions that I am more than happy to fulfil.'

'Right. Well, I hadn't got round to thinking...'

'About where you were going to bring up our child?'

'It's still some time away,' Maude said vaguely.

'So it is,' Mateo drawled in response. 'However, as you can see for yourself, the cottage is in desperate need of work. I suspect the purchase will be finalised within weeks and I already have a team on standby to descend the minute the signatures are in place.'

'That's very efficient,' Maude said faintly.

'I like to think so.'

'And you're going to move in…immediately?'

Mateo shrugged. 'I can't see why not. Naturally, I will maintain my place in central London, but the truth is I can always go there on the days when I won't be able to see my baby.'

'You make it sound as though I'm planning on keeping our child from you, and I'm not,' Maude said irritably.

'My mistake.' He gestured, an elaborate, rueful shrug, and smiled as she narrowed her eyes and viewed him with suspicion. 'Apologies if that's how it sounds. At any rate, yes, to answer your question. I'll be here whenever it's my turn. I'll have a nanny on call, and naturally I'll make sure you approve of my choice, although I intend to tailor my working to maximise the time I can spend with my child.'

He lowered his eyes and paused fractionally, and when he returned to the conversation his voice was serious and thoughtful. 'I have a couple of ideas for development in the area, as it happens. Could work. There are some natural underground springs here that could be put to use, and of course it will certainly be a way of integrating within the community. As a single father on his own, it'll be important to get some sort of social life going.'

'I beg your pardon?'

'Well,' Mateo pointed out reasonably, 'We're both in changed circumstances, and for the first time in my life I do concur that my free and easy bachelor days are at an end.'

Their eyes tangled.

Maude felt a frisson of *something*. She knew that she was being asked to join dots but she had a cold feeling that she wasn't going to like the big picture.

'Yes, well, that was never my intention.'

'What was never your intention?'

'Like I told you when I…er…came to see you to tell you about the baby, I wasn't asking anything of you. I had no intention of disrupting your life.'

Mateo's eyebrows shot up.

'That was a little short-sighted, Maude.'

'There's really no need for you to…to…'

'Ah, but you're missing the point, my darling.' His eyes hardened. 'There is *every* need to. You obviously thought that you were dealing with a different kind of guy when you broke the news to me. You maybe thought that you were dealing with someone with very elastic moral guidelines.'

'Of course not!'

'You're not. I may have enjoyed myself playing the field, because I never had any interest in settling down, but that never meant that I was someone who might be happy to relinquish responsibility in a situation like this in favour of continuing with my old patterns of behaviour.'

His dark eyes glittered like jet and absolute intent was stamped on every feature. 'Like I said, I grew up in a single parent family. I know what it's like to long for what I saw other kids have—two parents. It's one thing for two people to end up divorced, for whatever reason. It's a completely different matter for a child to have never been given a window into what a united family might look like.

'You've made your mind up, and I can't frog march you up an aisle, but I *can* and *intend to* do everything within my power to make this situation as good as possible for the child we will share. It therefore goes without saying that my days of playing the field are over. In due course, I will doubtless find someone with whom to build a unit. It might not be the ideal unit, but it will be a unit. As you say, it's a sign of the times—children moving between families, bonding with step-brothers and-sisters. These things happen. Life goes on.'

Maude's mouth dropped open as these bare facts were laid out before her with ruthless efficiency.

What had she expected?

Had she thought that he would somehow remain in a vacuum, a part-time father doing his own thing, accommodating her while she got on with her life and conveniently never settling down?

Here he was. He had willingly taken the first of the big steps and he wasn't sorry about it, wasn't voicing any regrets for the lifestyle he'd be leaving behind.

He would move into the perfect cottage, having thrown money at it, with the perfect garden where a perfect kids' swing set would sit nestled amidst perfectly pruned apple and pear trees, and he would integrate into the community, doubtless becoming the man of the moment and the resident of the year.

Why wouldn't he? He was beyond wealthy, interested in doing his bit for the town and eligible beyond description.

Maude felt faint at the picture gathering shape in her head. Women would be falling at his feet. A sinfully rich, sinfully handsome guy without a wedding ring on his finger, pushing a baby in a pram and in search of a partner? The queue of women lining up to net him would stretch for miles. All that would be needed to finish off the enticing image would be a cute puppy on a lead in tow.

Her heart was thundering inside her.

He thought that *she* would likewise move on in her search for Mr Right because wasn't that the whole point of her rejecting his marriage proposal—the fact that she wanted love to be part and parcel of the deal?

He would never be constrained by concerns like that. A man who wasn't in search of love could easily find a suitable wife, and she could see that he would be a faithful and principled husband.

'You've gone a little green round the gills, Maude. Have something else to eat and we can change the subject, move on to less contentious issues. Although, in fairness, it is a subject we will have to return to at some point...'

Maude's anxious gaze collided with concerned dark eyes and she licked her lips, debating which way forward to go.

What had she done? Could she really spend a lifetime watching as Mateo, this guy she loved with all her heart, settled into a life from which she would be excluded? Life with another woman by his side—how on earth would she ever be able to bear that?

In pursuit of the ideal, what would she end up sacrificing and what would their child end up missing out on?

She had seen the situation through hopelessly blinkered lenses. Presented with a marriage proposal she had never envisioned—a proposal where no words of love had been exchanged, no passionate getting down on one knee and asking for her hand—she had fast forwarded to a vision of a miserable marriage in which her heart ached permanently for what she wanted and what was on offer. Mateo, growing restless, would descend into resentment about a situation he hadn't asked for and, trapped in the middle, good intentions or no good intentions, a child would bind them together.

How happy would that childhood be? she had asked herself. Kids picked up on stuff. In time, when everything inevitably fell apart, how much more damage would they inadvertently have caused?

She had stuck to her guns because everyone deserved love and marriage, whatever the circumstances, should never be a trap. She had failed to see a middle ground, which was the one Mateo would now occupy. One in which there could be contentment, harmony and...who knew?...over time, maybe not the crazy love she had for him but something like love, couldn't there?

The alternative...the one he had just presented to her, made her blood run cold.

She felt very green round the gills indeed when she thought about that.

'No,' she said in a strangled voice. 'We have to talk.'

And, looking straight into her eyes, watching the shadows flit across her face, Mateo knew that he had succeeded. He'd never contemplated marriage before but it was coming at him now.

He was ready to embrace it.

'Marry me, Maude,' he urged huskily. 'Step up to the plate and do what you surely must know is the right thing to do. Trust me.' He covered her hand with his. 'You will not want for a better husband, nor our child a more devoted father...'

CHAPTER NINE

SHE'D THOUGHT THE proposal had been a one-off but now Mateo's eyes glittered with intensity.

Had the same thoughts crossed his head? Even as he had told her that he would one day find a woman to complete the circle, had he thought about how he would feel if *she* likewise found a man to complete her circle?

He had proved that he would do whatever it took for the baby she was carrying. The sacrifices he had laid bare for her were enormous. With that would surely come a sense of fierce possession? Had he recognised that it would be difficult to absorb the thought of another guy in his child's life?

Had there been an element of cunning blackmail in that vivid prediction he had given her of life with baby? Had he banked on the brutal truth weakening her defences, making her see just what the repercussions would be if she walked away from the offer on the table?

There were a lot of other things he could have said and was probably thinking. What would happen in the future if their child were to find out that marriage had been on the table but had been rejected out of hand? Would judgements be made?

Maude knew that it was crazy to worry about something that might or might not happen in the years to come but one thing she certainly knew—her parents would never understand. No one would. She would be on her own in that respect.

She would never find anyone else. She would be doomed to spend her days watching from the sidelines as Mateo got on with his life and replaced her with someone else. He would have no qualms about doing that. Why would he? He'd be a free agent in the emotional stakes when he couldn't love.

A wave of despair washed over her and, when it ebbed, she took a deep breath and met his dark eyes steadily.

'Why are you doing this?'

'Doing what?' He tilted his head to one side and frowned.

'Confusing me.'

'Because nothing in life is straightforward, Maude. We could pretend that we will remain the best of friends, amicably sharing custody, and then, when we find other partners doing all sorts of joint things together in a thoroughly modern way, but that won't be happening. Not on my part.'

'Is that some kind of threat?'

'No.' His voice was gentle but firm. 'Far from it. I would never stoop so low. I'm just being honest. I would find it very hard to watch another man make decisions about my child.'

Strip away the sentiment she was adamant about wanting, and the facts were laid bare. Why would he tiptoe around them? This was who he was—honest, forthright, and if he was a rock, immune to all that soft, woolly nonsense that ended up blowing away like gossamer at the first hint of an unfavourable breeze, then so be it. He could no more help being the man he was than she could help being the woman *she* was. Yet, with this baby in her, their worlds had to touch. He had shown her a vision of what would be if they didn't.

'I suppose,' Maude grudgingly conceded, 'I might find it difficult to watch another woman do things with my baby, my child.'

He held her gaze then lowered his eyes slowly and, when he next spoke, his voice was uneven.

'I'm really excited to see your body swell and grow with my child,' he murmured huskily and wild colour flared in her cheeks.

'If we decide to marry because of the situation, we shouldn't muddy the waters...'

'Those waters were muddied a long time ago. I think it's pointless trying to change that, don't you? Clear, open water has long disappeared and, I confess, I like it that way.' He smiled a slow, crooked smile that made her go weak at the knees.

Mateo was bursting with a deep-rooted sense of satisfaction. He could see a ring on her finger, his baby in her belly, unforeseen events that he didn't mind at all—not a bit. It would have been shocking if his brain wasn't currently wrapped up somewhere else.

'Let's go,' he murmured.

'Mateo...'

In response, Mateo reached to brush his finger across her cheek and watched as she shivered and blushed like a teenager. God, he'd missed that. Missed the way she responded to him.

'I've really missed you.' He breathed unevenly. 'Have you missed me?'

Caught between wanting to be cool and longing to be truthful, Maude gave a jerky nod.

She was going to marry this man and, like it or not, her heart was bursting with love and desire.

They didn't make it back to London. They made it out of the town, Mateo driving steadily with Maude's hand on his thigh, stroking in a way that made him clench his teeth as his erection pulsed steadily against the zipper. The first two villages they came to had offered nothing in terms of accommodation but the third had a pub with a sign advertising rooms and they made it in fast.

Small pub, small room, small bed...neither cared.

Mateo was stripping off the second the bedroom door was shut behind him. Maude's hands scrabbled over him, touching him everywhere, his chest, his shoulders, tracing the path down to where his erection was thick and rock-hard.

He couldn't get her clothes off fast enough and, as he stripped her of them, he whispered to her, voice thick with desire, stuff that made her skin burn and sent every pore in her body into instant, sizzling meltdown.

They stumbled their way to the bed and it creaked underneath them.

Her clothes were half-on, half-off, a barrier to his hands, which she wanted all over her.

'No need for protection,' he murmured as they fell on the bed, both naked, both hot for one another. 'It's liberating.'

'Yet we're here!' Maude laughed breathlessly. 'I'm having a baby, so it's safe to say we've been liberated before.'

'Touché.'

His hot gaze brushed her. He knelt and could only stare at her, lying naked for his hungry perusal. He rested his hand on her stomach.

'Have you…changed?' he asked.

'Changed how?'

'Your body. Does it feel different?'

Maude half-closed her eyes and thought that this might not be the real deal in terms of all her youthful dreams being realised—this might not be the fairy-tale ending she had always secretly longed for—but right now, with his dark eyes resting on her with interest and concern, things felt good.

He cared. Maybe not for her, but one hundred percent for the baby, and half a loaf was better than none at all.

'A bit. My…' she blushed '…my breasts are more sensitive,' she admitted. 'And I've gone off certain things. Coffee makes me feel a little sick…'

'Sensitive breasts,' Mateo murmured. He rounded them with his hands. 'They feel bigger.'

Maude laughed and went hot all over at the rampant hunger in his eyes as they rested on her.

'And they'll only get bigger.' She sighed. 'I'll look like a zeppelin.'

Mateo burst out laughing. 'Can't wait.'

Their love-making was slow, tender and thorough, making up for lost time, invigorated by a dimension to their relationship that hadn't been there before.

He touched her slowly, as though they had all the time in the world. He made her feel special. She wondered whether, subconsciously, he wanted to prove to her that what he had said was true—that they could have a good life together even though he didn't love her the way she wanted him to.

Afterwards, they lay curled into one another until he reminded her that there was still a little drive to London to do.

'Or we could just stay here,' he murmured. 'Now that you've reminded me of how much I've been missing, I might not be able to make it back to London without another stop somewhere.'

'I think we can manage it,' Maude murmured.

They did. Back to his place, which was another testament to his rise up the ladder, a marvel of blond wood, abstract art and pale furnishings.

It had been insightful of him to purchase the cottage, Maude thought as she walked around, running her hands along the white leather sofa and plunging her bare feet into the springy pale rugs. A toddler would wreak havoc in a place like this.

'That talk you mentioned we need to have...' She wandered towards him, looped her hands around his neck and drew him towards her.

'I can't say I'm in the mood for talking.' He kissed the tip of her nose and she smiled.

'Okay. Me neither. But Mum and Dad are back week after next. As soon as they're back, we can go and break the news.'

And with that Maude knew that there was no going back. She cupped the nape of his neck and leaned up to kiss him, then she kissed him a little bit more until she found she just couldn't stop.

It was drizzling two weeks later when they pulled into the courtyard outside her parents' house.

During that time they had talked and had the necessary conversations, sorted out where they would live and how that would work.

And they had made love.

On the surface, things couldn't have been better. Mateo had wanted his ring on her finger. He would get what he'd wanted. He'd shown her the down side of a relationship spent sharing custody, working out where weekends were spent and then, eventually, the messy business of other people having a say in the upbringing of the child he and Maude shared.

When he had put a bid on that cottage, then when he had taken her there, he had known just how much she would fall in love with it.

At heart she was a romantic, in love with the notion of being in love, and that cottage had all the hallmarks of just the sort of dreamy, fairy-tale place that would appeal to someone with a romantic heart. The urgent renovation element had added to the attraction.

When he'd told her that the cottage was meant for him, as his permanent residence once the baby was born, he had known that she would be swayed. Her imagination had gone into overdrive and it had accelerated even more when he had described the idyllic life of rural perfection he was effortlessly going to achieve, a life in which a suitable wifely candidate would barrel along within weeks, eager to take up the mantle of mother-figure.

Mateo had almost bought into the fantasy himself. In fairness, he would have made it work if Maude had stuck to her guns, but he had been over the moon when she had buckled and accepted his marriage proposal. He was a cool guy with a cool head and he had got what he'd wanted the cool way.

So why was this thread of unease running through him now?

* * *

'Are you nervous?' he asked, killing the engine and turning to look at her.

'Nervous?' Maude frowned but then smiled, doing her best to wipe out the vague sadness that had lodged inside her ever since she had accepted his marriage proposal.

She hadn't made a mistake. What she was doing was the right thing to do for a thousand reasons, not least because it was unbearable to think of this guy who had stolen her heart settling down with another woman.

Their child would have the sort of stable upbringing every child deserved, and she was in no doubt that Mateo would make an excellent father. Because it had become patently clear that he really cared about the baby. He might never have envisaged settling down with *her* or even prolonging what they had, however much he told her how much he still desired her and how much he had missed her, but he was fully engaged in his duty and she was the essential add-on.

She was and always would be the responsibility he had taken on board because he'd had no choice, not when he wanted the whole package with the whole full-time, hands-on two parents in the family unit he had never got the chance to have himself.

She had bowed her head and said goodbye to the dreams she had had growing up, and the reality of the life she was embarking on had settled like a mantle over her, spreading a sadness that she knew would never really go away, however much she told herself that she had done the right thing, the *only thing*.

Her body might still come alive when he touched it but

it came alive because she was in love with him, because it wasn't just about desire.

'About breaking the news to your parents.'

'No.' She smiled with more genuine warmth. 'They're going to be over the moon, and when Nick and Amy find out they will be as well, although they might be a bit miffed that we beat them to it.'

'Then why have you been so quiet on the trip here?'

'Have I?'

'Are you having…second thoughts?'

'No,' Maude said firmly. She cupped his face with her hand and smiled, because this was the way ahead and she was going to make the very best of it. She was going to enjoy what she had been given and not allow herself to be plagued with regret for what she would never have.

'Sure?'

'Of course I am.' She hesitated. 'What, out of interest, would you do if I told you that I *was* having second thoughts?'

'I would try and dissuade you. There's no way I would throw the towel in without a fight.'

'And all that because of the baby?'

'That's right. Why else?'

'Why else indeed?' Maude murmured, fighting back the sting of tears, knowing that time would take the sharp edges off and put everything into perspective.

'And don't tell me that there aren't distinct upsides to this situation…' He reached for her wrist and held her hand gently, turning it so that it was palm up and he could kiss the sensitive skin there.

On cue, Maude's whole body went up in flames. She sighed and her eyes darkened. Mateo looked at her with wolfish intent. 'I see you get where I'm coming from. Shall I spin the car around and we can find ourselves a nice little B&B ten minutes away? I'm sure your parents wouldn't mind if we're running an hour or two late.'

'You're terrible and, yes, they would send out a search party. I was so keen to fix a date to see them as soon as they came back that I'm sure they suspect something's up, and knowing my mother, she'll be bristling with all sorts of theories.'

Mateo relaxed because this was more certain ground. He didn't like it when he sensed something in Maude, something deep inside unvoiced. He couldn't deal with the nebulous suspicion that somewhere inside she was hurting. He hated the thought of that. This was much better.

'Well, if you insist.' He vaulted out of the car, loose-limbed, sexy and compelling and swung round to open the passenger door for her. When he helped her out, it was another reminder of the role she now played in his life—mother of his unborn child.

Her parents were waiting. The front door was flung open before Maude had time to reach for the door bell. Her finger was raised and poised to press it when her mother was standing in front of her, as brown as a berry, her hair even more white-blonde than ever and reshaped into a perky, shorter hairstyle.

'Maude!'

Her father was beaming in the background, ushering them in and making a fuss.

They looked like what they were, two people just back from a holiday in the sun.

'Mum, you *do* know that there's such a thing as sun

block?' Maude teased, laughing and hugging them and then standing to one side while Mateo did the usual and blended in as though he had known them his entire life.

He was so at ease and so drop-dead gorgeous in a pair of black jeans and a cotton tan and black jumper and loafers. He was effortlessly sophisticated. He had told her about his childhood one night when they had been lying in bed, wrapped around one another while the last embers from their passionate love making had died down.

'I grew up with nothing materially,' he had said pensively, stroking her hair as she rested on his shoulder, curled into him like a cat. 'And where I came from there was a choice of two roads to travel down to sort that out—drug dealing or pulling yourself up by your bootstraps and doing the hard graft to get to the top.'

'Was it tough going against the grain?'

'Less so than you might think. My father was great when it came to the straight and narrow. He'd clocked the importance of money the minute my mother jumped ship for a rich guy. He might not have been able to achieve wealth himself but he made damned sure that I was on the right track to have a go at it myself, and I did.'

'I had it easy.' Maude had sighed with a pensive frown.

'Not that easy,' he had murmured, 'Or else you would have ended up married to a rich man a long time ago and your career would have been knowing how to fold napkins and lay a good table.'

'That's a stereotype!' But she'd burst out laughing and thought how good it was to be wrapped up in this man, so big, so dominant, so self-assured, a guy with a strong sense of duty and a deeply ingrained moral compass.

Whatever he'd grown up with or without, his father

had been the bedrock when it had come to showing him the way forward, and he'd smiled when she'd told him, honestly, that she wished she could have met him.

That he was now the embodiment of everything that was uber-confident and crazily sophisticated showed just how much single-minded focus he had to get what he wanted out of life.

Such as power. Such as money. Such as this marriage, the passport to his child.

Maude felt his eyes thoughtfully watching her as they were ushered into the big family kitchen. Her mother was in her element, gesturing and describing their holiday while her dad smiled indulgently and went about the business of offering them drinks and nibbles, making the same well-worn jokes about having slaved to prepare the cheese sticks and dips, all of which were still in their wrapping.

'I would have done them myself,' Felicity said, 'But I didn't have the time. It's been a flurry of activity ever since we got back day before yesterday.'

They had migrated to the living room, which was comfortable and cosy with squashy sofas and a wide sideboard with framed family photos laid out along it, a parade of pictures depicting the sort of family life Maude had always envisaged for herself.

Her eyes slid away from the photos to clash with Mateo's. He was standing by the bay window, lounging against the ledge with a drink in his hand, legs lightly crossed at the ankles. Behind him, the back garden was shrouded in gloom, the days becoming shorter and announcing that autumn would soon be drawing in.

Their eyes held and, for a few moments, it felt as

though time was standing still, allowing him to get inside her head and see the sadness that had lodged there.

Then they were both brought back down to earth by her mother clapping her hands, almost as though she was addressing a crowd of people, bringing them to order.

'I know you two have something to tell me!' She beamed and turned to her husband. 'Don't we, darling? And you must be absolutely fed-up hearing about the holiday...'

'Wait until the photos get developed,' Richard Thornton said. 'Brace yourselves for a repeat performance, but tack on another hour poring over the snapshots.'

'Mum.' Maude smiled, very much aware that Mateo had strolled towards her, joining her on the sofa, his thigh against hers, his legs spread as he relaxed back, 'I didn't think anyone actually developed photos in this day and age.'

'Darling, you know I like putting everything in frames!' She smiled and winked at Mateo. 'I'm not a fan of scrolling through a phone to look at pictures.'

Mateo was smiling good-naturedly, duly glancing at the array of family snapshots on the sideboard and knowing that, if he did a thorough house inspection, he would find many dozens more strewn on surfaces in all the rooms.

This was what he had missed out on. These were all the tangible, physical manifestations of the life he had never had, however good his father had been when it had come to raising him. And this was what Maude had wanted for herself, the big thing she felt she had sacrificed, the thing that only love could bring to the equation.

The moment passed by, leaving an uncomfortable taste

in his mouth. Felicity, having got their undivided attention and having moved away from the holiday chit chat, fixed them both with a beady stare.

'Okay, don't tell me that you two love birds have hurried over here at full pelt because you couldn't wait a minute longer to hear about our holiday abroad. I know that can't be true because I usually have to force this young lady to come visit us…'

She grinned and rested her hand lightly on her husband's knee, an unthinking gesture of affection. 'I'd say spit it out right now, but Nick and Amy are popping over for supper, so if you have urgent news then maybe it can wait until they come? Which will be in…remind me what time they're coming, darling?'

'They'll be here in fifteen.'

'So, can it wait?'

'Mum, since when do you have to *force* me to visit?'

'Perhaps I exaggerated a little.' Felicity smiled and blew Maude a kiss.

'Well,' Maude began, 'As it happens, we *have* got…er…'

She was interrupted. The doorbell went and that was good. No, she was not going to back out of this agreement now, but the enormity of what she was embarking on was dawning on her. In thirty years' time, would she and Mateo have photos proudly displayed on every surface conceivable? Would they be taking romantic trips together? Or would their very functional relationship have evolved into two separate people leading separate lives, sleeping in separate quarters in the very big house only huge amounts of money could buy? Would they even still be together?

Maude knew this was a pointless direction for her

thoughts to take but she was still tussling with them when Amy appeared in the doorway and Nick behind her, his arm around his wife's waist, her head leaning back on his shoulder, both smiling, both radiantly happy.

Mateo watched this family gathering at its most relaxed, very different from when he had last seen them all at that pre-wedding do, and held back as Maude stood to move towards her brother and sister-in-law, along with her parents.

He had got what he wanted.

He had never felt the drive to be possessive about anyone in his life before. He had become an island, strong, powerful and utterly shatter-proof. Cassie had been his one and only weakness and, even then, he had never given her anything more than his sympathy. But this baby... From the minute he had known of its existence, Mateo had realised that he would do his utmost for it, and that included marrying a woman who, to be brutally honest, had had no interest in marrying *him*. He had been given a deck of cards and he had known how to play them to his benefit.

But Maude had been out of sorts on the drive here. Had the prospect of seeing her parents again wakened her to what she was in the process of giving up?

He had watched her and, for the first time, he had realised that when it came to anything that involved emotion nothing was black and white. In *his* world, the world he had created for himself, there were no shades of grey. When he had decided that marriage was the solution to what had been thrown at him, that too had been a black and white decision.

But he had looked at those photos on the sideboard, had watched Maude as she had looked at them, and had felt as though he'd been given an insight into how she thought without her having to say a word. It had been a sucker punch to his gut.

And then when Nick and Amy had come in, the very picture of happiness, he had seen the shadow that had flitted over Maude's face. She'd smiled and moved, arms open to hug, but something inside her had crumpled and it had crumpled because of him.

He was the one who had given her a chilling alternative to the perfectly reasonable picture she had painted of two adults leading their own lives while still loving the child they had accidentally created together. He was the one who had swayed her into thinking that it was okay to give up on the dream of a happy family she'd probably had since she was a kid because of a baby.

But now Mateo had had an insight into just what that meant. It meant taking away her chance to find someone she loved, who loved her back. It meant taking away her chance to follow in her brother's footsteps and aim for the happy-ever-after life, whilst he had given up on all of that a long, long time ago.

In the flurry of activity, and with Nick and Amy demanding all the holiday info Maude and him had already been given, Mateo took the opportunity to pull Maude to one side as everyone else trooped into the kitchen where the drinks and nibbles had been left on the kitchen table.

'You're having second thoughts.'

'No,' Maude said honestly. 'I'm not.'

'I can see it on your face, Maude.'

'What can you see, Mateo?'

'Being back here…seeing your parents, seeing your brother and his wife… Has the reality of what lies ahead kicked in for you? Have you discovered that you don't like the image you're looking at?'

'That's not important.' Maude looked down. She could feel a dull throb in her temples as she stared at his expensive shoes, knowing that to follow that line up, to follow the line of his beautiful body, would be a little heartbreaking just at the moment. She quickly raised her eyes to his face and looked at him steadily.

'You were right. What's important is the life that both of us can work towards to make sure our child has the best possible start. If that means…' Her voice trailed off.

'If that means sacrificing our personal chance for real happiness and everlasting love with someone else, then so be it?'

Maude shrugged. Her eyes were welling up.

'This isn't the time for this conversation,' she said unhappily. 'I don't know why we're having it. I… I've already thought about this and made my mind up, come to terms with it, and I'm not unhappy.'

But neither was she happy. The only thing that could make her happy was the one thing he couldn't give her.

'Maybe I'm the one with the second thoughts,' Mateo said quietly and this time her eyes widened and she drew in a sharp breath.

She had not expected this.

Shock and misery tore into her in equal measure as she realised in a flash that she had misread everything.

She'd concluded that Mateo was the commitment-phobe who had no interest in ever settling down, whose heart was buried under layers of ice, but maybe that was before he'd realised the enormity of becoming a father.

Had that shown him that love was more important than he had ever imagined? Had he made the case for the business arrangement where everything slotted in nicely, papering over the fact that he didn't love her, presuming that she didn't love him either, only to gradually realise that, for a true family unit to stand a chance, feelings had to be part of it? That love had to be part of it?

Had *she* been the one to come to terms with the sacrifices he mentioned only for him to gradually come round to *her* point of view? The unfairness of that hit her like a punch in the stomach.

'What do you mean?' she questioned jaggedly.

'I think,' Mateo said in a low voice, 'That we need to spill the beans about our little charade that got out of hand. You were right, Maude. You...*we*...can very happily make a go of bringing up a child without, as you so graphically put it, being shackled together, sacrificing all chances of finding real, lasting, *loving* happiness with someone else.'

'I don't think I put it quite like that...' She drew in a shaky breath and tried for a smile, before continuing. 'You're saying that you've decided that you're ready to fall in love now?' She loosed a brittle laugh. 'I thought you were adamant that that sort of thing wasn't for you.'

Mateo shrugged. 'I guess you must be wondering about the things we discussed. The cottage...living there... Maude, the cottage is yours, unless you have any objections.'

Maude realised that she didn't want the cottage. She didn't want anything but Mateo. She had dug her heels in and turned him away when he had first proposed. He didn't love her, would never love her, and she had stuck her chin in the air and rejected what he had offered because it hadn't fitted in with the picture of the ideal dream life she had painted for herself.

Then she'd seen sense, but now he was the one turning away, and it showed her just how bleak and unforgiving the very future she'd originally demanded looked in the cold light of day.

She might have felt sad when she'd done her comparisons with what she was going to have and what her parents had, what Amy and Nick had, but the sadness she felt now was without compare.

Not that she could turn back.

'Let's go talk to your parents, Maude.' He smiled. 'It's what you wanted, isn't it? So now I'm going to make it real for you...'

CHAPTER TEN

FROM OUTSIDE, Maude could hear the buzz of voices and laughter.

Holiday anecdotes were being exchanged. Voices were talking over one another and there was lots of laughter, teasing and the thrum of a happy family life, the very family life she had longed for and was now saying goodbye to.

Next to her, Mateo's purposeful stride filled Maude with suffocating panic, but what on earth could she say? That she'd had a change of heart? That she loved him and would take him at any price?

In short, push him into a trap when he had now discovered that there might just be something more rewarding out there for him?

How proud she'd been! How determined to dig her heels in because things hadn't been perfect!

She pushed open the kitchen door to four faces that turned, beaming, in their direction.

'Mum.' She cleared her throat. Some of her unhappiness must have been mirrored on her face because the smiles dropped and she could see concern replace the laughter.

'What's the matter, darling?'

'We should have been honest with you from the be-

ginning.' Mateo stepped in to take over, giving Maude
a reassuring squeeze on her shoulder before swerving
round to pull out a chair at the kitchen table, which he
nodded to Maude to take so that he could stand behind
her, his hands resting on the back of the chair while everyone stared at them in confused silence.

'Honest about what?'

Mateo gazed at the faces turned towards them. He had always been cool, collected, utterly in charge, but he could
feel himself getting hot under the collar. He could feel
Maude's tension flowing from her shoulders to his fingers like the buzz of an electric current.

This was for her.

He'd corralled her into following him but seeing her…
watching what she saw and what she had always expected,
all the things he had never really had a clue about…had
done something to him. He had felt the twist of a knife in
his gut and however determined he had been to get what
he wanted, to drive the situation in the direction he felt it
should take, that sick feeling he'd had watching her accept her dreams disappearing had changed everything.

'Honest about what?'

'Honest about the fact that, when I came here the first
time, I didn't come in the capacity of Maude's boyfriend,
which you were led to assume.'

'What are you saying? What *is* he saying, Maude, darling? I simply don't understand.'

In an unwitting show of unity, her parents had edged
closer together and were now standing side by side, arms
touching, while Nick and Amy hovered on the periphery,
as bewildered as Felicity and Richard.

Maude and Mateo both rushed in, their voices overlapping. Maude could detect the high edge of hysteria in her voice and she fell silent, listening as Mateo calmly took over the monologue.

His voice was low and soothing, making everything sound so rational.

From start to finish. The arrangement made way back when…an optimistic solution to two problems. The problem of Maude not wanting to show up without an escort but facing the prospect of that because her plus-one had bailed on her. And Mateo's problem with his ex which had become an ongoing saga, drifting into the dangerous territory of her becoming a stalker, leaving him the unpleasant option of having to take hostile steps to deter her.

'It seemed straightforward at the time,' Maude said to a silent, open-mouthed audience. When her mother apologised for making her feel that she was somehow *lacking* because she hadn't followed the expected path, Maude felt tears prick the back of her eyes.

'I never thought…' her mother said. 'I should have been a little more thoughtful. Darling, I so hope you can forgive me. You know I've only ever wanted the best for you.'

Mateo's jaw tightened. The family love around him was a stark reminder of what he had not had, and he kept focused on that, focused on powering past the desperate urge to do whatever it took to hang onto Maude, to build the life he wanted to build.

Without the love. Because he was incapable of loving anyone. He was too tough, too cold. Those doors had been firmly shut a long time ago.

Hadn't they?

Something shifted inside him and for a few seconds he lost the power of speech.

He felt his hand tighten on her shoulder and had to make an effort to loosen his grip. But he just couldn't remove his hand because he wanted to carry on touching her.

Maude and her mother were smiling patchily, half-laughing and sighing, going over old ground, talking about misunderstandings, both knowing that those misunderstandings were trivial in the great scheme of things because there was sufficient love between them to more than make up for them.

Mateo heard Maude pick up the thread of the conversation, returning to the charade they had cooked up between them. He noted the way she said almost nothing about Cassie. There was no hint of criticism of his ex who had been responsible for escalating the situation.

'She's a bit fragile, I guess,' Maude said vaguely, when pressed for details of how a fake engagement had come about, conjured up from thin air, or so it seemed. 'And you know how it is…she decided to be a little naughty, I'd say.'

Smart, sassy, soft as marshmallow underneath, kind, generous…

Mateo felt the steady beat of his heart and his pulses quickened.

He wasn't interested in relationships. He was interested in fun, in sex. In ships that passed in the night. Those were things he had made absolutely clear to Maude from the start, as if they hadn't been clear already.

She knew his history. She knew that staying power wasn't in his remit. Besides, it was self-evident that he wasn't her type and never had been. She'd more or less told him as much herself.

What they had should have been straightforward,

so how was it that he was standing here, his heart was thumping and he was perspiring and in the grip of the disconcerting feeling that he was suddenly standing at the top of a very perilous precipice, looking down into an abyss?

'Cassie was one of my more monumental mistakes,' he cut in, moving to sit next to Maude and keeping the chair close to hers, although she didn't look at him as he did so.

Tension radiated from her in waves and he badly wanted to reach out and hold her hand but he wasn't sure how she might react. A lot of water had flowed under the bridge and they were here now facing a situation neither had anticipated, spilling the beans to the very people he knew she had hoped would never find out about her deception.

'She sounds very vindictive. All of this... I guess things might have been worse...'

That from Amy, who then proceeded to marvel at the train of events that had led them to a phoney engagement and a world of coincidences while Nick watched her indulgently and affectionately.

'We never meant for things to go the way they did,' Mateo said quietly, capturing everyone's attention simply by the tenor of his voice. 'The engagement story broke and I decided that it might be an idea for Maude and I to disappear for a while. I have a house in Tuscany...'

'A mansion on an estate with vineyards attached,' Maude filled in wryly.

'Yes, one of those. Far from prying eyes, and handy, because I knew that there was some business there to take care of so I would be able to kill two birds with one stone. What happened was—'

'Wasn't meant to happen,' Maude jumped in hastily,

avoiding eye contact with everyone and focusing instead on the kitchen clock on the wall.

'But it did, didn't it?' Mateo murmured, turning to look at her, satisfied when she reluctantly turned to look at him in return.

Just like that, the room shrank to just the two of them.

Maude had been aware of him moving from behind to sit next to her, with everyone else standing, so the focus of attention had been squarely on them. But she hadn't realised how close he was until now because she had been making such an effort to keep her eyes averted.

'And you said…' Mateo locked his eyes on hers '… that there were no regrets.'

'No,' Maude said with wrenching honesty.

'And…like a broken record… I maintained that what you saw was what you got with me.'

'You don't have to repeat the mantra, Mateo,' she replied jerkily, 'I got the message loud and clear.'

'How can I begin to tell you that it was a message I was so accustomed to churning out that it never occurred to me that the day might one day come when it was no longer on point?'

'What are you saying?'

She started when her father cleared his throat, and when she blinked back to reality it was to find her parents glancing at one another and shuffling.

'I do think,' her mother said briskly, 'That these two might want to have a conversation without us all around picking apart every word they're saying.'

Maude opened her mouth to vigorously deny any such thing but was overruled by Mateo, agreeing that he would appreciate a little bit of privacy.

At which point, all four sidled out, with her mother leading the way, and the kitchen door was shut quietly behind them. Maude turned to Mateo to ask what the heck was going on but he silenced her with a finger on her lips.

'Let me talk,' he murmured. 'This is hard for me to say but I need to say it.'

'No, you don't. We've said everything there is to say. We can tell them about the pregnancy, but the ground work...' Her voice trailed off. She couldn't finish the sentence.

'The ground work has only just begun, my darling.'

The way he said *my darling* sent a thrilling frisson through her which she loved and loathed at the same time.

'I told you that the message I always imparted was the same—no commitment. I wasn't interested. As it happens, you are the only woman to know why. At the time, I didn't even stop to question how it was that I had shared that confidence with you because it had seemed so natural.'

'And I understood, Mateo. I *understand*.'

'I don't understand,' Mateo admitted quietly. 'I don't understand how I could have allowed my past to dictate the future to the extent that I simply shut the door on any hope of having a meaningful relationship with a woman. I just never questioned it.'

'You were hurt as a child. How could you not be affected? I don't blame you. I would have been the same, I'm sure.'

'You forgive too easily.' But he smiled crookedly at her and risked a light touch, his finger on her hand, letting it linger there for a few moments. 'I never anticipated going to bed with you, Maude, and, before you tell me the obvious, I know—you never anticipated going to bed with me either. Making love to you… It was mind blowing, like nothing I had ever experienced before. I told myself it was because you were so different from all the women I'd gone out with.'

'Tell me about it.'

'Appearances have nothing to do with it,' he admonished but gently, tenderly. 'I never got the appeal of a woman who enjoyed giving as good as she got, but of course you were always that woman. You never shied away from saying what you had to say when it came to work. You were always happy to shoot down anyone you thought had flimsy ideas on whatever structures you were working on and, if that person happened to be me, then that never stopped you from loading the gun.'

He paused and looked at her thoughtfully. 'Show me that woman and I would have told you that I wasn't interested because what I wanted was someone soothing and non-argumentative. Who needs extra stress when your work life is already stress-packed and lived in the fast lane? But how wrong I was.'

'Are you telling me that you enjoyed making love to me because of my mind?'

Oh, how Maude wanted to read a million and one things into every word leaving Mateo's beautiful mouth, but she had to keep a grip on reality. Was this all leading up to a convoluted explanation as to why he now wanted to give her the freedom she had demanded? Why he wanted to find his own way, begin his own search for a woman he could love?

'Or,' she whispered slowly, disengaging herself from the stranglehold of his dark gaze, 'Is this your way of kindly telling me that I set you on the straight and narrow.'

'Come again?'

'You're going to be a father, Mateo. You're entering a new chapter in your life. You might not have asked for it, but sometimes things happen not quite along the expected lines. Maybe that's opened your eyes to what I told you at the start. That a family unit is important, yes, but a family unit with all the right ingredients in place. Maybe going out with me for a while made you see that it's possible to have something with a woman who isn't afraid to argue with you…is that it?'

'Not at all.'

'What do you mean?'

'I mean that this is my way of humbly apologising for being a complete fool and bravely asking you whether you would consider marrying me for all those right reasons you talked about.'

'I don't understand what you're saying.' Maude looked at him in sudden confusion as the ground was swept away from under her feet, and the hope she had been keeping in check burst its banks and threatened to rampage over every iota of common sense she had done her best to put in place.

'I love you, Maude Thornton.'

'No, you don't. Don't say stuff like that, Mateo.' Her eyes welled up but she fiercely kept the tears in check. 'This isn't a game!'

'It's very much not a game, and if you'd look at me…' he tilted her chin so that she had no choice but to look at him '…you'd see that I'm being one hundred percent serious. Darling Maude, why do you think I suddenly decided that you were free to walk away?'

'Because…because…'

'Because I love you. We came here and I saw the way you were with your family, the way your family were with you. I realised that there was no such thing as black and white when it comes to family ties and the jumble of emotion that makes us stick at relationships, get married, have hope, believe in happy-ever-afters. I saw the sadness in your eyes and I knew that you were weighing up what you were sacrificing and what you were going to gain. Weren't you?'

It was a statement more than a question and Maude nodded imperceptibly. Her head was still buzzing with what he had just told her.

He loved her? How could that be? Dared she believe him?

Yes. She did believe him. She could see the sincerity in his eyes but, that aside, she knew this man and knew that he would never, ever say anything like that as a ploy to getting what he wanted.

'I couldn't help it,' Maude admitted. 'But, however sad I was at giving up on the dream of the perfect life, I was still going to marry you because...'

'Because I made a great case for it?'

'Because, when I sat back and really thought about what life would look like without you in it, I...was scared.'

'Are you saying what I hope you are?'

'I'm saying that I fell in love with you and, by the time I realised, it was too late to start being rational about it. It hit me like a sledgehammer.' She smiled ruefully but her heart was soaring and she was giddy with happiness. 'And then I found out that I was pregnant.'

'Maude, you've made me the happiest guy on earth. The minute you told me about the pregnancy, my whole world tilted on its axis, and suddenly everything seemed to fall into place. I love you so much, my darling. So again, can I ask...will you marry me for all the right reasons?'

'Oh, Mateo!' Maude breathed, cupping his face with her hand. 'I think I can do that.'

'In which case, it's time we carried on this conversation with your family...'

They married five weeks later. A wedding in Tuscany, where friends and family were flown over for the weekend, no expense spared. The wine was from home-grown grapes, the food had been lovingly prepared locally and Maude reconnected with some of the familiar faces she had seen when they had been there.

She could not have hoped for anything more wonderfully romantic. It was a small, intimate affair, just friends and family, not a reporter in sight. To think that they had escaped to this villa in Italy to avoid the glare of publicity instigated by a vengeful ex. Now the tabloid press was far too engaged dashing behind a minor royal who had been caught taking drugs and was facing a prison sentence to bother with their story. Indeed, their nuptials, duly reported without any gossipy fanfare, were announced in the discreet pages of the broadsheets and in the *Financial Times*.

She had seen the villa in the summer, but it was as spectacular in autumn, and Mateo had arranged for it to be wonderfully lit for the reception with fairy lights, lanterns and outside an elaborate, sprawling pergola entwined with flowers and slatted so that the moonlit, starry sky was visible when you looked up. The food was served there. It was perfect.

And then afterwards they'd moved into the cottage, which had been refurbished, and started on the business of preparing for the little arrival.

It was busy, joyous and dream-like.

* * *

Exactly six months after they were married, Maude woke to the dull throb of back pain. Lying in the king-sized bed, with Mateo curved into her, she watched this big man sleep and the love she felt for him was so huge that it brought a lump to her throat.

He would panic.

She smiled, but then winced, breathed in sharply and roused him, voice as calm as she could make it, to tell him that the time had come.

Mateo woke with the alacrity of a cat. He'd been waiting for this. He felt as though this was the very moment he had been waiting for his whole life and he flicked on the light switch, turned to her with concern and slid off the bed to get dressed, all without pausing to draw breath.

In his head, he had rehearsed everything a thousand times. He grinned when she said, casually, 'You're not going to panic, are you?'

Mateo looked at her, in the process of zipping his trousers, grinning.

'Do I strike you as the kind of guy who panics?'

'In a situation like this? Yep.'

At three-thirty in the morning, the roads were bleak and empty. It was a route Mateo knew well. Ever since they had moved to the cottage, he had become accustomed to roads that were largely free of traffic and had become accustomed to the way they spun and twisted round corners, often without warning and with the occasional tractor meandering along, not a care in the world for traffic piling up behind it.

Once upon a time, he had been a workaholic and, while he still worked hard, things had been put into perspective.

Life had been put into perspective.

He reached out to briefly hold her hand and felt her hang on tightly to it. He heard her trying to put the breathing method she had been taught into practice. Panic? He was on the verge of it.

He had wanted to go private for the entire pregnancy, but Maude had burst out laughing and told him not to be an idiot.

'We could have had a top consultant waiting for us right now,' he ground out, swerving into the hospital car park and helping her out.

'This is just fine, Mateo. I can't begin to tell you how many women successfully deliver their babies without a top consultant on speed dial.'

Eight hours later, Violet Felicity Moreno was delivered without fuss.

And there in the hospital, as Mateo sat and gazed in wonder at the tiny seven-pounds-and-eight-ounces scrap of dark-haired baby girl lying next to his wife's bed, he knew what peace, joy and contentment felt like.

It was something he thought he would never achieve, something he had never even thought about, a concept that had never cropped up on his horizons.

His beloved Maude was smiling at him, her love as unconditional for him as his was for her.

Happiness.

* * * * *

THE HOUSEKEEPER AND THE BROODING BILLIONAIRE

ANNIE WEST

MILLS & BOON

With special thanks to the lovely Franca Poli,
who is always so supportive and ready to help
with my queries.

This one is for Dottie Auletto, a good friend
who always had such faith in my stories
and who will be greatly missed.

CHAPTER ONE

HE STOOD BY the arched window, staring into the solid wall of mist that covered the lake. It would suit his mood if that grey pall stayed all day, locking the island in from the outside world, away from the rising sun.

This day didn't deserve light.

Nor do you.

Pain jabbed his ribs, piercing yet so familiar he almost welcomed it. Pain was now a permanent companion, a sign of life.

Alessio grunted with mirthless laughter. On days like this, life wasn't necessarily a positive.

He scraped his hand around his neck, easing taut muscles. He'd been awake all night, using the excuse of the auction in East Asia as an excuse to avoid bed and the sleepless hours he knew awaited him.

The staff in the Asian office were the best. All his employees were. They could run a high-profile fine art auction without his online supervision. Even an event as spectacular as the one they'd just concluded, where fortunes had changed hands to secure some of the most exquisite antiques, paintings and ceramics the market had seen in a decade.

It had been one of his company's most successful events. That was saying something since his family's auction house had been brokering the sale of precious items to the world's elite for two centuries.

Alessio should be jubilant. His staff were. His extended family would be when company dividends were paid.

Yet he'd felt no pleasure at the success of an event a year in the planning.

Not surprising. His life was as much a blank as the lake mist out there. No peaks of pleasure or even satisfaction. Not since that day three years ago. He worked harder than ever, relentlessly driving himself, because to take a break would allow too much time to reflect and feel.

He shoved his hands in his pockets. He'd never marked anniversaries, but today's date was seared into his soul. He'd done what he had to, kept going. So many people depended on him. Family, employees, locals who looked to the Conte Dal Lago for support as they had for hundreds of years.

But keeping going wasn't living. Not as he once had.

His mouth twisted. He'd made many mistakes. He refused to add self-pity to the list. Rolling his shoulders, he forced his mind to the emails waiting for him.

A shaft of early morning light broke the thinning mist and Alessio froze, heart stuttering to a momentary halt.

He blinked. He must be hallucinating. Lack of sleep was finally catching up with him.

Or is it guilt, playing tricks?

He didn't believe in ghosts, despite living in the *castello* where his family had been born and died for over five hundred years. But what other explanation could there be for the shadowy form that made his nape prickle and the hair on his scalp rise?

He leaned closer to the glass, but the image remained the same. Below the tower, on the island's only sandy beach, was a figure.

Not one of the locals heading across the lake at dawn on some business. Not a lost tourist pretending they didn't know the island was private and off-limits to all but invited guests. There *were* no invited guests these days.

Alessio blinked, telling himself the figure would disappear, a figment of his imagination conjured by the toxic mix of emotions this date engendered.

The mist swirled and the person disappeared. He was telling himself it had been illusion when there it was again. Not just a figure, but a woman, a young woman.

He heard the breath saw in his lungs, felt anguish sink razored talons into his belly as she walked out into the water. It rose to her slender thighs, then her waist, her fingertips sending ripples through the water.

Like in your nightmares.

Alessio grabbed the window frame for support. This wasn't real. She wasn't actually there. She couldn't be. She'd been gone for three years.

Three years today.

Still she kept walking, not pausing like any normal bather on encountering that first morning chill. Instead she paced steadily deeper into the still, dark water, mist curling behind her.

Alessio's head swam, pinpricks of light circling in his vision. The stonework around the window abraded his fingers as he clutched convulsively.

Was he going mad?

His aunt had threatened it would happen if he stayed immured here, but he'd brushed off her concern. There were reasons he wouldn't return to Rome or any of his old haunts. A penance to be paid.

Mad or not, Alessio refused to wait here, wondering. He turned and strode from his study, hurrying down the tower's ancient stone staircase, its steps hollowed from centuries of footsteps, and outside.

The cobblestones were damp from the mist, but spring sunshine was already piercing the fog. He felt its warmth on his face as he plunged towards the shore.

There was nothing. No evidence anyone had been here. Nor

any sound. Unless…did he imagine the soft splash of water towards the end of the cove?

He headed to the promontory, every sense alert in the foggy stillness, but heard nothing over the ragged rush of his pulse. He continued to the pier. The few boats there were familiar. Nothing to indicate a stranger's presence.

It had been imagination. A phantom conjured by guilt, regret and too little sleep.

Yet Alessio was too unsettled to go back to his office. He took the narrow, cobbled street that circled the island, past familiar buildings, some empty and some tenanted by families who'd lived here almost as long as his own, most of them reliant on his family for work. They were a tight-knit community.

Not for the first time, he felt grateful for the way they'd closed ranks when tragedy had struck. The paparazzi printed unspeakable things about him, and society gossips were agog with speculation. But not a word had escaped from L'Isola del Drago about the events on which the world continued to speculate.

He was a lucky man to have such loyalty.

Alessio's mouth twisted. Lucky? In his people's loyalty and in business, definitely. Three years of complete dedication to the company had brought unheralded success. As for anything else…

There is no anything else.

He inhaled the scent of freshly baked bread and realised he'd already circumnavigated the small island, reaching the tiny bakery that kept the residents supplied with bread and baked goods.

He could call on Mario for an early morning chat over a cornetto pastry. It had been weeks since he'd looked in on the old man. But he couldn't face talking to anyone today, even someone who'd known him from the cradle.

Especially someone who knew him so well.

Alessio was striding towards the *castello* when the mist on the lake lifted and with it every hair on his body.

She was there.

The woman he'd seen earlier.

A rogue shaft of sunlight lit her from behind, turning her into a silhouette as she emerged from the green depths and waded towards the shore, shoulders back and hips undulating in a gait that was pure feminine allure.

Alessio's heart threatened to burst the confines of his ribs as he took her in. Face in shadow, wet hair slicked back and clinging to her skull. Slender arms. Narrow waist and flaring hips.

He must have made a sound. What, he couldn't imagine, for his larynx had frozen. But she stopped, head jerking towards him as if she'd been unaware of his presence.

For another devastating second the illusion held, his brain telling him it was Antonia, or her wraith.

Except this was no wraith. Nor a haunting memory. The gap in the mist widened, the shaft of sunlight opening further, gilding the young woman's arm and one pale, wet thigh, turning her from shadow into cream and gold and slick, living flesh.

Alessio's lungs burst into life as the breath he'd held escaped and he dragged in oxygen so fast it slammed into his tight chest.

Of course it wasn't Antonia.

She'd been gone for three years. Nor had she possessed a sapphire-blue one-piece swimsuit. Antonia had preferred bikinis.

He blinked, taking in the sleek shape of the woman who'd stopped in knee-deep water, as if wondering if it were safe to come ashore.

He would have told her the place was cursed, warned her to go back to wherever she'd come from, except his throat had constricted so badly it felt wrapped in barbed wire.

So he stood, hands clenched at his sides, listening to his drumming pulse and staring.

The high-necked swimsuit should have been demure, except it clung to delectable curves and a slim waist. Dimly he thought of the Renaissance painting of Venus emerging from her bath that hung in the principal guest suite. But Venus lacked this woman's punch-to-the-belly sexiness. Even her pale bare shoulders, glistening in the first rays of the sun, looked sleekly inviting.

That, finally, freed him from stasis. This was no ghost but a flesh-and-blood woman.

It was confirmed by his body's abrupt, almost violent response, a rush of what he could only label masculine appreciation. Because he refused to be more brutally honest about that sudden surge of blood and testosterone.

Alessio widened his stance, locking his knees, enduring a sensation like the thawing of snow-numbed flesh, painful yet invigorating. It had been years since he'd experienced anything like this.

Had his physical responses been frozen along with his heart?

He strode forward, furious with this interloper who'd mystified and aroused him, drawing responses he'd never expected to feel again. Never wanted to feel again.

'You're trespassing. Go away.'

It emerged as a growl from his tight throat. So be it. He, more than most of his ancestors, deserved the ancient, whispered appellation, Dragon of the Lake.

Yet the woman moved closer, swinging her arms wide as she waded. Sunlight caught the rest of her now, revealing hair the colour of the old gold jewellery locked in the vault below the *castello*.

Alessio scowled. Didn't she understand Italian? He repeated himself in English.

Even then she didn't stop until she stood before him, ankle-deep in water.

'I understood the first time. But I'm not trespassing. I'm Charlotte Symonds.'

Then she smiled.

Charlotte kept her smile pinned on as she looked up into his sombre face. Years of practice with demanding guests came to her aid, even if a warning voice cried out that this man was unlike any challenging hotel guest she'd ever had.

He was in a league of his own.

She breathed deep, searching for the calm that would help her through this meeting, and saw his gaze flicker as her chest rose. Something flashed in his deep green eyes that sent a jolt of heat to her very core.

The hair at the back of her nape prickled at her unexpected response. She wasn't beautiful, but she'd encountered her share of male interest and had perfected the art of the deft brush-off.

At the moment she felt anything but deft. And for the first time in forever, her instinct wasn't to deliver a brush-off. That derailed both her smile and her confidence.

'I don't care who you are,' he growled. 'This is private property.'

He crossed his arms, his stance pure challenge, as if preparing to repel her physically if she tried to get past him.

The idea was ludicrous. His cheeks might look hollowed beneath those high, aristocratic cheekbones, but he was tall and powerfully built. When he stood like that, feet wide and crossed arms emphasising the width of his chest, he looked immoveable and impervious. Not a man she could tackle physically.

'What are you smiling at?'

Hastily she flattened her mouth. 'I'm not smiling. It must have been a trick of the light.' She reached out to shake hands. 'How do you do, Conte Alessio? I'm—'

'Not welcome here.'

That hard, beautiful face with its long, sharp planes and intriguing symmetry turned to stone.

Except for the pulse thudding at his temple. It proved he was flesh and blood. As did the dark shadowed jaw and shiny tangle of untamed black hair. The combination should have made him look like a scruffy pirate. And there *was* something piratical about him, the air of a man who'd break every rule without a second thought if it suited him. If it meant getting what he wanted. His expression told her he was used to getting exactly what he wanted.

Despite the chill air, a curl of heat low in her abdomen made Charlotte frown. As if she found such ruthlessness arousing, though she abhorred bossy men who expected to get their own way.

Instead of looking scruffy, the man before her looked…indomitable. Imposing. Intriguing.

Incredibly sexy.

Charlotte should have been prepared. But the old photos she'd seen—of him clean-shaven in a bespoke suit, the epitome of success, or impeccably casual and stylish boarding a private yacht—hadn't revealed his raw energy. The stark, grab-at-the-throat magnetism.

She swallowed hard, trying to snatch control of her thoughts.

'If you don't leave immediately, I'll personally see you off the premises.'

'That won't be necessary.' Charlotte stood taller, telling herself it didn't matter she was in a swimsuit instead of work clothes. 'I work here. I'm your temporary housekeeper.'

He didn't so much as blink. The scowl stayed firmly in place. The only change was the lift of one coal-black eyebrow in haughty disbelief.

Charlotte's lungs tightened. But she was used to sneers. Her father was an expert, though in his case it was closely followed by a barrage of furious bluster as he browbeat whoever had dared stand up to him.

She'd long ago refused to be cowed by her father's threats. Her new employer would learn that a mere raised eyebrow wouldn't deter her. She might be an employee, but she wouldn't be bullied.

'I arrived late yesterday. Anna was going to introduce me personally when you were available.' Because the Count was not, under any circumstances, to be bothered while working. 'But a call came from Rome in the middle of the night. She had to leave suddenly.'

His folded arms fell to his sides. 'Her daughter?'

She nodded. 'There's a complication with the pregnancy. She's in hospital.'

Charlotte searched for some softening in his expression, but his features seemed to draw even tighter while his large hands flexed at his sides.

Yet she could have sworn she saw a shadow cross his face, as if from pain.

Perhaps he wasn't as unfeeling as rumour had it.

Or maybe you're imagining things.

She'd always tried to see the best in people, despite close acquaintance with her father's nasty ways.

He pulled a phone from his pocket, scowling, then turned on his heel, lifting the phone to his ear, striding away on long legs. Charlotte heard him say 'Anna,' and then a stream of words that was beyond her nascent understanding of Italian. Moments later he'd put the phone away, presumably having left a message for his housekeeper.

Demanding she return?

Or enquiring about her and her daughter?

Charlotte had no way of knowing. His expression was just the same, hard and forbidding.

The stories she'd read about Alessio, Conte Dal Lago, crowded her mind. He was head of one of Italy's oldest aristocratic families. Descended from robber barons and warriors who'd carved a fiefdom for themselves in the lakes and mountains of northern Italy, who had prospered and finally turned genteel. Yet their reputation for ferocity continued. According to one site, the Counts from the Lake, as their title translated, were renowned as being the most loyal friends and the most savage enemies.

She shivered and rubbed her hands up goose-pimpled arms.

When she'd read about his family, she'd been snug in her cosy suite in Switzerland. It had been easy to assume the reports were exaggerated as folklore always was.

But as the Count, or Conte in Italian, turned and fixed her with eyes the colour of the cold lake behind her, Charlotte recalled more recent stories. About this man. The recluse. The unfeeling, brutish Bluebeard. The cruel tyrant with blood on his hands. Speculation was rife about how he'd sequestered his beautiful socialite wife here, hinting she'd died of a broken heart, married to a pitiless tyrant.

Charlotte had dismissed that as media hype.

Had she been too hasty?

His eyes narrowed, almost as if he read her thoughts. Then his mouth lifted up at one corner. She couldn't call it a smile. There was nothing warm or carefree about it. Nevertheless, she couldn't drag her gaze away from that hint of dark amusement, if that's what it was.

She stood transfixed, wondering how sensible her plan to work here for three months really was.

'My temporary housekeeper?' he mused.

Gone was the gruff challenge. His voice was soft as velvet and dark with something she didn't recognise, an undercurrent that eddied around her suddenly wobbly knees. Whatever it was, it made her wish, again, that she wore her housekeeping clothes, instead of a wet swimsuit.

Not that he leered as some men did, who thought hotel

staff might provide extra *personal* services. The Conte kept his eyes on hers.

But for the first time in years, Charlotte felt out of her depth. Unsettled by the unfamiliar coiling heat low in her pelvis.

And the uncanny suspicion he knew it.

'I'll see you in my study in thirty minutes.'

His tone suggested her first day was going to be even more difficult than she'd feared.

CHAPTER TWO

THIRTY MINUTES LATER, Charlotte tapped on the oak door of what she hoped was the study.

There'd been no time for a proper handover from Anna, and the map the housekeeper had left of the *castello* and its cluster of surrounding houses was sketchy. The idea had been for Charlotte to work with Anna for several days before the older woman left to be with her daughter for the birth of her first child. Instead, as Charlotte's arrival late yesterday was swiftly followed by the medical emergency in Rome, there'd been time to pass on only a few nuggets of information.

One. The Conte's privacy was paramount. Charlotte couldn't take photos on the island or discuss anything she learned about him, this place or anyone else here. As if the hefty penalties in the nondisclosure agreement she'd already signed hadn't made that absolutely clear.

Two. Visitors weren't allowed on the island without express permission. See rule one above.

If Charlotte had had any doubts on that score, her meeting with her employer had banished them.

Three. If the Conte was working in his study, he was never, under any circumstances other than a fatality, to be disturbed. No matter how long before he chose to emerge.

Again, see rule one above.

Four. If she couldn't make a perfect espresso, there was no point staying.

Charlotte's lips twisted in a tight smile. Apparently the demon count could be pacified with decent coffee. Though perhaps *pacified* was too much to ask. Given his mood earlier, she doubted a little arabica would make much difference.

What would it take to conjure a smile from those flinty features?

That, Charlotte Symonds, is none of your business.

She pushed her shoulders back, checked her still-damp hair was in its usual impeccable chignon, and rapped again.

'Avanti.'

She stepped forward, then halted on the threshold, her heart rising in her throat. Not because Conte Alessio was scowling, though this time his foul temper was directed at his phone rather than her.

It was the extraordinary room that stopped her in her tracks. It took up almost the whole of the massive round tower, with high windows on three sides through which morning light streamed. Beyond was an arresting view of steep-sided mountains falling down to gentler green slopes and the misty lake. It was like being in an eagle's eyrie.

The round walls were fitted with bookcases that must have been custom-made for the circular room. Beneath the windows were deep padded window seats that would be perfect for curling up with a book or some embroidery.

Charlotte stepped inside, surveying the vast, extraordinary space. That first impression of cosiness altered as she took in the sleek modern cabinets near the door and the impressive array of computer monitors on the vast desk. Even the lounges grouped by a fireplace large enough to roast an ox had the look of modern design that married comfort with cutting-edge dynamism.

'Is that coffee I smell?' he asked.

He didn't even look up. His dark eyebrows were still angled in a V of irritation or concentration.

She'd give him the benefit of the doubt since it was clear he hadn't known of her arrival. Charlotte understood from Anna that she wouldn't see much of her employer. He hadn't interviewed her. Anna had done that after an initial interview by a formidable recruitment advisor, and the employment contract had come from a very superior legal firm in Rome.

Yet annoyance tickled her spine. She was used to providing an almost invisible service to wealthy guests, but surely he could acknowledge her as more than the bearer of coffee.

She walked, unhurried, around the desk and held out the tray she carried.

'Thank you,' he murmured, still looking at his screen. At least he had some manners. Charlotte recalled her father ignoring the staff on their estate, expecting them to anticipate his wishes and when they couldn't read his mind, blasting them with a violent tirade.

She saw the moment when Conte noticed the second small cup on the silver salver. He blinked as if it had never occurred to him that his housekeeper might appreciate an espresso after her early morning swim and his peremptory summons, leaving her no time for breakfast.

Or maybe you've gone too far, making a point.

At the small but ultra-exclusive Alpine hotel where she'd been head of housekeeping, she'd been treated as an equal by the manager. This was different, working for a titled aristocrat in his own home.

Yet Charlotte's mother had been an aristocrat, and Charlotte knew that a true gentleman treated his staff with consideration, not merely peremptory orders.

Why had *this* man's attitude irked her when she'd spent years placidly dealing with the most demanding guests? Even his gruff attitude was nothing in comparison with her father's furious rants. She had an unnerving suspicion she'd overreacted to his earlier dismissal of her, not as an employee but as a person.

Forest-green eyes locked on hers, probing. 'Please, take a seat.'

'Is there news from Anna?'

'Her daughter had an emergency caesarean overnight, but she's doing okay, and so is her baby daughter.' His mouth softened, and Charlotte sensed his relief. Perhaps his furrowed brow was a sign of focus rather than disgruntlement as he read the message. His next words seemed to confirm it. 'We arranged for them to go to a private facility with the best care in Rome, so hopefully there'll be no complications.'

We? Charlotte suspected *he'd* arranged it. She doubted Anna would be able to afford top doctors, nor would her daughter and son-in-law, who she'd said were saving every penny for a home.

Yet the Conte didn't have the smug look of a satisfied benefactor. There'd been unmistakeable tension in his tone earlier.

Face it, he's impossible to read. And it's not your job to try.

She moved towards a straight-backed chair before the desk, but the Conte gestured towards a pair of leather sofas. 'Over there.'

She took a seat, put the salver on a nearby table and sipped her coffee, eyelids half closing in appreciation at that first taste. When she swallowed, she looked across to find him sprawled opposite her, long legs stretched out, eyes narrowed. Had she pushed him too far? Surely he wasn't contemplating firing her before she'd started?

No, he was a man used to being waited on. He wouldn't choose to fend for himself until he found someone to replace her. *She hoped.*

Charlotte sat back, crossing her legs. They felt cool, a reminder she'd had no time to pull on the tights she usually wore with her skirt and jacket as she raced to get ready and make his coffee.

As if he read her thoughts, he said, 'You don't dress like a housekeeper.'

The words emerged before she thought about them. 'You think I should wear a white frilly apron?'

'That's a French maid, not a housekeeper.'

His expression didn't change, yet she felt the blood rise in her cheeks and knew he was laughing at her. She couldn't believe it. She never let belittling or sexist remarks get to her.

Yet for once her usual calm deserted her. Her new employer sparked responses that were anything but professional, which was curious given she prided herself on her unflappability.

Had she bitten off more than she could chew, coming here?

'Is there a problem with my clothes?'

His gaze flickered over her straight skirt and down her legs. 'No problem. But Anna doesn't dress formally. You don't look ready for cleaning, more for a business meeting.'

Charlotte shrugged. 'In my previous position I had to look tidy for the guests, but I take my jacket off when I have to scrub anything.' She offered him a tiny smile. 'Sometimes I even wear trousers.'

His expression didn't soften. 'And what *was* your position?'

She frowned. It might have been Anna who'd interviewed her, but she'd assumed the Conte would review her decision. After all, he was a renowned recluse. Was he really so uninterested in who lived under his roof?

No, that wasn't right. That was exactly why he asked about her work now.

'I was head of housekeeping at a luxury Swiss hotel. I also filled in as manager for a short period.' It had been that experience which prompted her to look for a move. Charlotte was good at her job, but it was time for new challenges. She named the hotel and saw those expressive eyebrows rise in surprise. 'I can get my references.'

'That won't be necessary. Anna would have checked those.'

More confirmation that he hadn't been involved in choosing her. Yet now, it seemed, he had doubts.

Charlotte repressed a shiver of apprehension. This job was important to her. Most especially because one of the reasons she'd been offered her next position, a promotion to a famed

Venetian *palazzo* hotel, was that she'd mentioned she was coming here to work as the Conte's temporary housekeeper. Her interviewers had been visibly impressed. The Conte Dal Lago had a reputation for accepting nothing but the finest in everything. Working for him was a sure stepping stone to future success.

And she was undermining herself, trying to score cheap points against him because he rubbed her the wrong way!

Get a grip, Charlotte. You can't afford to get the sack.

'I know the place. It's very well-regarded.' He paused. 'You seem young for such a position.'

Charlotte sat taller. 'I'm twenty-six in a few months. I've been working in the hotel industry for over eight years.'

This wasn't the first time people had underestimated her because of her age. But she was dedicated, determined and organised. Growing up helping her mother had taught her so much before she'd even begun her first job in a Swiss chalet hotel.

People had looked at her mother and seen glamour and privilege, the country estate and high society guests. Her mother had made it look easy as she managed the estate and its employees, ran her equestrian business and acted as society hostess. But behind the grace and calm had been hard work, excellent planning and social skills, plus the ability to handle any crisis. Charlotte had been her apprentice until the year she turned seventeen.

She swallowed, thrusting aside painful memories. She hadn't been home since the year her mother died.

The truth behind Charlotte's career success boiled down to one thing. *Desperation.*

Her career meant everything. It had saved her from her father's appalling plans and filled the void of all she'd lost. It gave her hope for a future built on *her* terms. Where *her* choices and *her* happiness mattered, and she wasn't a pawn in her father's endless quest for more influence and money.

Charlotte looked up to find that steady green gaze fixed on her. 'They haven't been happy years?'

Charlotte blinked, horrified that she'd been unguarded enough to reveal emotion. Blanking out her thoughts was something she'd mastered early as a defence against her father.

'On the contrary...' She made her smile easy. 'I loved Switzerland. I enjoyed my job and I met wonderful people. I've been very lucky.'

It was a matter of pride that the girl who'd left school with barely passable grades, the daughter her father saw as valueless because she'd never follow him into the world of high finance, had done so well. He'd deride her since she worked in the service industry, but it was honest work and she excelled at it.

'There's no need for the hard sell.'

This time it was Charlotte who raised her eyebrows. 'You don't believe me? It's true, I assure you.'

'Okay, tell me three things you liked about it. Off the top of your head. Don't stop to think.'

The Conte leaned forward, and she caught the scent of cedar and something smoky, like incense. Instinctively she drew a deeper breath.

'I...'

'No thinking, just tell me, quick.' He snapped his fingers. 'Three reasons you liked it there.'

'The mountains,' she found herself saying.

'And?' He was in her space now, forcing her on. 'What else?'

'Doing a job well.'

'And?'

'I could be me there.'

Charlotte gasped as the words emerged. Her heart hammered high and hard as if she'd run up one of those mountains she loved so much. As if he'd probed too deep, making her reveal things that felt too personal. She put her cup down, barely resisting the urge to cross her arms protectively over her body.

'What do you mean, you could be you?'

Of course he'd locked onto that unguarded revelation.

Amazing how that confession felt so visceral. Even after all these years, it felt like prodding a bruise, thinking of the life and expectations she'd left behind in England. Of how she'd never measured up, no matter how she tried. Not that she had regrets. She loved her life.

'Ms Symonds?'

Charlotte met his stare, hiding resentment at the way he insisted on probing into her personal life. If he had doubts about her ability to do this job, he had only to follow up her references.

Slowly she shrugged, allowing her mouth to curl in a small smile as if she were totally at ease. 'I told you I enjoyed the people, both the ones I worked with and the guests. And I made the most of the location. I enjoy hiking and skiing. I even did a little climbing.' She didn't bother to mention her other, sedentary pastimes. She couldn't imagine this man taking an interest in embroidery or cooking. 'The place suited me.'

Alessio surveyed the woman before him. She was hiding something. But was it something significant or something personal yet irrelevant to him?

He had no doubt she'd answered him truthfully. That brief moment of wide-eyed surprise had told its own story.

But Charlotte Symonds made him wary. He felt a jangle of the nerves, a frisson of warning, or perhaps awareness.

That stopped his musing. He hadn't been aware of any woman in that wholly male way since Antonia. He'd even noticed the fact his new employee didn't wear stockings. It didn't fit her conservative image, but maybe she'd run out of time. He'd been surprised when this poised woman, bearing excellent coffee, met his deadline.

She sat with her ankles demurely crossed but then shifted,

crossing one leg over the other, and he couldn't help but imagine the slide of smooth bare skin against his own.

His belly clenched. A snaking chill crept through his veins, and the flesh tightened over his backbone.

He was *not* interested in this woman as anything other than an employee. His libido had been dead for years, and even if it weren't, he had only to think about the end of his marriage to kill his sex drive all over again.

Alessio's curiosity was prompted by self-interest. He had to know he could trust someone living under the same roof.

More fool him for not taking a hand in selecting her. He'd buried himself so deep in work he'd left that to Anna and his legal team. It was only today, faced with a stranger in his home, and one with an uncanny knack for unsettling him, that he faced the consequences of his determination to ignore the changes Anna's absence created.

'You understand no one else lives in the *castello*? It's just me and my housekeeper.'

Slowly she nodded, giving a good appearance of confidence, but he guessed from that flicker of her lashes that this was news.

Was it enough to make her turn tail and leave?

He almost wished she would. Something about Charlotte Symonds spelled trouble, though he couldn't put his finger on what. The discomfort he'd felt since he'd first seen her was instinct telling him life would be easier without her here.

Life? What life? According to Beatrice, you don't have a life. You just exist.

Only his Great-Aunt Beatrice, who'd known him from the cradle, taking an interest him while his parents were off enjoying themselves in Rome, Gstaad or the Caribbean, would dare say such a thing.

'Living quietly doesn't bother me,' said his new employee. 'In fact, it rather appeals.'

His eyebrows rose. 'You think looking after this place, looking after me, is an easy job?'

A husky laugh escaped, reaching out and curling hard around his innards, until she bit down on the sound and wiped the amusement from her face.

Alessio was stunned to feel regret. That laugh, warm and low—a woman's laugh, not a high-pitched giggle—sounded... attractive.

It had been years since he'd heard anything like it.

'Not at all. I researched the *castello* before I came. No one could call it easy, maintaining scores of rooms across four floors, all filled with enough precious antiques for several museums and galleries.'

She *had* done her homework. There wasn't much information online about the interior of the *castello*. It was his family's home, carefully guarded from prying eyes.

'Six floors,' he murmured, 'if you count the basement and dungeons.'

That punctured her assurance. Her eyes grew round. 'Dungeons?'

'Several of them, and a torture chamber.' He felt one corner of his mouth climb higher in an unfamiliar smile because the look on her face was priceless. Desperate poise vying with shock. 'Don't worry, it's not in use. It's been generations since my family used such violent methods. These days we get what we want in other ways.'

He paused, watching the muscles in her slender throat work as she swallowed.

She looked wary rather than scared, and he had no interest in terrifying her by sharing any of the creepier tales about the old place. But she needed to understand her work here, if she stayed, would be no sinecure.

He sat back, eyes holding hers. 'That's the family motto, you know. *I take what I want and I hold what I take.*'

Unaccountably an image flashed into his head, of this

woman in one of the stone-lined underground rooms. Her blond hair was unbound, spilling around bare shoulders because instead of a neat skirt and jacket, she wore that clinging blue swimsuit. She was reaching towards him, arms outstretched, not in supplication but invitation.

Alessio's heart gave a sudden leap and he sat back, rubbing a hand over gritty eyes. Even exhaustion didn't excuse such wayward imaginings.

'Don't worry.' His voice was gruff. 'There are maids who'll come in to help you. Plus carpenters, stonemasons and glaziers who live on the island and do maintenance here as needed. Most have jobs on the mainland as well. Anna oversees all maintenance work for the *castello* as well as domestic housekeeping, though if it's anything particularly significant or an item needing extra care, it's always done in consultation with me. Anna should have left the work roster.'

'I'll look for it,' she said quickly.

'That's the *castello*. Then there are my requirements.'

He had to respect her composure. She looked politely interested, back straight, chin up, her expression serene.

Alessio knew what they said about him. Some people, eager to show their sympathy, had painted him as a pathetic, heartbroken hermit after his wife's death. When he'd rebuffed their public attempts to offer sympathy, and thereby worm their way into his life, the stories had changed. Many regarded him as a cruel monster who'd forced his wife to drop out of society and kept her here, a virtual prisoner.

His gaze went to the family crest carved above the doorway. There was the winged beast, talons out, ready to seize whatever treasure took its fancy.

Sharply he turned his head. A thousand needle pricks tingled along his spine as Charlotte Symonds' blue gaze meshed with his.

'You have no qualms, working for me?'

'Should I?' She shook her head. 'You need to know I don't

believe everything I read or hear. I've learned to judge people on their actions, not what the press says.'

Alessio was surprised she'd referred to the stories about him when most people were too scared to, and fascinated by that hard note in her voice that sounded older than her years. The sound of a woman who'd faced some harsh truths.

'Besides,' she continued, 'you had great references.'

Startled, he sat straighter. '*I* had great references?'

She nodded. Was that a tiny smile flirting at the corners of her mouth? It disappeared before it could settle, and he told himself he was glad. 'Anna clearly cares for you very much, and after putting me through one of the most thorough interviews of my career, I respect her judgement.'

'She gave me a reference? What did she say?'

There it was again, that ghost of amusement curving the edges of her mouth. It made her regular but rather ordinary features suddenly compelling. He found himself noticing the attractive shape of her pale pink lips, the intriguing way her eyes tilted at the corners with laughter. The change accentuated her cheekbones too, giving definition to her round face.

'That would be telling. I'm sure you understand that we housekeepers know how to keep confidences. But it was, on the whole, positive.'

For one astonished moment, Alessio felt a bark of laughter rise in his throat. It was so unprecedented his whole body stilled. Laughter belonged in another life.

'On the whole?' He raised one questioning eyebrow.

She nodded. Then, as the silence lengthened, she added, 'I was warned under no circumstances to approach you in the morning unless I came with excellent coffee.'

This time Alessio couldn't hold back. His laughter echoed around the room, the sound like a ghost from the long distant past.

That recognition instantly dimmed his humour. He was amazed he could laugh today of all days, but he refused to let the thought take root. If he'd paid more attention to the world outside himself, he wouldn't now be confronted with a temporary employee he wasn't sure he wanted in his home.

'Your lawyer was also reassuring.'

'It didn't occur to you that he was biased because I pay his fees? For that matter, Anna might not have been wholly truthful.'

The woman before him narrowed her eyes. 'I believe she's honest. Besides—' she paused '—one of my hotel guests vouched for you.'

Alessio frowned. So much for the confidentiality clause she'd had to sign before arriving.

It was unexpected and disturbing when she continued as if she'd read his mind. 'Don't worry, I didn't discuss the job or you. I mentioned that I was thinking of coming to work in this region, and Signor Lucchesi mentioned the *castello* and a major charity event you host here. He was full of praise for it and for you.'

She must be talking about the spring festival. It had been a tradition for generations, celebrating the fruitful seasons, and in more recent years, Alessio had hosted a grand ball, raising money for projects to improve the lives of people in the region. The sort of projects that often slipped through the cracks of government funding.

Anna had pestered him about reviving the celebrations this year, but he'd deferred giving a decision. It was easier to follow his policy of ignoring things he didn't want, knowing people would eventually give up bothering him. After all, he personally funded many local initiatives. He didn't need a festival to remind him of his obligations.

Yet you forgot about the arrival of your temporary housekeeper.

Not forgot so much as ignored it, not realising how much time had passed, thinking Anna's departure was still in the future. Though long-suffering Anna had tried to shift his attention to domestic matters. He'd brought this situation on himself.

He met Charlotte Symonds' wary blue gaze and admitted she deserved better than the gruff welcome she'd received. Anna would have been ashamed of him.

'I'm afraid it hasn't been the most auspicious start for you.'

She blinked, and shock crossed her features before she smoothed them into a placid mask.

Had he been such an ogre that the tiniest hint of warmth surprised her?

Not just an ogre. You've been ungracious and arrogant, the creaky voice of his conscience whispered.

She might as well get used to the working conditions now as later, replied the ogre.

'I lost track of the dates,' he explained. That was anything but the truth. He'd been fixated on today's date for months. This sombre anniversary had consumed his thoughts, and he'd ignored anything peripheral. 'I'd planned to discuss Anna's replacement with her before now. I hadn't realised you were due to arrive so soon.'

Charlotte Symonds stared back, frowning. She didn't believe him. But like a perfect employee, she nodded, the sunlight through the window catching her gilded hair.

'I understand. It must have been a shock, seeing a stranger on your private island.'

Not as much of a shock as seeing her in the lake on the very anniversary of the day his wife had drowned there.

'Conte Alessio? Are you okay?'

She looked about to rise. And what? Put one slim hand on his brow? He could almost feel her touch, not only on his face but elsewhere.

His chilled body thawed and ached. He told himself pain always followed a thaw. But this ache low in his body was different, something he'd never expected to feel again.

Abruptly he lifted his chin, looking down his nose. 'Of course I'm okay.'

But Alessio didn't feel it. His thoughts frayed, and making conversation was difficult. Images of this woman emerging half-naked from the lake kept playing across his mind, merging with older, less pleasant pictures.

He couldn't remember when he'd last eaten. Yesterday? The day before? No wonder he wasn't handling this well. He'd gone too long without food or rest, working for days straight. These unexpected sensations had nothing to do with Charlotte Symonds but with the way he'd neglected his body's needs.

He looked at her and felt his groin grow heavy and tight as he considered those needs.

Ones beyond craving sleep and sustenance.

Something punched him hard in the gut. *Shame.*

He shot to his feet and strode to the desk. 'We'll continue this later.' His voice was a growl.

'But you haven't told me about *your* requirements.'

Her words stroked fire through his belly. A fire he doused with the chill of remembrance.

Alessio sank onto his desk chair, opening a computer screen, not allowing himself to look her way.

'Later, Ms Symonds. Settle in and find your way around the *castello*. We'll talk about my requirements later.'

CHAPTER THREE

LATER MEANT *MUCH* LATER.

Several times through the day, Charlotte went up the tower's curving staircase to his study. Each time the door was shut. She'd been warned never to interrupt the Conte at work, and his expression when he'd dismissed her this morning made it clear their discussion wasn't a priority.

He'd already been looking at his computer screen, eyes narrowed in concentration as if he'd forgotten her presence.

Was it business that put him in that tetchy mood? His deep green eyes had held a febrile glitter that spoke of something more than concentration.

Emotion, and deep emotion at that.

She'd glimpsed hints of it despite his aristocratic hauteur and his grouchiness, like a bear disturbed in its den. He didn't like dealing with a newcomer, but instinct told her there was more to it than that.

You're not being paid to understand him.

Yet no matter how busy she'd been during the day, her thoughts strayed back to that fierce, daunting man who'd ruffled her composure as no one had in years.

He had the arrogance and brute power of his robber baron ancestors. If she really had been an interloper, he'd probably have tossed her back into the water.

She'd felt his nearness as a physical force. The angry glide of his gaze creating friction on her bare flesh. The aura around him, like a force field, was palpable. The flick of one eyebrow, the flare of chiselled nostrils, igniting a rush of heat inside her.

It was inexplicable. In Switzerland, many guests had been fit and athletic, there for the skiing or climbing. But none had such an overtly physical presence.

If his stare had been sexual, it would have been easier. She could deal with unwanted attention. It came with the job, sadly. But the Conte hadn't leered. He wanted her gone. Even when he discovered who she was, it felt like he'd prefer it if she ran away and left him to his own devices.

Charlotte frowned as she grabbed a tray and cutlery.

Whatever the Conte did all day, it didn't seem to involve eating. She'd taken stock of the supplies in the huge pantry, and nothing had disappeared.

All day, as she explored the ancient building and talked to the maids who'd arrived to clean the grand reception rooms, she'd waited for his summons.

There'd been none.

Was he still deciding whether to employ her? Charlotte's breath snagged. She couldn't get the sack on her first day!

Nor could she wait endlessly for him to remember her existence. She had to know where she stood.

She'd take him dinner, knock on the door and leave it there if necessary. But with luck he'd invite her in, and she'd at least have a chance to schedule a meeting.

Charlotte laid the tray, adding some of the scrumptious bread the baker had delivered. At least *he'd* been friendly, and the maids too, if inquisitive. Their welcomes had gone a long way to restoring her faith that this *was* the wonderful opportunity she'd hoped.

Minutes later she arrived at the study to find it empty. On a hunch, she took the stairs up another floor to the Conte's private suite. She'd explored it earlier, changing towels, dusting, and noticing that his vast bed was already professionally made. As if he hadn't slept in it since the morning before, when presumably Anna had tidied the room.

Or maybe he's incredibly self-sufficient and neat. Maybe he prides himself on his hospital corners and smoothing every last crease from that gorgeous dark green-and-gold bedspread.

Charlotte snorted at the idea of the Conte erasing creases when he hadn't bothered shaving in days and his hair was a wild tangle.

Wild but indecently attractive.

Her fingers clenched on the tray's handles.

No, no, no! She never thought of clients like that.

The door to his sitting room was open. She paused and cleared her throat. There was no growling response. 'Conte Alessio?'

Nothing. She pushed the door wide and stepped in. It was empty, but the door to the bedroom was ajar. Presumably he was in there.

Charlotte took a moment to survey the room. The vase of ferns and spring greenery she'd left earlier looked good. As did the order she'd brought to the art magazines she'd found spilling across the coffee table.

It wasn't that she needed those seconds to slow her quickened pulse before meeting the demon count again.

Of course not.

When he thought it through, he'd realise he needed her. She could enjoy the job's challenges, knowing she wouldn't have the embarrassing, potentially catastrophic task of explaining in Venice that she hadn't worked for him after all.

Charlotte set the tray down on a table near the window.

'If I'd wanted you, I would have asked for you,' the deep voice drawled, and she stiffened, almost dropping the meal.

The idea of that velvet-over-iron voice summoning her because he *wanted* her awoke a feminine yearning so profound it shocked her.

Firming her lips and ignoring the way her nipples thrust against her bra, Charlotte took her time straightening. He would *not* discompose her or make her apologise for doing her job.

Fleetingly she wondered if his attitude was a deliberate ploy to make her leave. But why?

'I did call out before coming in,' she said as she turned. Whatever she'd been going to say next disappeared into brain fog as she saw him.

Towel slung around his shoulders. Lustrous, damp hair tousled from being rubbed. Faded, low-slung jeans, undone at the top. Bare feet. Bare torso. Acres of taut olive-gold skin.

Charlotte took in the image in a second of awed admiration, because, despite the now-familiar scowl, he was, quite simply, the most beautiful man she'd ever seen.

Except beauty implied softness, and there was nothing soft about all the lean strength in that imposing V-shaped torso. Nothing soft except perhaps the dusting of dark hair that shadowed and accentuated the shape of his chest and narrowed to a tantalising hint of darkness arrowing down into snug denim.

Charlotte snapped her attention back to his face and kept it there. But it didn't help. Something about his particular style of masculinity was emblazoned on her brain. Even the low curve of abdominal muscle and hip bone seemed branded on her retinas.

She swallowed, her throat sandpaper-dry.

'Next time, don't come in unless you're asked.'

'Of course.' She almost added that it was good to have him spell out some of his expectations but knew he wouldn't appreciate the reminder of their overdue talk. 'Shall I take the food away?'

Alessio looked into that butter-wouldn't-melt expression and had to force his jaw to unlock. He didn't want to scare her, precisely, but her refusal to react as expected was unsettling. Why was she here when he'd told her to keep away?

Even more unsettling was that today, for the first time in ages, he was so aware of himself physically. Of sensations and hungers he'd long forgotten.

The food smelled wonderful, and his stomach was empty. 'Leave it, now you've brought it.'

He was being churlish. Anna would have stuck her hands on her hips and scolded him for bad manners. Yet this woman merely stood, unblinking in the face of his bad temper, calm and collected.

When he was anything but. He'd managed an hour's work after she left his study, because he didn't want to go to the kitchen for food in case she was there. He'd needed solitude.

Finally he'd stretched out on a sofa and shut his eyes, knowing if he did manage a fitful sleep, he'd be haunted by Antonia's sorrowful brown eyes and fragile beauty. Instead he'd slept the day away! And woken to the recollection of sparkling blue eyes and an unfamiliar, husky female voice.

Woken aroused too, for the first time in years. Hence the bone-jarringly icy shower he'd just endured.

Because of this woman?

Impossible.

'I'll leave you to it,' she said, yet she didn't move. 'Shall we make a time to meet tomorrow for our discussion?'

So that was it. She wanted to know where she stood. She was as pushy as Anna. No wonder the older woman had hired her. She'd seen the similarities between them. Though Anna knew when pushing too far was counterproductive.

'We'll do it now.' He sighed. 'Give me a minute.' Then there'd be no more need to interact with this disquieting stranger.

When Alessio emerged from the bedroom, he was fully dressed. A place had been laid with fine bone china, polished silver and a linen napkin. A crystal goblet caught the light.

He wanted to say she was trying too hard. He was happy with simple meals. But to be fair, no one had told her his preferences.

Whose fault is that?

He took his place at the table and gestured for her to join him. A sensational aroma hit his nostrils from the steaming soup.

'Mario, the baker, brought a basket of fresh mushrooms. I assumed you like them.'

Alessio nodded, his mouth watering. But instead of sitting, she lifted a bottle for approval. 'May I?' He recognised it as a vintage sherry. 'It was the first sherry I found. I hope that's okay.'

Alessio shrugged. It would take several lifetimes to empty the fine wines in the cellar. 'Sherry with mushroom soup?' It wasn't a wine he usually drank.

'Trust me,' she murmured as she poured a measure.

The wine glowed like autumn sunshine. He swirled it, admiring the colour, then the nose, then finally the taste. A complex flavour of nuts and dark honey exploded on his palate, warmth trickling down his throat and into his veins.

How long since he'd noticed what he ate and drank? He eyed the old bottle, telling himself it was because this was an exceptional wine, but knowing that was only part of the explanation.

Ignoring the conundrum he dipped his spoon and tasted the soup.

'My compliments. This is excellent.' He took another mouthful and another, suddenly realising he was ravenous. He broke off some bread. 'Sit and tell me about yourself. Why you want to work here.'

She took the seat opposite, her posture erect. 'As I told Anna—'

'Anna's not here. Just tell me what I need to know.'

He had faith in Anna, but reserved the right to his own judgement. After all, it was his privacy being impinged on.

'I'm English, but I've worked most of my career in Switzerland. I began in ski chalets. I have experience in housekeeping, reception and management. I—'

'Why not work in Britain? Don't you miss family and friends?'

Alessio watched her eyes narrow and her brow furrow until that blank, professional expression returned. 'My mother's dead, and I'm not close to my father. I found good opportunities in Europe and took them because my career is important to me.'

What did that tell him? She didn't have strong ties to her family. She was focused on success. He had to admire that— it was something they shared.

Yet working here was an unusual choice. He couldn't shake the suspicion she was here for more than work. To pry and sell a behind-the-scenes exposé?

Yet she'd signed a nondisclosure agreement. He'd checked today and found the document from his lawyers.

'You see yourself managing a significant hotel? Is that your goal?'

She shrugged. 'I'd like to work for myself eventually.'

'Surely a job like this doesn't fit your career plan.'

'I didn't answer an ad. A friend recommended me to someone Anna knew.'

Alessio put down his spoon and took a slow sip of wine. A personal recommendation rather than the usual process? 'Is that how you get your jobs, personal recommendations?'

She wasn't a stunning beauty, but there was something about Charlotte Symonds that attracted male attention. Attracted even his, which until today, he'd thought impossible.

Had she won jobs through *personal favours*? The delicious flavours on his tongue turned sour.

He would have sworn his expression was unreadable, yet it seemed she'd read his thoughts. 'Not in the way you're thinking.'

Her chin tilted, and she regarded him as imperiously as his Great-Aunt Beatrice, the tyrant who terrified the younger generations of the Dal Lago family. No one else would dare look at him that way, yet he felt no anger. He'd take offence if someone implied such a thing about his success.

'You don't know what I'm thinking.'

'I take my work and reputation very seriously.' Those blue eyes fixed on his unwaveringly. 'I've won every job on merit. It's not surprising I receive personal recommendations when I do my job well. Surely you find the same in business, that those who excel are recommended?'

Alessio nodded. 'So why this position? It's not an obvious stepping stone for a career in hotels. Plus it's only for a short time.'

She eased back in her seat. 'I need to practice my Italian. My next position is in Venice. And...'

'Go on.'

'And I was ready to move on to something new.' Still Alessio waited. There had to be more. Finally she shrugged, her gaze flicking away, then back again. 'You must know your reputation. Working for you, even for a few months, will be impressive on my resume.'

He'd long since ignored the outrageous stories told about him, yet he found he still had pride enough to be annoyed. 'Because surviving to tell the tale will prove how good you are? Because I'm such a monster?'

That's what some labelled him.

Her eyes rounded. 'No! Nothing like that.' She drew a deep breath that pressed her breasts against her crisp white blouse. 'I meant your reputation for insisting on the finest. Your auction house is renowned for quality, and so is your personal taste. You only employ the best experts.' She shook her head. 'I never meant…'

'It's all right, Ms Symonds. I understand.'

Only too well. He really had been mired in his own dark thoughts too long.

Maybe Beatrice was right, and isolation was skewing his perception. But not without reason. Too many people had tried to wheedle their way into his world via one excuse or the other. All wanting a piece of him. In the old days, it had been his money and influence or even his body. More recently there'd been a prurient interest in his suffering, in uncovering the salacious details of his marriage.

'Conte Alessio—'

He raised his hand. 'My apologies, Ms Symonds. It seems at least some of what they say about me is true. There's something particularly…ungracious about jumping to such a conclusion about you. I'm sorry. Maybe I've begun to live down to my reputation.'

It wasn't a welcome thought. He might be a recluse, but he wasn't a barbarian. Or he hadn't been.

'I suggest you go now,' he said. 'It's late, and I'm sure you've had a busy day.' She opened her mouth, he guessed to protest. 'Tomorrow morning we'll go through everything you need to know about the job.'

Finally she nodded and rose. 'I'll bring some more soup. If you're hungry, there's also—'

'No need.' His appetite had died with the realisation of his boorishness. 'This will be fine.'

'Very well.' Was that *concern* in her gaze? For *him*? The possibility scored what was left of his ego. 'I'll see you tomorrow morning.'

When she'd gone, Alessio finished the superb soup and crusty bread. He might have no appetite, but his years in hell had taught him he still needed fuel for his body.

Who'd have imagined he'd spend the anniversary of Antonia's death fixated not on the painful past but the present and the woman who'd interrupted his peace?

Charlotte Symonds was the first new face on this island in three years. A reminder of life beyond this place. Despite working seven days a week, and online discussions with staff and clients around the globe, the outside world had never impinged on him as it had today.

Now he felt...different. More aware. More alive.

As if this stranger had changed the dynamic and jolted him out of his stupor.

Or like an animal coming out of hibernation. There'd definitely been something bearish about his attitude when he'd confronted his new housekeeper. It was a wonder she hadn't left on the spot.

She had backbone.

And more. His fingers twitched as he thought of her breasts against that clinging blue swimsuit. The gentle arc of her hips down to slender legs.

Heat stirred in his belly. A heat that had nothing to do with the soup.

Alessio shot to his feet, too wired to sit. He needed a distraction from his new employee.

For he'd keep her on as his housekeeper. He owed her that since it appeared she'd come in good faith. But that didn't mean he had to fall headlong into the dangerous temptation she brought with her. The temptation to forget the lessons of guilt and responsibility and think simply like a man faced with an attractive woman.

More than attractive. She was fascinating with her uppity defiance mixed with calm competence. And there was something else about her, something he didn't yet understand, that set her apart.

Alessio planted his hand on the cool mullioned glass and

surveyed the dark lake, its edges marked here and there by the sprinkle of lights from small towns.

Three months. She'd be gone before he knew it. Nothing would change. All he had to do was ensure she kept out of his way so he could concentrate on work.

Simple.

So why the disquiet? The sense that his peaceful life was wobbling on its foundations?

CHAPTER FOUR

CHARLOTTE POWERED THROUGH the water, the morning chill bringing her still-waking body to tingling life. She'd discovered cold swimming in the Alps, and it was better than coffee for energising her for a day's work.

Though, if she'd wanted, she could have lazed the days away. The Conte wasn't interested in her work, so long as she provided coffee and meals on time.

In the week since she'd served him dinner in his suite, she hadn't seen the man. Not once!

She seethed at how he'd avoided meeting her again, as if she were contagious. Even for a recluse, his deliberate avoidance felt like an insult.

On her second morning, she'd gone to the kitchen after dawn to discover a note in spiky black script on thick cream paper. The Conte had left a list of his expectations rather than meet her face-to-face.

He'd given times for his meals. Contact details for suppliers and a few other, sparse instructions. He'd ended with food preferences: none, and key requirement: privacy.

He was never in the small dining room when she served his meals, and she waited until she heard him leave before clearing away.

The Conte Dal Lago was unlike any employer or guest she'd known. It should have been easy to meet his demands and ignore him, yet perversely Charlotte was more than ever aware of her elusive employer. And, as if his lack of interest were a challenge, working harder than ever to make the *castello* shine and her hermit boss's meals delicious.

Charlotte heard him on the stairs and would stop, breath tight for reasons she couldn't identify. She'd enter a room and *know* he'd just left it, though she couldn't explain why. It was only later that she'd notice something had been moved, like books or those glossy art and antiques magazines.

Making his bed, she was always aware of the imprint of his head on the pillow and that distinctive hint of earthy woodiness and frankincense. The enticing scent was stronger in the bathroom, especially if it was still steamy from his shower. She'd find herself pausing to inhale, a fluttery sensation stirring inside.

Clearing his neatly folded clothes, she was sensitive to the fact he'd worn them. Occasionally she felt the warmth of his body on the fabric and caught that other faint scent, of healthy male, that made her stomach dip.

It was appalling, reacting so to a man who wanted nothing to do with her. Not only appalling but new.

She hadn't been so stupidly focused on a man since high school, when an earnest science teacher had tried and failed to help her grapple with chemistry.

The Conte was no well-meaning young man. He was like a force of nature. Elemental. Harsh. With an inner darkness that should repel her.

Instead it fascinated her. Perhaps because, while proving himself to be every inch the brusque, demanding lord of the manor, he'd betrayed hints of deprecating self-awareness. He'd apologised for his assumptions about her. And when he'd laughed, the rich sound curling around her as amusement blazed in those extraordinary green eyes...

She bit her lip. This fixation had to stop. Yesterday she'd found herself in the great hall, staring at a painting of a dragon-like creature emerging from a lake. Presumably it was the fabled local monster she'd heard mentioned. But what had drawn her wasn't any legend but the fact the creature's scales were the exact deep green of the Conte's eyes.

That had tugged her closer, and she'd noticed another figure in the small painting. A blonde woman in a long dress. She faced the dragon with a surprisingly calm expression, given the hungry way it surveyed her.

A shiver had sped down Charlotte's spine. She'd felt an instant affinity with the golden-haired woman, facing down a terrifying beast. Especially as its sharp, devouring stare felt familiar. But in her unruly mind, her boss surveyed her with an entirely different type of hunger.

Charlotte set her teeth and turned for the shore, furious with herself. She didn't need his company, or for him to look at her the way a man watches an attractive woman. She didn't need anyone. It was a luxury having time to herself. She spent evenings nestled in her window seat, sewing and watching the sun set beyond the mountains, bathing the lake in peach and gold before the sky turned indigo.

She was putting her feet down to wade out onto the beach when movement behind her made her twist around.

There was a hiss, a powerful ripple and tug in the water that instantly made her think of the legendary monster.

Charlotte's eyes widened as, through the last patch of mist, a sleek form sped past the island.

Her heart thudded, then eased as she recognised the shape. Not a monstrous creature but a rowing scull, moving at speed. She saw a black hull and a tall figure and exhaled in relief.

That's how he stays so phenomenally fit.

She'd seen him half-dressed and knew he couldn't spend all his time at a desk.

He's got a rower's shoulders and powerful thighs. And that's none of your business, Charlotte Symonds.

Pushing back her shoulders and setting her jaw, she marched up the beach and grabbed her towel. She had things to achieve today, and that included cornering the man who'd done everything to avoid her.

The question was, which of them would find the meeting more challenging?

'*Buongiorno.*'

Alessio stopped midstride as a door opened and a warm, slightly husky voice slid through him. A pang of something sharp pierced his belly as light spilled into the dark corridor, revealing the trim figure of his housekeeper.

His pulse quickened. Because of the ambrosial smell of coffee and fresh baked pastries she carried.

Not for any other reason.

Yet he couldn't stop his gaze drifting from her shining old-gold hair down her slender frame.

'Good morning.' His voice was gruff.

'I saw you rowing and thought you might like coffee as soon as you came in. Shall I bring it up to your suite?'

'No need. I'll carry it myself.'

Her thoughtfulness pleased him, but he didn't want to encourage her. He'd been unsettled all week, unable to give work his usual total focus, mind straying too often to the stranger in his home.

The stranger who looked remarkably svelte in plain black trousers and a crisp white shirt. Even her severe hairstyle, scraped back in a bun, accentuated the purity of her features, the wide eyes, straight nose and cupid's bow mouth that was surely even more plush than he recalled.

Slamming a door on those thoughts, he reached for the tray, only to see her shake her head.

'I need to speak with you, so I might as well bring it.'

And have her in his rooms again? He didn't need that distraction.

All week her presence had curtailed his concentration. Everywhere he looked he saw reminders of her. From the meticulously plumped cushions to neat stacks of books and magazines that he'd left open and spilling across surfaces. Vases of foliage and flowers had appeared in all the rooms, even in the deep window ledge of the turret staircase. Not huge, ostentatious arrangements, but artfully simple concoctions that pleased the eye and made him feel grumpy with himself about resenting them. As for the luscious hint of vanilla and cinnamon on the air after she'd passed by...

He crossed his arms, belatedly feeling chilled as his body cooled from that workout. 'I'm busy this morning. What do you need to know?'

She blinked, and he realised her gaze was fixed not on his face, but on the ancient T-shirt that stuck to his sweaty chest. Slowly she lifted her head, her expression glassy, and his pulse revved.

Half-forgotten sensations stirred. Foremost was satisfaction, because there was no mistaking that look for anything other than feminine appreciation. The other was anticipation.

Once he'd have taken her interest as a green light for—

Alessio stiffened. Women had no place in his life, not even for short affairs. As for messing around with an employee... Absolutely not.

'It's the chapel,' she said finally, her voice thick in a way that made his blood beat slow and heavy. 'One of the stained-glass panels is broken. You said to speak to you about significant repairs, and I didn't want to have it fixed without consulting you. That glass looks very old.'

'It's medieval. One of the *castello*'s treasures.'

Alessio swallowed a sigh. So much for losing himself in work. He took the espresso from her tray, careful not to brush his hand against hers. Yet he couldn't avoid that light drift of enticing scent. Was it a commercial perfume, or had she been baking?

'Give me time to shower and dress,' he said through gritted teeth. 'I'll meet you in the chapel.'

Fifteen minutes later they stood below a high, arched window. Sunlight poured through, bringing a kaleidoscope of colour.

'It's such a shame,' she said, looking at the glass. 'It's beautiful.'

She hadn't met his eyes since he'd arrived.

Because she knew he'd read her earlier lascivious stare? The idea both pleased and annoyed him. Pleased because there was no room for a male-female relationship between them. Annoyed because, despite that, part of him, the dark, dangerous part, responded eagerly to the notion.

Alessio gritted his teeth. What madness had invaded his blood?

He wasn't pining for female company. He'd been content all this time. His eyes narrowed on her upturned face. She was unremarkable, pleasant but not stunning.

He yanked his gaze away. This wasn't about looks. There was something about Charlotte Symonds that teased him, hooked him and wouldn't give him peace. Something that, impossibly, had woken a vital part of him.

'It was my favourite window as a child. All those animals lined up ready to go onto the ark fascinated me.'

Blue eyes caught his, and heat shimmered in his belly.

'Really?' Her crooked smile was somehow enchanting. 'I have trouble imagining you as a little boy.' Her eyes widened. 'I'm sorry. I didn't mean to—'

'It's okay. I suspect I was always older than my years.'

As the only child of absentee parents with high expectations, he'd spent his time under the control of a series of strict tutors, working hard to become worthy of the proud Dal Lago name.

Stolen hours with Anna, Mario and other locals had never made up for a lack of parental love. Was it any wonder that when he was old enough to attract female adulation, he'd sought respite from the demands of family responsibility in hedonistic indulgence?

Alessio moved to the window. 'It must have been that storm a few weeks ago.' He swung around when he sensed the house-keeper's eyes on him, and a once-familiar frisson rippled down his backbone. Awareness. Sexual interest.

Instantly she turned to stare at the broken glazing.

Wise woman.

'There's a father and son team here on the island who can fix this.'

'Really? Surely it's very specialised work.'

'It is. There's no one I'd rather trust with this. Their family has been working glass for centuries. It was probably one of their ancestors who made this panel.' Pride warmed his voice. 'One thing we've managed to do here is support our artisans. Many are in demand internationally because of their specialist skills. My family values excellent craftsmanship, and we've done what we can to support it.'

'I read something about that,' she said, surprising him. 'There was an article about specialist goldsmiths here, trained in a scheme run by your company.'

Alessio shrugged. 'My family has collected rare and pre-cious things for generations. We've made that our business, brokering the sale of valuable art and antiquities. As a result, we need access to the best artists and craftspeople when re-pairs are needed.'

Alessio didn't add that he would still sponsor that and other schemes even without the auction house. While he appreci-ated skilled work, it was equally important to ensure employ-ment in the region. They were his people. He took seriously his family obligation to care for those around him. Support-ing elite craftsmen was a single strand in the complex web of initiatives designed to keep the area prosperous.

'How did you notice the broken window?' The chapel was rarely used.

'I had a call from the priest in Florence about his visit, and I wanted to check everything was all right first. I'll bring in fresh flowers and—'

'Visit?' He frowned. 'I know nothing about a visit.'

Her expression grew guarded. 'He said he rang last week and spoke to the housekeeper. He was following up to check everything was okay for this weekend.'

Alessio was already shaking his head. 'Anna didn't mention it to me.' But maybe she'd had no time, given her sudden departure. 'No matter. Ring him and tell him it's impossible.'

'Why is that?'

Her voice was soft yet there was no mistaking an undercurrent of—was that criticism?

As if his housekeeper had a right to judge his decisions!

'I don't receive visitors.'

Assessing eyes met his, and Alessio felt both curiosity and something else in Charlotte Symonds' stare. Disapproval? Or could that be...pity? He stiffened.

'You don't have to receive them.'

'Them? I thought it was a priest?'

'He wants to bring a group. A *small* group to see the chapel, half a dozen. He spoke in glowing terms about the artwork here and—'

'No.'

'You needn't see them,' she continued as if he hadn't spoken. 'They'd come straight from the pier to the chapel and be gone in an hour. They wouldn't come into the *castello* itself.'

Alessio shook his head. 'It's not possible.'

'Very well. I'll...' But she stopped, brow furrowing. 'It would help to know why. I mean, clearly a visit is *possible*.' Something flashed in her eyes. Definitely disapproval. 'I understand select groups used to visit in the past.'

She paused as if waiting for him to explain himself.

Alessio drew himself up to his full height. The Conte Dal

Lago didn't need to explain his motives, especially to a temporary employee.

'Surely you have so much, so many beautiful things, that you can afford to share a little?'

His head snapped back as if she'd slapped him. 'You think I'm a miser, hoarding this?'

The idea stunned him. His wide gesture encompassed the exquisite chapel with its rare artworks, glowing stained glass and sumptuous furnishings. It was a remarkable place.

But he hadn't been in here for years, not since Antonia's funeral. A shiver sucked the heat from his bones.

It was easy to fill that chill void with anger.

'I regularly lend treasures for display,' he bit out. 'Half the family jewels are in an exhibition in Rome. The tapestries are just back from being displayed in Paris, and several paintings are on loan to galleries and museums for study or display.'

Those grave eyes regarded him, filled now with puzzlement rather than disfavour. 'That's very generous of you.'

Now she pandered to his ego? That goaded Alessio. He didn't need her endorsement. He did it because it was the right thing to do. He felt a deep responsibility to care for and share his family's treasures.

For years he hadn't given a damn what anyone, relative, friend or stranger, thought of his actions. He'd cut himself off from people and their opinions. Now he found himself irked by an employee's assumptions. Not just irked but trying to prove himself!

His skin prickled under her stare. Did she think him greedy? Uncaring? Or maybe she believed the wild speculation about him, hiding away from the world.

Aren't you hiding? Beatrice thinks so.

As if his great-aunt or anyone else truly understood the situation.

'If it hurts you to have people around, of course you shouldn't do it.'

That serious, sympathetic gaze held his. *Sympathy. For him!* As if he were someone to be pitied instead of the Conte Dal Lago, wealthy and powerful, a man who supported and cared for thousands. Whose business success was lauded worldwide.

'If you tell me how to contact the glaziers, I'll organise the repairs, then ring the priest in Florence—'

'Wait.'

Alessio hadn't planned to interrupt but now heard the word, sharp and silencing, reverberate between them.

What harm could it do? When they came, he'd be in his office, working—

Hiding out, said his great-aunt's voice in his head.

He looked down at the woman before him and consciously unlocked his jaw. 'Confirm the visit.' Her eyes widened. 'But I want you with them at all times. They go straight from the boat to the chapel and back. An hour maximum.'

'Of course. I'll see to it all.'

Her gaze softened, her mouth curling at the corners. Then she turned as if to leave. Or to hide her satisfied smile?

Alessio marched beside her down the aisle, wondering why he'd agreed to this. It had been his decision, yet he felt he'd been outmanoeuvred.

Because he cared what Charlotte Symonds thought? Because he was sick of Beatrice's carping voice in his head? The pair deserved each other, judging and interfering.

They walked out of the chapel, and Charlotte was aware of how he reined in his long-legged stride to match hers. Of the swing of his hand just centimetres from hers and the high ridge of his shoulder at her eye height.

Her heart fluttered stupidly at being close to all that vibrant masculinity. She was still catching her breath after their confrontation when he returned from rowing.

Wearing shorts and a T-shirt that clung to his body, his powerful musculature had been front and centre. He might have a rower's shoulders, but those sculpted thighs were works of art in their own right.

A weak part of her had fallen in a fluttery heap. It had been all she could do not to let his coffee cup rattle on the tray she clutched.

No wonder she'd avoided his eyes in the chapel.

Until anger and curiosity had made her confront him. Anger because he'd reminded her of her father, a man who hoarded wealth but without a generous bone in his body.

When Charlotte's mother died, he'd sacked many estate staff, people whose families had worked there for generations. He'd pushed them out of their homes, remodelling them into 'executive-style country houses' to sell for a tidy profit.

But what she'd seen in Alessio's eyes had made her think again.

Not Alessio. Conte Alessio to you!

His pain, the dark void of suffering glimpsed in an unguarded moment, had stunned her.

And made her thoughts skew to the gorgeous modern bedroom she'd found on the far side of the castle, complete with a huge ensuite wet room, and through an adjoining door, a nursery in sunny shades of yellow. Her heart had clenched as she stood in that bright room with its empty cot, knowing instinctively it had never been used.

It clenched again now.

How much had this man lost?

The press spoke about his wife. But was there more...?

'Not so quickly, Ms Symonds.'

His words stopped her as she turned towards the kitchen.

Charlotte pulled up, head swivelling towards him. There was no grief or weakness in that severe, aristocratic face. The Conte Dal Lago looked totally in control. More, the gleam in his moss-dark eyes hinted at something disturbingly like anticipation. That, coupled with his air of untamed masculinity, accentuated by his darkly stubbled chin and unruly hair, made tension dance across her nerves.

'Yes, sir?'

Frown lines appeared on his broad forehead as if he didn't like being called *sir*. But formality seemed appropriate.

Charlotte clasped her hands and waited. What he said next stunned her.

'I'd like your assistance. Let's discuss it over coffee.' He nodded in the direction of the kitchen and reached out to open the door at the same time she did.

Long fingers brushed hers, brushed and tangled. For that skimming touch sent a sizzle of shocking heat through her, making her hand curl instinctively so that instead of sliding free it caught his. Her breath hissed in but didn't fill her lungs. Her eyes rounded on the sight of long olive fingers locked with her paler ones.

Fire swept her features as she realised she was holding his hand. The moment was brief yet seemed to stretch forever. Trying to persuade her locked fingers to open. Trying to pretend her body hadn't gone into spasm at the merest touch. Trying to ignore the awareness that shot through her, settling like a glowing ember deep in her pelvis.

'Sorry.' It sounded like she spoke over grated glass. Felt like it too.

Charlotte dropped her hand, curling her fingers tight over the hypersensitive throb where they'd touched. She didn't look up, didn't want to read his expression, but watched those long fingers turn the knob and open the door.

This wasn't static electricity. It was more. Something connected to the disquiet she experienced whenever she was with the Conte. Or thinking about him. Or recognising that dark velvet voice as it wound through her dreams.

The door opened, and Charlotte shot into the kitchen, relieved to be in her own territory.

Yet it felt different now.

The vast space, a vaulted room that combined massive stainless-steel ovens and refrigerators, several pantries and an ancient fireplace big enough to roast a bullock, shrank in size when her employer entered. He didn't loom but sat in a chair at the enormous table. Yet his presence changed the atmosphere completely.

Or maybe that was embarrassment. She'd overreacted to a chance touch like some cloistered virgin.

Fiery trails still ran along her veins. What did that mean?

The air crackled, and Charlotte felt his scrutiny as she moved to brew fresh coffee. There was a clatter and she looked over her shoulder to find him piling fresh pastries on not one, but two plates.

The Conte met her stare with a raised eyebrow. 'It was early when you accosted me in the corridor. I'm assuming you haven't eaten breakfast either.'

Accosted? He made it sound like physical assault rather than a request for guidance. But she said nothing, too busy digesting the fact he not only wanted her assistance but planned to share a meal. What had happened to her reclusive employer?

'Don't scowl. You'll put me off my food.'

Given the voracious bite he'd taken out of a pastry, it was on the tip of her tongue to scoff, for he was clearly a man with a healthy appetite, much healthier, it seemed to her, than when she'd first arrived.

Which is none of your business.

Even if she'd been reluctantly worried about her unfathomable boss.

She focused on the coffee and calming her pulse rate.

'That's better,' he sighed, minutes later after his first sip. He was already halfway through a second pastry. Charlotte pushed some fresh fruit in front of him and a jar of heaven-scented honey that came from his own bees. She was rising, intending to cook some eggs, when he reached out.

He stopped short of touching, yet she felt the phantom

weight of long fingers on her wrist. The sizzle under her skin was familiar now. Did he feel it too? Is that why he'd stopped short?

'Sit, Charlotte. I want your attention.'

He had it. Especially when he called her Charlotte rather than Ms Symonds in that dark chocolate voice.

A shiver ripped through her, and her nipples peaked against her bra. Disconcerted, she reached for her coffee and hugged it close. Maybe she was succumbing to a fever.

'I'm listening.'

A quick look confirmed his haunted expression had disappeared. So too had the anticipation she'd seen lurking in his eyes. But she couldn't relax. The curl at the corners of his expressive mouth warned he was enjoying himself. Was he about to test her? Set an impossible task she had to perform or get the sack, because she'd had the temerity to question his motives?

What had she been thinking in the chapel? The client was always right. She'd learned that years ago. Why persist in questioning him?

Because she'd hated to think he was like her venal father.

'I have a special favour to ask, Charlotte.' His eyes locking with hers made her pulse slow to a ponderous beat. 'You don't mind if I call you Charlotte, do you?'

Was it his deep, smooth voice, or that musical lilt of an accent that made her prosaic, old-fashioned name seem almost alluring?

'Please do.' To her relief, the words emerged crisp and clear. Unlike the rest of her, which seemed to be melting.

'Thank you.' He paused. 'What I'm about to ask doesn't fall within your duties. It's far more…personal than that.'

Charlotte told herself she imagined his emphasis on the word *personal*.

Yet she didn't imagine the satisfaction in his tone. Or the lambent heat in those stunning sea-green eyes, or the half-lidded expression of expectation as he sprawled back in his seat. It was the look of a confident man, fully expecting her to say yes to his request.

Her heart hammered as she considered what he might ask.

Charlotte recalled the man her father had wanted her to marry. She'd barely known him, but he'd had the same air of lazy self-assurance, of casual anticipation as he undid his bow tie and backed her into an empty room, telling her there'd be no engagement until he'd had a chance to 'try before buying'.

'I hope you don't mind bending the rules a little and providing a little extra service. I'd be very grateful.'

The Conte had caught her gawping at his muscle-packed body when he came in from rowing. Had he registered her response to his touch? The way her skin flamed and her breath seized from the casual brush of flesh on flesh? A man with his reputation knew when women were attracted. He'd been a renowned playboy before he settled down to marriage.

Did he think she was available on request?

CHAPTER FIVE

'DON'T LOOK SO WORRIED, Charlotte. I'm not asking you to slay a dragon or do anything morally questionable.'

He wasn't?

'I'd ask Anna, but I don't want to interrupt her in Rome.'

Charlotte sagged back in her chair, torn between relief and...was that disappointment? If this was something Anna could help with, he wasn't talking about physical intimacy.

She lifted her coffee cup to hide her burning cheeks.

Of course he wasn't going to ask you for sexual favours.

Look at him! He probably had women queuing from here to Naples, eager for his attention. He might be reclusive, but he was a fit, healthy man in his prime. Until his marriage, he'd dated a long line of gorgeous, talented women, and then married the most beautiful, most talented of them all. His little black book probably bulged with the numbers of amazing women.

He would never be interested in a housekeeper whose idea of a fun evening ran to a long bath, then watching a film or doing needlework, or preferably both at the same time. Whose own father had dismissed her as a domestic dormouse.

'Though, now I think about it, I suppose I *am* looking for a dragon tamer.'

His mouth curved infinitesimally higher, and she wondered, if he did that often enough, whether he'd actually smile. She recalled how his unexpected laughter the first day had cut through her professional reserve and tapped into a shockingly responsive part of her.

Light danced in those devilish green eyes.

Was that a dimple in one lean cheek? It was gone so fast she might have imagined it, yet she *knew* he was amused. It was there in the smug way he folded his arms over that broad chest and the almost-smile ghosting his lips.

The effect was devastating. If he ever really smiled at a woman, or, Lord help her, *with* her, the female in question would dissolve with delight.

Charlotte sat straight, pressing knees and ankles together and clasping her cup tightly, annoyed that she couldn't keep her thoughts in order.

'You've got me worried.' Though not as worried as she'd been, wondering if she could withstand a proposition from the only man who'd ever made her feel so sexually *aware*. 'Can you please explain?'

'It's quite simple, and I'm sure you'll be just the person to deal with it.'

'*It* being your dragon?'

'Figuratively speaking.' He shook his head, and Charlotte was intrigued to see his expression soften. 'I lost track of dates. It's my great-aunt's birthday soon, and I need an appropriate gift.' He rubbed the back of his neck. 'You seem like a people person.' At her questioning look, he shrugged. 'You were very concerned not to disappoint our visiting priest, whom you haven't even met.'

There was a hint of steel in his tone, reminding Charlotte that she'd pressed her case perilously far.

'I'm hoping you can find something to satisfy her.'

Charlotte was about to protest that she knew nothing about his great-aunt. But hadn't she done that sort of thing before? Chosen gifts for high-paying guests to take home? She'd even found the perfect eternity ring at short notice for a guest who'd forgotten his wedding anniversary.

This was no different. Except she sensed the Conte enjoyed the prospect of her failing.

She had no intention of failing. She needed this job, she was good at it, and she'd excel.

'Tell me about your aunt.'

'Great-Aunt Beatrice.' He paused. 'Eagle-eyed. Sharp-tongued. She doesn't suffer fools and has an opinion on everything, particularly the foibles of her relatives.' Including, Charlotte guessed, her great-nephew.

'What does she like?'

'Apart from telling everyone what to do? Travel. Gossip. Fine food and wine. Jewellery.'

'What did you give her for her last birthday?'

'A Renaissance gold ring with a flawless cabochon ruby.' He paused. 'She complained it didn't have a secret cavity for poison she could use to dispose of annoying time wasters.'

Charlotte stifled a giggle and was surprised to see amusement lighten his stern features. 'And the year before?'

'Ruby earrings.' At her raised eyebrows, he spread his hands. 'Red is her favourite colour.'

'But she doesn't want more jewellery?'

'No, that year she complained the rubies were too heavy on her ears.'

'She sounds like a woman of definite opinions.' Charlotte rather liked the sound of the old lady, but she didn't relax. This would be a tough challenge. 'What else does she enjoy?'

'Quaffing champagne with cronies and bemoaning the younger generation. You'd think her harmless, sitting with her needlework, until you realise she heard every salient point of every conversation and has an uncanny knack of dredging them up at the most inconvenient—'

'What sort of needlework?'

'Sorry?' The Conte stared, and Charlotte stifled a groan. She hadn't meant to interrupt, but it was the first real lead he'd given. 'I don't know. Decorative stuff. Embroidery. I remember she made a tapestry cushion cover too.' For the first time since they'd met, he looked unsure of himself.

'Cross-stitch?'

He spread his hands wide, shoulders lifting, and she repressed a smile at his cluelessness in this, at least.

'You've given me an idea. Give me a few days and I'll see what I can do.'

The prospect of solving his dilemma and proving herself capable gave Charlotte the fillip she needed. And helped banish the memory of her earlier bizarre reaction.

As if the *Conte* would ever be interested in *her*.

There was no mist this morning as he trod the lakeside path. Already spring was advancing. Alessio felt its warmth and something else, an expectancy, a vigour in his blood he hadn't known in what seemed forever.

Change was in the air. And in him? He felt different. Unsettled.

Yesterday he'd stood at his window, watching the visitors leave the chapel. Charlotte had waved them off, the sun burnishing her blond head, and he'd wanted, badly, to go down and bask in her warmth.

Even when she was annoyed with him, she was concerned about him, trying to feed him up or make him more comfortable. It was her job. Yet Alessio felt she actually cared about his well-being.

Sure! Enough to accuse you of being an egocentric miser.

But maybe that's what he was, trying to make the world stop because he was too guilt-ridden to face it.

A sound made him halt, and there was the woman herself, leaving the bakery.

She looked alluring even in dark trousers and a white shirt. Her neat uniform couldn't conceal those curves or long, supple legs. But it was the way she walked, head up, shoulders back, as if ready to face anything, that drew his focus. A more imaginative man would say she had an inner strength that would see her through the toughest times. A woman who could vanquish dragons.

Alessio stifled a bitter laugh. That proved he should have nothing to do with her. According to local lore, he as the Count Dal Lago *was* the dragon of the lake, descended from a line of rapacious strongmen who'd plundered what they wanted— lands, riches, even women.

Which made it farcical that he'd timed his walk to coincide with her visit to Mario's bakery. So their meeting would appear accidental because he was too proud to send for her. But it wasn't mere curiosity about yesterday's chapel visit that brought him here. He wished it were so simple.

He wanted her.

He'd tried to pretend it wasn't true.

He'd told himself he was overtired. But it wasn't sleep he craved.

He'd only seen her half a dozen times, but there was no mistaking the attraction. It had been there from the first, snaking through his belly and disordering his thoughts.

After years wanting nothing more than solitude since he couldn't find oblivion, suddenly Alessio wanted so much.

He moved closer. Charlotte swung around. *And smiled.*

That blaze of welcome punched him in the chest. Alessio's lungs squeezed, pulse quickening as adrenaline shot through his bloodstream. His stride lengthened, greedy hands curling tight as he imagined reaching for her.

Then, in the blink of an eye, her smile faded, and she looked away. When their eyes met again, her expression was blank of everything but polite enquiry. She was the perfect housekeeper, no sign of the vibrant, welcoming woman whose smile had lit the fire smouldering in his belly.

A chill of understanding prickled his scalp.

'Conte Alessio. You're up early.'

'Just Alessio,' he ground out, unreasonably annoyed at her

use of his title. Because it was a reminder of the barriers between them.

He'd let himself forget. As her employer, he had power over her, a power he could never abuse. He abhorred men who used their authority to coerce unwilling women.

Would Charlotte be unwilling? Had he imagined her eager grin? He'd believed he read interest, more than interest, in her eyes when she looked at him before today.

'I couldn't call you—'

'Of course you can.' He sounded grumpier than ever. But he *was* grumpy, and with good reason. 'Anna calls me by my first name.'

'It's not the same. She's known you for years.'

Alessio paused, acknowledging her point.

But an obstinate part of him refused to be ruled by caution. He couldn't have Charlotte in the way he craved, not only because he was her boss, but for so many reasons, including that he had just enough decency left not to want to taint her with his darkness.

Yet how he wanted…

Surely he could have *this* at least? The sound of his name on her lips. Not combined with the formality of a title, but said simply the way a woman would speak to a man? As if they were equals. Or lovers. As if they connected.

In the world's eyes, they weren't equals because he paid her wage. To some, his inherited title and wealth put him above her. But Alessio knew the truth. Such things didn't matter against the true soul of a man. As his soul was lost, he felt no superiority.

In fact, having her interact with him as an equal would be the closest he was likely to come to a blessing. She occupied a world he merely viewed from the outside. A bright, wholesome place he no longer felt he knew.

'Conte Alessio? Is everything all right?'

Charlotte moved closer, and he caught a drift of cinnamon

and vanilla. She even smelled wholesome, though she attracted him like the most flagrant seductress.

Had years of solitude warped his perception? No. This woman with her unexpected combination of practicality, determination and sensuality drew him at a visceral level.

'Everything is fine. I was considering your comment. Shall we walk?' He glanced at the open door to the bakery and was glad when she fell into step. 'The fact is, Charlotte, I'm not used to sharing my home with strangers. We're a close-knit community here, even more so since my wife died.'

He paused, stunned. It was the first time he'd willingly mentioned the traumatic event that had so changed him. Even more surprising was the absence of crucifying pain that always accompanied that memory.

'I'm so sorry for your loss.'

Bright eyes met his, but Alessio saw only regret there, not prurient curiosity. More and more this woman seemed exactly what she appeared, hardworking, decent, capable and, he suspected, warm-hearted.

All the more reason to leave her alone.

As if! He might have enough shreds of decency not to pursue her. But he needed something for himself. Just a taste now and then of her generous warmth, even at a distance.

How the mighty had fallen! He'd once had the world, and any woman he wanted, at his feet. How shallow that seemed now.

'Thank you. The *castello* may be grand, and it's also my workplace, but above all it's my home, the place where I unwind.' In theory, at least. In reality, most of the time he felt wound too tight. 'It took a long time to convince Anna and the others on the island not to use my title, at least when we're alone. I would…appreciate it if you'd do the same. You'll be living here for several months, and it will be more comfortable for both of us.'

He slanted her a sideways look as they approached the *cas-*

tello. Her knotted brow warned she had misgivings, but she nodded. 'If that's how everyone here addresses you, then of course I will.'

'Excellent.' He held the door open for her. 'I have a little time before my first online meeting. I suggest we share those pastries with coffee while you update me on yesterday's chapel visit.'

He should have known better, he reflected as he leaned back in his chair, savouring his second coffee. He'd only permitted the visitors because Charlotte had prodded and queried and he'd wanted, for reasons he refused to identify, not to disappoint her.

He should have followed his instinct for privacy rather than pander to a woman. Yet even now he found himself warmed by the enthusiasm in her bright eyes.

'Let me get this clear. He not only wants to bring another party of visitors to the chapel, but you want to make an event of it?'

'Not a big event,' she hastened to assure him, placing a sugar-drenched pastry on his plate. This woman had all Anna's determination and even more wiles.

Dangerous, murmured a voice in his head.

Delectable.

Alessio grabbed the pastry and bit deep into buttery, sugared layers. He'd be twice his usual body weight and suffering from tooth decay if he kept using food as a distraction from Charlotte Symonds. 'Go on.'

'It would still be a small group, no more than a dozen. But they'd stay for an hour or so extra. The first group got into conversation with the glaziers removing the window. Did you know that as well as repairing old glass, they make stained-glass lamps and windows of their own design?' She met his eyes and smiled crookedly. 'Sorry, of course you do. But the point is, the visitors were fascinated and eager to buy.'

'So this is to be a buying trip? I don't see the value if it's just a dozen people.'

'A dozen influential people, all interested in fine art, some working in galleries. And it's not only the glass. When they heard about the gold-and silversmiths, the woodcarvers, jewellers and—'

'Enough.' Alessio raised his hand. 'I get the idea.'

Charlotte tilted her head as if doubting. 'I know one visit won't solve everyone's difficulties, but from what I hear, it's been tough for some of the artisans. Given the economic troubles recently, there have been fewer commissions.'

'So an opportunity to showcase their work to the right people is welcome,' he finished for her. It made sense. So much sense he should have thought of it himself.

He'd been too wrapped up in his own misery to do more than what was absolutely necessary. Why hadn't Anna or someone else raised this with him?

The answer was obvious. He'd given orders not to be disturbed, and his people had respected that. But instead of respecting them by paying attention to their needs, he'd wallowed in his private darkness. Sourness filled his mouth, and he grimaced.

'Truly, it won't disturb you. We can—'

'It's fine. It's a good idea.' It should have been his idea, if he'd been thinking straight. Guilt gnawed at his belly. What else had he missed?

'You agree?'

'No need to look so astonished,' he said gruffly. 'If it helps the island, it's good.' In fact, it might be worth considering a more organised event on a regular basis, something the locals could rely on.

Charlotte beamed, and Alessio realised he'd do a lot to win her approval. If he couldn't have the woman, he could at least have her smiles.

'I'm glad you think so. It would be a good opportunity for

Mario too. He wants to try some new products to keep his great-nephew interested, but he wasn't sure the locals would take to them.'

'Great-nephew?' Alessio frowned.

'Mario mentioned him this morning. He got into trouble with some other teenagers in his hometown, and his parents sent him here for a break. Mario is trying to convince him to become an apprentice baker.'

Alessio sat back, fighting a scowl. Not at Charlotte's news but because it was she, an incomer, telling him. Time was when he'd have known about it straightaway, especially if Mario was looking to organise an apprenticeship.

Alessio hadn't stopped by the bakery for a few weeks. For that matter, he hadn't been in personal contact with a lot of the locals recently, relying increasingly on Anna to pass on important news.

His stomach hollowed. What sort of Conte was he? What sort of custodian or, for that matter, friend? He didn't just have a duty to these people. He liked them, was tied to them, cared about them. They'd been there for him through those lonely growing up years. And more recently, guarding his privacy.

What had he given in return?

Not enough. Not recently at any rate.

Alessio's chair screeched on the tiled floor as he shoved back from the table. 'That all sounds good. Meanwhile I need to—'

'Can you spare me a couple more minutes, please? It's about your aunt's gift.'

The perplexed look on Alessio's face was priceless. Charlotte had to stifle a smile.

'But it's blank.' He examined the package of fabric and coloured threads through its clear cover.

'That's the idea. Your great-aunt will sew it herself.'

She found herself staring at his handsome face as he studied the cross-stitch kit, a knot of concentration turning his features from imposing to breathtakingly attractive.

Her throat tightened. She couldn't explain her feelings for this man. Even when he'd made her anything but welcome, he'd fascinated rather than repelled her, attracted her when he should have been no more than a difficult client. Today he'd shown another side of his personality. He'd been genuinely concerned about his community. Far from blustering about protecting his privacy, he'd readily agreed to her plan.

Now his concentration on the gift and his puzzlement made him look endearing.

Abruptly he raised his head, and Charlotte's breath caught as their eyes met and fire raced through her veins.

Endearing? The man should come with a health warning. He looked away almost instantly, but that moment of connection reinforced the fact that she was out of her depth with him.

'If I could show you?'

She took the package, careful not to touch his hand.

'A friend designs these to order. As a special favour she created this in record time. Fortunately the express delivery was even quicker than I expected.'

Charlotte was babbling, her fingers all thumbs as she wrestled to open the plastic. That moment of searing intensity, when she'd met Alessio's green eyes, had rattled her. Even though she knew she'd imagined something more than curiosity in his stare.

At last she found the design sheet and held it out to him.

He said, 'It's the *castello*.' He shifted his chair closer to hers, angling his head to see the sheet better, lifting his hand to trace the design. 'And the village, and the mountains beyond the lake. But how?'

'Simple. I took some photos and sent them to her. My friend specialises in making cross-stitch designs of real locations. Though this one was a bit more work than usual, especially given the short time frame.'

He nodded, his focus still on the design. 'I'll compensate her for her time. This is remarkable.'

'I'm glad you like it. All your aunt has to do is follow the design to create an image of the *castello* on its island.'

She'd gone out on a limb, ordering this without consultation, but she'd had to act quickly to have it done in time. If he hadn't liked it, Charlotte would have kept it to do herself, a memento of her stay.

Charlotte frowned, feeling an unexpected pang of regret at the idea of moving on.

'It's brilliant. Beatrice will adore it. Thank you, Charlotte. This is the sort of personal, thoughtful gift I'd hoped for.'

He lifted his head and smiled.

All thoughts of the future and leaving disintegrated.

She'd been right.

When the Conte Dal Lago smiled at a woman—*really* smiled—she melted into a puddle of pure longing.

Nothing had prepared Charlotte for this. Not her clear-eyed understanding of humanity's foibles developed over years working in hotels, nor her experience warding off entitled men.

Every strength she'd taken for granted, every defence she'd carefully built, crumbled as she returned that blazing smile.

She was in so much trouble.

CHAPTER SIX

CHARLOTTE HUMMED AS she dusted the top shelf of the towering bookcase. Despite her misgivings, things were going well.

For 'misgivings' read 'a profound weakness for her boss.'

Her breath snagged for a second, but she ignored that, reaching further along the shelf and humming louder.

So he was attractive. Deeply attractive.

What woman wouldn't feel a little flutter inside when he smiled at her? There was no harm in it, as long as she remained professional. It wasn't as if he were pursuing her. Far from it.

Their relationship had improved enormously, but it was still a *working* relationship.

Alessio seemed to trust her, unbending more and proving himself to be a man she could like. That didn't sound like much, but given some of the men she'd known, it was high praise. He respected her, regularly thanked her for her work and since their discussion a couple of weeks ago, had been out in the village more. She'd seen him talking with locals, and he'd taken over plans for the next chapel visit.

Charlotte put back the book she held and, grabbing the shelf, pulled herself on the tall library ladder further along the built-in bookcase. She smiled. This sliding ladder reminded her of her mother's precious library at home, the one her father had cleared out when she died.

The ladder stopped short of the end. Charlotte jiggled her weight, trying to shift it but it wouldn't budge. There must be a problem with the track. She could climb all the way down and try to fix it or lean just a little further to reach the end of the shelf.

Time was short. She'd promised herself she'd finish the top shelf before getting Alessio's lunch.

Leaning sideways, she reached for the last books. But as she stretched out and up, the ladder suddenly shifted in the opposite direction. She clutched for safety. A heavy book knocked her forehead and she winced. Then came an almighty thud as it tumbled to the floor.

Charlotte didn't look down to see the damage. She was too busy holding on. The bookcases at this double-storeyed end of the library were magnificent when viewed from the ground but too far to fall. Perspiration prickled the back of her neck, and her arms were rigid as she fought panic. She was stretched at an ungainly angle, but as soon as she caught her breath, she'd pull the ladder back.

Except it wouldn't budge.

She was just getting really worried when the ladder moved again. Not another jerky slide but a rhythmic vibration.

Seconds later heat surrounded her. A living heat.

'Let go of the bookcase, Charlotte. I've got you.'

She felt Alessio's warm breath riffle her hair, the brush of his big frame behind her, and felt relief that he was here.

Yet she couldn't unlock her fingers.

'Trust me, Charlotte.'

On the words, gentle fingers covered her hand, prising it loose from the woodwork. Her heart galloped as she realised she wasn't hanging on to the stability of the bookcase any longer, but then Alessio's hand folded around hers, pulling it back and curling it around the ladder.

'Thank you. I'm okay now.' And she was. She was perfectly capable of climbing down the ladder even if her knees trembled.

'Of course.' His chest brushed her back as he spoke. and

now she was aware of his arms around her, grasping the ladder on either side. It was…comforting to have him there. 'But we'll descend together, just to be safe. Ready?'

'More than ready. I can't wait to get down and have a cup of tea.' Her words belied her unsteadiness, but did he hear the wobble in her voice?

'Take a step down, Charlotte.' He moved lower, and she hurried to follow him, surprised at how much she disliked the idea of being left behind.

They descended like that all the way to the marble floor, one step at a time, his arms encircling her. But when they reached the bottom, to her horror, Charlotte couldn't pry her fingers from the ladder.

'I'm sorry about the book. I'll pay for any damage.' Which could be expensive if it was rare.

'Out of the question.' His voice was sharp. 'It's my fault for not warning you about the ladder. Anna mentioned a problem with it, but it slipped my mind.' He paused. 'Are you going to let go now?'

She laughed, the sound brittle. 'In a second, when I persuade my fingers to work again. It's silly. I'm not afraid of heights, but…'

As she watched, Alessio reached around her, covering her hands with his and gently pulling them free. His voice soothed. 'You've had a shock. We both have. If you'd fallen…' His deep voice turned to gravel.

His hands left hers, and she was surprised at how bereft she felt. Until the world tilted and she found herself, for the first time in her life, held off the ground in a man's embrace.

Stunned, she looked up past a firm, familiar jaw with its dusting of roguish dark stubble to piercing eyes the colour of deep water. Except deep water was cool, and Alessio's eyes blazed fire.

Her heart leapt at what she thought she saw there. Not the disinterested look of a stranger. Nor annoyance at the potential damage to his precious book. Alessio's stare was intent, charged. Devouring.

Charlotte shivered, not with weakness or dismay but excitement. She closed her fingers tight against the temptation to reach up and stroke his hard jaw. To slide her hand higher, into that lustrous black hair. To clutch his skull and pull his head down.

She snapped her eyes shut, willing the crazy thoughts away. Yet without vision, she was more conscious of his tall frame against her. Those strong arms supporting her. The rise of his chest. The cushion of soft cotton and solid muscle against her cheek. The heady scent of clean male skin just a breath away.

Too soon, or not soon enough, he lowered her to a chair. Charlotte stiffened, eyes opening and hands lifting instinctively as if to keep him close. One grazed his jawline, the other catching his hand.

Energy pulsed between them. A quickening that she felt deep within. For a second their fingers clung, and in that moment, it felt perfectly right. As if they'd touched that way a thousand times.

Alessio's pupils widened, darkening his eyes, and she leaned closer. His fingers squeezed hers, and she *knew* he was about to lean in and kiss her.

His gaze dropped to her lips, parted in readiness. The air thickened.

Then his hands slid free and he moved back, straightening to his full height.

'You're all right now. No harm done.'

He stood less than a metre away, yet the distance between them was immense and unbreachable.

A lump of ice settled in her middle.

The man doesn't want to kiss you. He can't get away fast enough.

Embarrassment flooded her, heat roaring up into her cheeks. 'I'm sorry. I—'

'There's nothing to be sorry about. It was an accident, and if anything, my fault. I'll have the ladder fixed straight away.'

He was deliberately misunderstanding, letting her save face by pretending to think she was talking about the trouble on the ladder instead of how she'd grabbed him.

Charlotte was grateful, of course she was, but the idea of him pitying her futile attraction ripped a hole through her self-possession. Fortunately years of practice at appearing unmoved in the face of her father's tirades and putdowns came to her rescue.

She rose, only slightly unsteady, and pinned on her professional smile. 'Thank you, Alessio.' Her throat constricted on his name. 'I'll leave you to check the book. You know far more about it and what repairs might be necessary. I need to go and see about lunch.'

'Charlotte...'

Already she was walking to the door. 'But I *will* pay for any damage.' Then, mercifully, she was out in the corridor and hurrying back to the staff section of the *castello* where she belonged.

CHAPTER SEVEN

ALESSIO SWORE UNDER his breath. Then swore aloud.

It was no good. He couldn't settle. For the last three days, since that incident in the library, he and Charlotte had both kept their distance, yet his concentration was shot.

A chill frosted his bones. That *incident* could have ended in serious injury if she'd fallen onto unforgiving marble.

It would have been his fault. Anna had mentioned a problem with the antique ladder, and Alessio had said he'd inspect it himself. Then forgotten.

What if Charlotte had fallen and cracked her skull?

Another woman's life on his conscience.

Though it hadn't come to that, he'd still hurt her. The pain in her dazed eyes when he'd pulled back from her...

She'd needed comfort and reassurance, and he'd been too scared of the need roaring within him to give it to her. Scared that instead of offering comfort, he'd take what he needed so badly.

Each night he was haunted, no longer by thoughts of his drowned wife, but his housekeeper. That felt like a betrayal of Antonia's memory.

In his dreams, Charlotte's earnest eyes fixed on him as she reached out, and he didn't hold back. In those fevered imaginings, gentle caresses turned to animal lust, fervent demands and desperate orgasms.

Alessio scrubbed a hand around the back of his neck, feeling the tension that grew daily.

It was unreasonable to blame Charlotte. The problem was his obsession. Yet right now, Alessio would happily dump some of the guilt on her slim shoulders.

What the hell was she doing downstairs? Muffled sounds distracted him from important business. No matter that he kept his study door ajar hoping to catch a glimpse of her. He'd heard voices. A male voice too, not just the maids chatting as they worked.

She must have brought someone in to assist with a specialist job. Not the library ladder. He'd fixed that personally the night of her almost-fall.

Alessio shoved the chair back from his desk and stalked to the door. There it was again, a male voice. Then, unmistakeably, Charlotte's laugh.

Suddenly it felt like a savage, sharp-toothed animal gnawed on his gut.

If he didn't know better, he'd put it down to dog-in-the-manger possessiveness. Jealousy that Charlotte shared her carefree laugh with another man instead of him.

That was impossible. Alessio had never been jealous about a woman. He'd had his share of lovers, and his relationships had been easy, never fraught with emotion. Even with his beautiful wife, there'd been no question of jealousy. They'd shared complete trust.

What he felt now couldn't be possessiveness. Yet he couldn't think of any other explanation.

Alessio took the stairs two at a time.

He found them in the vast gilded ballroom. One of the enormous antique Venetian glass chandeliers that lined the centre of the room had been lowered to just above the parquet floor. A vast trestle table had been set up nearby, where three maids were carefully cleaning individual glass drops. Ennio, the specialist who cared for the *castello*'s many antique clocks and was an expert in the mechanism that lowered the price-less chandeliers, was at the other end of the room, intent on a control panel hidden in the wall.

And Charlotte, looking far too seductive in a grey skirt that sculpted her buttocks as she leaned forward, was up a ladder, reaching for a cluster of crystal drops.

His pulse quickened and his mouth dried.

What was it with this woman and ladders? Hadn't she had enough of heights in the library?

He opened his mouth to order her down, then stopped. No need to startle her. Instead he stalked across the room, vaguely aware of heads turning, but he didn't stop till he reached the base of the ladder. Even then she didn't notice him. Slowly she descended, one hand on the ladder as she cradled precious crystal to her chest. It wasn't until she reached him, his hand braced on the ladder where she was about to put hers, that she stopped.

'Alessio!'

She sounded breathless, and as her gaze caught his he read more than surprise. It was the same expression he'd seen the day he'd held her in his arms. Yearning. Excitement. Arousal.

His heart leapt.

That was why his feelings for her ate him up. Because he knew he wasn't the only one attracted.

He'd told himself that day in the library that he'd imagined it and she'd only wanted comfort. But he was a man who knew women and desire. Charlotte desired him, though she tried to hide it behind a facade of professionalism.

And he, a man used to indulging his desires, found it pure torture, holding back.

Because she was his employee.

Because he had a duty of care.

Because he was ultimately responsible for his wife's death, and he had no right to enjoy the delights of a sexual liaison when Antonia lay dead in the cold earth.

He drew a slow, shuddering breath and stepped back.

He was tainted, and he couldn't spread that miasma to an innocent woman.

'Are you all right?' she murmured.

That was another thing he hated. Her perceptiveness. Charlotte saw things in him no one else did. Emotions. Weaknesses.

Alessio couldn't get his head around it. He was used to being controlled, contained and unreadable.

Even Anna, who'd known him from birth, knew better than to prod about his well-being. But this woman who gave the impression of being the perfect employee, competent, efficient and adept at anticipating his needs, crossed vital personal boundaries.

He abhorred that. It made him feel...vulnerable.'With me. Now.'

He spun on his heel and marched from the room. He didn't pause until he was on the flagstone terrace on the west side of the building, where water lapped below the balustrade.

Even here Charlotte Symonds had made her mark. Last time he'd been here, the great stone urns had been empty. Now they were planted with bright red flowers, so vivid in the sunlight they made him think of days long ago when parties had spilled out here, the air filled with laughter and music.

The memory hurt.

Damn it, everything hurt. Surely life had been easier when there'd been nothing to interrupt his solitude, or make him yearn for things he couldn't have.

Alessio stalked to the edge, sparing a glance for the deep, still water that hemmed in his world.

Finally he turned, leaning against the balustrade to survey the woman who'd followed him, mastering the urge to take her in his arms and kiss her. It was too tempting. He could *feel* her body against his, the waft of her breath on his face, the softness of her mouth as she pressed close and begged for more.

His head cleared, and he saw her face was unreadable.

It struck him that Charlotte, like he, had practice at hiding thoughts. Because of her work? Or because of something else? What secrets did she conceal?

'What's going on?' he asked.

'Going on?' Behind that bland expression, he read something in her eyes. Turmoil. Guilt?

'Yes, going on.' Alessio gestured to the pieces of crystal she clutched to her breast. 'That's not the usual dusting you're doing. I didn't give you permission to open up the ballroom.'

Charlotte stiffened, and despite his annoyance, he admired the way her chin came up and she looked down that unremarkable nose at him, undaunted. Inevitably, his admiration took the form of a burst of heat low in his body. He shifted his weight, planting his feet wider.

'I wasn't aware I needed your permission to enter the room. You and Anna said I had free access to the whole building, apart from your study when you're working.'

'You're avoiding the issue, Charlotte.' He took his time, savouring the taste of her name, hearing his voice drop to a hungry drawl. He was rewarded with a rosy blush to her cheeks as her gaze fell to his mouth. His groin tightened.

The man he'd once been would have scorned such a cheap triumph as making her blush with awareness, but the man he'd become revelled in knowing she responded to him. That this sexual awareness wasn't one-sided.

'The question isn't permission to go into the ballroom. It's what you're doing there.' He folded his arms and narrowed his eyes. 'You're up to something.'

She bit her lip, and he stifled a groan at the way that drew attention to her lush pink mouth.

'There seemed no harm in a proper spring clean. We're being extraordinarily careful. Every piece of glass is numbered and—'

'That's not in question.' He kept his voice even. 'What. Are. You. Up. To?'

Charlotte sighed and walked to a nearby table, carefully depositing the antique crystals. The sunlight caught them, casting a rainbow reflection across her face. But when she turned, there was no hint of radiance on her features, just wariness.

'I found a list Anna had left in a drawer in the kitchen. A list of...plans.'

'Go on.'

'The main item was preparation for the island's spring festival.'

A weight plunged through Alessio's gut. 'There's been no festival for years.' Not since he and Antonia moved here from Rome.

'So I gather.' At his stare, she spread her hands wide. 'I asked Mario about it. He said it was enormous fun, the highlight of the whole year, not just for the islanders but for those beyond the lake.'

'*Was* being the operative word.' This was no time for inane festivities.

'So Anna hadn't talked with you about it?'

'Not this year.' Alessio gritted his teeth. She'd raised the possibility last year, but he'd squashed it. He hadn't been able to bear the idea of noise and gaiety, his island invaded by partygoers. Not when he needed peace and solitude.

'I see.' Again that almost martial look from under her finely arched brows. 'You refused last year, and she didn't have time to raise it again before she went to Rome.'

Or she'd been biding her time, waiting for the best opportunity to raise it, hoping to catch him in a weak moment.

'You guessed she hadn't,' he said slowly, watching her expression shutter. 'That's why you didn't mention it. What was the plan? To get so far along with the preparations, you hoped I wouldn't have the heart to put a stop to it?'

Her flush deepened, but instead of apologising, she folded her arms, mirroring his stance and inadvertently giving him a

tantalising glimpse of cleavage where a button had come undone as she'd unburdened herself of the crystal.

'Why would you stop it, Alessio? Is it such a bad thing?'
Despite her challenging stance, far from being confrontational,
Charlotte's tone turned soft. As if she pondered and was concerned about his motivations. As if she guessed at some of the
black burden of remorse weighing on his soul.

He pulled in his wandering thoughts. No one understood.

'This isn't up for debate. It's my decision, and my answer
is no.'

For a full minute, silence expanded between them. In the
distance, he heard a motorboat crossing the lake, and nearer,
a bird calling to its mate.

'You know how much this celebration means to people
here?'

Alessio stood taller. How dared she assume to lecture him
on *his* people?

But she'd known about the need for a new commercial opportunity for local artisans. She'd known about Mario's great-
nephew. Things Alessio should have known. Anger rose at
himself more than anyone else.

'The festival was always at the prerogative of the Conte
since he pays for it.'

Her eyes widened. 'You're worried about the cost?'

'Of course not!' He couldn't believe she'd thought that or
had the temerity to ask. Money had never been a problem for
his family, and under his stewardship, the family business had
gone from strength to strength.

She shook her head, her eyes never leaving his. 'So it's just
that you, personally, don't want to be bothered? I can do a lot
of the work, and I know from speaking to some of the locals
that we could set up a committee—'

'You've already discussed this with them?' Alessio's voice
was sharp with warning.

Charlotte heard it. Her crossed arms and tight shoulders now looked defensive rather than challenging.

'After I asked Mario about it, he mentioned it to some of the others. A couple of them spoke to me.'

In other words, she'd gone behind his back. Alessio's chest rose and fell as he reined in anger.

Anna had asked about a festival last year, but she'd understood, as had the other islanders, that such a celebration was inappropriate given his loss.

'This is none of your business. You're an outsider.'

Once again Charlotte's cheeks flushed pink. Then the colour faded, leaving her features pale and taut. Piling another layer of guilt onto Alessio's conscience.

'I apologise if I've overstepped the mark.' Her voice was brittle but not, he realised, with apology. 'I've followed the guidelines you and Anna set. Given your instructions not to interrupt you, I haven't had a chance to raise the issue with you before now.' She paused as if daring him to disagree. Her eyes flashed fire, and his skin prickled. 'So I decided to start at least preparing the *castello* in case you agreed.'

Her breasts rose against her pale shirt, and Alessio couldn't help but wonder what it would be like if Charlotte shared some of the passion she tried to suppress with a man. With him. His groin grew tight and heavy, and that annoyed him even more.

Alessio was trapped in a never-ending cycle. Solitude brought little relief. But being with people again brought more problems. He couldn't even manage his feelings for his housekeeper. He was wracked by libidinous urges he couldn't relieve and bound by past mistakes to live out his penance alone.

'Well, you know now. No festival.'

'Even though the people here want it? Just because you want to bury yourself here, don't they deserve their celebration?'

Alessio stared. Was she accusing him of being selfish? She hadn't used the word, but the implication was clear. He saw the judgement in those blazing eyes. As for *burying himself,* no one bar his Great-Aunt Beatrice had the nerve to say such a thing.

'Wouldn't the festival be another, bigger chance to show-case the island and local businesses? A showcase they badly need. I've heard people come from Rome and beyond for the celebrations. It would be a huge boost locally. From what I've heard, they badly need that.'

The truth of her words stopped his automatic refusal.

Alessio grew hot and then cold with shame. He'd made a point recently of visiting his neighbours, gauging how they were doing. Most were highly skilled craftspeople, many in specialised fields. A few had weathered the recent economic difficulties well, but others hadn't. He had plans to help them but hadn't even considered the festival as a springboard for those plans. Now he realised it was an obvious starting point.

Not that anyone had mentioned the festival to him. Because they respected his mourning? Or because they knew he'd dismiss it out of hand?

Self-absorbed. Selfish. The words circled in his head.

Had his rejection of the outside world meant he held his own people to ransom? His gut curdled, and his mouth tugged down in a grimace self-disgust.

He spun around and planted his hands on the stone balustrade, feeling his lowering head drag heavily at his shoulders. Feeling the lead in his belly as he stared at the beautiful, unforgiving waters that had shaped his life.

'If you're concerned about being with strangers...' She faltered to a stop as he swung around.

He'd had enough of Charlotte analysing him. It was clear she believed he was hiding away, a skulking hermit too scared to leave his home or meet others.

Yet you haven't left the island in three years.

That didn't matter. That was his choice. He had everything he needed here. Yet her pity grated.

Out of the plethora of emotions bombarding him, guilt, dismay, determination and even unwilling arousal as he watched Charlotte's breasts rise with each quick breath, the strongest was anger. At himself above all, for being blind and thoughtless, burying himself in his own needs instead of doing his duty by his people.

Anger at Charlotte too, for seeing what he hadn't and making him face it. He knew he was at risk of shooting the messenger. She hadn't actually done anything wrong, but his fury needed an outlet.

Alessio leaned back against the balustrade, planting his hands on the stonework and crossing his ankles with a nonchalance he didn't feel. She thought him pitiable? A shadow of the man he'd been, scared to face the world again?

Battered pride rose. It was easier to cling to that than admit she was right and thank her for forcing him to see what he'd done.

'Very well. The festival will go ahead.' Her eyes rounded and her lips, those sweet lips that haunted his dreams, curved in the beginnings of a smile. 'I'll take care of it.' He'd get started today. 'Except for the grand spring ball. That's what you're cleaning the chandeliers for, isn't it?'

Before Charlotte could respond, he continued. 'There'll be several hundred guests. Some locals but many more from elsewhere. The cream of European high society.'

His mouth twisted. He had no doubt every invitation would be accepted. Everyone would be eager to see how he fared after his wife's death. To try to discover the truth of the rumours they'd all been spreading.

'Apart from the invitation list, I'll leave every detail of that in your capable hands. As well as spring cleaning the *castello*, of course.' Alessio smirked, knowing preparation for the gala ball alone usually took a team months of work. Charlotte's arrested expression told him she was beginning to guess as much.

Good. That would keep her busy and out of his way.

'If you manage that to my satisfaction, I'll give you a glowing reference to take to your next position.'

He straightened and headed for the *castello* entrance.

'One more thing.' He paused beside her, knowing he was being unreasonable, knowing he'd owe her a massive apology later, yet unable to prevent himself taking out his simmering fury on the woman who'd brought all this to a head. 'I want you there through it all, but not behind the scenes. I want you front and centre as my hostess.'

It was one thing to work for rich hotel clients, quite another to mix with them as an equal in a social setting. Charlotte Symonds would learn how tough that was.

Maybe then she'd have some tiny inkling of how appalling it was for him to face the prospect of society's curious gaze. The whispers and gossip. The false sympathy hiding eagerness for juicy details of his personal life.

If he had to suffer through the spring festivities, so could she. With luck she'd resign when she realised what she was facing. Then maybe he'd have some measure of peace in his home.

The thought should have pleased him. Yet as he stalked inside, Alessio's mood was grimmer than ever.

CHAPTER EIGHT

CHARLOTTE LIFTED HER head and stretched cramped fingers. She'd missed the sunset again, her favourite time of day. Now the island and lake were bathed in deepening indigo.

The place had a special quality she'd felt from the beginning. A beauty and peacefulness that she appreciated more the longer she stayed.

Even now, with preparations for the festival in full swing. The silence was regularly broken by the sound of power tools, boats and voices as structures were made for outdoor celebrations and seating to view the boat races. For the peace was about far more than silence. The island drew her, welcomed her. She'd miss it when she left in two months.

Her mouth flattened and she rose, rolling stiff shoulders and walking to her window at the sound of voices.

Alessio approached down the cobbled lane with three other men. They stood close, gesticulating as they talked, pointing to the shoreline and arguing the merits of putting banked seating there. Alessio murmured something, and there was a roar of laughter.

This wasn't the first time she'd witnessed his easy interaction with the locals, though a mere week ago they'd seemed more reserved, as if they weren't used to his company.

Had he cut himself off from *everyone*? Her heart squeezed.

Clearly, though, they respected and liked him, and he felt the same about them. No wonder they'd protected his privacy.

Alessio might enjoy adopting the role of lofty lord of the manor with her sometimes, but he wasn't always so stiff-necked.

Something pulled in Charlotte's chest. Pleasure, seeing him interacting easily when once he'd been so reclusive? Delight at his resonant, deep chuckle that, even from this distance, melted some of the tension in her weary body?

She tried to summon anger. It was his fault she was exhausted, working through the evenings. He'd set her an almost impossible challenge because she'd dared to interfere.

Still, Alessio undid her as no man ever had.

Just as well they didn't spend enough time together for him to notice. Though, to his credit, he increasingly sought her out to check how she was faring and, she suspected, to give her the chance to ask for help. But she'd been too proud, determined to prove herself.

Her father had consistently underrated her, jeering at what he called the humdrum domestic skills she'd learned from her mother. Charlotte didn't know if she was working herself to the bone to prove herself to Alessio or to the father who'd never see the fruits of her labour.

And she thought Alessio had problems, letting the past shadow the present too much!

Face it. It's not your father you're trying to impress. It's Alessio. You want him to be stunned by how wonderful the ball is, how successful and grand. You want him to look at you with admiration and respect.

She watched the men walk away and drew a deep breath, scented with sweet-smelling flowers.

Slowly Charlotte turned, her gaze falling on rich, blue velvet. The dress she was making for the ball.

Alessio had wanted to punish her for daring to question him. She'd read his temper. No doubt he'd expected her to be out of her depth and turn to him, begging for help.

Her lips twisted. For once her past was her secret weapon

instead of a burden. She'd been born and bred for events like this. Even in her teens, she'd worn designer evening gowns.

Later, after she'd spurned her father's schemes and had no money, she'd learned to sew her own clothes. She could have dipped into her savings now to buy something special but had no time to travel to a city boutique. Nor did she trust online shopping. This had to be something stunning, made specifically for her.

Because you want Alessio to look at you with more than admiration and respect. You want him to want you. You want him to feel that same trembling tug of awareness.

Charlotte pressed a hand to her thundering heart.

It was ridiculous. She'd seen photos of his glamorous wife with a film star's poise and beauty to match. Her glossy dark hair, sculpted features and stunning body cast other women into the shade.

No ordinary woman could compare.

Yet there'd been times when Charlotte felt Alessio's hungry stare. Been *sure* he experienced that desperate attraction too. But he'd pulled back, and she didn't know what to do with the jumble of emotions and longing inside her. It felt like her skin was too tight, and nothing would soothe her but his touch.

She should be grateful he'd withdrawn. An affair with her boss was impossible. It broke every professional rule.

Yet an unfamiliar part of her, oblivious to propriety or duty or even the future, craved the impossible.

For the first time, she desired a man with all her being. He infuriated her yet drew her like metal to a magnet.

She wanted Alessio to find her desirable in her own right. Not as simply convenient as she'd been to the man who'd considered marrying her to cement a deal with her father. Or to the hotel guests who'd assumed too much about the services hotel staff provided.

Even if it could go nowhere. Even if Alessio still grieved for the wife he'd lost.

Shame burned in her, yet that didn't stop this yearning. It was utterly selfish, but to know just once that he too felt this, even though he'd never pursue it, was vital.

To her self-esteem? Surely not. She didn't need a man to make her feel good about herself.

But maybe it was time to come out of the self-imposed hibernation she'd embraced after her mother died. She'd been grieving and lost when her father tried to force her into an engagement. Her first and only sexual experience had been the deliberate, crude groping of a man who thought himself entitled to her body because her father badly wanted to do business with him.

Charlotte smoothed her palm across the rich fabric. She imagined it against her skin, but from there her imagination leapt to the idea of Alessio's strong, capable hands stroking her flesh.

Fabric crumpled under clutching fingers as she shivered. Primal instinct warned that she courted disaster. Instead of trying to attract Alessio, she should find an excuse to leave. No matter how much explaining she had to do in her next job.

That would be sensible. Trouble was, for the first time in forever, Charlotte didn't feel sensible.

'There you are. I've been searching for you.'

Charlotte sat back on her haunches and looked up. Her head swam, and she told herself it was because she'd been leaning deep into the cupboard in the butler's pantry. Not because Alessio filled the doorway, making her pulse gallop.

'I'm taking inventory of the silverware for supper on the night of the ball.' She held up a huge platter engraved with his coat of arms. There were at least a dozen such platters, plus tureens, gravy boats, goblets, cutlery and a multitude of other items.

'If you need more, let me know and I'll open one of the vaults.'

One of the vaults?

'I'm sure that won't be necessary.' Charlotte scrambled up, feeling at a disadvantage on the floor. 'What can I help you with?'

She kept her gaze on his chin rather than his eyes, but that was a mistake because she found herself staring at those superbly sculpted lips and remembering the feel of his hair-roughened jaw beneath her fingertips.

'For once, Charlotte, it's me wanting to help you.'

Startled, she looked straight into fathomless eyes and felt the tide of longing ripple through her bloodstream.

Yes, please. Can you soothe away this jittery feeling? Maybe with a kiss?

As if that would ever happen. Even if Alessio was attracted, he was obviously grieving for his wife. And he never forgot they were employer and employee.

Yet the way he looked at her with all that lambent heat...

It took a moment to realise he was holding out a card. Gingerly she took it. Embossed in gold were the name and contact details of a world-renowned couturier in Milan.

'A driver will take you tomorrow to be fitted for a ball gown.' He paused. 'It was remiss of me not to organise it sooner.'

'Thank you, but I don't need it. I have a dress sorted.' Though it wouldn't be a patch on a designer gown.

Alessio shook his head. 'I invited...ordered you to attend.' His mouth firmed. 'I apologise. I wasn't at my best that day, and I took it out on you. But I'm not so unreasonable as to expect you to pay for a formal dress that you'll only wear once, because I demanded your presence.'

Charlotte stared, torn between competing impulses. To smile and accept this olive branch. Because it was just that, with an admission of guilt, no less. Yet at the same time, it rankled that he assumed she'd never wear a ball dress after she left here. Because her life was about serving others, not ever being the belle of the ball.

'Thank you. Apology accepted. But there really is no need. I have a dress that's suitable.'

She'd tried the jewel-coloured gown on last night and been stunned. For the first time in her adult life, Charlotte had felt glamorous and seductive. Not at all like the practical, down-to-earth woman she really was.

Alessio frowned as if he didn't believe her, or maybe didn't trust her to know what would pass muster at such an exclusive event.

'Don't worry, Alessio. I've served at some very elite events. I won't embarrass you.'

'I know you won't.' The certainty in his voice surprised her. 'What colour is the dress?'

'Deep blue.'

He angled his head as if to get a better look at her. Why? She hadn't altered. She wore her usual uniform with her hair neatly up, the barest hint of make-up and no jewellery. Yet as his scrutiny touched her face and hair, dipping briefly to skim her body, that too-familiar heat built in her pelvis.

'If you change your mind about the dress, let me know.' Charlotte nodded. 'And as of today, I've assigned someone to assist you.' He raised his palm as if anticipating a protest. 'No arguments. You're doing a fine job, but I don't want you too exhausted to attend the ball.'

Then, without waiting for further argument, he turned on his heel and disappeared, leaving Charlotte confused. Was he just ensuring he had a hostess available on the night? Or was he genuinely concerned for her?

He *had* apologised for being unreasonable and making her solely responsible for the ball. And he could have offered to get her a dress from a nearby boutique without arranging for her to go to a world-class designer.

She hugged the massive silver tray to herself. The trouble was, she wanted him to be aware of her as a woman when every sensible bone in her body knew that was dangerous. What she felt for him was dangerous.

She'd see the ball done and then leave. Because staying, feeling the way she did about her employer, was a recipe for disaster.

Charlotte paused outside Alessio's study, smoothing her long skirt. When she'd looked in the mirror, she'd seen a woman she didn't know. Someone glamorous and intriguing. Not at all like a housekeeper, but like...

Who? Cinderella?

She snorted. She might be going to the ball, but she was still staff. Nothing changed that. Her dress wouldn't compare with the haute couture of the guests. And when every other invitee was tucked up in bed after the festivities, she'd be the one organising the clean-up.

Tonight is work.

But as she rapped on Alessio's door she couldn't scotch a tingle of anticipation at the thought of standing beside him to receive his guests.

'Come in, Charlotte.' His low voice curled around her, and strangely, her flutter of nerves settled.

He had his back to her. But he swung around as she approached, and she faltered to a halt midway across the room.

He was magnificent.

Her gaze roved his features, taking in neatly trimmed hair and scrupulously shaved skin that revealed a proud, well-shaped chin. His formal evening suit, snowy shirt and silk bow tie set off his austere good looks so well that he literally stole her breath.

Charlotte pressed a hand to her churning abdomen, trying to still her reaction.

She'd dreamed of Alessio as a marauding pirate who swept her off her feet and did things to her no man ever had. She'd thought nothing could surpass that secret fantasy. Now she realised her error. In formal clothes, the Conte Dal Lago was the sexiest, most handsome man she'd ever met.

And then he smiled.

Pleasure curled his mouth and lit his eyes, and her breath snagged in cramped lungs.

'You look beautiful,' he told her.

It was ridiculous to be undone by his words. But no one had called her beautiful and really meant it since her mother died. Passing compliments from men looking for quick sex didn't count. Charlotte viewed her round face and ordinary features as pleasant, not outstanding, though her blond hair was a pretty colour.

But meeting Alessio's gleaming eyes, she believed he meant it. She stood taller.

'Thank you. So do you.'

He laughed, the sound snagging in her chest. He didn't seem like the proud, reclusive aristocrat now. 'You're very kind.'

Not kind at all. It was an understatement. She hurried on, needing to change the subject. 'You wanted to see me?'

'I did. I wanted to loan you this to wear.'

Charlotte looked down to the case in his hands. Inside lay a necklace of flawless sapphires, the centre one as large as a pigeon's egg.

She couldn't prevent an audible gasp. 'You were going to lend that to *me*?'

He put the case on the desk beside him, where the gemstones glowed under the overhead light. 'You're my hostess tonight, and I—'

'Was afraid I wouldn't measure up?'

Alessio's eyes narrowed. 'No. I was going to say I regretted putting you in a situation where you might feel out of your depth.' He paused as if choosing his words. 'I wanted to make amends and do what I could to make the evening feel less daunting.'

Charlotte was stunned. She'd seen a change in him as he

spent more time with others, busy working with his community. But this was an extraordinarily generous offer. She had
no doubt the gems were priceless heirlooms.

'You said you were wearing blue.' His voice dipped and
dragged through her middle. 'I wanted to see you wearing
this. Sapphires would be perfect against your creamy skin.'

She swallowed hard. The way he spoke, it sounded like he'd
made a study of her complexion. Deep inside, a tight knot of
pent-up emotion loosened and frayed.

'But I see my offer is unnecessary. Your own jewellery is
perfect.'

Her hand went to her pendant. 'Thank you. It's precious
to me.'

It was the only jewellery she had from her mother. Her
father kept the rest locked away, though it was technically
Charlotte's. Because Charlotte had dared to defy his wishes
in not marrying the man of his choice. Her father couldn't
abide being crossed.

Alessio moved closer. 'May I?' He nodded to the necklace.

'I...of course.'

Deft fingers lifted the pendant from her décolletage, but that
barely-there brush of skin on skin felt like so much more. Charlotte clamped her lips together and fought a shiver of reaction.

'Baroque pearls and a fine ruby. Exquisite.'

He stood so close his words were a puff of warm air across
her skin, and she caught the slight tang of clean male skin,
cedar and exotic incense. Valiantly she fought not to meet his
gaze, but the draw of him was too strong.

Had Alessio's eyes always been that dark? Not with anger
or impatience but something she'd never seen before.

She was leaning closer when she realised what she was
doing and stepped back. Instantly he released her pendant and
it fell to her breast, warm from his hand.

Her breathing faltered. To her overwrought senses, it felt
like he'd touched her.

'It's an unusual design. Several hundred years old.'

Of course he could date it. He specialised in antique treasures. 'I was told it came from a much larger piece that was broken up.'

Wealthy as her mother's family had been, they'd fallen on difficult financial times. Until Charlotte's mother married a successful businessman. But, as Charlotte and her mother had learned to their cost, money didn't guarantee happiness.

Since her mother's death, Charlotte had kept the piece in a bank deposit box, afraid of losing it or being tempted to sell it when she'd struggled to make ends meet. She'd only retrieved it before coming to Italy, not wanting to leave it behind.

'Well, you wear it admirably.' Alessio inclined his head. 'Now, shall we go?'

Charlotte was just full of surprises, Alessio mused, torn between rampant curiosity, admiration and lust. And a piercing sliver of annoyance at having been naive enough to underestimate her. He didn't enjoy feeling like a fool.

Far from being out of her depth, she'd come alive at the ball, as if born to such grand events. He'd had no reason to feel guilty, berating himself for placing her in an impossible situation.

Somehow she combined overseeing the staff and catering and acting the gracious hostess as if it were easy.

Alessio could attest that dealing with his guests' curiosity was anything but easy. His champagne turned sour and his flesh prickled whenever he faced the never-ending curiosity about his dead wife and his own solitude. Or felt clutching female hands on his arm as one eager socialite after another made it clear they would happily distract him from his sorrows.

He shuddered, repulsed, and his gaze turned again to the enigma who was his housekeeper, waltzing down the centre of the room in the arms of one of Italy's most eligible bachelors.

Alessio's hand tightened around his wineglass, and he shoved his other bunching fist into his pocket.

Charlotte looked serene and carefree. And it didn't feel like an act. It felt real.

As real as the way she'd chatted easily with billionaire businesspeople, minor royalty and trophy wives. She'd made introductions, guided an eligible dance partner towards a reserved young woman, and fielded queries about her employment here with good humour and poise.

More than once, she'd even deflected the conversation of someone intent on interrogating him about Antonia.

As if he needed protection!

He was the Conte Dal Lago. He fought his own battles.

Yet it was curiously…nice having Charlotte wield that gracious smile like a weapon on his behalf.

Who is this woman?

She couldn't have learned those skills in housekeeping school. For all the time he'd spent fixated on her, he'd done nothing to uncover her past. It was clear she had almost as many secrets as he.

'If the wind changes, your face will stay like that.' Great-Aunt Beatrice's hoarse chuckle made him turn. 'Not that you look ugly. In fact, that Scandinavian princess seems quite taken with your scowl.'

'Beatrice.' He smoothed out his expression. 'I hope you're enjoying yourself.'

'I've never had so much fun.' The gleam in her black eyes would make a lesser man uneasy. 'I find her delightful, by the way, your Charlotte.'

Alessio was about to snap that she wasn't his Charlotte but knew any sign of emotion would be minutely scrutinised. He didn't need Beatrice, who already interfered too much, to realise he lusted after his housekeeper. Or that he was jealous of the never-ending line of men eager to dance with her.

He'd let it be known he wouldn't dance tonight. It was tough enough, facing the glare of avid public interest. Keeping some personal distance was vital.

Beatrice didn't wait for a reply. 'She and I had a lovely chat earlier. So...informative.' He tensed, until she added with a sideways look, 'About embroidery, mainly. I *knew* that gift must have been someone else's idea. You wouldn't know embroidery silk from tapestry wool.'

'I'm pleased you like it.'

The old girl raised her eyebrows at his laconic answer. But he refused to discuss Charlotte. With anyone.

'I like the way she's shaken things up around here.'

Shaken things up? Shaken *him* up, more like.

'Such an interesting background she must have too. I was chatting earlier with George Somersby. He was surprised to learn Charlotte's your housekeeper. He remembers her attending exclusive black-tie events at a stately home in England. But she definitely wasn't a member of staff.'

Alessio's eyes widened. It was more than *interesting*. It was more proof that she was an enigma. He shot an assessing look at Charlotte, circling elegantly in her partner's arms, and felt his jaw clench.

His great-aunt nodded briskly as if confirming something. 'Good night, Alessio. Giorgia's ready to leave.' He'd invited Beatrice to stay overnight, the only person to receive such an invitation, but she preferred to stay with an old friend. 'It's been... illuminating.' Her grin was sly, and Alessio was instantly on guard. 'I can't remember a more entertaining evening.'

After escorting Beatrice out, he returned to the doorway, surveying the scene.

The ballroom glittered, every glass and mirror polished. Flowers in decorative jardinières and enormous formal arrangements scented the air. In the supper room, visible through open doors, tables covered in finest linen and antique silver groaned under a spread of gourmet delicacies.

Chatter filled the air, and everywhere he saw smiles. The

ball, the opening event of the festival, proved he'd done right, agreeing to it.

Charlotte had been right.

Musicians performed in the minstrels' gallery, and the floor was packed with people in their finery, from locals in neat suits and pretty dresses to the monied elite in bespoke tailoring, fabulous jewels and designer gowns.

Amongst them all, Charlotte stood out.

It wasn't merely the way the light caught the rich gold of her hair. Or the way said hair was styled in a luxurious, softened upsweep that revealed her slender neck yet left tendrils free. It gave her a seductive look, inevitably making him imagine her just risen from bed.

Her dress was the rich blue of lapis lazuli, shaping her body like a lover's hands before falling in folds to the floor. A band of fabric rose in a V from deep over her cleavage to the points of each shoulder, making him wonder how securely that bodice was held up. It left a wide swathe of perfect pale skin bare.

Except it wasn't pale now. She glowed with exertion from dancing. Or maybe from delight at the sweet nothings that Roman playboy was whispering in her ear.

Pain exploded in Alessio's jaw from grinding molars. He wanted to stalk across and wrest her away from those grasping hands. Pull her into his arms and then...

It's not dancing you have in mind, is it?

All night, every time he'd seen her in the arms of another man, his tension had screwed tighter. He remembered holding Charlotte against him. How right it had felt. How much more he'd wanted. And how wrong that was.

Alessio stood, fighting the impulse to make a scene and march off with Charlotte in his arms while the world gawked. Then he turned and pushed his way from the room.

Charlotte caught Alessio's eyes on her. Again. All evening she'd felt that spark of heat and turned to find him glaring at her. So much for the sensual awareness she'd hoped for. With the guests, he was all smiles and urbane charm. It was only when he looked at her that he frowned.

What had she done wrong? The evening had turned out wonderfully. Even his dragon of an aunt had proved herself impressed and approving, albeit disconcertingly outspoken.

She couldn't think why he wasn't thrilled. She'd worked so hard and deserved his appreciation. More than one guest had said it was the best party they'd attended in years.

But it's his feedback that matters, isn't it?

Alessio scowled and turned away. Charlotte's heart plummeted even as she shored up her indignation. But she was too deflated to concentrate on anger at the man she'd tried to impress, not as his efficient employee but as a seductive, alluring woman.

She focused on her companion, discreetly moving his roving hand higher. Not long to go now. Soon she could ditch the long dress and heels and put on work clothes for the clean-up.

So much for romantic yearnings.

So much for Cinderella.

They stood together at the main entrance to the *castello*, waving goodbye to the last of the guests heading to the boats that would take them to their luxury accommodations. While the Conte Dal Lago had opened his doors for a fabulous celebration that guests would talk about for years to come, there'd be no overnight guests.

The chatter and laughter died away, and still Alessio said nothing. Not one word of praise. In silence he closed and bolted the vast iron-studded doors.

Charlotte had had enough. She'd done her best, but clearly it wasn't enough to satisfy him. And it wasn't as if the night were over. She had hours of work ahead.

She spun on her heel, lifting the long skirts that had made her feel, for a little while, like a princess in a fairy tale. Her jaw clenched at her futile imaginings. Nothing would make her more than his domestic drudge. She flattened her mouth, fanning anger at her own stupidity.

'Where are you going?' Alessio's voice was sharp.

She didn't bother to turn back, instead marching towards the grand staircase. 'To my room to get changed, ready to supervise the clean-up.'

'No.'

Nothing else. Just a single word.

'Pardon?' She was forced to swing around, and discovered him right there, so close she could see the hint of tiny dark bristles beginning to form on his jaw.

'I cancelled tonight's clean-up and sent everyone home.'

'You did what?'

'It can wait till tomorrow.'

'Everyone will be busy tomorrow. There are boat races and a festival and—'

'Then the cleaning can wait till after the festival.'

Charlotte opened her mouth to argue. Then she read his expression, and her breath disappeared. A finger of disquiet tracked down her spine, making her shiver.

He looked...dangerous.

Yet she felt no impulse to flee. On the contrary...

'Aren't you going to ask me why I sent them away, Charlotte?' Alessio's voice was silky smooth, yet tight with whatever emotion clamped his jaw.

The air between them thickened, and she had to moisten her suddenly dry mouth. 'Why, Alessio?'

His eyes flared as her voice turned husky on his name. Then his mouth curled in a harsh smile, and he stepped close, his arm encircling her waist and drawing her up against him. 'Because of *this*.'

CHAPTER NINE

ALESSIO'S ARM AROUND her felt shockingly familiar, stopping her angry retort.

Charlotte might be infuriated and confused, but she knew what she wanted.

This. The weight of his arm around her waist, pulling her hard against his lean, muscular frame. The press of powerful thighs against hers. The spark of awareness that turned his usually cool green gaze to fire.

She felt that fire inside, racing along her veins, pooling in her pelvis, heating breasts that seemed to swell and press against the tight fabric of her bodice.

'What *do* you want, Alessio? You need to be more specific.'

She was amazed to hear herself sound so calm.

His eyes crinkled at the corners. 'With pleasure.' Did she imagine he gave the word *pleasure* lingering emphasis? 'It's a ball, Charlotte. I want to dance with you.'

She shook her head, spirits plummeting. Was he making fun of her? 'The ball's over. We could have danced earlier.'

She ordered her unresponsive feet to step back, but they didn't move.

'Impossible. If I'd danced with you, then I'd have been obliged to dance with others.' His eyes held hers, and his voice deepened to a luscious rumble. 'I didn't want to dance with anyone else. Just you.'

As if she alone, among all those sophisticated women, attracted him. Charlotte swallowed and discovered her throat had constricted. Her heart beat too fast, and her thoughts scrambled.

Danger, screamed a warning voice in her head.

But, oh, what glorious danger.

When he looked at her that way, Alessio undermined all her caution. After years protecting herself, maybe it was time to live a little. To choose danger instead of safety.

Still she resisted. 'There's no music.'

Alessio took her resisting hand and placed it on his shoulder, where her fingers instantly spread and clung, absorbing his heat and hard strength. He took her other hand, lifting it in a waltz hold.

'You can't hear the music?' He drew her closer. 'Listen to your heartbeat.'

Then they were moving, slowly but in perfect unison in a circle that took them from the vaulted entry hall into the brilliantly lit ballroom.

Charlotte was floating, the steps coming easily, without thought. As if they'd danced together a thousand times, their bodies totally attuned.

Alessio swung her faster, and now they swirled down the grand room, her skirts flaring, their legs pressing close, and not once did he lift his gaze from hers. She could almost hear the music, its powerful rhythm urging her on. They reached the end of the room, and his arm tightened around her waist, swinging her up for a second off the floor.

A laugh escaped her. The sound of pure joy as they circled back along the polished floor, faster and faster. Yet Charlotte felt totally secure in Alessio's embrace, ready to go where he led, caught up in heady excitement.

'Why were you angry?' she asked him. 'You marched out of here in a temper.'

The words emerged as a gasp, but Alessio didn't slow. If anything he hugged her closer, spinning them faster on the next turn. Charlotte didn't care. Never had a dance felt like this, like they were flying.

For a moment, for two, it seemed he wouldn't answer. Then they slowed to a more decorous pace. 'The simple answer?'

His eyes glinted, and arousal arrowed to her core. Charlotte nodded. It was more and more difficult to concentrate on words. 'Simple will do.'

'Frustration.' His chest rose high in the first indication that their reckless speed affected him. But his next words proved it wasn't that shortening his breath. 'I wanted you in *my* arms, Charlotte. Not dancing with every womaniser and layabout in Italy.'

Charlotte stumbled, and Alessio's hold tightened. Their steps slowed until they barely moved.

'They weren't all womanisers and layabouts.'

He huffed out a laugh, and the sound stroked deep inside her. 'I wanted to throw them out when I saw how they looked at you.'

Her eyes grew huge. Alessio had been *jealous*? Her chest clogged. 'And are you enjoying it now, dancing with me?'

To her surprise, he shook his head. Charlotte pulled back in his embrace, but still Alessio held her securely.

'I was. But it's not enough.' He swallowed hard, and to her astonishment, this man who'd always controlled every situation looked suddenly desperate. 'I want more, Charlotte, much more. Too much.'

That teasing smile was gone, his features harsh as he frowned down at her. Then she turned cold as he released her, sliding his arm away and stepping back so her hand on his shoulder dropped to her side.

His voice was rough when he spoke again. 'This was a mistake. You work for me. I remind myself all the time, but tonight I keep forgetting and—'

'Couldn't we pretend for tonight that I don't?' Did he hear her longing? 'Couldn't we pretend I'm someone else?'

He shook his head so vehemently that obstinate lock of hair tumbled forward over his brow. All night Alessio had looked perfectly groomed, perfectly in command. Now he was more like the marauder she'd first met.

'No pretending. It's you I want, Charlotte. The woman who drives me to distraction with her unflappable efficiency. Who makes even navy trousers and flat shoes sexy! A woman of secrets who's anything but a simple housekeeper.' He watched her jump of surprise. 'Oh, yes, I see more than you think.'

His words were a potent caress, smoothing doubts and fears, stroking her sensitised skin and stoking the need deep inside.

How could she resist a man who said such things and meant them? It was rare for Alessio to let down his guard, but now he did, enough for her to see the truth in his eyes. The raw hunger, the loneliness that matched hers.

Charlotte's heart squeezed. 'If you see so much, then you know how I feel.'

He wasn't letting her off the hook. 'Tell me.'

She held his gaze. 'I want you, Alessio. I've tried to pretend there's nothing between us, but it doesn't work. I've never had a sexual relationship with an employer.' Now wasn't the time to admit she'd never had sex, lest he think twice about this. She lifted her chin. 'I want to be your lover.'

For weeks it had been her guilty secret, but in admitting it, Charlotte felt stronger than ever before. No matter what the world said, they were simply a woman and a man caught in an utterly natural attraction. In her case, a very overdue attraction, because her early experiences of the opposite sex had left her wary and wounded.

Alessio's face drew tight. His nostrils flared, and the pulse at his temple throbbed urgently.

She'd done that. Charlotte had never realised the heady excitement of having a man want her with such intensity.

She took a step closer, but he stopped her with an abrupt gesture.

'I can't give promises except to treasure your body and give you all the pleasure I can.' Described in his low, sexy voice, that sounded absolutely perfect, yet Alessio looked grimmer than ever. 'I can offer short-term delight. But nothing else. If you're harbouring thoughts of the future–'

'Absolutely not!'

She might have fantasised about him, but Charlotte was a realist. She'd learned to face unpalatable facts early in life.

'You're the Conte Dal Lago. I'm a temporary housekeeper. Our worlds only intersect a little.' Though once upon a time, before she and her father disowned each other, she'd moved in similar circles to his, albeit in another country. But that past was dead, and she didn't regret it, because she loathed the ugliness that had been the price of staying in it. 'I have a career and long-term goals, and you have...' She floundered for a second when the only word that came to mind was *sadness*. A strange, hollow feeling opened up inside. 'Responsibilities.'

For a long moment, Alessio didn't respond, just scrutinised her as if sifting her words for truth. Then, abruptly, he inclined his head. 'I don't want to hold out false hope of a longer-term relationship.'

For a second Charlotte let herself wonder what it would be like if Alessio truly cared for her. To be loved by a man of such intensity and, she'd learned, integrity. His wife must have felt...

No, she couldn't go there.

'Nor would I. I'm leaving for Venice in a couple of months. It will be a huge career move for me, a step towards achieving my goals.'

Yet tonight she'd take a chance. Ignore the world's rules and her own and follow her instinct.

Suddenly Alessio smiled, and something inside her melted. It wasn't a carefree smile, more a twist of the lips that looked almost painful. Yet that look, and the blazing heat in his eyes, turned her knees weak.

'Then we've no time to waste.' A second later he held her in his arms, not in a waltz hold this time, but cradled up high against his chest, her long skirts trailing.

It was so sudden Charlotte was still catching her breath when he strode out of the room towards the grand staircase.

She opened her mouth to protest that he couldn't possibly want to carry her up several flights of stairs. But she didn't say a word.

His display of machismo did the strangest things to her common sense. Instead she rested her head against his hard shoulder and relished every moment of those powerful arms sweeping her ever higher in a possessive embrace that spoke to the primitive heart of her.

'At last.' Alessio wasn't even breathing heavily as he lowered her to her feet beside the vast bed that dominated his room.

Charlotte's heart beat wildly somewhere up in her throat as she palmed the lapels of his dinner jacket, her hands a little unsteady. Because they really were going to do this. Because, against the odds, Alessio wanted *her*. It seemed remarkable, but she had no intention of pausing long enough to question her good fortune.

She wished she had more experience to draw on.

At least she had enthusiasm on her side.

'What are you smiling about?'

'Us. This.' She lifted her face to his. 'Sometimes, rarely, life can be a gift, don't you think?'

His eyes widened as if the thought had never occurred to him. Charlotte felt a pang of regret that he'd lived in the shadows of grief for so long.

Then, to her surprise, Alessio grinned. It transformed him, and she clutched at his lapels for support. What wouldn't a woman do to make him look like that every day?

'I do like gifts.' His voice was a sensual thread that wove around her, teasing erogenous zones and trailing awareness through her. This man had brought her once-dormant body out of hibernation with a vengeance. 'I especially enjoy unwrapping them.'

His fingertips skimmed the wide neckline of her dress, making her shiver and lean closer. He still hadn't kissed her. Would it be gentle and sweet or urgent?

As if reading her thoughts Alessio bent his head, but instead of touching his mouth to hers, he pressed an open-mouthed kiss to her bare shoulder. She shuddered as a tumult of sensation thundered through her. His hands slid around her back as his mouth followed the line of her bodice across to her breasts. He paused, his breath hot against her cleavage, but not as hot as the molten desire pooling low in her body.

'Alessio!' Her knees sagged, and she might have slid to the floor but for his encompassing embrace.

'Patience.' Yet there was nothing patient about his deft hand dragging the long zip down her back, then sliding the material off her shoulder and down her arm.

Cool air brushed Charlotte's skin, her back and breast, for she didn't own a strapless bra and only wore knickers beneath the dress. She felt her nipples pucker, exposed to the night air.

There was a hiss of indrawn breath, then a low, heartfelt flood of Italian that she couldn't understand. Except when she opened eyes she hadn't realised had closed, she read Alessio's expression, his reverence and delight as he cupped her breast in his warm, capable hand.

He looked as blown away as she was, and Charlotte felt a punch of triumph that indeed this wasn't one-sided. Whatever tomorrow brought when they returned to their positions as boss and employee, they were equals now.

Her eyes fluttered shut at the onslaught of profound bliss as he brought his mouth to her breast and the world fell away.

'Alessio.' It was a hoarse plea of encouragement and wonder as he took her nipple between his lips and sucked. Fiery darts zapped from her breast to her groin and back. The knees that had nearly collapsed stiffened, and she pressed closer, moving restlessly, needing contact.

He planted his feet wide, one hand splayed across her buttocks. He pulled her to stand in between his legs, bringing her into contact with that swollen ridge of masculine potency as he lifted his head.

She saw stars then. Tiny glimpses of light in those deep green eyes as if he glowed from within. Or perhaps the stars were in *her* head, products of the explosion of sensation within her.

'Charlotte.' He held her gaze as he lifted his left hand to her right shoulder and pushed the narrow velvet band down her arm. Now her other breast was exposed, yet instead of feeling hesitant, standing half naked before a man still fully dressed, she felt powerful. Because of what she saw in his expression and the throb of his erection against her belly.

Far from wanting to cover herself, Charlotte pushed her shoulders back, offering her bare breasts to him while unconsciously her lips formed into a provocative pout.

She'd never pouted in her life, or offered her body for any man's delectation. But this wasn't one-sided. She got as much pleasure revelling in Alessio's ardent response as he did from her actions.

But even more pleasure when he groaned, deep at the back of his throat and pulled her higher, drawing his tongue the length of her breast before circling her nipple and finally catching it in his teeth.

She screamed then. Not words but a strangled sound that melded desperation and delight as her body caught fire. She was aware of her fingers digging into the fine fabric at his shoulders, of the restless arch of her lower body into his and the certainty that only Alessio could satisfy this consuming craving.

'Too many clothes,' he muttered against her breast, and she agreed, reaching for his perfect bow tie.

But Alessio wasn't talking about himself. In a single movement, he shoved the heavy fabric down from her waist to her hips, from where it slid to tent around her ankles. She was so turned on that even that brush of fabric on bare skin overloaded her senses.

Charlotte swallowed hard, her tongue flicking out to moisten suddenly dry lips. She saw his heavy-lidded gaze track the movement.

'I want to eat you all up. Slowly.' His accent had thickened as his voice dropped to a sensual burr that sent a ribbon of heat straight to her sex.

'Yes!'

Restlessly she shifted her weight, trying to mould herself to his body again, but her high heels caught in her discarded dress.

Once more deft hands caught her, encircling her bare waist in a way that made her feel delicate and almost tiny against his superior size. Charlotte was fit and active and by no means weak. Yet now she was consummately aware of the profound physical differences between male and female.

She didn't even gasp when he simply lifted her off the floor, stepped over the discarded ball gown and put her down on his bed. Instead, she delighted in his strength.

Sitting on the side of the bed, wearing nothing but ivory lace knickers, while well over six feet of fully dressed, pure male magnificence towered over her, Charlotte should have felt out of her depth. Instead it felt like freedom after a lifetime of shackles.

She leaned back a little to take in the view, resting on palms planted on the bedspread that she tidied every morning. She might even have opened her knees a little wider as Alessio's hot gaze ran the length of her body. The silk and lace between her legs was wet with arousal. Could he see that?

She saw the enormous bulge in his trousers and the way his chest rose mightily as if he couldn't suck in enough air.

Yet he didn't move, and though his eyes glittered with hunger, something about the harsh twist to his lips made her wonder if he'd changed his mind.

Her confidence splintered as a chill doused her. She sat up straight and for the first time felt the urge to cover her breasts, except pride forbade that.

'Having second thoughts?' Charlotte wanted to sound understanding, but the words came out scratchy. And full of a regret she couldn't hide.

Of course he has second thoughts. He's still mourning his wife. How could you possibly think...?

'No.' His laugh was harsh and totally lacking amusement. 'I should be but, for my sins, I'm too selfish for that.'

She was torn between relief and curiosity, but before she could ask more, he spoke. 'Are *you* having second thoughts?'

She was shaking her head before he'd stopped talking. So much for pride.

'Good,' he growled. 'Because I meant what I said, Charlotte. I want to devour you, every inch of you. I need you so badly—'

'Then stop talking and take off your clothes.'

Nerves made her voice strident, and she saw his mouth curve as speculation gleamed in his eyes. 'You like giving orders? Maybe later if you're very, very good...'

How had she ever imagined he was anything but totally in control? Just the teasing flick of one raised eyebrow and that glimmer of humour in his dark face had her shifting on the bed, trying to ease the desperate ache between her legs where the pressure built so high it felt like she might explode. If she didn't have him soon she'd go crazy.

Or maybe she was already crazy, thinking this could work. This man had been a legendary lover before his marriage. He'd expect someone experienced.

Should she tell him?

And risk rejection?

The inner debate ended the moment he ripped his bow tie off and flung it towards a chair. It slithered to the ground.

So different to the neatly folded clothes he left for laundering each day.

Charlotte yanked her gaze back in time to see his gold cufflinks drop onto the bedside table. One circled and rolled off, but he didn't seem to notice, and she couldn't move to pick it up because he'd already discarded his jacket. Now he was unbuttoning his shirt. Halfway down he lost patience and tugged. She heard something tear, threads undoubtedly, but at the same time she felt something shear free within her. A last lingering thread of caution?

There was no time to follow that thought, because Alessio's hands dropped to his trousers, and her capacity for conscious thought died.

She leant forward, reaching for the tiny buckle that would undo her shoe.

'Don't! Let me do that.'

Alessio shucked his trousers, freeing himself too of socks and glossy shoes. He stood before her in nothing but black silk underwear and his own magnificence.

Charlotte felt her eyes grow round. She'd seen him shirtless. She'd seen him in rowing gear. But standing there, arms akimbo, lamplight spilling across his olive-gold skin and picking out in loving detail every line and curve of that impressive musculature, he looked like some fantasy hero made flesh. From his wide, sparely fleshed chest to his solid thighs, he was potently masculine.

Her gaze dropped to the fine line of dark hair that disappeared below the silk waistband, and instantly his erection twitched as if in response. Stunned, she met his eyes and saw his tight, rueful smile.

He lifted his shoulders. 'What can I say? I want you, Charlotte, so very, very badly.' He shook his head. '*Bad* is the operative word, isn't it? I shouldn't be doing this. I pay your wages—'

'If you say that again I'll…!'

'What will you do?' One sleek eyebrow rose as his voice turned silky. 'Punish me?'

Excitement sizzled through her. Not at the idea of punishing Alessio, but at the thought of doing with him whatever she wanted. Not that she was experienced enough to have too many ideas on that score, but with time, she'd definitely think of some.

'Stop talking, Alessio. I'm tired of waiting.'

And there it was again, that pout, that slackening of thigh muscles that spread her knees wider, that straightening of her spine that thrust her breasts towards him.

For once he didn't argue as he closed the space between them and dropped to his knees between her feet. In fact, she realised, his eyes looked a little glazed as they raked from her lips to her breasts and down to her sex.

One large hand closed around her ankle as nimble fingers plucked at the tiny buckle. Carefully, almost tenderly, he slid the sandal from her foot, then paused to press his thumbs to her instep, pushing slowly up her sole and sending lush, decadent heat pouring through her.

Charlotte bit back a moan of ecstasy.

'You like that?'

When she managed to open her eyes, it was to discover his smug expression had slipped, replaced by something raw and hungry that called to the very heart of her being.

'You can't tell?' she purred. His smile was brief as he massaged her foot again, working tired muscles and eliciting shudders of arousal. So much arousal. 'I don't think...'

Her words stopped as his lips feathered her heel, her ankle, then followed his smoothing palm up her calf. She knew about foreplay. Theoretically. She'd watched films and read books, but nothing had prepared her for Alessio focusing all that single-minded intensity on pleasing her. And he hadn't even got to the good bits.

Alessio lifted her leg higher, pressing an open-mouthed

kiss to the groove behind her knee, and she shuddered as heat arced through her. Her fingers clutched the bedspread so tightly she'd probably shredded it. But the housekeeper in her, whose business it was to be concerned about such things, was nowhere to be found.

To her astonishment, Alessio propped her calf across his shoulder as he reached for her other shoe. With one leg up high, it felt natural to give in to the weight of gravity and lax muscles. She slumped back on the bed.

Her eyes drifted shut as he repeated the procedure, removing her sandal and massaging her other foot until she wondered if she might come from the sheer bliss of his touch. Kissing her slowly, deliberately, up and up her leg, building tingling anticipation in all the places he hadn't yet touched.

Her nipples pinched hard and her hips circled with need, but still Alessio made her wait.

Finally, feeling drugged with arousal, she opened her eyes to find him watching her. A dark flush coloured those high cheekbones where his flesh pulled tight. His mighty chest rose and fell, and she felt his breath hot against her thigh.

A noise escaped her throat that she'd never heard before. A protest and a plea. She wanted to reach for him so she could finally feel him inside her. Yet another part of her adored this exquisite, sensual torture.

'Are you very fond of this underwear?'

His voice was so thick it took her a second to understand his words.

She frowned. 'No, it's—'

'Good.'

Warm knuckles brushed her inner thigh. Then, in one urgent tug, he ripped the fabric free of her body.

Charlotte's mouth hung agape as ivory lace sailed through the air. She just had time to read Alessio's satisfied smile before he pressed her thighs open with those big, gentle hands and buried his face between her legs.

Her senses overloaded as he located her clitoris. His tongue circled, then stroked, and her pelvis lifted eagerly because it was impossible to stay still. Not when each lap of his tongue sent another bolt of lightning through her.

He traced her entrance with his finger, delving in time with his tongue, and Charlotte gasped.

She quivered all over, pleasure rising to impossible levels as his intimate caresses breached every expectation. How had she thought she'd understood her body when it was clear she'd known so little about how good it could feel? She was filled to the brim with heat and light and a welling sensation stronger than anything she'd ever known.

One finger became two, and she heard the slick sound of their easy slide, felt the draw of his mouth against her most sensitive spot.

And suddenly she was flying, racing up through the clear, bright air, sobbing in ecstasy so powerful it edged towards fear. Till heat surrounded her, strong arms pulling her close, and there was Alessio, his chest crushing hers, whispering reassurance in that velvety voice till the fear disappeared and there was only rapture and this man. This one amazing man who'd given her more than she'd ever expected to receive.

Charlotte sobbed his name, clutching him close, and for the first time in her life, let herself go completely.

CHAPTER TEN

WATCHING CHARLOTTE CLIMAX, holding her to him as she embraced rapture, was the most extraordinary experience. As if he shared that rapture. As if her delight were his and he'd flown to the stars with her, even though he was tight to the point of pain with unfulfilled need.

Alessio had known plenty of women and was always a gentleman about sex, ensuring his partner's pleasure before his own. Yet he couldn't recall ever feeling like this with a lover.

His arousal was torture because he'd never been so turned on in his life.

Yet gratification wasn't uppermost in his mind. Charlotte was.

He basked in the glow of knowing he'd brought her to a shattering high. But there was something more, a primal instinct that spoke of a deeper bond. She clung to him, his name a soft sigh on her lips, as she tucked herself tight against him, and part of his brain went into meltdown. At the knowledge she needed him still, even after that climax.

And at the strange jumble of emotions rampaging through him. Protectiveness, triumph, excitement and tenderness.

Alessio had never felt like this about any other woman.

Even Antonia, his dead wife.

He waited for piercing guilt to stab him. After all, this was the first time he'd been with a woman since Antonia.

Yet it didn't come.

Gently he brushed Charlotte's damp hair off her cheek, his chest squeezing as she turned her face to follow the gesture, pressing her lips to his palm and sending a shudder of exquisite pleasure arrowing to his groin.

No, it hadn't been like this with Antonia. They'd known each other for years and been friends with occasional benefits, neither looking for or expecting commitment.

Until everything changed and they'd married.

And everything went wrong.

'What are you thinking about? You look upset.'

Alessio tried to gather his thoughts. He met eyes of rich lapis lazuli, felt himself fall and keep falling. As if nothing could be better than to lose himself in those depths.

'Alessio? I'm sorry. I should have waited for you. That was selfish of me.'

Charlotte's hand fumbled between them, sliding across slick skin to hold him, and send him into one of the darkest circles of hell. Because resisting the urge to spill himself was almost impossible.

'No!' He grabbed her hand, pulling it away, wincing at the desperate effort of not coming in her hand.

The thought brought him to the edge of control, chest heaving, every muscle strung taut.

'You don't want me to touch you?' Had Charlotte's eyes always been so wide and wondering?

He shook his head. 'Of course I do, but not now.' The words emerged as a harsh growl, and he felt her delicious body stiffen, a frown corrugating her brow.

Instantly Alessio was contrite. He stroked her bottom lip with his thumb, realising they hadn't even kissed yet. There was so much he wanted to do with her, he almost didn't know where to begin.

'Because I need to be inside you when I climax, *cara.* Nothing else will do. I'm so on edge that if you touch me again, I won't be able to hold back.'

From dismay, her expression turned to delight, and he watched a rosy blush rise from her breasts to her cheeks. Almost like a woman unused to talking about sex.

Crazy how even that added to his arousal.

Face it, everything about her arouses you.

Even those damnable uniform trousers. Just as well Charlotte had no idea how perfectly they outlined her buttocks as she stretched and reached.

Which made Alessio imagine taking her from behind, pumping hard against her curvaceous rump while he found her sweet spot with his hand between her thighs.

His retreat off the bed was frantic rather than dignified, but Alessio didn't have time for smooth moves. Other than smoothing on a condom, which would be test enough of his willpower.

Fortunately he didn't disgrace himself, though his hands were shaking and his teeth tightly clenched by the time he'd put on protection. From the corner of his vision, he saw Charlotte watching him intently from under lowered lashes, and suddenly he felt as sophisticated as a schoolkid.

As if this were new. As if it wasn't something he'd done multiple times before.

Yet it felt... Alessio shook his head. He didn't have the mental capacity to work that out when every blood cell in his body was draining down to his groin.

He knelt on the bed, mouth drawing into a predatory smile as Charlotte scooted further across the bed to give them more space. He felt her eyes on him as he ran his fingers up her inner thighs, and she jumped before letting her knees loosen and open for him.

Propping himself on one hand, he stroked her sex, watching her shiver and give that eager little twist of the pelvis as if trying to follow his caress. The way she responded...

'Alessio—'

He barely caught her voice over his thundering pulse, but

when he raised his gaze to hers, some of his excitement died. She gnawed her lip as if uncertain about something. About continuing?

His long-denied libido screamed denial at the thought, but he forced himself to lift his hand from her body, nostrils flaring at the unique scent of cinnamon, sugar and female orgasm.

Razors scored his throat as he swallowed. 'What is it, Charlotte? Do you want me to stop?'

Instantly she shook her head, and relief slackened his muscles. 'No. I want you, Alessio. I just...' She heaved a shuddering sigh that made her breasts jiggle and Alessio's erection pulse. 'Nothing. Nothing at all.'

Yet there was something. He knew it. He was about to ask again when soft fingers fluttered across his shaft and he spasmed hard, on the brink.

Curiosity died, swamped by the need that had been building since she'd arrived on the island.

He caressed her sex, slipping a finger deep, then another, to be rewarded not just with slick heat, but the undulation of her hips anticipating his possession.

Suddenly he could hold back no more. Alessio settled between those pale thighs, braced himself high to save her from his full weight, and drove home in one urgent thrust.

He'd died and gone to heaven.

Ecstasy beckoned. Every sensation was perfect. Charlotte's softness. The tight velvet embrace of her body. The friction of her breasts against his heaving chest. The clamp of her hands on his shoulders and the warm stroke of her breath on his face.

Except even on the edge of losing himself, he couldn't ignore how her lax, pleasured body had stiffened. Or that tiny tugging sensation when he'd thrust, as if dislodging a barrier.

His eyes snapped open, and what he read on her face answered the question filling his mind.

Charlotte was a virgin.

Had been a virgin until seconds ago.

Her lovely mouth was pulled tight as if in discomfort, and her eyes were foggy. With pain?

Horrified, Alessio moved to withdraw.

Sharp fingernails dug into his skin, and she looped her slender leg over his as if to hold him still.

'I hurt you?' His throat was thick.

'Only for a second. And not hurt really, more...' She paused and dragged in air, making her breasts torment him as they slid against his labouring chest. 'I feel fine. More than fine.' She wrapped her other leg around his thighs, then jiggled her hips so she could encircle his buttocks with her legs. 'I want you Alessio. *Please.*'

Those words banished a rusty conscience that told him he should withdraw completely. Because he didn't mess with virgins.

She's not a virgin anymore.

It wasn't logic that convinced him, it was that pout, that sexy moue of pink lips, as if she begged for something only he could give her.

When in fact it was she giving everything to him.

The realisation sank deep into his soul, past the years of pain and isolation, to a place he hadn't known existed any longer. A place that craved warmth and connection. And Charlotte's beguiling body.

Knowing he'd have to battle his conscience and his curiosity later, Alessio gave in. He was only a man, after all, more flawed than most, and no man could resist the irresistible.

Holding her close, he rolled over so she lay above him. He watched her eyes widen and felt a tiny punch of satisfaction as her legs slid down to straddle him, and he tilted his hips, sliding deeper into welcoming heat.

'Hold on to my shoulders and sit straight.'

She was delightfully eager, and each movement sorely tested him. But it was worth it to have her seated there, taking all of him.

'Okay?' he grunted, barely leashing the need to set a driving rhythm.

'Oh, yes.' Her fingertips curled against his shoulders, digging deeper as she shifted, eyes widening at the sensation of them sliding together.

Alessio grasped her hips, urging her up. Somehow, even as he battled the compulsion to lose himself, it was Charlotte's look of wonder and delight that took centre stage.

She sank back and he thrust up, feeling her tell-tale shiver of response inside that made the sweat break out on his brow as he fought to go slow. Her skin flushed a deep rose, and he wanted to taste her again.

He held back. As her first lover, he had a duty to make this as good as possible for her. Yet it wasn't duty driving him. He wanted her in ecstasy even more than he needed his own release, even though it felt like waiting any longer might kill him.

Charlotte found her pace, her breaths quickening, her bright eyes holding his as he cupped and fondled her breasts, feeling the momentum build within her. Finally, as they both sped towards the inevitable peak, he gave in to his body's desperate urging and drew her down against him so they touched all the way down their bodies. He took control of their rhythm when she faltered and captured her lips with his.

Her mouth tasted as sweet as he'd imagined through all those lonely days and nights. She tasted like the promise of spring after the longest drear winter.

Restraint was impossible. Her silken hair tangled in his fingers as Alessio grabbed the back of her head and held her to him. Their lips fused as he plundered her mouth in time with the desperate plunge of their bodies.

Charlotte moaned, and he swallowed the sound.

He didn't understand how, but that felt every bit as intimate as the age-old dance of their striving bodies.

That sound, the taste of her on his tongue, the indescribable perfection of their thrusting bodies were too much. Alessio felt the surging rush of sensation from the back of his skull to his groin, knowing he couldn't wait any longer. But then it didn't matter because at last her spasming muscles signalled her climax, drawing him tighter, milking him into ecstasy.

His last thought was to hold her safe and tight against him as they leapt together into fiery oblivion.

Alessio hugged her to him as their thundering pulses finally slowed. How long he'd lain with Charlotte in his arms he didn't know. Just that he wasn't ready to relinquish the lingering remnants of bliss.

Finally he rolled onto his side and Charlotte with him so she lay facing him, their bodies still welded together.

Her hair was in disarray, her eyes closed, and those soft lips slightly swollen from the desperate way he'd plundered her mouth. It amazed him how touching his lips to hers had undone him when he'd been able to withstand earlier temptations.

Her skin was flushed and she'd never looked more alluring.

A tiny shudder rippled down his spine.

Her eyes opened in a flash of blue, brighter than any gem in the Dal Lago treasure vault.

'Are you all right, Charlotte?'

She blinked, that sweet mouth turning up. 'More than all right. I feel fabulous.'

The stirring guilt in his gut eased. It shouldn't have been him taking her innocence and initiating her into the world of erotic delights, but he'd done no immediate harm.

With relief came a rush of other feelings. He slid his hand to her hip, shaping that delicious arc, before sliding his fingers along her silky thigh.

'You absolutely do feel fantastic.'

Another ripple of sensation, except this time in a part of his anatomy that should be completely dormant after that stunning climax. Alessio's brows twitched in a perplexed frown.

Gently but firmly, because her hands clung, he withdrew before she could realise the effect she still had on him. He needed time to think.

Alessio headed to the bathroom to dispose of the condom. But instead of lingering to get his head straight, within minutes he was back in the bedroom, drawn by a force stronger than the need to master himself.

Charlotte lay on her side in exactly the same position as when he'd left, except she cuddled a pillow to her chest. Missing him? Something shifted in Alessio's chest.

Wearing that blissed-out smile, totally naked in his bed, she was irresistible. He moved the pillow and climbed in next to her, pulling her to him.

Instantly she shaped herself against him, one knee between his, a palm open on his chest, her other arm around his waist as she settled her head under his chin.

Alessio closed his eyes and savoured the sensation of body against body, the thrum of her heart against him, the gentle caress of her breath.

It felt peaceful. Special.

Only because you've had no physical contact with another person in over three years. This is just you relishing the comfort of an embrace.

But since when had he needed such comfort? As a kid he'd learned never to expect cuddles from absent parents intent on their pleasure-seeking lives. As an adult he enjoyed the company of lovers and friends but never *needed* anyone.

He was the one who comforted others, most notably Antonia. Though towards the end she'd avoided physical contact. His breathing stalled on acrid memories until gentle fingers smoothed along his chest as if massaging his reluctant lungs back into motion. As if Charlotte sensed his distress.

He allowed himself a moment's stillness to absorb the comfort of her touch, realising how rare it was.

How different from past experience.

Antonia had set a benchmark for him. He'd never been closer to any woman than her. Not because they'd fallen deeply in love as the world thought. The strength of their relationship had been a friendship built over years. They'd fallen into sex, becoming friends with benefits rather than soul mates. So that when the world fell apart, they'd drawn on that friendship and trust.

Not that it had been enough to save her.

'Are *you* all right, Alessio?'

He found Charlotte regarding him steadily and realised she'd quoted his own question back at him. There was something so genuine about her gaze that pierced too deep.

'Never better.' Yet her palm against his chest meant she felt his heart pounding.

Alessio didn't do vulnerable. He'd been trained from childhood to be self-sufficient and strong. So he followed a lifetime's training and took charge of the situation, changing the subject. 'Why me, Charlotte? Out of all the men you might have slept with?

No woman stayed a virgin until her midtwenties without good reason. Choosing to lose her virginity had to be a major decision.

It was only because they were so near and he watched so closely that he saw the minuscule change in her expression, the way her gaze darted away, then back again.

Despite the heat of their bodies against each other, he felt his bones frost. He knew that look.

Prevarication. Evasiveness.

She is about to lie.

Because, despite his warning earlier, she hoped for more than sex from him? That had been a problem when he was younger and not experienced enough to spell out his limits to potential lovers.

Was Charlotte hoping to tie him into a relationship?

Or perhaps use their boss-housekeeper situation and twist

what had happened into something ugly, hoping for a financial settlement?

Alessio had lived in the world, and a world driven by money, long enough to know anything was possible. He'd had more than his share of avaricious women target him for what they thought they could get. Even after Antonia's death, they'd tried to push their way into his life, or at least his bed. He felt sick at the idea Charlotte might be like that.

'I could ask the same, Alessio. Why me?'

Her voice grazed his skin, a reminder that, wary as he was, she still had the capacity to undermine his willpower with the siren call of sex.

The best sex of his life.

The thought startled him. And made him yet more determined to scotch any unwanted expectations on her part.

Alessio shrugged one shoulder and raised a deliberately provocative eyebrow. 'Presumably you know my reputation. I enjoy sex. How could I resist?'

Charlotte didn't even blink. Yet he felt her shrink in his hold. Twin streaks of colour slashed her cheekbones as her expression clouded.

'You make me sound like a sweet treat that caught your eye in a shop window,' she snapped.

Her chin angled up in that familiar way she had when he'd been particularly difficult. But this time he hadn't just been difficult, but insulting. He'd hurt her.

Because he'd stepped into the unknown and it scared him!

Remorse was bitter on his tongue. Whatever Charlotte's motivation, she deserved better.

'You're right. I apologise. That made it sound like what we shared, that *you*, were a commodity. That's anything but true. Tonight was special.'

Alessio halted, trying to find a line between the truth and maintaining his pride. In the end he gave up and admitted, 'I told you in the ballroom. I've wanted you for so long. Ever since you came here.' He forced himself to go on, making the truth his penance for hurting her. 'My reputation as a lover was in the past, Charlotte. You're the first woman I've been with in years.'

CHAPTER ELEVEN

THE FIRST WOMAN in years. In years!

Charlotte stared across the water at the racing boats, adorned with fluttering flags and elaborate decorations, but didn't really take them in, instead remembering Alessio's expression as he said she'd been his first lover in years.

Since his wife?

Charlotte assumed so but hadn't liked to ask.

For despite his gentle smile, as if making up for his harsh words immediately before, there'd been a starkness in the depths of those green eyes, a seemingly infinite pain that she couldn't probe.

Not because she didn't want to—her curiosity about Alessio was deeper than the rules of politeness. But because she didn't have the heart to dredge up more hurt.

She'd seen him stiffen and turn into the stony-faced feudal lord more than once last night when some gushing female offered saccharine sympathy for his wife's death. The sympathy might have been real, but so had been the avaricious curiosity and blatant sexual interest.

Charlotte had felt jealous and protective.

Her lips twisted. Alessio didn't need her to fight his battles. Most of the night he'd used charm like a weapon, leaving eager women in his wake while steering clear of cosy chats. It was only as the evening wore on that the severe autocrat had shown through the surface gloss when people got too close.

Charlotte shouldn't have had time to notice, but no matter how she'd tried to concentrate on her hostess duties, she'd found herself fixated on Alessio.

A grunt of harsh laughter escaped. What was new?

She'd been fixated on him since the day he'd stood, blocking her way up the beach with folded arms and something curiously like dismay in that stern, beautiful face. And after what they'd shared last night, not just the amazing sex, but the unexpectedly tender way he'd held her close until she fell exhausted into sleep, that fixation was only stronger.

'What's the matter? You're not enjoying the race?'

Charlotte pivoted to see Alessio's formidable great-aunt beside her. She wore couture fashion, a scarlet pantsuit and matching suede shoes, with the panache of a woman decades younger. The light caught stunning ruby earrings that made Charlotte think instantly of Alessio.

Again.

'I'm afraid I wasn't really paying attention.'

'No doubt you have a lot on your mind.' Gleaming black eyes met hers, and Charlotte had the unnerving conviction that the other woman saw right into her head. 'With the festival and such. Last night was a triumph but a lot of work. I know my great-nephew better than to expect he exerted himself over a ball.'

It was true. Alessio had left everything to Charlotte as a punishment for daring to challenge him. Yet indignation rose at hearing his relative say so.

'Actually, Alessio has been behind the success of today's festival. He's worked incredibly hard and took the lead in planning the events.'

The old woman lifted her eyebrows. '*Alessio*, eh, not the *Conte*? And so quick to jump to his defence.'

'I—'

'No, no, don't explain. There's no need. It's a relief to see him out in the world again, not just masterminding more business success from his tower but actually *engaging* with people.'

The softening in her expression stopped the words forming on Charlotte's tongue. For it revealed a depth of feeling that surprised her. Suddenly the other woman looked her age, lines of concern obvious in her features where before Charlotte had noticed only pride and determination.

'Would you like to sit?' she said. 'There are a couple of seats free in the shade over there.'

There was a crack of husky laughter. 'Worried about the old lady standing too long, are you?' But there was warmth in her gaze as she nodded. 'Sensible of you. These legs aren't as young as they used to be, and you could probably do with the rest too. I've seen you running around all day making sure everything goes well. You'll need your strength for the dancing later.'

Charlotte was about to respond that she wouldn't be dancing, but her companion wouldn't be interested in her plans to spend the evening cleaning the ballroom. That was something she felt guilty about deferring, though she'd had no choice in it.

Because you were too busy making love to Alessio.

Having sex, she corrected herself. Love didn't enter into it.

'Just as well you found seats in the shade,' the old woman's voice interrupted. 'You look quite flushed.'

Guiltily, Charlotte met the other woman's eyes and was almost sure she read amusement there. But she couldn't know...

'Ah, here they come. The last and most important race of the day. And there's my great-nephew.'

There was no mistaking the pride in her tone, and Charlotte felt any annoyance at the other woman's perspicacity fade. Dutifully she turned to see several long rowing boats emerging from around the point. At this distance, they looked a little like Venetian gondolas with sleek lines and raised prows, but with space for several rowers.

As they drew closer, she realised the bows were different.

Each had a figurehead. Charlotte saw a lion, a mermaid, a bear and even a unicorn with a rainbow-coloured mane. There was also a rather severe saint with a halo and, streaking up past the other boats, one whose figurehead was a green dragon, breathing fire.

It was the dragon she saw everywhere in the *castello* and which always made her think of Alessio. Not just the green of his eyes but the way his initial gruffness hid such fire.

That was his boat, of course. He was easily recognisable with his broad shoulders and athletic physique, pulling at the oars with enviable strength. The boat picked up speed, scudding past first one then another of the competitors and a huge cheer rose. Her companion leaned forward, as eager as the locals.

Another boat put on a burst of speed, almost matching Alessio's, and another group cheered rowdily.

All around people jumped to their feet, barracking for their favourite boat. Charlotte's heart was in her mouth as she urged Alessio's boat on, which was crazy because it was just a boat race. But something deeper than logic made her hope he'd win.

Because she wanted to see him smile?

Because he deserved something to celebrate after what she guessed were years of grief? Yet Charlotte thought Alessio would hate being the object of her sympathy.

When his boat sped across the winning line first, she was on her feet like the woman beside her.

A gnarled hand grasped hers. 'There. He always was a superb rower.' Then, as if suddenly aware that she'd grabbed Charlotte's hand, she moved back, and when she spoke again her voice was cool. 'I'm glad it was a team of islanders who won. No doubt he had the whole crew practising hard each morning.'

'He did. Morning and evening.'

'He always did take things seriously. When he commits to something there's no turning back.'

Yet she didn't make that sound like a positive thing.

The older woman sighed and slanted her an assessing look before saying softly, 'His wife died here, in the lake, you know. He didn't row for at least a year after that. Wouldn't go out on the water or swim. It's such a relief to see him active again.'

Charlotte stared, hearing the emotion in her companion's voice and seeing a bright glint that might even have been tears in those dark eyes. Her heart ached for Alessio, so grief-stricken by his wife's death, and for this old lady who clearly cared so much.

He wasn't the ogre he sometimes went out of his way to appear. Charlotte was more and more convinced that Alessio felt too much. He was a proud man battling demons by locking himself away with his grief.

Something deep inside her chest twisted savagely.

How much he must have loved his wife.

Charlotte had no experience of such love. Her father had viewed her mother's death is inconvenient rather than a tragedy. She'd grown up convinced that romantic love was a fantasy spruiked by poets and playwrights.

'Silly boy,' the old lady murmured. 'As if he'd have been able to stop her drowning even if he'd been here.'

Charlotte frowned. That didn't make sense. If Alessio had been here, surely he'd have been able to prevent the accident that took his wife's life? He was so confident on the water, she suspected he was a powerful swimmer.

She was about to ask for clarification when the other woman urged her down into the crowd to watch the victorious team come ashore, and the opportunity disappeared.

The incomers had all left the island and the sun had set when Alessio finally had an opportunity to be with Charlotte. All day there'd been so much to do, not just as the festival's official host, but as one of the islanders, participating like everyone else in the activities.

It had been a strain at times, but he'd found it strangely therapeutic, plunging back into the life of the island on the most raucous day of the year.

He'd caught Beatrice watching him more than once, a satisfied look on her lined face, but to her credit, she hadn't said 'I told you so' despite three years of nagging, trying to draw him out into the world again.

The trouble was that, while today had been satisfying, he still carried the terrible burden of guilt that nothing could erase.

Except being with Charlotte last night. You didn't feel guilty then. You felt alive in a way you hadn't done for years, even before you married Antonia.

The hairs on the back of his neck prickled. He told himself it was with shame that he should feel so much for a woman he hardly knew.

Yet it felt like he knew her. Not all the details of her family or her past, but at some visceral level, deeper than words.

He looked across the cobbled square, strung with lights and filled with islanders in colourful, festive clothes, dancing to live music. He located her easily. All day he'd been able to sense unerringly where she was, no matter how thick the crowd.

Alessio's belly tightened as something rose inside him. Desire, yes, but more too. Need? Possessiveness? Relief?

She danced with Mario's ne'er-do-well great-nephew, her golden hair flying free around her shoulders as her red summer dress flared around her legs.

Charlotte looked fresh and pretty in that casual dress. The first sight of her in it this morning had dried Alessio's mouth. He'd wanted to hustle her back to his room and lock the door to keep her to himself.

But he'd had obligations, and she'd been looking forward to the festivities.

Who is this woman?

She seemed equally at home acting as chatelaine in a castle as mixing with this tight-knit community. She took Beatrice in stride, mixed easily with Europe's elite yet had been a sexual innocent. She had the backbone to stand up to Alessio, yet at other times she fitted perfectly into the role of discreet housekeeper.

He'd seen the appreciative and speculative looks she'd received last night. No doubt having her as his hostess would ignite a whole new round of gossip, but Alessio didn't care what the world thought. He was too busy puzzling her out for himself.

That English banker last night had recognised her, not as a housekeeper at a Swiss hotel, but as a guest at exclusive society events in Britain.

Alessio had been determined to get to the bottom of that last night and demand answers from her. But when he'd farewelled the last of his guests and turned to Charlotte, he'd been sidetracked by need.

And it hadn't dimmed. Last night had been intense, but if he'd hoped it would cure him of this burning hunger, he'd been mistaken. His need had merely intensified.

Alessio shouldered his way through the dancers as the music died. He'd done his duty, dancing at this final event just for locals with everyone from eighty-year-old Rosetta to fourteen-year-old Sonia. Now it was *his* turn.

As arranged with the band, the final tune of the night was a slow number. He reached for Charlotte. 'My dance,' he growled.

Her young partner read Alessio's expression and melted away.

'You scared him off.' Her gaze challenged him, yet she moved eagerly into his embrace. Alessio felt himself finally relax.

'He'll get over it.' Alessio didn't have sympathy to spare, not when he'd spent the whole day bereft of Charlotte in his arms.

Years of celibacy—that had to be the reason for this craving.
Yet he wasn't sure the explanation was so simple.

He pulled her to him, uncaring of curious eyes, knowing that he needed these moments with her pressed close, her body moving with his. A reward for all he'd endured, facing the public again, pretending all was right in his world.

Except he discovered to his surprise that things hadn't been as onerous as expected. He'd enjoyed a lot of today. Especially when he'd looked up and caught Charlotte smiling at him and felt anticipation sear through him.

'You've enjoyed yourself?'

Her smile was wide and unstinting, hitting Alessio's chest like a shaft of sunlight. 'Absolutely. It's been marvellous. The music, the people, the food. Congratulations on winning the boat race, by the way. That was impressive.'

He shrugged and held her closer. 'We had a good team.'

'Today's market seemed successful too, don't you think?'

'It was. Very.' He paused. 'Thank you, Charlotte. It mightn't always seem like it, but I appreciate what you've done here. Making me see what I should have noticed long before.'

She shook her head. '*You're* the one who's made the difference. You're the one who got the festival off the ground.'

Only because she'd forced him out of his eyrie and back into his community.

The music ended to applause and cheers, and Alessio forced himself to release Charlotte. He turned in response to calls for a speech and found his fingers tangling with hers. He tightened his grip for an instant before forcing himself to let go. But the touch of her hand stayed with him as he closed the festival. He didn't rush, acknowledging everyone involved while nodding and smiling in response to the crowd's thanks.

They deserved thanks too for their understanding and forbearance over the last couple of years. He might have been in a dark place, but he'd had no right to curtail their celebrations.

Seeing them all in holiday mode today had brought home to him in stark clarity how self-absorbed he'd been.

'You're very quiet.' Charlotte said as they approached the *castello* together, a careful arm's length apart.

Alessio turned and caught her expression. Reserved. Impenetrable. Like when she'd been simply his housekeeper. As if they'd never been intimate. As if she hadn't given him her virginity and more besides. It felt like she'd ignited a light in the darkness of his soul that, once lit, still glowed brightly.

The idea of her retreating appalled him. Last night had changed things in so many ways, and despite the complications that brought, he couldn't wish it undone. For good or ill, they'd embarked on an affair, and he wasn't ready for it to end.

'It's been an eventful day.'

Alessio pushed open the big door and gestured for her to precede him. Once inside he bolted it, feeling a stab of satisfaction that finally they were alone.

But when he turned, Charlotte had moved away, not quite meeting his eyes as she spoke. 'I suppose I'd better make a start on the ballroom.'

'Because it bothers your efficient heart to think of it not gleaming?' He paced towards her, watching her eyes widen as they locked on his. 'Do you have a secret cleaning fetish? Or is it an excuse to avoid being alone with me?'

He stopped before her, reading her answer in her face. She was unsure of herself, and suddenly Alessio was remembering how it had felt last night as her first lover.

A carnal shudder ran down his spine and shot through his belly to his groin. He knew now that this sparking heat between them was new to her. For that matter, it felt unique to him.

'I want you, Charlotte. Still. More.' His voice was a rumbling note deep in his chest. 'Last night wasn't enough for me. But if you don't feel the same, I won't pester you—'

'No! It's not that.' She planted one hand over his quick-thudding heart. 'I wondered if last night was a one-off and today we'd return to our normal lives. We agreed to something brief.'

'Brief, yes, but not that brief.' The idea of not having her again was impossible.

She surveyed him solemnly, her expression at odds with the way she leaned in, and it took everything he had not to sweep her into his arms.

'It's your decision, Charlotte.' He still had some scruples left.

'So you won't object if I walk away.' He stifled a groan. He'd been so sure she wanted him still. 'My head says I should,' she whispered, 'but...'

She moved then, lifting her mouth to his. Instantly he hauled her close. Lightning sheeted through him. His blood sizzled, and the erection stretching his trousers was instantaneous as their bodies pressed and all that feminine softness strained against him.

But more than that was the wave of relief that engulfed him. Alessio had waited all day for this. Even pulling at the oars of a racing boat or welcoming dignitaries to the events, at least half his mind had been on Charlotte and the need to hold her, have her.

He slid his fingers through her silky hair, cradling the back of her skull as he leaned into the kiss. She opened her mouth eagerly, drawing him in and stroking her tongue against his with barely a hint of the sweet clumsiness that had intrigued him last night. As if it wasn't just sex but kissing that was new.

That thought finally made him break the kiss. Though he almost changed his mind at the way Charlotte lifted her head to follow his mouth with hers. Heat doused him and his hands shook as he gently held her away. This woman undid him so easily.

All the more reason to set some ground rules.

She pouted up at him, almost undoing his resolve. 'Alessio?'

'Soon, *cara*.' He couldn't resist stroking that sensuous bottom lip with his thumb, pressing it open and then swooping down for another kiss, swift but ravaging. He heard her tiny moan, and it sent a thrill of temptation winding through his body till he almost forgot his good intentions. It was only as he felt his hands shaping her buttocks, lifting her off her feet and up against his erection, that he realised what he was doing.

Rather than release her, Alessio compromised, wrapping her close and carrying her into the nearest room. It was a formal salon, antique furniture upholstered in pale green silk. He walked stiff-legged across the honey-coloured parquetry and lowered her, centimetre by delectable centimetre, down his throbbing body.

Someone gasped. Her hands clutched, and he gave in. Instead of sitting beside her on the long lounge, he sank onto it and drew her onto his lap, his arm around her back, her breast snug against his chest.

'We need to talk,' he said.

Talking was the last thing he wanted.

'Go on.'

'I need to know exactly what you want, Charlotte.' He needed to be sure she didn't feel pressured.

A smile he could only describe as lascivious unfurled across those pink lips and made his erection pulse against her buttocks. Her eyes rounded in shock, amusing him but at the same time damping his arousal. Because it was a reminder of her inexperience against his.

Was he taking advantage?

Alessio loosened his arms, but it was beyond him to move away. He wasn't a saint. He was a sinner through and through. Despite her inexperience, despite being her employer, he craved her with every particle of his newly awakened libido.

A shadow passed over his heart as he looked into Charlotte's clear, questioning eyes. What was he doing, even thinking of an affair with her?

'What do I want? That's easy,' she said in a husky voice that twisted his gut inside out. 'I want *you*, Alessio. I want more of what we did last night.'

A delicate blush coloured her cheeks, but her look was direct.

Alessio shut his eyes, a prayer of thanks forming in his head when he couldn't remember the last time he'd prayed.

'I think we can arrange that.' As if he wasn't already fighting the need to ravish her out of that red dress and lose himself in her sweet body. Heat drenched his skin as he imagined it.

'But we need to set some boundaries,' Charlotte said, dragging him back from his eager thoughts.

He inclined his head. 'I agree.'

'You first,' Charlotte said. Her tongue cleaved to the roof of her mouth at the way he devoured her with his eyes, but this was important, and she strove to concentrate even as she shifted on his lap, relishing the feel of his rigid shaft beneath her buttocks. Had she really taken all that length inside her last night? The thought made the muscles inside clench needily. 'What boundaries?'

'I told you I can only offer sexual pleasure.'

She nodded, biting off the impulse to admit he'd done that to perfection.

He didn't need her gushing about his sexual prowess. He knew the effect he had on her.

'I want more than a single night.' His voice ground deliciously low, and she felt her nipples peak in response. 'I want an affair.' Sea-green eyes held hers, and she wanted to dive into those depths and lose herself in the tide of passion rising through her body. 'But I can't offer more than that.' He frowned down at her as if to make sure she heard every word. 'Not *won't* but *can't*, Charlotte. That's never going to be an option.'

Because he's still in love with his dead wife.

Hadn't his great-aunt said as much?

Charlotte had known it, yet having it spelled out made some fragile, barely formed hope sink like a pebble tossed into deep water.

'But I don't want to take advantage of you. If you don't want that, I promise not to touch you again.'

The jut of his clenched jaw and his febrile gaze told her that while Alessio would be as good as his word, it would be difficult for him. Silly how wonderful that made her feel. 'Or if you prefer to leave now, I'll write you a glowing reference for the work you've already done, and not stand in your way.'

'So,' she said slowly, moistening dry lips and feeling heat explode in her pelvis at the way his eyes followed the movement. 'My choices are hot sex with you for however long this attraction lasts. Maybe a week or—'

'Months.' His voice, thick with desire, made her feel more confident. 'It will take a while to satiate this.'

'Or I could get up and walk away now and never have you touch me again.'

Appalling how desperate that made her feel. She could no more turn her back on Alessio than she could scale the Matterhorn.

'Guess which I choose.' She lost herself in those mesmerising eyes. 'I want more too. I've got a lot to learn, and you're just the man to teach me.'

The subtle shift in his expression, the flare of aristocratic nostrils and the softening of his taut mouth, told her he wanted this as much as she did.

'But I have my own plans, and they don't include being known as a rich man's mistress.' She felt him stiffen, his eyes turning unfathomable. 'My reputation is important to me. I can't have it damaged by gossip that I'm sleeping with my employer.' No matter how much she wanted Alessio. 'Acting as your hostess last night probably already set tongues wagging.'

'You're right. I'm sorry.' Concern furrowed his brow. 'I'll do what I can to scotch any rumours. As for our relationship,

I'll take every precaution to keep it private. There'll be no more dancing together at local fêtes.'

Charlotte felt a pang of loss. How wonderful it would be simply to enjoy this extraordinary attraction. To be carefree, not fretting over what others thought or where this might lead.

But it couldn't lead anywhere.

She sat straighter. 'Venice is calling, and I'm not looking for a long-term partner.'

Work had been her salvation and she clung to its security—the only security she'd known since her mother died. Her goal was to run her own upmarket guest house. Working in other people's hotels wasn't enough. She wanted to use the hostessing skills she'd learned from her mother to create a warm, intimate atmosphere in her own home that guests would come back for again and again.

'That makes you different to most women I know.' He paused, his look searching. 'Did something bad happen, Charlotte? Something that put you off sex?'

She blinked, stunned at his perspicacity. No one else had picked up on her reserve around intimacy.

No one else knew you were a virgin until last night. Strange how with Alessio, she'd been anything but reserved.

'Nothing I couldn't cope with.' It was only half a lie, but she didn't want to talk about it. She'd got away with a torn dress and badly shaken nerves. And a mistrust she'd never lost. 'Other than meeting too many men out for what they can get, who don't care who they trample in the process.' She met his arrested stare and hurried on. 'I didn't mean—'

'It's okay, Charlotte. I understand.' Another pause as he surveyed her intently. 'A guest last night recognised you, said he'd met you at a spectacular party in an English mansion. But you weren't working. You were one of the guests.'

Instinctively Charlotte pulled away, except his strong arm still encircled her. 'You think I'm some imposter?'

His gaze pinioned her. 'I simply think there's a lot more

to you than you let on. Last night you fitted in as if you'd attended balls for years. Don't tell me it's because you're used to meeting guests. It was more than that.'

Charlotte's skin prickled. She had nothing to hide, yet it felt like she'd been caught out in a lie. 'My parents were wealthy,' she said eventually, 'and they liked to entertain. I attended a lot of formal events.'

'They're dead? My condolences.'

'My mother died, but my father's very much alive.' She lifted tight shoulders. 'We're not in contact.' Still Alessio regarded her. 'I don't want to talk about him.'

'Okay.' Alessio pulled her close, and suddenly thoughts of her father and the past fled as she responded to the promise of his virile body. He planted his palm on her thigh and heat drenched her, moisture blooming at her feminine core. 'I'm sure we can find other things to discuss.'

Instantly unhappy memories were replaced by urgent physical need. Charlotte embraced it eagerly. Never had she known anything so perfect as being with Alessio.

In some distant part of her mind, a warning clanged, but then Alessio's hand slid under her dress to inch up her thigh, and caution died as bliss beckoned.

CHAPTER TWELVE

BEYOND ALESSIO'S BROAD SHOULDERS, she caught the pink glow of dawn streaming into his room. But then he moved down her body, peppering a line of kisses from her breast to her navel, across to her hip, before sinking between her open thighs.

Charlotte gasped, body arching, electrified by the devastating touch of his tongue. They'd been lovers nearly a month, and he still made her feel like it was the first time again with all its wonder and power.

She trembled as he settled deeper, one hand beneath her bottom, lifting her into his caress, the other splayed across her thigh in what felt to her bemused brain like possessiveness.

Like the way, even in sleep, he anchored her to him.

Like the gleaming look in his eye every time she emerged from a swim to find him waiting on the beach with her towel, ready to rub her dry before carrying her indoors to the nearest sofa and having his wicked way with her.

Wicked, that's what it was, to make a woman so blissed out she couldn't think.

He'd indolently lean against the doorjamb, watching her make the bed, then saunter over and tumble her onto it, saying he was so turned on from watching her he couldn't resist.

She loved it all. Loved *this*. The rising tide of excitement as her body thundered towards fulfilment, the feel of his silky hair in her clutching hands and his abrasive morning stubble against her inner thighs. How his eyes held hers, watching her tumble towards ecstasy.

Charlotte shuddered, overcome by the enormity of it all. And the need not to be alone as he drove her to climax.

'Alessio!' It was a gasp so hoarse she wasn't sure the sound registered. 'I need you with me.'

He rose on hands and knees, prowling up her body, a magnificent predator. Except his eyes held something more than sexual hunger.

As he closed the gap between them, blocking the dawn light with his broad shoulders, her throat clogged. She had no name for the expression he wore, yet it filled her with something profound. Tenderness, a sense of belonging and connection at the deepest level.

Her heart rolled over.

'Charlotte.' He made her name sound like a welcome and a prayer as she opened her arms, drawing him down.

This was what she adored above everything else. His weight on her. The oneness as he sank into her. She was so aroused physically but also emotionally. This felt...

She squeezed her eyes shut, fighting the hot prickle of tears that had nothing to do with pain or distress but came from being completely overwhelmed.

A calloused palm cupped her check. Alessio's warm breath on her face was a benediction. '*Cara*, look at me.'

She did, seeing the familiar excitement melded with an affection that echoed her feelings.

'I'm all right,' she whispered before he could question her. 'Just a little...overwhelmed. I need you, Alessio.'

She wrapped her arms around him, one hand on his taut buttock, the other around the satiny, hot skin of his back.

Better that he think her response purely physical than guess her tangled emotions.

'It's okay.' Slowly he moved, thrusting deep and creating a

heavenly symphony of delight. 'I've got you, *tesoro*. I'll look after you.'

Her smile was wobbly, and then it disappeared altogether as their bodies quickened, taking up that now familiar, triumphant tempo that led them both into bliss. They stayed wrapped in each other's arms, riding out the wonder of it, locked together as if nothing could ever separate them.

Even when it was over, neither moved. Their hearts thundered in tandem, their desperate breaths in sync, sharing shudders of ecstasy as they came back to the real world together.

Except the real world had changed, she realised.

Nothing would ever be the same.

It changed the moment you met him.
The moment you gave yourself to him.
The moment you fell for him.

Charlotte closed her eyes, as if that way she could avoid the truth. But she was in Alessio's arms, tucked close, her favourite place in the world.

She breathed deep, inhaling the spicy scent that she'd associate with him forever. Warm, male skin, cedarwood and something exotic like frankincense. And the primal scent of sex.

Except in her case she feared it wasn't mere sex. It was love.

She'd never expected that to happen. Not after seeing her parents' unhappy marriage and the way so many men treated women as disposable assets, available for their convenience.

Yet although Alessio had made it abundantly clear this could only be a short-term liaison, he'd given her far more than she expected. The sex was brilliant, energising, satisfying, addictive. At the same time he gave her respect and consideration. Plus his tenderness was beyond price.

Far from being an ogre or uncaring playboy, she suspected this man had a heart bigger than he let on. He was caring and thoughtful but seemed determined not to let anyone, apart from those on the island who'd known him forever, realise it.

Because he'd been hurt. Was still hurting.

She wanted to heal him.

She didn't want to leave in another month. She had a horrible feeling it might break her heart.

How had it come to this?

Yearning for the impossible, for a man still in love with his dead wife.

A sound of distress escaped, and instantly he stroked her hair. 'Charlotte?'

She gathered herself and opened her eyes, forcing a smile. 'You're a little heavy.' He wasn't. His body covering hers was bliss, but it was the only excuse she could think of.

Instantly he rolled onto his side, hugging her close. 'Sorry. I should have moved.' He paused. 'Are you sure you're all right?'

There it was again. Concern. An awareness of her emotions that she'd never encountered in anyone else. She needed to change the subject because she couldn't talk about her feelings. She was too churned up.

'I've never been better.'

She slanted him what she hoped was a mischievous smile though she couldn't meet his eyes. Quickly she looked away, hoping for inspiration. Her gaze landed on a small, very old painting that had fascinated her from the moment she saw it. Like the one downstairs, it showed a creature that looked like a cross between a dragon and a sea serpent, its coiling tail encircling a beautiful woman.

'What is it with your family and dragons, Alessio? I know there was supposed to be a local monster, but they're everywhere in the *castello*.'

He shifted as if settling more comfortably. 'You don't know the story?' He stroked her hair, and some of her tension eased. She shook her head.

'My family have dominated this region for centuries, so long that they've come to represent the place. Legend is that there was a monster in the lake, and the people would appease it by giving it something precious every year. One year instead of the best fruits of the harvest or gold and jewels, for some reason they offered a beautiful blonde virgin. They left her on this island for the monster to take.'

Charlotte shuddered. 'I don't like this story.'

A laugh rumbled up from his chest beneath her ear. 'Don't worry, it ends well. The official version is that a saint saved her by killing the monster and setting her free. There's a monastery dedicated to him on an island at the far end of the lake.

'But the *real* story is told by the locals. They say the dragon was actually the Conte Dal Lago, the rapacious baron who ruled with an iron fist and took whatever he wanted. Until he met his match, in the form of a golden-haired virgin.'

Charlotte's eyes met Alessio's.

Stupid, the way her heart leapt. At the weird coincidence that she was blonde and had been a virgin when they met. And because part of her yearned for the Conte Dal Lago to claim her as his, not for a brief affair, but for life.

Because you want Alessio more than you've ever wanted anything.

More than the career that had been her salvation when she'd lost her mother and cut herself adrift from her father. More than the independence she'd thought her greatest asset.

But life was no fairy tale.

'It doesn't sound like a match made in heaven. If he were used to taking whatever he wanted, he probably grew tired of her once the novelty wore off. And she didn't have much choice in it, did she?' She gave Alessio a smile she hoped was coolly amused. 'Just as well it's a myth.'

Alessio frowned, not sharing her brittle amusement. He regarded her intently as if seeing something in her expression that she'd hoped wasn't there.

Charlotte turned towards the bright daylight streaming through the windows. 'It's later than I thought. I need to shower and get moving.'

She leaned across and pressed her lips to his, savouring his welcoming kiss, knowing this was a short-term privilege that would end all too soon.

When she pulled away, she avoided his eyes. 'If you don't mind, I won't join you for breakfast. I have to meet some suppliers.'

She was out of the bed before he could answer, hurrying towards the bathroom.

Which meant she didn't see Alessio's assessing look.

Charlotte had been like a cat on hot bricks all day.

Whenever Alessio tracked her down, it was to discover her bustling off to some new task. At first he'd thought she was disturbed by the continued speculation about her in the media. The world seemed fascinated by his mysterious, glamorous hostess. When he'd mentioned that, she'd shrugged it off. Yet it felt like she avoided him, always with a good excuse.

Alessio was edgy. Something had happened this morning. Something that felt like an invisible wedge driven between them. He'd seen and felt her withdrawal even as he held her in his arms.

It had been...disquieting.

Even if his saner self said that was a good thing. Better that Charlotte didn't grow comfortable in this relationship.

Because it had to end.

Strangely, instead of bringing relief, the thought made Alessio's gut spasm.

As if he didn't like the idea of Charlotte leaving.

He wasn't ready for her to withdraw, much less leave. The suspicion that *she'd* have no regrets about going unsettled him.

Which was why midafternoon found him searching for her, only to pull up short, his heart beating a sickening rhythm when he discovered where she was.

Alessio stopped in the doorway of the sunny room, stiff fingers clutching the doorjamb, stomach churning.

'Alessio!'

She put down a duster and smiled. But only for an instant because then he saw it again—her withdrawal—as if she put up an invisible barrier.

Something sour exploded on his tongue. Disappointment? Loss?

'What are you doing in here?' Her eyes widened at his brusque tone, and he tried to temper it. 'There's no need to clean here. The room's not used.'

The empty nursery mocked him. He hadn't been here in three years. The sight of it unleashed regret and pain.

He watched Charlotte's gaze travel from the picture books that had never been read to the pristine cot and the rocking chair where he'd last seen Antonia, curled up in a ball of misery.

He drew a shuddering breath, fighting memories.

'I'm sorry, Alessio.' Charlotte approached him, regret and understanding in her eyes as she reached for him. 'This must be hard for you. I—'

He jerked his arm away. 'You think I need your sympathy?' His voice was sharp like the brittle darkness inside him. It was easier to lash out than let himself think. 'You presume too much!'

He stepped back, dropping his arm from the doorjamb, but the miasma followed, clouding his thoughts and tainting the air. When it cleared, Alessio saw she'd paled, her body rigid.

The churning in his belly intensified, but this time with self-disgust. 'Charlotte...' He crossed the threshold, but she recoiled and he slammed to a stop.

It wasn't just shock in her eyes—it was hurt. He'd wounded her because she'd glimpsed his pain and regret. And because, after the happiness they'd shared, the sudden bleak memories felt overwhelming.

What did that make him? When had he become a man who'd hurt someone whose only crime was to care? Not just anybody, but his lover. A woman who brought him pleasure and a measure of peace and joy he'd never expected to experience again.

His heart slammed against his ribs and shame thickened his throat. 'I'm sorry, Charlotte. You didn't deserve that.' Still she stood, unmoving and wary. Alessio almost wished she'd berate him. Her silent appraisal scoured him to the bone. 'I've hurt you, and I'd do anything I could to undo that.'

He drew a breath and found himself saying something totally unexpected. 'Can we go somewhere and talk about it?'

Eventually she nodded, and he led her to a window seat at the end of the corridor looking out over the lake. He waited till she was seated beside him, ankles crossed primly and hands clasped in her lap, but he read the tension in her narrow shoulders. He wanted to hug her to him for his own sake as well as hers, but he didn't have the right after the way he'd ripped up at her.

Alessio scraped his hand around the back of his neck, trying to ease rigid muscles. 'You're right. It was hard, being in the nursery. I haven't gone through that door in three years. I should be thanking you for noticing and caring, not attacking you.' He met her dark blue gaze and let the truth out. 'I've got in the habit of pushing people away, especially sympathetic ones.' He shrugged. 'In the past most of them had an agenda, to get the gory details of my marriage to share with others or to insinuate themselves into my life for their own ends.'

It was amazing how blatant some women had been, offering physical intimacy supposedly to ease his wounded heart. But he'd read the avaricious glitter in their eyes.

'You don't think I...?'

'No!' He covered her hands with one of his and felt something inside him ease when she didn't pull away. 'Not for a second. That's why my reaction was unfair. I knew you saw my pain, and that made me feel...vulnerable.' His mouth curled in a tight smile. 'I've spent years telling myself I don't do vulnerable.'

'So you attacked instead.' Her voice was unreadable.

'I'm appalled, because I know you genuinely care. You've got no hidden agenda, and I know how rare that is.' Maybe that's why this affair felt different to anything he'd experienced. 'Obviously you've guessed some of what happened.'

Her fingers twitched beneath his, but she didn't pull away, and he felt himself relax a little. Charlotte was, he realised, the first person he'd reached for, emotionally or physically, in a long, long time.

'You and your wife hoped to have a child.'

'Antonia, my wife was Antonia.' How long since he'd spoken her name aloud? 'She spent so much time and effort designing the nursery. It had to be perfect.' And it gave her a distraction from other things.

Alessio looked at his hand joined with Charlotte's, fascinated that such a simple touch should feel so good. He met her eyes and read understanding and sincerity. He could trust her not to share his secrets.

'We weren't just hoping for a baby. Antonia was pregnant.' He felt Charlotte's jolt of surprise. 'That's why we married.'

'I see,' she said carefully.

No, she didn't, but it was enough to explain about the baby without discussing his marriage.

He and Antonia had been friends for years and occasional lovers, but as soon as she found herself pregnant, both had wanted to bring up their child as part of a family. Both had wanted to be better parents than theirs had been.

'We left Rome and settled here because it was quieter.' That was true as far as it went. For a second, Alessio contemplated blurting out the whole story to Charlotte. But he wouldn't burden her with that.

Her hand turned in his, squeezing. 'It would be a great place to bring up a child.'

Alessio shrugged. 'We hoped so. My memories of growing up here are mixed. My parents were the absentee type, but I loved the lake and the people here.' He paused. 'But it's academic. The baby died. Antonia miscarried.'

Charlotte covered his hand now with hers, her touch solid and comforting. 'I'm so sorry.'

Just that. Nothing about trying to imagine how he'd felt or some platitude about time healing. Yet Alessio felt his wound-too-tight grief ease just a little. Grief for their unborn child and for Antonia. Even for himself.

'Thank you,' he said eventually, his tongue thick. 'I haven't talked about it. Only a few people knew...'

'I won't tell anyone.'

That's not what he'd meant. It had been a simple statement of fact. Maybe Beatrice was right and he should have found a grief counsellor. Alessio couldn't imagine discussing his private life, and Antonia's, with a paid stranger.

Yet talking with Charlotte felt natural.

'Thank you.' He squeezed her hands, then withdrew his. It wouldn't do to grow too accustomed to her ready sympathy. Though it was harder than expected to pull away. 'My anger in the nursery was misdirected. I—'

'It's okay, Alessio. I think I understand. You were hurting, and you lashed out.'

'You make me sound like a toddler having a tantrum.'

Her mouth curved in a crooked, tender smile that shot a dart of longing right through him. Not longing for sex but for Charlotte in his arms, making him feel as if, for once, things would be all right.

Hell! He *was* like a needy child. Maybe the toddler analogy was right.

'We all have our moments.'

He met her understanding look and wondered about Charlotte's emotional moments.

She was remarkably poised, with a sangfroid many public figures would envy. It was only when they made love, or danced, or laughed together, that she revealed the warm, vivacious woman he'd always suspected lurked behind the professional image. She was so contained, rarely giving a hint about her past. Curiosity consumed him. He needed to *know* Charlotte in more than the carnal sense.

It was something he'd never felt about any previous lover except Antonia. But that was because they'd agreed to share their lives. Yet his feelings for Charlotte weren't like what he'd felt for his wife.

Thankfully. He'd never marry again. He shuddered, remembering the fraught drama of it all. The loss of control. The never-ending guilt.

It was definitely time to change the subject. He'd satisfied Charlotte's curiosity. Now it was her turn.

Unable to resist any longer, he reached for her hand, threading his fingers through hers, enjoying the way they fitted together despite their differing sizes.

'Tell me something important about yourself, Charlotte. Something from your past.'

'Because you shared a secret with me?'

Alessio met her steady look. 'No. Because I want to understand you.'

There it was again, the feeling that Alessio *saw* her. That she *mattered*.

It was tempting to read too much into that. The reality was probably that Alessio was uncomfortable talking about his painful past and wanted to change the subject. Yet as their gazes meshed, it didn't feel like that.

What did she have to lose? It wasn't as if she had a guilty secret. 'What you want to know?'

'Tell me about your family, about your father.'

She must've flinched, for Alessio gently squeezed her hand. 'You go straight for the jugular, don't you? No wonder you're so successful in business.'

'The last thing I want is to hurt you, Charlotte. But I suspect I'm not the only one who might benefit from a listening ear.'

Was it that obvious? Charlotte had thought she'd done an excellent job of getting over her past.

Except she'd let it colour so much of her life. She hadn't returned to England in all these years. She'd never dated, much less taken a lover until Alessio. She'd never trusted a man enough to let him into her life.

At least with Alessio she knew he wasn't scheming for anything apart from her body. She admired his honesty even if she found herself wanting more.

Yet he was grieving for his wife and child. She couldn't expect more from him. He might have married Antonia for their baby, but he was so distraught it was clear he'd fallen in love with her. Her heart squeezed, remembering his expression of stark loss.

Charlotte curled her fingers around his, drawing strength. 'There's not much to tell. I adored my mother and despised my father. I haven't seen him since she died.'

'Do you miss home?'

The sharp, hollowing sensation in her chest was instantaneous. 'I miss the home I used to have, but it doesn't exist any more.'

'It's been sold?'

She met his concerned stare and felt annoyed with herself. The man had just spoken of the most intimate personal tragedy. Her past was nowhere near as traumatic, yet here she was, hoarding her misery as if it were unique.

'No.' She gathered her thoughts. 'My mother was the last of an aristocratic family and lived on a country estate. She was on the point of selling up when she married my father. He was a businessman with pretensions to grandeur. Acquiring a country pile where he could entertain distinguished guests with an aristocratic hostess helped him climb the social ladder. As for my mother, she'd been desperate to save the estate not just for herself but for the tenants and employees. My father's money accomplished that.'

Alessio nodded.

'Most of my childhood I was happy. I loved the estate and my mother, and my father was away a lot.'

'We have that in common. I rarely saw my parents.' Another revelation from Alessio. What had happened to the taciturn man she'd first met? 'Sorry. I shouldn't have interrupted. Go on.'

'There's not much to tell. My father is a bombastic bully. He demanded absolute obedience from everyone, and if he didn't get it instantly, you paid dearly.'

Alessio's voice was sharp. 'He was violent?'

'Not physically. He had other ways of hurting people.' Though the last time she'd seen him, he'd been so apoplectic with rage she'd half-expected physical assault. 'My mother ran a stable. One day I badly disappointed my father.' It was something she'd done often, not getting the right marks in school, not making friends with the right people, not being nice enough to his slimy friends. 'The next day when she went there, she discovered her horses gone. They'd been packed up in the night to be sold without her knowledge. She'd bred some of them herself.' It had almost broken her heart, and Charlotte had been distraught with guilt.

Alessio muttered something in Italian that sounded like a curse. 'He controlled you through your mother?'

'And vice versa. My mother put up with a lot for my sake.' Too much. 'Then, suddenly she died. One day she was fine, and the next she had an aneurysm and died instantly.'

'I'm sorry.' He moved closer, putting his arm around her, and Charlotte leaned in. 'That must have been appalling.'

She nodded. 'I still miss her.'

After a few moments he said, 'Without your mother, there was no one to protect you.'

Charlotte shook her head. 'I was seventeen. I protected

myself.' She sat straighter. 'That was the year he introduced me to the man he wanted me to marry. A man with the right pedigree and business connections that would help him. I was supposed to be especially nice to him, but the guy was like my father. He thought other people existed for his convenience. Including me.'

Alessio's arm tightened. 'He must have got a shock when he realised you wouldn't stand for that.'

She lifted her head, noting the glint in his eyes and the grim set of his jaw. He looked angry. On her behalf.

Her throat closed. At seventeen she'd been out of her depth and terrified when her would-be fiancé tried to force her into sex.

What wouldn't she have given for Alessio by her side then? But she'd managed alone.

Charlotte stifled the realisation she didn't want to manage alone any longer. That knowledge threw her, making her blurt out more than she'd intended.

'It wasn't pleasant, but I managed. I ended up with a badly torn dress and bruises to my wrists, but he needed to have his nose reset. Needless to say, the business deal didn't go through.' She paused. 'That's why I never dated. I...'

'You don't need to explain, Charlotte.' He lifted her hand and pressed a kiss to her knuckles that softened every tense muscle. 'I'm sorry you had to defend yourself in that way. I'm sorry your own father caused so much pain.'

He paused, his expression full of an emotion she couldn't read. 'You are a remarkable woman, a strong and valiant woman. One I'm proud to know.'

Strong? She'd always tried to be. But now her feelings for Alessio had grown far deeper than sexual attraction.

Looking into his eyes, she feared she might not be strong enough to cope with leaving him.

CHAPTER THIRTEEN

CHARLOTTE WALKED DOWN the cobbled street, barely taking in her picturesque surroundings. Not because she'd grown too accustomed to the quaint lakeside town, but because her world had just slipped off its axis.

She blinked against the bright sunlight, pausing outside a shop that sold beautifully wrapped nougat and boxes of almond biscotti. In the window she saw her reflection. Wearing a blue summer dress and with her hair down, she looked like any carefree tourist.

Except she was anything but carefree.

Days ago she'd recognised her feelings for Alessio had deepened into love. That had scared and thrilled her, for she'd had no expectation of and precious little experience of love. And while Alessio was clearly capable of deep love and loyalty, she knew she couldn't take Antonia's place in his affections.

Alessio had been at pains to ensure Charlotte understood he could offer only sex. She'd gone into the affair with her eyes open.

Except he'd unwittingly given her far more than sex. His passion, respect, tenderness, even the challenges he set her, had given her something unexpected. A belief in her own value. Confirmation of what she'd told herself for years but never completely believed. She'd spent too long listening to her father's putdowns, then feeling cheapened by the appalling situation that last year at home.

Alessio made her feel strong, proud and sexy. A woman who had the right to demand whatever she wanted from the world, or a lover.

Charlotte drew a shuddery breath as tingles of excitement and anxiety rippled through her.

There was only one lover she wanted, and he was already spoken for.

He was in love with his dead wife.

No matter what she wanted from him, there could be no future with Alessio. Or could there?

She turned and started walking. Her boat to the island was due to leave soon.

But she wasn't ready to return. She felt numb, her brain whizzing in too many directions at once. She needed time away from the island, away from Alessio, to think and decide what to do, because her life had changed irrevocably. Whenever she was with him, it was too tempting to believe in happy-ever-afters instead of cold, hard reality.

She'd talk to the boatman and negotiate a later ride back.

Slipping on her sunglasses, she stepped into the piazza, surrounded on three sides by shops and restaurants and on the fourth by the lake. Instinctively she paused, taking in the gorgeous scene, the holidaymakers in bright colours milling around under the trees, the outdoor tables filling and the sun glinting off the water. And across the water L'Isola del Drago.

How she'd miss it. Miss *him*.

'Charlotte.'

She turned and there he was, as if her troubled thoughts conjured him. Something snagged in her chest, and it took a moment to catch her breath.

How could that be when mere hours ago they'd made love until they were exhausted? She should be growing immune to his spectacular looks.

It's not his looks. It's him. The whole flawed, fascinating, wonderful man you've fallen in love with.

He strode towards her with that deceptively lazy gait and heads turned. Women stared and stood taller, straightening their clothes and hair. Some locals hailed him and he returned their salutes. But he didn't stop until he reached her.

His slowly unfurling smile made her jittery stomach settle, and for a moment her worries fled as she basked in his attention.

'What are you doing here?' She'd never known Alessio to leave the island. His great-aunt had hinted he hadn't left it since his wife's death. 'Is something wrong?'

He shook his head. 'Everything is fine…now I've found you.'

Charlotte felt winded. By his unexpected presence and the implication that things hadn't been fine until he'd found her. Was she misreading him? Her thoughts were so jumbled and her emotions so chaotic she didn't know what to think. Today's news had already unsettled her.

'I'm piloting your boat back to the island,' he said.

'You? But you don't come here!'

One black eyebrow rose lazily. 'Yet here I am.'

But Charlotte was aware, even if Alessio wasn't, of the way staff in the surrounding restaurants whispered and stared. No matter what Alessio said, his presence here was noteworthy.

If there wasn't some emergency, surely it was a positive thing that he'd left the island? Like it was positive that he spent more time with the other islanders instead of living like a total recluse as he'd seemed to earlier.

'*Why* did you come, Alessio? I thought you had meetings.'

He shrugged and looked towards the gleaming speedboat at the end of the pier. It wasn't the boat she'd arrived in, and she guessed it was his private vessel.

'It was time for a break from work.'

He held out his arm but didn't meet her eyes.

Because he knew she'd find that hard to believe? This was the man who lived for his work. It was only in the last few weeks he'd begun keeping anything like normal business hours. Now they spent every evening together as well as the nights and increasingly long siestas.

'Shall we go, or would you like me to buy you a coffee or a gelato first?'

'Nothing, thank you.'

Her stomach had been churning with nerves all morning, and she didn't want to test it with coffee. She slipped her hand through his arm and let him lead her towards the boat.

The idea that he was here because he'd missed her sent delight dancing through her. Could it be as simple as that? As simple and profound?

He'd changed so much from the surly recluse she'd first met. She knew he enjoyed being with her, not just for sex. Now they knew each other as friends as well as lovers since they talked about anything and everything.

Except his marriage. Other than explaining about Antonia's miscarriage, he was still taciturn about that.

That squashed her leaping excitement. Yet as they walked through the sunlit piazza, his tall frame brushing close, she couldn't help wondering if his following her off the island was significant.

Her heart missed a beat as she thought about why she'd come here. He couldn't know about her earlier appointment.

Which meant she'd have to tell him. She swallowed hard and leaned closer to his comforting warmth, revelling in it while she could.

Everything was about to change, and she had a premonition it wasn't going to be easy.

Alessio matched his stride to Charlotte's, nodding to acquaintances but not stopping to talk. Another time. For now he needed to leave. Not because coming to the town for the first time in years was difficult. On the contrary, it had been remarkably easy.

No, what made his skin prickle as if it were too tight to contain him was the need to be alone with Charlotte.

All morning he'd been restless. Sheer determination had seen him through the first of several online meetings. But he kept thinking of Charlotte, wondering what she was doing, wishing he could be with her.

The castello *was empty without her.*

That realisation had brought him up short. The place was his haven, even if it held awful memories. But today, for the first time, he needed to get away.

To Charlotte.

He tightened his hold and slanted a glance at her. With her gilded hair loose over her shoulders and her breasts budding against that pretty blue dress, she looked fresh and irresistible.

Something lurched in his gut. The knowledge that he shouldn't have initiated this affair. He was too tainted for a woman like her.

Yet how could he resist?

Part of him he didn't recognise had taken over today. A reckless, fun-loving Alessio that reminded him of the man he'd been before marriage and disaster.

He guided Charlotte onto the boat, saw her settled, and cast off. Minutes later, throttle in his hand, the boat leapt to life beneath his touch. The way his heart leapt when she touched him.

'Where are we going?' Because the boat wasn't headed towards the island.

'You haven't eaten lunch yet, have you?'

She shook her head and Alessio felt his mouth curve in a tight smile. Tight because his growing need for her, the fact that he'd had to interrupt his day because he missed her, rang warning bells he'd deliberately ignored.

'Good. I raided the larder and have a picnic packed.' His smile became a grin as he saw her eyes widen. 'Don't worry. It's all delicious. I have an excellent housekeeper.'

Her mouth curled primly. 'So I hear. I have it on good authority that you're lucky to have her.'

Alessio laughed, the sound torn away as he pushed the throttle and they sped along the lake. The sun shone brightly and the wind was fresh on his face, while beside him Charlotte looked flushed and happy.

Life was good.

Even if just for this day, life was good.

It was a revelation, a benediction, and Alessio thanked whatever fates had led Charlotte to him.

A short time later, he pulled in to a private pier. Once the boat was secured, he grabbed the picnic blanket and basket and helped Charlotte ashore. She was nimble enough to get ashore herself, but he liked how her hand turned in his, accepting his help, then stayed there, as if she too needed the physical connection.

'Who lives here?' she asked.

Alessio looked up at the pale pink three-storey villa as they walked through the rambling garden. 'Nobody at the moment. I own it, and a cousin lived here until recently. I'll look for a tenant soon, but for now it's empty.' He turned to Charlotte. 'We're totally alone.'

Dancing blue eyes met his, and heat shafted through him. '*Totally* alone?'

'Absolutely.' His voice was gravel and heat as that ever-present need for her surged anew. He saw it reflected in her face, felt it in her hand squeezing his.

Something passed between them. An understanding, an urgency. An unspoken primal message that had him dropping the picnic basket and drawing her into the deep shade of a spreading chestnut tree.

'Charlotte.' He tossed the picnic blanket down, but spreading it out would mean relinquishing his hold on her. Instead he backed her up against the tree trunk. 'I want you, Charlotte. Now.'

Such simple words, yet they revealed a devastating truth. Alessio had wanted her from the moment he'd seen her, dripping wet, emerging from his lake. He hadn't stopped wanting her since. If anything, his need had grown and grown until it was all-encompassing. He couldn't imagine life without her once she'd gone to Venice and her stellar career. If he had to, he'd—

Her hand on his cheek brought him back to the present. To eyes that held the same mix of desperation and anxiety that he felt. Was it possible Charlotte felt the same?

His tense shoulders eased as if a weight had been removed, and something unfamiliar fluttered in his belly. Hope. It had been so long, he almost didn't recognise it.

'I want you too, Alessio.' Her hands were already busy at his shirt buttons, spreading the fabric wide so she could plant her palms against his heaving chest.

He scrabbled in his back pocket for a condom as her nimble fingers undid his trousers.

'I love your efficiency,' he murmured as he sheathed himself.

Her laugh was a throaty gurgle that went straight to his groin. 'I love how aroused you are,' she countered. 'So strong and virile and—'

Charlotte gasped as he lifted her off the ground and pinioned her with his body against the tree. She grabbed his shoulders and with his help, put her legs around his hips. Alessio was rigid with anticipation and delight. How could he ever get enough of this woman?

He delved between her legs, tugging aside lacey fabric to be sure she was ready. Her slick folds and convulsive shudder at his caress gave him the confirmation he sought. No time now for foreplay. He *needed* her urgently.

'Charlotte…' Her name was a sigh of delight as he pushed in slowly, watching her pleasure as he settled at the heart of her. *'La mia ragazza d'oro.'* His golden girl.

'Alessio.'

She held his gaze with eyes so bright they scorched him to the soul. When she took his hand and planted it on her breast, he couldn't wait any longer.

He swallowed to clear his throat enough to apologise because he couldn't do slow and thorough, not now. Not with her gazing up at him with such yearning. Except her sweet body moved against his. His throat closed, and words failed him as he tumbled into abandon.

The union of their bodies, and he could have sworn, their souls, was perfect. They moved in sync, every thrust and twist perfection in that ancient dance that had never felt so right. The tension built with each touch, each slide, each gasp. She was with him all the way, drawing him deeper, making her own demands to match his.

Thunder roared in his ears as his climax exploded. He felt Charlotte jerk and clench, her fingers digging deep into muscle as she arched her head back and rode the same seismic waves of pleasure as he.

Had he ever known anything so superb?

They clung together, and Alessio was glad for the tree at her back to prop them up when it seemed nothing but instinct kept him upright.

How long it took for his mind to re-enter his body, he had no idea. As for lowering them both to the ground and the discarded blanket, he had no real memory of it. He just found himself lying, with Charlotte clasped tight in his arms, as they rode the aftershocks.

The sun had shifted by the time they roused enough to do up their clothes and think about food.

'I owe you a button,' he murmured as he watched her sit up and straighten her dress. A row of small buttons ran down the front of the bodice, and one was missing, creating a tiny gap that tantalised him with its glimpse of creamy flesh. He'd tugged the buttons undone, needing to fondle her bare breasts, and in the process had torn one free.

Charlotte slanted him a look that pretended to admonish but was all satisfied woman. 'I should set you to find it in this grass. You'd be here for hours.'

'Maybe you could help me.' He shifted closer, following the line of buttons with his index finger. 'We work better together.'

He saw her expression shift, an arrested look in her eyes, before she turned away. 'Maybe we should eat first.'

It wasn't Charlotte's desire for food that caught his attention but the indefinable difference in her voice.

Alessio's instinct sounded a warning. Something had changed. Her incandescent brightness had dimmed, and she was putting distance between them.

He leaned across, covering her hand with his. 'Something's wrong.'

It wasn't a question. It was a certainty, confirmed when she didn't immediately deny it but kept her attention fixed on the picnic basket. Except Alessio sensed she wasn't seeing the wicker box.

Where were her thoughts? What was it that made her jaw tense and her brow furrow?

He didn't even stop to question his need to understand and help. She was more than a casual sexual partner. She was important, special in ways that he couldn't articulate.

'Charlotte.'

Slowly she turned, and he read anxiety in the glitter of her overbright eyes. 'I went to the doctor this morning.'

Alessio's heart dipped and shuddered. His fingers tightened into a vicelike grip as he fought rising fear. In the past he'd heard the worst from a doctor. It took every atom of control not to panic and assume the worst now.

He fought to keep his voice even. 'What's wrong? Are you sick?'

How sick? Pain hemmed him in, pressing down on his chest and shearing through his gut.

'I'm okay. I'm not sick.'

Alessio stared, watching her mouth move, hearing her assurance but taking extra time to digest that. He swallowed, his throat thick. 'But there's something.'

She nodded, the movement jerky. 'There is.' She took a deep breath and that tiny gap in her bodice stretched wider. 'I missed my period. I'm pregnant.'

CHAPTER FOURTEEN

ALESSIO'S FACE TURNED sickly pale. His hard yet comforting grip on her hand ended when he dropped it as if it burned.

There was silence as his gaze raked her. Silence but for the thunder of her pulse and the hiss of his indrawn breath.

Not happy about the news, then.

What had she expected? Brilliant smiles, talk of shared parenting and a future together?

Charlotte hadn't been that foolish. But nor had she expected the look of complete horror that made his flesh shrink back against his bones, emphasising the harsh austerity of his features.

'Pregnant.'

It wasn't a question, yet she sensed he couldn't quite believe it. She didn't blame him. She'd been astounded when her regular-as-clockwork period failed to materialise. Even more when the doctor this morning had confirmed her suspicion. Charlotte had put her faith in the protection Alessio always used, even knowing it wasn't one hundred percent effective.

Trust her to be that point-something-percent exception!

'Yes.' She cradled her fingers in her other hand, but it wasn't the same as *his* touch. 'I'm pregnant with your child.'

The words turned him to stone. She couldn't even see his chest rise or a pulse flicker. And somehow, in that instant of total stillness, Alessio seemed to draw in upon himself so that now he resembled not the lover who had taken her to bliss but the forbidding stranger who hadn't wanted her in his home. As if their weeks of intimacy had never happened.

Except they had. There was proof of it as tiny dividing cells in her womb.

Charlotte took a sustaining breath, still grappling with her own shock and mixed emotions. She hadn't planned on a baby and didn't feel remotely ready. Yet at the same time, beneath the anxiety and uncertainty lurked excitement at the idea of having Alessio's child.

Apart from the fact that she loved him, she recognised a yearning to have someone to care for and love. If she couldn't have Alessio, and his expression indicated that was unlikely, she could have a child of her own. It struck her how terribly she missed the warmth of her mother's love.

Instinctively she wrapped her arms around her middle in a gesture that made Alessio's eyes widen. He shot to his feet, muttered an apology and strode away so fast on those long legs he almost ran.

Charlotte stared, unprepared for such a reaction. Surprise, yes. Even anger. But not this.

Yet you knew he'd already lost a child. And a beloved wife. You should have understood this would open up all sorts of memories for him.

Charlotte hunched in on herself, watching as Alessio stalked the length of the garden to the lake, to stand staring out at his island home. Every inch of his tall frame looked tense, from his wide-planted feet to the high set of his shoulders and the grim cast of his profile.

It was impossible to believe this was the man who a short time ago had lost himself in ecstasy with her, so driven by need that he'd taken her up against a tree, fully clothed and desperate for release.

Now he looked like a man who wished he was anywhere but here.

Charlotte wilted as if her spine slowly melted. She'd gone

into this affair with her eyes open, yet when she discovered herself pregnant, she'd harboured the tiniest hope that this would bring them together even more.

As if a baby would make Alessio love you.

She winced at the scoffing voice in her head. It was too like her father's. Like the brutal voice of her would-be fiancé, hurling abuse as she ran from him, clutching her torn bodice after he'd tried to rape her.

Desperately she tried to gather her composure. She should be used to facing life's challenges alone. If she had to do that now, so be it.

She was busy fending off anxiety when a sound made her look up. Alessio stood before her, hands deep in his trouser pockets, his face blank of emotion except for the troubled knot on his brow.

'I beg your pardon, Charlotte.' His deep voice sounded clipped and unfamiliar. 'That was not well-done of me. I apologise.'

She cleared her throat. 'It's a shock for us both.' She didn't want him thinking she'd planned this. 'I'd never thought of getting pregnant. I'd assumed condoms would be enough.'

'I understand.' His mouth lifted at one corner in a mirthless smile. 'I should have known better, since this happened once before.' He dragged in a breath so deep his chest heaved. 'I'm sorry for not protecting you better. I should have thought to suggest backup contraception, but—' his smile turned wry '—I was too busy enjoying myself to think.'

That wasn't what she'd expected. 'It's as much my responsibility is yours.'

She might have been a virgin, but she had a responsibility to take care of her own body. Why hadn't she sought extra protection? Surely it couldn't be because she'd wanted… No, that was impossible.

Alessio sank to the ground nearby. Not close enough to touch, Charlotte noticed with a sinking heart. He might accept joint responsibility for the pregnancy, but keeping his distance didn't bode well. Not for her or the baby.

'There are things I need to explain.' His voice was gentle, his expression stark. She understood, as if she hadn't before, that she wasn't going to like what he had to say.

'Go on.'

Alessio watched her push her shoulders back as if preparing for bad news. Her chin angled up and her gaze was clear, yet her arms were still wrapped protectively around her middle. It almost killed him to think of how badly he was about to let her down. His gut grabbed painfully. Because he'd be yet another man, after her father and her fiancé, who'd abused her trust.

The realisation made his tongue stick to the roof of his mouth.

He wanted to be the man she wanted.

A man she could rely on to be there for her and her child. He felt torn in two by that need and the knowledge he could never be that, no matter how much he wished it.

His mouth was full of the dull tang of failure. The sharp ache of regret pierced his chest, and his cramped lungs struggled to draw in enough breath to fuel his words. But he owed Charlotte the truth. Even if it made her hate him more than she was already beginning to.

'You know Antonia and I married because I accidentally got her pregnant.'

He watched Charlotte's mouth turn down at his choice of words. To her this was a unique event. For him it was history repeating itself. He shuddered as cold enveloped him.

'We'd been friends for years, so at least we had that to build on when we married. Like me, she was an only child, but unlike me, she had no relatives. I became her only family. She relied on me.'

Alessio felt his throat tighten and paused. 'We were living in Rome but came here soon after the wedding.' Charlotte had said it was a good place to raise a child. But that's not why they'd moved. 'She wanted to live quietly, away from the paparazzi and the gossipy social scene. She didn't want people seeing her.'

'I'm not surprised. It must be hard having the press snapping photos of you all the time.'

'There was more to it than that.' He felt like there was a boulder lodged in his chest. He hadn't spoken about this with anyone. 'On a routine medical check, the doctor noticed something wrong and sent her for tests.'

Alessio remembered in minute detail hearing her news. Their lives had transformed from that moment.

'Antonia was diagnosed with a terminal illness.' He heard Charlotte's gasp and made himself continue. 'She could have had treatment that might have lengthened her life, but she chose not to because she wanted, more than anything, for our baby to have a chance to survive. She was playing a waiting game, hoping and praying she'd live long enough for that.'

There was a rustle of fabric as Charlotte moved towards him. Then, as his eyes met hers, she sank back where she was. He couldn't cope with anyone's touch right now. He teetered on a knife-edge of self-control.

'Oh, Alessio! I'm so sorry.'

He nodded. 'It wasn't that she minded the world seeing photos of her pregnant. It was that she didn't want everyone to see her waste away. She was a proud woman, vivacious and glamorous, and she couldn't bear the world to see that change. She didn't want sympathy or attention. She needed privacy. As time went by, she cut off ties with friends, relying more and more on me.' As if he'd been able to give her what she needed! 'I promised to look after her and the baby. To do everything possible to protect them.'

He'd promised, but he'd failed abysmally.

'How appalling for her, and how incredibly difficult for you.'

Alessio's head jerked up again to meet Charlotte's sympa-

thetic stare. He wanted to bask in it, take every good thing
she offered, all the warmth and tenderness, the understanding and generosity of spirit, and hold them close. But he didn't
deserve that.

'The doctors believed there was a hope for the baby. In fact,
things went so well that I went to Rome overnight on business.' He paused, remembering. 'That night she miscarried.'

There was nothing he could have done, they'd said. Nothing anyone could have done. But he knew, and he knew Antonia knew too, that if he'd been at home, she might have rested
more, letting him look after her as he always did, soothing her
fears and reading to her in the evening until she fell asleep.

Gentle fingers touched his and he wanted, so badly, to turn
his hand to hold Charlotte's, clinging to her as if she could
eradicate the dark maw of guilt.

Instead he slipped his hand away.

It was time to end this. 'After that, Antonia gave up, and I
watched her waste away before my eyes, mentally even more
than physically. It was hell. Then suddenly she seemed to
rouse. She looked almost like her old self, with a determination I hadn't seen in ages. She talked of reconnecting with
friends and making the most of the time she had left. I'd been
asked to visit an estate to advise on an auction of rare heirlooms, but I'd refused. Antonia urged me to go, said I needed
a break from her and the *castello*.'

He looked away, unable to hold Charlotte's eyes. 'She waited
until I'd left. Then she somehow found the strength to walk
out into the lake and drown herself. She'd planned it all along.'

He heard Charlotte's muffled sound of distress, but wisely,
this time she didn't reach for him. He couldn't blame her.

'The only thing I could do was manage the public narrative to make it seem like a swimming accident. I owed her
that much.'

Especially as he'd failed her and the baby. He'd sworn to

protect her, but he hadn't been able to stop her descent into depression and suicide.

'You poor man.'

He caught Charlotte's troubled gaze. 'Poor Antonia, don't you mean? I promised I'd look after her. I should have suspected—'

'How could you have known that's what she planned? You said yourself she seemed better, talking about connecting with friends.' She leaned in, her expression earnest. 'You did your best to care for her, Alessio. And at least she had the solace of knowing you loved her.'

He jerked back then, and found himself on his feet, towering over Charlotte. His voice, when it came, was harsh. 'But I didn't. I cared for her as a friend, a good friend. I tried to be a decent husband, but I never loved her or she me. Maybe if I had...'

Alessio shook his head and turned away, his gaze turning inevitably to the island that was his beloved home and at the same time, his prison.

He turned back to Charlotte, drinking in her gentle beauty and, even now, her sympathy. As if his revelations hadn't proved how undeserving he was.

'I know the situation's different now. *You're* different. But I can't go there again.' His throat closed convulsively. 'I can't be a father and husband. I can't be the man you and the baby deserve. I'll support you both. Anything you need, you can count on from me, and I won't interfere with any decisions you make about the child. But that's all I can offer. Nothing more.'

CHAPTER FIFTEEN

CHARLOTTE SLEPT ALONE that night for the first time since the ball when Alessio had swept her into his arms, carried her up to his bed and taken her to heaven.

It seemed a lifetime ago.

She stared at herself in the mirror, seeing the evidence of a sleepless night. But there was some small comfort in pulling on familiar work clothes. For years her work uniform had been a concealment, useful when she wanted to keep her distance, especially from men.

She shrugged into a jacket, feeling the need for extra armour in case she saw Alessio at breakfast. But instead of wearing her usual navy or black, today she'd chosen her one colourful outfit. The dark crimson lent colour to her cheeks and made her tired eyes sparkle. Or maybe that was anger at the way he'd cut himself off from her so completely.

They'd talked on the way back to the *castello* yesterday, and later. Rather, she'd talked and Alessio had politely listened. But it was like addressing a brick wall. Not quite that bad, for he'd nodded from time to time, acknowledging her words. But nothing she'd said had made any difference.

She blinked fiercely as her eyes prickled, and she concentrated on yanking her hair up into a businesslike bun.

She'd considered leaving it down around her shoulders, knowing Alessio liked it that way. But this wasn't a problem to be solved by using her femininity or trying to seduce him.

She grimaced. If anything, *she'd* be the one seduced, for even furious and hurt by his rejection, she was still weak as water around him.

To her shame, she'd spent the night missing his lean strength. Not even for sex but for the comfort of being held close and that sense of blissful intimacy where it felt everything was right in the world.

Alessio was the most stubborn man she'd ever known to believe himself responsible for two tragic deaths when it was clear to any impartial observer that neither had been his fault. Antonia had planned her suicide carefully, getting him out of the way so he couldn't stop her.

But his guilt showed him to be a man who cared deeply and who took his responsibilities to heart, even if he hadn't loved Antonia.

Guiltily Charlotte recalled how her heart had jumped at that news. As if that meant he was free to love her.

She spun away from the mirror, unable to meet her haunted eyes.

He doesn't love you and never will.

He made that clear from the start. He spelled out the rules for a short-term affair.

A baby won't change his feelings, no matter how hard you wish it.

Charlotte breathed deep, trying to find at least an appearance of calm. She should be used to it by now—being alone. Being unloved. But today it felt harder than ever to face a new day.

The scent of coffee reached her as she paused in the kitchen doorway. She frowned, pulse quickening as she saw the man busy at the counter, squeezing fresh orange juice into a glass.

He looked up, dark eyes locking on hers, and Charlotte felt that familiar tremble of longing. To hide it, she smoothed her hands down her straight skirt and entered.

'What are you—?'

'Getting you breakfast. You work too hard, and I want to be sure you have a decent breakfast instead of waiting on me.' He paused, and what he said next stole her breath in a great whoosh of air. 'You have to think about the baby.'

The baby you don't want.

The words hovered on her tongue.

But *she* wanted it. The more time passed, the surer she became. Charlotte had no illusions that being a single parent would be easy, even with Alessio's financial support, but she'd manage. She always managed.

She walked to the table, her legs only a little wobbly, and took a seat.

'What if there *is* no baby? There's always termination.'

Alessio's olive skin blanched, turning his face the same sickly shade as when she'd told him she was pregnant. He couldn't bear the thought of being a father, but it seemed nor could he bear the idea of ending the pregnancy.

'That's what you're thinking of?' His tone was sharp.

Charlotte thought of letting him believe so, but despite how much she hurt, she couldn't torture him that way. 'No. I'm not.'

She found it telling that Alessio hadn't suggested that option. Many men would have.

Alessio set the glass of juice in front of her. 'Or there's milk. I wasn't sure if you'd want coffee.'

'Juice is fine.'

He didn't meet her eyes but busied himself at the kitchen counter as if he found this as difficult as she did.

'We need to talk, Alessio.'

'I know.' He swung around, carrying a plate of pastries and a bowl of thick yoghurt topped with fresh berries. 'There are things to sort out, arrangements to be made. But later. For now, concentrate on your breakfast. Would you like an egg?'

Charlotte blinked up at him. Eggs, dairy foods and fresh fruit. Had he been researching dietary needs for pregnant women? Did he intend to supervise all her meals for the remaining weeks she was in the *castello* to be sure she looked after herself?

She didn't think she could bear that parody of a caring partner, solicitous and excited about her pregnancy.

'Actually, I'm not very hungry. I'll eat later.'

'Charlotte, you need to—'

'Don't tell me what I need to do, Alessio. You're in no position to give orders unless it's about my job.'

Her chair scraped as she shoved it back and stumbled to her feet. She felt queasy, but surely it was too soon for morning sickness. No, what made her nauseous was this situation. A man she loved who would never return her feelings. A decent man whose instinct was to care but who was so caught up in grief and self-blame that she feared he'd never be free of his past.

Charlotte's hand curled around the back of the chair. 'Tell me this, Alessio. If our baby is a boy, he'll be the next Conte, won't he?'

Slowly Alessio nodded, his expression grave.

'How will he ever be able to take up the role if you have nothing to do with him? I've seen for myself that the title is the least part of being the Conte Dal Lago. It's about taking a lead in the region and supporting people. That's not something you pick up overnight.'

Alessio shrugged. 'I had to learn for myself. My father was too busy enjoying a life of luxury elsewhere to worry about his commitments here. But I wouldn't do that to my...' He paused. 'If the child is a boy, when he's old enough, I'll make sure he learns what he needs to know.'

Charlotte looked at Alessio's set face, the determined angle of his jaw and those broad shoulders that carried so many burdens. He was so resolute that she felt the last of her hopes tumble and crash. It didn't matter what she said or did. She wouldn't change his mind.

'It's all about duty with you, isn't it? You married out of duty. You tried to be the perfect husband because it was your duty. Now, when the very mention of a new baby makes you turn green with nausea, you're determined to do your duty, to ensure there's someone else to carry on your responsibilities when you're gone.'

She couldn't look at him anymore. The pain was too great, clamping her lungs so she could barely breathe, making her heart ache as if it bled. She turned to the window, where she could see a glorious sunny day beginning.

'Let's leave that discussion about the arrangements you want to make. I can't face it today. I've had enough of your concern and your duty.'

Charlotte spun away and walked to the door, conscious all the time of Alessio's gaze heavy between her shoulder blades. She waited for him to speak, to acknowledge the truth of what she'd said. Or even protest she was wrong about his feelings for her and their unborn child.

But he said nothing. His silence enveloped her like a chill cloak, dousing the heat in her cheeks and frosting her heart.

She'd lost. There was no argument she could make that would reach him. Nothing she could do to make him love her.

Midnight had struck. The Cinderella fantasy which had crept into hopeful life was dead.

Alessio stood at his office window, staring sightlessly at the view.

Instead of the lake, in his mind's eye he saw Charlotte, her mouth crumpled with hurt while her eyes blazed with desperate determination. Charlotte walking out on him, her shoulders stiff and head high while he'd wanted to do anything, say anything, to make her turn back to him. To have her walk into his arms, smile up at him, lay her head against his chest and lean close.

His heart thudded a ponderous beat as he relived the effort it had taken not to relent but to watch her walk away.

Because walking away was best for her and the child, no matter how much he yearned for the light she'd brought into his life.

She didn't understand how his failure with Antonia had stained his soul, marked him as a man who couldn't be trusted to protect those he cared for. He knew all the logical arguments about it not being his fault. Beatrice had berated him with those more than once, and he was no fool. He understood what she said. Yet in his heart, in his dark soul, the guilt remained.

He couldn't, wouldn't taint Charlotte with that darkness. He couldn't risk failing her and her unborn child.

At the same time, he couldn't sustain the current situation. For days, Charlotte had avoided him. He'd let her, rather than force his presence on her, because he'd seen her confusion and hurt. That only reinforced the knowledge that he did the right thing, keeping his distance.

Nevertheless, they needed to talk. There were arrangements to be made for her care during pregnancy. For the child.

A great ache opened up inside him like a yawning chasm at the thought of her alone and pregnant somewhere far from him. He wanted to be with her so badly. Because he was selfish. He craved—

Sounds on the pier interrupted his thoughts. He looked down and recognised Mario loading his boat for a trip across the lake. He carried a big basket aboard, baked goods for a nearby market. But then he loaded a large suitcase.

Alessio frowned. Mario hadn't mentioned a trip. He was pondering that when another figure emerged. A slender woman with hair the colour of old gold.

Charlotte. Alessio stiffened. She climbed onto the boat and took a seat near the suitcase.

His heart stopped beating, and the bright morning light faded towards darkness. When he remembered to breathe, he found himself clutching the window frame, hauling air into cramped lungs.

Something like panic rose inside him, a great wave of dread. Charlotte was leaving like he wanted. But too soon, far too soon. He wasn't ready.

Deliberately he tightened his grip on the window, forcing his feet to stay planted where they were. This was best. It wasn't ideal. He'd rather have sorted out the practicalities of his support for her first. But that could be remedied. All he had to do was stay here and let her do the sensible thing.

Alessio blinked, his gaze blurring, as Mario started the engine and Charlotte left him.

They were halfway to the shore, Mario chatting over the putter of his engine, when a roaring made Charlotte turn. She frowned. Was that…?

'The Conte's in a hurry.' Mario watched the speedboat approach.

Charlotte turned to stare at the town ahead of them. She didn't want to talk to Alessio, especially in front of someone else. Her emotions were too close to the surface, and she felt scraped raw.

But instead of passing them, the faster boat slowed. Alessio called out and Mario answered, conversing in the local dialect she couldn't understand. Then the other boat surged away, and she felt stupidly let down.

Because Alessio hadn't addressed her?

She shook her head at her neediness. The sooner she left and started a new life the better.

Thoughts turning inward, she paid no attention to her surroundings until the boat bumped gently against a pier and Mario offered her a hand to disembark.

'No thanks. I'm fine. Can I help you with the basket?'

A deep voice came from above. 'Mario isn't getting off here.' She looked up and there was Alessio, his windblown hair and darkened jaw making him look more like a pirate than ever. Or maybe it was the hard glitter in his narrowed eyes as he reached down to take her hand.

Startled, Charlotte looked beyond him. They weren't at the town but at the villa they'd visited together days before. In the distance she saw the spreading tree where they'd made love, where she'd told him about the baby and he'd explained why he could never be part of her life.

Instinctively she pulled back, but Alessio was too quick. 'We don't want an audience for this, Charlotte,' he whispered in her ear. Then more loudly he added, 'Mario doesn't want to be late for the market.'

Charlotte opened her mouth to say she had her own plans for the day, but she was already letting him lead her up off the boat. Where was her willpower? She feared this weakness she couldn't control.

He led her away from the water, not even dropping her hand when the engine revved behind them and Mario left.

Sunlight kissed her bare arms and his fingers encircling hers were hot, yet Charlotte shivered, cold to the bone.

'What do you want, Alessio?' Her voice was harsh, rough with emotions she didn't dare identify.

He stopped and turned towards her, the morning light behind him. 'You're leaving. Without even telling me!'

'I—'

'How could you do that?'

Charlotte stood taller. 'Do what? Go? That's what you want. You're the one pushing me away. The one who can't bear to think about, much less see our child.'

He shook his head. 'But to leave without a word.'

'We've said everything that matters. Besides, I—'

'No, we haven't.' Alessio shifted, and now she could read his expression. What she saw startled her. He didn't look angry but haunted, desperate even. His nostrils flared and his broad chest rose as if he struggled to drag in enough oxygen. 'I need to explain.'

'No more explanations! I understand your feelings.' She tugged, trying to slip out of his grasp.

'That's just it. You don't.'

For a long moment, his glittering eyes held hers. Then abruptly he let her hand go. Instantly she cradled it in her other hand, missing his touch.

She should march away rather than prolong the agony of being with him, but she couldn't. 'What don't I understand?'

'I want you, Charlotte. I don't want to give you up, or our child.'

The shock waves from his words thundered through her, making her weak at the knees. 'That doesn't make sense.'

Alessio's laugh was harsh. 'I'm not surprised. I'm an emotional mess, not the logical man I used to be. Since you arrived on the island, I haven't been able to think straight. I haven't been able to resist temptation. Haven't been able to sleep, except with you in my arms.'

His voice hit that gravelly note she knew from lovemaking, and some of her hard-fought resistance melted.

Charlotte struggled to be sensible though every instinct urged her to hug him close, since he made it sound like he suffered the same tortures she did. She feared that would resolve nothing and simply ignite the sexual attraction still burning between them.

'Tell me, then. Explain what's going on.' She folded her arms rather than reach for him.

'I said I wanted you to leave and bring up our baby somewhere else. I believed it as I said it, but it wasn't the truth.' He nodded at her shocked gasp. 'I told you that because I thought it better, both for you and the child, to be far from me. My track record is…abysmal. I had one role in my marriage, to protect, and I failed. I couldn't bear to fail you or our baby.'

Charlotte didn't recall deciding to move, but now she was in his space, gripping his shirt front, tilting her head up to hold his gaze.

'You might be a brilliant businessman, Alessio, but in some things you have absolutely no idea. The only way you could fail me, fail us, is to turn your back, the way you have the last few days.'

Strong arms wrapped around her back, pulling her up against his hard body. Heat seeped into her, and it felt like the first time she'd been warm in days.

'I wasn't turning my back. I was hiding.' He grimaced. 'I told myself I needed to give you space, but really I was too scared to see you in case I blurted out the truth.' He drew another deep breath, his chest pushing against her. 'I was even afraid to give a name to my feelings, until I saw you leaving.'

'It's not—'

'Shh.' He put his finger on her lips, his expression gentle, his mouth curling up in a wry smile. 'Let me finish, please.' Yet he paused before continuing as if he found the words hard. 'I saw you get into Mario's boat, and something broke inside me. That's amazing in itself, because not so long ago I thought everything inside me was completely broken. Until you made me see differently. You made me wonder if there could be good things in life again. You made me hope even though I tried to resist. You made me love.'

Charlotte blinked, telling herself she'd misheard. But it was too late. Already her blood effervesced in excitement. 'Alessio?'

'I've never been in love. I never saw it modelled by my parents or felt any love from them. I didn't recognise it. I told myself it was lust, and fun, and companionship. Gratitude even, because you shone a light where in the past there's only been darkness.' His mouth twisted. 'What you saw in me, I have no idea. I've been a grumpy, difficult b—'

This time it was Charlotte's hand that covered his mouth. She shivered as he pressed a kiss to her palm, and she felt it right to the core of her being.

'You were in a bad place, but *you* weren't bad,' she assured him. 'Your bark was worse than your bite—'

'Most of the time.'

'And there were reasons you found it hard having someone new your home.'

'The main one being that you interrupted my attempt to wallow in self-pity. You kept appearing, demanding things, expecting me to act and get involved, tempting me as no woman has ever tempted me before.'

Sizzling green eyes held hers, and fire crackled in the air between them.

'I mean it, Charlotte. I've never felt like this about any woman. Never *loved* before.' His mouth turned down. 'That only added to my guilt. I'd married Antonia and promised to protect her, but I'd never *loved* her.'

'Oh, Alessio.' Her heart felt so full she thought she might burst. 'You can't blame yourself for that. You two married for the good of your child. You tried your best.'

'I know, I know. But what I feel for you makes me realise how little I really had to give Antonia. I was her carer and her friend but that's all.'

'I'm glad you were her friend. She needed that. But it sounds like she wasn't in love with you either.' She paused, knowing she didn't have the right words, if there were any. 'You both did the best you could in extraordinarily difficult circumstances. You did all you could, Alessio.'

He said nothing, but his expression wasn't nearly as bleak as it had been earlier. Maybe one day he'd believe that.

Finally she couldn't hold back any longer. 'You really love me? It doesn't seem real.'

'I truly do. Which is why I'm hoping you'll give me another chance. For the baby's sake, if not mine.'

'What about for my sake?' Charlotte paused, fighting her learned instinct to keep her feelings to herself. 'I'm in love with you, Alessio.'

His eyes widened, and he lifted her right off her feet, drawing her up till her face was level with his.

'Say that again.' His voice was husky as if he couldn't believe it.

'I love you.'

She watched her words sink in. The stark lines around his mouth somehow lessened, and the furrows on his forehead disappeared. He looked younger, lighter. Happier.

'I haven't even apologised yet. I need to grovel at your feet for the way I've behaved.'

Charlotte shook her head. 'You can kneel at my feet anytime you like, but there are other things you could be doing there apart from grovelling.' She saw the familiar, hungry glint in his eyes that softened the muscles at the apex of her thighs.

The blaze of joy in his face and the wicked gleam in his eyes spoke of a man ready to turn his face towards the future, even if it wouldn't always be easy.

A great weight lifted off her heart. This really was happening!

'Can we take it as read that you're sorry and I'm sorry too?'

'You've got nothing to apologise for, Charlotte.'

'Apart from wrecking your peace and making you face lots of things that have been painful for you.'

She'd seen how deeply his guilt ran over the past. Ever since he'd explained what had happened to his wife, Charlotte had been horrified at how much he'd had to endure, and how she'd inadvertently dredged up so much pain.

But she couldn't regret anything when Alessio smiled at her like that. Slowly, oh, so slowly, he lowered her to her feet, and the delicious friction between them felt like a promise.

'I have a confession to make,' she murmured. His eyebrows rose. 'I wasn't leaving today. Mario was just giving me a lift to the market.'

'But the suitcase?'

'His great-nephew's. He left yesterday with a friend who

didn't have room in his car for a suitcase. Mario is taking it ashore to send on after him.'

Alessio shook his head, his expression brimming with laughter. 'I've never run so fast as when I saw you leaving with that case. I told myself I was doing the right thing, staying there, but I only lasted thirty seconds. I swear my feet didn't hit the stairs going down the tower.'

'I'm glad you came after me, even if it was a mistake.'

He shook his head. 'It was no mistake, Charlotte. It was the best, most sensible thing I've done in my life. I intend to stick close, woo you and persuade you to stay with me, always.' On the last word, his voice dropped to a resonant note she felt deep in her heart.

'You want me to live with you in the *castello*?'

'I want you to live with me wherever you like. Here or in Rome or...'

'I like it here.' Suddenly she felt shy. Because of the way Alessio watched her, as if she were utterly precious.

'I want to make you my *contessa* if you'll have me. I know I have a lot of ground to make up, and you may not want to marry—'

'I can't think of anything I'd like more. And *not* for the sake of our baby. I'm being totally selfish.'

'Excellent.' His smile was that devastating one, guaranteed to melt her bones. Just as well he was holding her tight. 'Because I am too. I want to marry you because you make me happy, Charlotte, happier than I've ever been.'

His head swooped low, his mouth covering hers reverently as if sealing a lifetime's promise.

Charlotte kissed him back with her whole heart.

It wasn't long before she was grateful he'd had the foresight to lead her deep into the garden. For what came next was utterly joyous and just for the two of them.

EPILOGUE

ALESSIO SMILED AS he looked into the cosy room. 'I thought I'd find you here. Aren't you coming downstairs to help welcome the guests?'

Beatrice lifted one imperious eyebrow. 'Stop bothering an old lady. I'll be down in my own good time. You and Charlotte are perfectly capable of managing without me. The recent *castello* balls have been a huge success.'

He smiled, surveying the real reason his great-aunt was taking her time. The dark-haired toddler almost asleep in his bed, one hand clutching his teddy bear, the other resting on the picture book the old lady held.

The bond between little Luca and his great-great-aunt was an unexpected joy. And it kept Beatrice so busy she had less time for poking her nose into Alessio's affairs.

'Very well, we'll expect you soon. Remember the Swedish ambassador is coming early and wants to talk with you. And Luca's babysitter is waiting.'

'If the ambassador's coming early, what are you doing here? Shouldn't you be downstairs supporting your wife? Marrying her was the best thing you ever did, but you can't afford to take her for granted. She's turned you and this place around completely, and you need to support her.' Beatrice paused. 'It's months since you took Charlotte to that beach resort at Langkawi. You should plan another trip soon. Maybe to Switzerland since she loves it so much.'

Alessio repressed a smile. Beatrice just had to give advice. And it had been she who'd asked him to call her in good time before the guests arrived. 'Yes, Aunt Beatrice. I couldn't agree more.'

'Oh, you...' Beatrice narrowed her gaze. When he was a child, that beetling look might have made him nervous. Now Alessio read her silent laughter. 'Begone with you. Go to your wife, immediately!'

Chuckling, he headed a few metres down the hall. Pushing open the door, he halted, stunned. When he'd left their bedroom, Charlotte had still been wearing a wrap, putting on her make-up.

Now she stole his breath.

'La mia ragazza d'oro,' he murmured when he found his voice. 'You look more and more beautiful every day.'

In a dusky pink strapless gown, its full-length skirt sprinkled with what looked like thousands of diamonds, Charlotte rivalled any fairy-tale princess.

Alessio wrapped his arm around her waist and planted a kiss at the base of her neck so she gasped and clung to him. The subtle scents of vanilla, cinnamon and fragrant female hit his sense receptors and hardened his body.

'Alessio.' Her welcome never grew old. Nor did the shimmering delight in her smiling eyes when he lifted his head. 'You look more and more handsome. Sometimes I can't believe this is all real.'

'Believe it, Charlotte.' His voice deepened as emotion rose. 'All I am I owe to you. I've never been so content and fulfilled.'

She beamed, her eyes so bright they rivalled the brilliance of the ruby and antique pearl earrings he'd given her to match her heirloom pendant.

'You know,' he murmured as he kissed her, 'I don't think I ever told you the end of the family legend.'

'About the baron who claimed the virgin who'd been left for the lake monster?'

'That's the one.' Alessio traced the soft flesh at the edge of her bodice, unable to resist torturing them both with what they couldn't yet have. 'Tradition has it that they were supremely happy, loyal and loving. And while most of my forebears were greedy, grasping types, every generation or so, one of them fell for a blue-eyed, golden-haired virgin, and his fate was sealed. His destiny lay with hers.'

'You're joking!'

'It's true. I didn't tell you before we were married because I didn't believe it myself. Now I know it's true. I love you with all my soul, Charlotte, and always will.'

'That's just as well.' The emotion in her eyes belied her faux brisk tone. 'Because I'll love you forever, my darling Conte.'

Neither moved for long moments, lost in their good fortune. Then Alessio thought of the arriving guests. Regretfully he ushered her out towards the grand staircase. 'I'd much rather spend the evening alone with you.'

'We only have to wait a few hours.' Yet her voice told him she felt the same. 'Did you see Beatrice? I thought perhaps we should tell her our news.'

Charlotte's hand pressed to her abdomen in a gesture as old as time, and Alessio felt that familiar surge of protectiveness. He lifted her hand and pressed a kiss to her knuckles, holding her close.

How had he ever thought to survive without Charlotte and the family they were making?

'You know Beatrice. She'll fuss over you and try to give orders. Let's keep it our secret a little longer.'

'I like the sound of that.' For a second longer they shared the moment. Then Charlotte sighed. 'The ambassador's coming early. We'd better go.'

'Practicality as well as passion. No wonder I love you with all my heart.'

Tenderly, proudly, Alessio led her down the stairs.

This woman had given him back his heart and given him a future as well. What more could he ever want?

* * * * *

COMING SOON!

We really hope you enjoyed reading this book. If you're looking for more romance be sure to head to the shops when new books are available on

Thursday 11th May

To see which titles are coming soon, please visit

millsandboon.co.uk/nextmonth

MILLS & BOON®

Coming next month

WHAT HER SICILIAN HUSBAND DESIRES
Caitlin Crews

"Truly," he said, in that low voice of his that wound around and around inside her, "you are a thing of beauty, Chloe."

"So are you, Lao," she said softly, then found herself smiling when he looked surprised she should compliment him in return.

It made her wonder if he was so overwhelming, so wildly intense, and so astronomically remote in every way that mattered, that no one bothered to offer him compliments. But any such thoughts splintered, because he carried her hand to his lips and pressed a courtly sort of kiss to her knuckles.

It should have felt silly and old-fashioned, but it didn't. Not in an ancient castle, perched here above an island so steeped in history.

And not when the faint brush of his lips across the back of her hand made everything inside her seem to curl up tight, then begin to boil.

"Welcome, little one," he murmured, the heat in his gaze making everything inside her take notice, especially the tender flesh between her legs. And that heart of hers that would not stop its wild thundering. "To our wedding night. At last."

Continue reading
WHAT HER SICILIAN HUSBAND DESIRES
Caitlin Crews

Available next month
www.millsandboon.co.uk

LET'S TALK

Romance

For exclusive extracts, competitions
and special offers, find us online:

 facebook.com/millsandboon

 @MillsandBoon

 @MillsandBoonUK

 @MillsandBoonUK

Get in touch on 01413 063 232

For all the latest titles coming soon, visit
millsandboon.co.uk/nextmonth

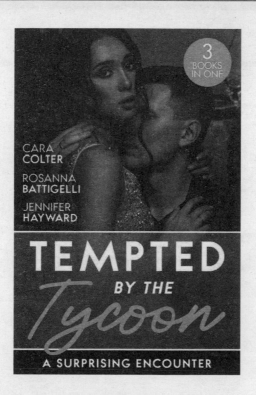

MILLS & BOON

THE HEART OF ROMANCE

A ROMANCE FOR EVERY READER

MODERN
Prepare to be swept off your feet by sophisticated, sexy and seductive heroes, in some of the world's most glamourous and romantic locations, where power and passion collide.

HISTORICAL
Escape with historical heroes from time gone by. Whether your passion is for wicked Regency Rakes, muscled Vikings or rugged Highlanders, awaken the romance of the past.

MEDICAL
Set your pulse racing with dedicated, delectable doctors in the high-pressure world of medicine, where emotions run high and passion, comfort and love are the best medicine.

True Love
Celebrate true love with tender stories of heartfelt romance, from the rush of falling in love to the joy a new baby can bring, and a focus on the emotional heart of a relationship.

Desire
Indulge in secrets and scandal, intense drama and sizzling hot action with heroes who have it all: wealth, status, good looks…everything but the right woman.

HEROES
The excitement of a gripping thriller, with intense romance at its heart. Resourceful, true-to-life women and strong, fearless men face danger and desire - a killer combination!

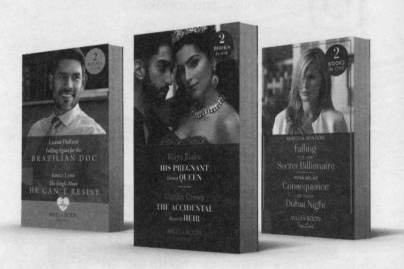

GET YOUR ROMANCE FIX!

Get the latest romance news,
exclusive author interviews, story
extracts and much more!